Praise for Juli Zeh

"Zeh challenges readers to consider how complicit
we are in our current political dilemmas."
Los Angeles Times

•

Praise for About People

"Juli Zeh has proven herself as an adept novelist of
social satire. *About People* has been on the bestseller
list ever since it was published last spring: it is a
Zeitroman for the corona-pandemic era."
Dialog International

"A revealing novel about the state of our nation."
SWR

"Juli Zeh's new work shoots straight to the heart of
Germany's excessive demands: with a lot of wit and
compassion and also with a large portion of hope for
a more conciliatory society."
ZDF

"The first real corona novel, which takes place in
the middle of lockdown in spring 2020 and subtly
describes the social and very private consequences
of the pandemic."
Süddeutsche Zeitung

"A coolheaded and politically astute portrait of a village
where life is precarious, beset by a dying infrastructure
and right-wing attitudes."
Bayern2

"Juli Zeh has caused a stir with *About People*. The novel is gripping and doesn't make it easy for itself or its audience."
rbb Inforadio

"*About People* goes beneath the surface of ideologies and attitudes."
Stuttgarter Zeitung

"A deft, imaginative, and absorbing novel about a post-heroic protagonist who is sweating from hard work rather than fear, caught between stoicism and struggle."
Kölner Stadtanzeiger

"A conciliatory novel that does not conceal evil, but demonstrates that the world, viewed less ideologically, could be a little more humane."
Deutschlandfunk Kultur

"A novel for our times, especially our Covid-times, in which much is clarified and intensified, including failure, loneliness, and sanguine fits of hatred."
WDR3

"I would love to recommend this to everyone to read, to break down all these walls that somehow exist between the different groups in society."
Rbb Kultur

"Juli Zeh is a master of satire, and her dialogues are always on fire, sparking and glowing fiercely, keeping the reader alert at all times. And yet Zeh also creates vivid and fascinating portraits of the characters that

inhabit the novel. The way the relationship between Dora and Goth ends is just heartbreaking, and at the same time it shows how skillfully Zeh balances the thin line between comedy and grief. I cannot imagine a more important and timely message than the one that is delivered in this novel."
ANNE LOUISE MORSETH-NORDBRYHN, Gyldendal Norsk

•

Praise for New Year

"Because the thriller and the analysis of society are here so densely intertwined, *New Year* is perhaps Juli Zeh's best book to date."
Süddeutsche Zeitung

"*New Year* is an impressively original book whose elegant construction testifies to Zeh's writerly prowess."
New Books in German

"Past experience is part of us, like a code in computer software—Zeh, in her usual straightforward way, has condensed this to make a compact novel."
Stern

"A thrilling, cinematic story."
VPRO Boeken

"With *New Year*, Juli Zeh has succeeded in writing a lost-memory thriller and at the same time an accurate psychogram of today's overwhelmed fathers."
WDR 3

"With *New Year*, Juli Zeh shows that good entertainment can indeed be easily coupled with depth and literary quality. This psycho-thriller is well on its way to becoming a bestseller."
SRF 2 Kultur

"A compact, highly concentrated story with gripping dynamics and a superb 'aha' effect."
SWR2

"Juli Zeh has written not only an enthralling psychogram of a man, but also quite nearly a classical tragedy."
Südwest Presse

"This book develops into a rapid, exciting drama, of a kind you might have never read before."
Der Kleinborsteler

"*New Year* dives deep into the psyche of modern, emancipated man and investigates to what extent experiences in our childhood influence how we live our lives as adults."
JAN

"Juli Zeh maintains suspense, homes in on the moments of unreality, the sense of magic, and offers an unexpected twist at the end."
Libération

"The landscape is a metaphor, the natural elements an allegory of the main character's inner turmoil and traumas by means of which the reader, witness to

a progressive, gripping psychological unveiling left unresolved until the final page, sees this hidden inner world resurface."
Diacritik

"*New Year* explores the profundities of being and attempts a decryption of the mechanisms of the unconscious, all the while following the codes of the thriller to ensnare the reader. Juli Zeh successfully constructs a psychological novel, all the while avoiding the pitfalls of the genre. This hypnotically written novel is one you devour."
La Provence

"An intense and gripping psychological thriller. The second part of this novel, impressive in its mastery of narrative, will cost you some hours of sleep."
Midi Libre

"Juli Zeh marvelously describes the traumatism of abandonment. Reaching the summit is an effective allegory for Henning's dive into himself. The German novelist brilliantly succeeds in launching him into the depths of himself and of what he left unsaid, all the better to liberate him of it."
L'Alsace

"Juli Zeh wields the mechanisms of the psychological thriller and adds her own trademark, which is to let the heroes brush with catastrophe without always drowning in it. The tension the novelist keeps going isn't resolved until the final page. *New Year* manages to

open up the silent depths of lives that are too plotted out, much like the potholes that shake up rental cars on the roads of the Canary Islands."
Le Monde des Livres

"Juli Zeh dramatizes the resurgence of that which has been suppressed by means of an efficient thriller that leaves the reader breathless and deeply shaken."
L'Obs

"The suppressed drama suddenly unravels before our bewildered eyes, leaving our hearts pounding and our minds racing. Once devoured, *New Year* obsesses its reader for days on end. Juli Zeh strikes hard and strikes home."
Transfuge

"An experience of psychological dissection. *New Year* is a vertiginous plunge into the psyche of a man straining under the weight of what he believes he must achieve and, in a subtle game of smoke and mirrors, into our own neuroses. With the tale of a mad ascent, the novel defuses, with the author's characteristic scathing and elegant irony, the diktat of perfection and permanence extolled by the media that has invaded the sphere of social life and intimacy, and invites us to respond with a middle finger stuck up with pride."
Lire

"You don't know where you're going, but you unconsciously feel that you are going far, very far away, a lot farther than the Lanzarote roads. To tell you more would be to spoil the pleasure provided by this novel,

which is as brilliant and amoral as can be and explores
our most common depths."
Page des libraires

"It is genuinely admirable how, page after page, Juli
Zeh manages to develop a truly nerve-racking thriller.
Ever changing register, she always starts with ques-
tions rising from the conditions of life in today's
society."
DNA

"Juli Zeh adapts adult distress to children's terrors, joins
a faltering present with a foundering past. As always in
her novels, she shows a formidable mastery of time.
New Year is an intimate drama, as well as a promise."
Julieamimots.com

"In this harrowing thriller, Juli Zeh evokes children's
solitude, their panicked fears of abandonment, their
incapacity to see their parents as anything but perfect."
Arts Libres

"In this gripping tale, Juli Zeh interrogates relationships
with childhood, the couple's power games, free will in
a conformist and demanding society."
Le Matricule des Anges

"*New Year* is an inspired portrait that manages to touch
upon something essential about this character we
begin to follow, love, and desire to see get better. Juli
Zeh makes this mirage of an insular Christmas look
very real indeed."
YAËL HIRSCH, *Toutelaculture.com*

About People

Juli Zeh

About People

Translated from the German
by Alta L. Price

WORLD EDITIONS
New York

Published in 2023 by World Editions LLC, New York, USA

World Editions
New York

World Editions is committed to a sustainable future. Papers used by World Editions meet the FSC standards of certification.

Library of Congress Cataloging in Publication Data is available

ISBN 978-1-64286-133-4

First published as *Über Menschen* in Germany in 2021 by Luchterhand Literaturverlag, a division of Penguin Random House Verlagsgruppe GmbH, München

Company: worldeditions.org
Facebook: @WorldEditionsInternationalPublishing
Instagram: @WorldEdBooks
TikTok: @worldeditions_tok
Twitter: @WorldEdBooks
YouTube: World Editions

Contents

Part One: Right Angles

Part Two: Seed Potatoes

Part Three: Mass Effect

PART ONE

Right Angles

1

Bracken

Keep going. Don't think.

Dora rams the spade into the ground, pulls it out again, cuts through a stubborn root with one jab, and turns the next piece of sandy soil. Then she tosses her tool aside and presses her hands into the small of her back. Back pain. At—she pauses a moment to do the math—thirty-six. Ever since her twenty-fifth birthday, she's had to stop and do the math regarding her age.

Don't think. Keep going. The narrow strip of dug-up earth has a long way to go before resembling anything like an achievement. When she stops to look around, she's overwhelmed by an existential hopelessness. The plot of land is far too large, and looks nothing like anything you might call a "garden." A garden is patch of lawn with a tidy little shed, like the ones in the suburb outside Münster, where Dora grew up. Or maybe it's a miniature flowerbed around a tree, like the little slices of verdure in Berlin-Kreuzberg, where Dora last lived.

The thing surrounding her now is no garden. Nor could it be called a park or a field. Honestly, it's a "parcel of land." That's how the land register puts it. From that same land register, Dora knows that the house sits on exactly one acre of property. She just didn't fully grasp what one acre meant. It's half a soccer field, with an old house on it. An overgrown wasteland, matted down and bleached by the winter that wasn't. A botanical catastrophe that Dora's efforts will transform into a romantic garden beside her rural home. And not just a garden—a garden with a vegetable patch.

That's the plan. Dora might not know a soul within a fifty-mile radius, and she might not own any furniture, but she wants her own vegetables. Tomatoes, carrots, and potatoes will provide daily confirmation that she's done everything right. That the sudden purchase of an old estate manager's house, in desperate need of renovation and far from any hint of suburban sprawl, wasn't just some neurotic knee-jerk reaction, but the next logical step on her adventurous life journey. Now that she owns a country house, complete with garden, her friends from Berlin will come for weekend visits, plop down on the antique chairs in the tall grass, and sigh, "You sure have it good here." If she can even remember who her friends are by the time it's all fixed up. And if they're ever allowed to get together again.

The fact that Dora doesn't know the first thing about gardening is no obstacle. That's what YouTube is for. Luckily, she isn't one of those people who thinks you need a degree in mechanical engineering before you can read the electrical meter or set the thermostat. She's nothing like Robert, with all his second-guessing and perfectionism. Robert, who just tossed their relationship out the window and fell in love with the apocalypse. The apocalypse is a seductress Dora can't compete with. The apocalypse demands allegiance, and calls for a collective coming to terms with fate. Dora's no follower, that's why she had to leave. And Robert just didn't get that it wasn't about the lockdown. As she toted her things down the stairs, he looked at her like she'd lost her mind.

Don't think. Keep going. The internet told her the planting season starts in April, or even earlier this year thanks to the mild winter. It's already mid-April, so she has to hurry up and turn the soil over. Two weeks ago, just after she moved, it suddenly snowed. That was the first snow this year. Big flakes floated from the sky looking almost artificial, like some special effect engineered by Mother Nature. The plot disappeared under a thin white blanket. Finally all clean and tidy, all quiet. For Dora it was a moment of profound peace. Once the snow melted, the desolate, neglected plot resumed its incessant nagging. Dora had her orders: get everything in shape, stat.

Dora isn't your typical urban refugee. She didn't come here to learn how to slow down with the help of organic tomatoes. Of course, city life is often stressful; the trains are overcrowded, the streets are crawling with crazies—not to mention all the deadlines, meetings, pressures, and high competition at the agency. But some people love all that, and at least the city's stresses are reasonably well organized. Out here in the country, it's complete anarchy. Dora is surrounded by objects that have a mind of their own, that never do what they're told. Here, there are so many half-functional, filthy, neglected things either in need of repair or utterly destroyed. On top of which are all the things that don't even exist here, even though they're desperately needed. At least in the city things are partially under control. Cities are organizational centers for the material world. For everything in a city there's at least one person in charge. There are places you go to get things and places you take them when you don't want them anymore. Here in the countryside, on the other hand, Dora's the only one in charge, and it's her against the domineering natural world, which grows over everything it gets its creeping fingers on.

A couple of blackbirds fly over, scanning the dug-up soil for earthworms. One of the birds perches on the handle of Dora's spade, a bold move that makes Jay-the-Ray, Dora's little dog, raise her head. In reality, Jay-the-Ray is just soaking up the spring sun in an attempt to warm herself after another night in their cold country house. Her dignified bearing betrays her big-city roots, even as she's forced to get up and give these feathered country bumpkins a piece of her mind. Then she goes straight back to her sun-warmed spot, sinks onto her belly, and spreads her hind legs, which gives her body the angular shape that, in turn, determined her name.

Sometimes Dora's mind gets stuck on sentences she's read somewhere. Actually, it's more like the sentences stick to her, and her mind picks at them like a scab she can't scratch off. One such scab is the second law of thermodynamics, which states that chaos always tends toward a maximum unless enormous energy is expended to restore order. Entropy. Dora can't help but think about that as she looks around—not just at her parcel of land, but all over the village, all over the county. It's rife with crumbling roads, half-collapsed barns and stables, former pubs overgrown with ivy. Mountains of scrap metal rise above the fallow fields and abandoned lots, and the woods are strewn with trash from burst-open bags. The freshly painted houses and newly fenced-in gardens are islands amid a sea of entropy. It's as if any given person has just enough power to tend only a few square yards within the wider world. Dora doesn't have an island yet. She's standing on a raft, armed with rusty tools scrounged up in the old shed, steeling herself, bracing against entropy.

She had googled the village six months ago, back in another era, in another world, when she first spotted the ad on eBay classifieds. According to Wikipedia, "Bracken is a locality in the township of Geiwitz near the village of Plausitz in the district of Prignitz in the state of Brandenburg. It includes Schütte, a now uninhabited historic settlement. The earliest mention of the village appears in a deed issued by Bishop Siegfried in 1184. Slavic artifacts excavated nearby suggest that Bracken was originally settled by Slavs."

The technical term is linear settlement, which just means it's your typical East German one-horse town. At its center lies a church overlooking the village square. There's a bus stop, a firehouse, a mailbox. 284 inhabitants. 285 with Dora, although she hasn't yet made it to the town registrar's office. It's currently closed to the public due to Covid. A banner on the Geiwitz town office website delivers this news.

Dora didn't even know she was part of *a* public, let alone *the* public. Who else is in this crowd? Don't think about it. Don't get stuck. There are so many weird new words and terms now. *Social distancing. Exponential growth. High mortality* and *mortality displacement. Spit guards* and *face shields.* N95s and KF94s. Dora hasn't been able to keep up for weeks. Maybe it's been months or even years—Covid has made it clearer than ever that it's impossible to keep up. New terms buzz around her head like flies you can't shoo away no matter how wildly you wave your arms. So Dora has finally decided all these words are no longer any of her business. They're from a foreign language in a foreign land. In recompense, she's been given the word *Bracken*, which in German has nothing to do with ferns. This word—a name, actually—still feels foreign, too. It sounds like a mashup of *Brachen*, meaning "fallows" or "plow," and *Baracken*, "barracks." It sounds like something done at construction sites, using heavy equipment accompanied by a lot of noise. Tomorrow we'll *bracken* the whole place. We need a few more day-laborers to *bracken* over there. Before the foundations can be poured, we'll have to thoroughly *bracken* the ground.

En-tro-py, en-tro-py, her thoughts chant. Keep going, Dora consciously counters. That's one thing she knows how to do: keep going, even when it feels impossible. Back at the ad agency, moving on was a part of everyday life, and *keep going* was everyone's mantra. New pitch, new deadline. Too few people, too little time. Presentation went well, presentation bombed. Budget came, budget went. Client won, client lost. We need to think digital, we need to think multidimensional, the full 360 degrees, from carousel ads to radio spots to social media to vlogging, Susanne, founder of Sus-Y, would say at every Monday Breakfast, which was just a two-hour meeting disguised as a meal. She'd go on and on: Creative excellence and unique positioning are what set us apart. They pay the bills. That plus the fact we really understand our customers, and help them solve their problems sustainably. Dora doesn't miss Monday Breakfast; the mere thought of it makes her feel like Covid might as well last forever.

If you keep going even when everything feels impossible, sometimes you start to feel like you're gagging. As if there's something rotten on your plate, but you have to swallow it anyway. And then the only thing to do is close your eyes, hold your nose, and get through it. Shove the spade into the ground. Entropy. En—dig in. Tro—dig deeper. Py—haul out the next shovelful.

She chose a lovely spot among the fruit trees, between the apples, pears, and a cherry tree just barely beginning to bloom. The vegetable patch will be separated from the house, but close enough that you can see the beds from the kitchen window. The area is reasonably level and not as densely overgrown as the front part of the parcel, which feels partially caged off by young tree trunks that are already as thick as her thumb. Mostly maples and locusts. Dora knows her trees. Robert studied biology, and during every stroll through the Tiergarten he'd tell her all about the trees: how they grow, how they reproduce, what they think and feel. Dora enjoyed those conversations, and even learned quite a bit.

Locusts are an invasive neophyte, an immigrant in tree form. They reproduce quickly and displace other species. Bees, however, absolutely adore locusts. Removing all these little trees using only garden shears and a handsaw will take weeks.

There's no locust thicket growing between the fruit trees, but there are blackberries. When Dora arrived they looked like a tangle of dry vines left over from last year, so dense the ground was almost invisible below the brambles. She can swing the old scythe alright, but doesn't know how to sharpen it properly, even after a YouTube tutorial, which is why she's been bludgeoning the brambles with the dull blade as if trying to hack her way through the jungle with a machete. Her first day there, after a chilly night, she went outside still wrapped in winter clothes: long cotton shirt, thick sweatshirt, lined jacket. Fifteen minutes later, she started peeling layers off like an onion, and soon she was standing next to a mountain of clothes in just her undershirt. Since then, she only goes out the door in a T-shirt, no matter how frosty the morning air first seems. Early each day the air feels freshly washed, and her goose bumps are invigorating. The house stays cool inside as the outside temperature climbs almost to seventy Fahrenheit over the course of the day, much to the delight of Jay-the-Ray, who spends each night under Dora's bedspread. During the day, Jay roams the garden like some little ambulatory solar cell in search of sunshine.

Easter came and went in complete silence. People say lockdown magnifies many differences, but it obliterates any difference between weekdays and weekends, working days and holidays. After clearing the selected area, Dora cordoned off a ten-by-fifteen-yard rectangle between the fruit trees with a taut string. This borderline is superbly straight, each corner a perfect right angle. The red line made the newly cleared area look like a bona fide construction site, such that the rest of the task seemed little more than a mere formality.

Which soon turns out to be a delusion, of course. For days on end Dora has been thrusting the spade into the earth, removing large chunks of turf. This turf is anything but grassy though; "weedy topsoil" would be a better descriptor. The roots hold the soil together so tightly that Dora has to stand with both feet on the spade's blade and jump up and down, several times, to drive it into the earth. It's back-breaking work, and that's only the beginning of it. The real challenge lies just a bit deeper, in the leftover legacies of a system based on a never-ending battle against entropy—a battle in which no one, apparently, felt personally responsible for their role. Whoever lived in the old estate manager's house back when this was still East Germany apparently thought the garden was the best place to toss all rubble, scrap metal, and garbage. Dora's spade constantly hits pieces of old bricks, rusty bits of metal, plastic buckets, broken bottles, orphaned shoes, and rust-encrusted pots. And then there are the toys: colorful sandcastle molds, wheels from matchbox cars, once she even found a doll's head eerily gazing up at her from the soil. Dora collects everything she finds and sets it all along the border, lining the strip of dug-up earth.

She picks up the spade and leans on the handle. Strength slowly flows back into her arms and legs. After just two weeks in the countryside, her hands are red and calloused. Dora turns them back and forth, looking at them like objects that do not belong to her body. The hands have always been too big. Sometimes Dora worries they might take on a life of their own, and move without her even meaning them to. It's as if a taller person is standing behind her and has put his arms through her sleeves. Her brother Axel used to tease her about it. "Dora-dinkypaw!" he'd shout, at which she would always fly into a violent rage. Until the death of her mother. After that, they no longer teased each other, but were steadfastly nice instead. As if everything, even Dora's huge hands, had turned to fragile glass.

Robert always claimed he liked her hands, at least he always did back when he liked anything about her. Before she'd turned into a carbon-footprint problem, and then into a potential coronavirus vector.

Dora knows from experience she shouldn't rest too long. If her break lasts too long, her brain starts calculating, and her calculations invariably turn into questions about the meaning of life. She'd begun clearing the land nearly two weeks ago; for the last three days she's been overexerting herself turning the soil. The row she's already finished is about a yard and a half wide. Which means she's not even a sixth of the way through. At this rate, it'll be mid-May before she can sow anything. The problem with that is that it's no real problem at all. She could just buy veggies at the supermarket. That's probably even more affordable, if you factor in the cost of watering the garden. Stay-at-home orders are worrisome, but neither menacing nor serious enough to make anyone *have* to grow their own potatoes. There's no real reason to start a vegetable garden, aside from a desire to indulge in cottagecore Romanticism or impress visiting friends. But Dora has no use for cottagecore, nor does she have any friends. Back in Berlin it made no difference; work left her with hardly any leisure time, and Robert had enough friends for them both. But here in the countryside the total non-existence of friends loomed on the horizon like some gloomy, rumbling cloud.

Trying to tackle such a huge plot right off the bat had been idiotic. It was a classic rookie mistake. Fifteen square yards, instead of 150, would've been more than enough to start. But Dora doesn't want to undo the perfectly plotted lines she's already drawn. After all, for the past several years she's banked on her ability to finish whatever she's started, no matter how absurd it might feel. Dealing with clients who change their mind on a daily basis, who always want to see more options, whose briefs are full of contradictions, and who are too afraid of their superiors to ever come to a decision—all that is, without a doubt, harder than gardening.

Keep going. If she can't make this garden happen, she'd have to ask herself why she even bought this place.

The answer would be easy if she could claim to have intuited as early as last autumn that Covid was on the move. Then a place in the country would've been a refuge, a place she could hide until the pandemic passed. But she hadn't seen it coming. When

Dora started eyeing real-estate listings online, climate change and right-wing populism seemed like the biggest problems. In December, when she secretly stopped by the notary's office in Berlin-Charlottenburg, the coronavirus was making headlines, but you still had to scroll way down, it was just something going on in Asia. By the time she scraped together the modest inheritance from her mother and her life savings to make the down payment, Dora still wasn't even sure she wanted to move to the countryside. All she knew was that she needed that house. Urgently. Even if it was just an idea. A mental survival technique. A hypothetical emergency exit from her own life.

Over the past few years, Dora kept hearing about people buying houses in the countryside. Usually as a second home. They did it in hopes of escaping the endless cycle of projects. Everybody Dora knows is familiar with this cycle. You finish one project and then you dive right into the next one. For a while, you believe your current project is the most important thing in the world, and you do whatever you can to complete it on time and as well as possible. Only to then discover how, the moment you finish it, any and all significance it held evaporates on the spot. Simultaneously the next, even more important project pops up. It never ends. You never reach your goal. There's no "making it." Strictly speaking, you never even make any headway. You can only circle around, again and again, and everyone just keeps orbiting because they're afraid of coming to a standstill, of getting stuck. Meanwhile, almost everyone's secretly realized it's all utterly pointless. Even if they're loath to talk about it. Dora sees it in her coworkers' eyes, in their deeply insecure gaze. Only newbies still think you can "make it." But "it" is unattainable, because "it" stands for every project you could ever imagine, and because, in truth, the greatest, ever-mounting catastrophe wouldn't be the arrival of the next project, but its non-arrival. The attainability of "it" is the foundational lie upon which the modern world of life and labor is built. A collective self-deception, a bubble that has already, silently, burst.

And now that an awareness of all that has seeped into the subway tunnels of every major metropolis and continues to circulate at every coffee machine, water cooler, and in every elevator on every floor of every office in every skyscraper, people are burnt out. And at the same time, the wheel spins faster. As if you could escape from the pointlessness of running by simply running faster.

And you can. Or at least Dora always has. She never resisted the cycle of project after project. Instead, she accepted it as a way of life. But then something changed. Not in Dora, but around her. She just couldn't keep up, and the idea of a house out in the country gave her un-keep-up-ability a proper home. That was last autumn, and now here she is out in Bracken, in her fine fallows, and she's starting to smell a hint of fear. The never-ending cycle of projects could spiral out of control. The sight of the ground all around her makes this clear. This plot of land is her next goddamned project, and this time it might be too hard a row to hoe.

Annoyed, she decides to *not* keep going. She'll force herself to endure doing nothing for a half hour. She lets go of the spade and stomps off toward the house, through last year's stinging nettles, to a spot below the linden tree, shading a few chairs. Dora found the rickety old furniture in the shed, just like all the other props for her future country-home lifestyle. What had the realtor said? "A comfy life is the idyllic life." That's probably just one of the many canned phrases people come up with just to sell run-down houses in places like this.

Dora sits down on one of the chairs, stretches her legs out, and wonders whether she's just as nuts as the people back in Prenzlauer Berg who cram yoga and meditation sessions into their already over-booked schedules solely in order to slow down. She knows the never-ending project cycle is a trap, a tough one to escape. It can even turn plans to un-project-ify one's entire existence into yet another project. Otherwise it wouldn't leave millions of victims in its wake. Dora takes a deep belly breath and tells herself her problem is rooted elsewhere. Her problem isn't projects, it's Robert. Something's happened, and she just can't keep up.

2

Robert

Dora can't remember when it all started. All she remembers is that, even back in Robert's climate-defender phase, she occasionally felt he went overboard. Like when he sniped that all politicians are idiots, and all his fellow human beings are self-absorbed ignoramuses. When he got all riled up at Dora's tiniest recycling mistakes, as if improper sorting were a criminal act. He sometimes seemed a bit overzealous and unforgiving, and it occurred to her he might have some kind of neurosis, a politically induced form of OCD that had turned the gentle, thoughtful person he had been into someone possessed.

In the beginning she'd mostly marveled at him, although admittedly that sense of wonder came with a hefty dash of bad conscience. Robert took things seriously. Robert got involved. Robert became a political activist. At the online magazine he worked for, he founded an entire department devoted to climate issues. He also started making changes in his day-to-day life, going vegan, buying earth-friendly clothes, and regularly attending Fridays for Future protests. Dora didn't want to go along, and that bothered him. Didn't she believe in climate change, and that human activity was responsible for it? Couldn't she see the world was headed for disaster? Statistics started dotting their conversations. Robert referred to numbers, experts, and the science. Dora sat before him as a stand-in for the stupid people, the unthinking masses who refused to be convinced by anything. When he really got going, he even blamed her career choice. He claimed her job stoked consumption. That she made people buy things they didn't even want, let alone need. He saw Dora as an agent for throwaway society, consumer culture run amok, wasting energy, piling the garbage dumps ever higher. She didn't feel any need to defend the advertising industry. But still, it hurt when Robert wrung her out like that.

After all, it's not like she needed convincing. Of course she knew climate change was a serious problem. It was just the rhetoric that paralyzed her. His tone was always more *how-dare-you* than *I-have-a-dream*, and tone makes all the difference. Instead of bickering about target temperatures, she felt people should focus more on the bigger picture, the important stuff— the end of the fossil-fuel era would never come unless people were more informed, so the focus had to be on rebuilding infrastructure, transit, and industry. Seen from that perspective, Dora found Robert's pride about not driving a car rather misguided.

Dora doesn't like absolute truths or any supposed authority that relies on them. There's something bristly deep within her, something that always wants to resist. She has no desire to fight to prove she's right, and refuses to take part in any kind of groupthink. Normally her resistance doesn't take the form of self-defense. You don't notice it. She adapts. Her form of resistance is more a kind of quiet yet stubborn defiance, an inner battle against outer circumstances. Which is why she finally had to tell Robert he'd better be careful when his statistics were less about arguing a valid point and more about proving he was right. Taken aback, he stared straight at her and asked if she'd prefer the alternative facts of someone like Donald Trump.

That was the first time the problem with Dora's thoughts came to light: they were unintelligible, perhaps even reprchensible. She couldn't talk about them. At least not with Robert. Not anymore. He sat there before her like an authority, radiant, self-assured. The plane he existed on was above all error, all doubt. He belonged to a group that had transcended all human character defects. And that's where Dora not only couldn't keep up, she refused to follow.

But at the same time, she was ashamed of her reluctance, her resistance, her stubbornness. At the end of the day it didn't make any difference why Robert was in it, even if it was just to prove he was right, as long as he actually was right. Climate policy was and is important. And Robert seemed content, while Dora was often wracked with self-doubt. It must feel good to really fight for something important. Robert no longer had to wonder what it was all for. He'd even overcome the endless cycle of projects, by substituting the overarching, probably unachievable, large-scale aim with a bunch of smaller, more readily attainable goals. That move was genius, a clever castling. It changed the entire game.

Dora decided to put in an effort. She gave up meat. She only bought organic. For Robert's sake, she even switched agencies. Sus-Y is a boutique advertising firm specializing in sustainable products and the non-profit sector, and it's pledged to support responsible companies implementing ecologically sound social goals. Instead of ads for canned soups, luxury cruises, and insurance behemoths, at Sus-Y, Dora develops campaigns for vegan-friendly shoes, bring-your-own-bag days, and fair-trade chocolates. The fact that her business card now features only the lonely little word *Copy* instead of *Senior Copywriter* never bothered her. Nor does the fact that she earns a little less than before. But in Robert's eyes, none of that sufficed. Not by a long shot. Finally Dora realized what he wanted, and she couldn't give it to him. He wanted acolytes. He wanted her to pledge allegiance to the apocalypse, and her inner defiance increasingly enraged him. She wasn't prepared to march on the front lines with him, and he couldn't stand it. He was disappointed in her, and their life together brought far fewer laughs than in the past. But somehow, despite it all, they were still a team.

Then along came Covid, and Robert discovered his true calling. As early as last January, with the fine-tuned sensitivity of a seismograph forecasting catastrophe, he'd said it would escalate, soon encompassing the entire globe. His online columns urged the German government to invest in face masks, while the rest of the world still thought this was just another Chinese problem.

At first his journalist colleagues dubbed him a Cassandra, ridiculing him for crying wolf. Soon thereafter they viewed him as a veritable clairvoyant. Robert became a Covid expert. As if he'd been expecting it for years, just waiting for this pandemic. And finally the wait was over, catastrophe wasn't near, it was here. The ship had been hit, we're going down, and now finally something can be done. Everything and everyone is ready to follow orders, any doubt tantamount to mutiny. Finally everyone's thinking the same way. Finally everyone's talking about the same thing. Finally there are hard and fast rules for a world that's spun out of control. Finally globalization is faltering, is on its knees. Finally there'll be an end to all this borderless mess, all the unchecked migration of people, goods, information, ideas.

Dora gets it. She understands Robert. Fighting climate change is exhausting. Everyone's used to kicking the can down the road. But now the dawdling's over. All of a sudden, look what's possible. Things that were inconceivable a moment ago are now no problem whatsoever. Predatory capitalism is canceled, all movement must be sharply curtailed. Covid itself might be invisible to the naked eye, but its effects have a graphic clarity. It's swift, dramatic, easily charted. Its consequences are measurable. And the virus appears to have an inherent, almost biblical inevitability. How long has it been five minutes to midnight on the doomsday clock? At some point the worst was bound to happen. Everybody knew. Everyone sensed it coming. Western culture has been flirting with disaster for a long time, maybe forever. And now it's here, the great plague, punishment for all our sins, our greed, our exploitation, our unbridled consumption, our whole outrageous lifestyle.

And now everyone Robert has been accusing of inaction for the past two years is finally coming around. Startled from their slumber, they're now sprinting, suddenly ready to listen to the experts. Political parties, private corporations, the left, the right, the rich, the poor, all united by fear.

Dora couldn't shake the suspicion that Robert somehow took satisfaction in this generalized state of panic. He dove headlong into a post-apocalyptic script. *The Walking Dead* in Berlin. He filled the larder, stocked up on toilet paper, ordered tons of hand sanitizer online, and constantly talked about how everybody should prepare for the worst. Dora felt uneasy. Sometimes she was downright scared. But she figured it was best to stay calm. Hit the pause button. Wait just one minute. And then trust the politicians to accurately assess the situation and make the right recommendations. Robert laughed in her face. He jeered at the politicians, too, because in his eyes they couldn't do anything right. Too little, too late. When Dora reminded him they live in a democracy, and that decision-making takes time, he flew off the handle. His nose and mouth shielded behind a respirator he'd procured early on, he rode his bike around town and surveyed people's opinions at the entrances to office buildings and out on the streets. He spent days out on his bike, and nights in front of the computer, stoking his own fanaticism with constantly updated notifications, numbers, calculations. He was drunk on data. His column grew more successful by the day. More and more, he became a stranger to Dora. He ended every text message, email, DM, everything with *stay safe!*

It was like the watchword of some secret society had now become a mass movement.

Living with Robert had already been stressful last year. In January it became aggravating, in February, unbearable. In March all schools, restaurants, and businesses shut down. New words entered everyone's vocabulary by the day. *Stay-at-home orders, lockdown, shutdown, flattening the curve. Infection rates, mortality rates, ICU occupancy rates.* Panic spread, as if illness and death were newfangled notions.

From one day to the next, Dora found herself back in her home office. Her WFH setup, as it was now known. And it wasn't so bad. On the contrary, she found it had its advantages. Sus-Y, like most ad agencies, didn't give members of the creative team their own offices. Instead, on any given day, Sus-Y HQ had about twenty-five people dotting its so-called open-plan office, a space that effectively became one big, noisy echo chamber. The consultants were the worst, since they were on the phone all day trying to wring intel out of their clients while simultaneously keeping morale high. Their job was to talk non-stop, although it never added any real value to the equation, whereas the copywriters' job requires immense concentration, so tossing consultants and creatives into the same space made the copywriters' lives difficult. A home office was undeniably quieter, even when Jay audibly sulked around. Back at Sus-Y HQ she had been the unofficial office mascot, and all the attention had spoiled her. As Dora waited for the coffee machine to spit out the morning's first Nespresso, Jay ran from desk to desk being petted and getting doggy treats from the special stashes her fans had brought in just for her.

The first days working from home went well. Dora and her coworkers used WhatsApp to brainstorm. Meetings moved to video conferences. The only accoutrement she really missed was the office fridge, perpetually filled with organic microbrews ever since Sus-Y had won the Kröcher account.

But then their Kreuzberg apartment started feeling too small. As a freelance journalist, Robert had always worked from home, so the proper home office was already occupied. Back when they moved in, Dora had thought the rooms huge. Now everything was shrinking down around her. Now that a stay-at-home order had been issued, Robert limited his excursions to one hour per day. Apparently his work fit the label *essential*. The rest of the time he, Dora, and Jay were relegated to sharing their 850 square feet of living space. The living room only had a low coffee table, so Dora had to work in the kitchen, on her laptop. She took a lot of walks with Dora. Dog owners were lucky, now that walkies had gone from being a burden to a privilege.

Out on the empty streets the atmosphere was eerie. Few cars, hardly any passersby. All the walkers in Viktoriapark had vanished. A pharmacy's front window framed faces covered in white. Robert said those were the people fighting on the front lines. Dora found his wording disturbing. The pandemic was bad, but it wasn't a war. Wars were waged against people.

One time, a man walking his dog out on the street hastily yanked the leash aside, lest Jay-the-Ray spread the virus. The quadrupeds' panting and the paws and claws scratching the sidewalk were disturbing. Another time, a young mother shouted at a jogger that he shouldn't breathe so heavily. Signs began appearing in windows: *Stay home, save lives.* These people were all part of something, even if Dora couldn't say exactly what. They hunkered down behind their homemade placards and hoped it wouldn't be as bad in Berlin as it was elsewhere.

Dora's walks were both depressing and at the same time a relief. These brief escapes let her break out of the now omnipresent claustrophobia. Robert, on the other hand, found it unthinkable that Dora would take Jay out three times a day. He was getting more and more riled up at the citizenry's lack of obedience. While she sat at the kitchen table trying to transform her clients' desires into creative concepts, he marched around the apartment ranting and raving, cursing people's unfathomably dumb behavior. He expected Dora to give some kind of signal that she agreed. A nod, at least. But she couldn't. She didn't know whether people were dumb. And which people, exactly? The ones who yanked their dogs away, or the ones who mounted group protests by hanging out quaffing beer in front of their neighborhood Späti?

Who's good and who's evil? Dora doesn't know, nor does she care to. She finds the question itself quite dangerous. She knows she doesn't like hearing people talk about "historic proportions" and "turning points" while far worse things are happening around the globe, albeit usually elsewhere. She insists there's no need to take sides when there aren't any easy solutions, and at the moment there are even fewer solutions than usual. Neither politicians nor virologists have any hard-and-fast truths that would make everything okay again if people just obeyed. Life is largely trial and error, and people are capable of comprehending and controlling far less than they often believe. Faced with such a dilemma, neither brash action nor utter idleness can possibly be the right answer. From Dora's perspective, it's a matter of remaining able to logically size up each situation, and communicating as honestly as possible. Honesty requires the awareness that you might not actually know for sure, or have all the information. That's why she resists the presumption that people all have to think a certain way. She has nothing against rules in and of themselves. She can follow rules, she just doesn't want anyone telling her that she has to like them. She doesn't need to hang out with ten friends in front of the Spätis clinking bottles just to prove that she's free, that she's important. If social distancing is the strategy society at large has opted for, she's ready to go that route. Within the bounds of reason. Not as a trailblazer. Maybe the Swedish approach would be more her style, but she's here in Berlin, not Sweden. She follows the rules and regulations. But her thoughts remain free. Nobody can force her to view the beer drinkers outside the Spätis as treasonous public enemies.

Except, apparently, Robert. He wants her to go along with him. But there she goes again, refusing to be his vassal. Failing to pledge permanent allegiance to the apocalypse. And because Dora stubbornly stared at her computer instead of just sitting there and agreeing with his hate-filled tirades, his aggression was increasingly directed toward her. Her laptop got in the habit of crashing at least once a day, forcing her to completely reboot. *Runtime error 0x0. We are sorry for the inconvenience.* Dora caught herself suspecting it somehow had something to do with Robert. She nearly broke into tears. He had been her partner, her companion, her best friend. And now she believed his aura was causing her computer to crash.

Out on one of her walks she saw a guy who'd devised his own social-distancing device. Whenever it beeped, he'd start flailing his arms and screaming, "Stay away!"

That scared her more than anything else. Was it possible for an entire society to collectively lose its mind? When she told Robert about it, he dismissed her as ignorant. He accused her of being insufficiently informed, of turning a blind eye to the danger right in front of her face. He said the guy with the beeping box was sensible. Dora felt like a little kid who just didn't get it.

Robert's accusation that she was ill-informed struck a sore spot, because as soon as the pandemic broke out, Dora had chosen to strictly limit her news intake. She doesn't want to turn a blind eye, but she can't stand the idea that, all of a sudden, Covid is the only news. As if the war in Syria, the refugee crisis, neo-Nazi terrorism, or grinding poverty on a global level had never been real problems. Just a bunch of infotainment, the pastime of bored mass-media consumers. Now that there's a pandemic, nobody needs all that other rubbish. Dora finds it downright shocking. She feels sick to her stomach even reading the headlines. At the same time, she's secretly ashamed to admit she doesn't know the latest infection rates. As if there were some new ordinance forcing everyone to consume the same media and information. Like Robert seems to believe, since he finds it veritably criminal that she's abstaining from the news.

Aside from all the mental wrestling, there was also the issue of space. They were constantly in each other's way. Whenever Dora closed a window, Robert cracked another. When she was in the bathroom, there'd inevitably be a knock on the door, followed by Robert's voice asking how long she'd be. Just as she sat down to crank out page after page of taglines and catchphrases, or to find the right radio producer who could not only handle a long-running campaign but also garner a bunch of awards in the process, he was suddenly motivated enough to empty the dishwasher that happened to be less than an arm's length from her elbows. Robert tripped over Jay and stepped all over Dora's documents, which, in lieu of anywhere else to put them, she'd distributed on the floor. When she wanted to get something from the fridge, he'd invariably already be opening its door. When she went to brew herself a coffee, he'd appear at her side and make it evident he couldn't wait for her to finish. When she took a cigarette break out on the balcony, he'd yell that the stench was filling every single room. Working on articles for his column, he'd pace up and down the hallway, talking to himself out loud. When Dora asked if he could cut it out, he said that was the only way he could be productive.

Although they split the rent, it seemed like every room belonged to him. After all, he had always worked from home, whereas Dora had always gone to the office. What's more, her unpreparedness when it came to apocalyptic thinking hadn't stopped her from implementing her newfound right to exist. Dora's resistance grew so overpowering that she started the whole deposit-bottle thing, which to this day makes her cringe every time it pops back to mind.

She was staying out longer and longer, too. She'd sit on a park bench just outside a closed playground, hoist Jay into her lap, and try to read a book on her phone. Usually she gave up after a few minutes and just sat there, staring straight ahead. All of a sudden everything fell silent. Voices, thoughts, headlines, fears. Her large hands stroked her dog's warm fur. All around her, space expanded, and for just this moment it belonged to no one. Dora could stay silent. She could simply sit. Then she went home and Robert asked why she'd been out for so long, and what she'd been doing. In her head she started dubbing him Robert Koch, after the famous bacteriologist. In Bavaria the police declared sitting on park benches a forbidden activity. Soon after, Robert informed her he'd no longer tolerate her walks. He spoke slowly and clearly, as if Dora were somehow cognitively impaired. Any and every movement in public space carried a risk of infection. Insofar as her behavior was irresponsible, she was placing him, Robert, at risk as well, and he was no longer willing to take it. It would be completely sufficient for Jay to do her thrice-daily duty at the nearest tree pit.

At first Dora thought it was an April Fool's Day joke. She pointed to the fact that Berlin hadn't issued the strictest form of stay-at-home order. Going for a solitary stroll was still allowed, especially with a dog.

Robert replied that wasn't the point. The issue was that, in the current situation, they should do everything possible to stop the spread. Everyone should help, as much as they could. Every movement, every outing that isn't absolutely essential would best be avoided.

Dora reminded him that he himself was still rolling around town on his bike, even if it was just for an hour a day.

Robert furiously shot back that that was part of his job. He's writing about the current crisis, and his articles are now among the site's most-read pieces. His work is absolutely essential, which is one thing that, with all due respect, cannot be said of hers.

She asked one last time whether he was actually trying to forbid her from leaving the house.

Robert thought about it for a second, even giving an embarrassed smirk. And then he nodded. On the kitchen table behind him, Dora's laptop crashed. *Runtime error 0x0. We are sorry for the inconvenience.*

That's when a switch flipped in Dora's mind. She looked at the black screen, and then at Robert, who was still standing right in front of her. She realized she no longer knew this man. There were three possibilities: Either she'd fallen into some absurdist film in which she had to play her part without having read the script. Or Robert had lost it. Or she herself had lost it. Dora had had it. She wanted out. Her brain couldn't keep up, couldn't process what had just happened, or simply didn't want to follow. She felt no pain. She was just perturbed, overcome by the sudden urge to flee. Between fight or flight, the latter won. She told Robert she'd be living elsewhere for a while, and packed her bags.

She still hadn't said a word to him about the house out in the countryside, and this definitely wasn't the moment to bring him up to speed. He didn't even ask where she planned to go, anyway. Maybe he was in shock. Or relieved she was leaving. Maybe he assumed she was temporarily relocating to Charlottenburg, to stay at her father's place, which was mostly empty since he only came to town fortnightly, for operations. Robert didn't help her carry her things downstairs. Maybe he didn't even see what she was taking. Two suitcases and three moving boxes of clothes, books, bedsheets, bath towels, a few kitchen utensils, and her work stuff. Dora dragged the heavy mattress pad off her side of the bed and lugged it out, letting it slide down the staircase.

The city grew smaller in the rearview mirror of her rented moving van. With each mile, her mood improved. She wasn't just leaving Robert behind, she was leaving the big city, the distress, the barrage of information and emotions behind her. It felt as if she were leaving the known world behind, as if she were in a spaceship headed toward new galaxies. She recognized the exhilaration from her stealthy real-estate visits the previous autumn.

Getaway. She liked the word. It sounded a bit like an abbreviated form of Get-the-hell-out-and-breakaway. She'd gone solo on most of her house-hunting outings, which the realtor didn't mind at all. It was a bit far, the commission a bit low. PDFs, pics, addresses, external viewings. The mere thought that it was actually possible to buy a home electrified her. If you went far enough, the prices were still within reach. At her age, with her career, getting a mortgage should be no problem. Interest rates were at an all-time low, and Dora had reserves: the modest inheritance from her mother, plus the money she had set aside every month since she'd become a senior copywriter, a job that earned as much as a tenured teaching post in Germany's relatively well-funded high-school system. A house amid the greenery. It would've pleased her mother. She would've loved it. And she'd have laughed at the fact that Dora hadn't told a soul. "My little bandit," she'd have said, stroking her daughter's head. Sometimes Dora couldn't help but think her obstinacy, her inner resistance, was her mother's bequest.

Nevertheless, those secretive house-hunting trips still weighed on her conscience. Why wasn't Robert by her side? Why was she going off behind his back instead of with him? It was like she was cheating on him, and getting a thrill out of it. But it just felt so good. Broad fields, muted colors, a vast sky. It had been a long time since Dora had enjoyed something so deeply. Even when she didn't like the houses she saw. When they were too small, too big, or too soulless. As the leaves began to fall from the trees, she no longer thought she'd find anything. But she kept going anyway, and all the while Robert thought she was attending a weekend workshop.

And then she stumbled on the old estate manager's house in Bracken. She pulled up next to the rickety fence in her rental car and just knew: That's the one. Big trees, overgrown yard, grey stucco. At the edge of the village. Six weeks later she was in the local real-estate lawyer's office signing the contract.

Then came Christmas, New Year's Eve, then Covid, and now here she was, driving back to Bracken in a rental van with all her worldly possessions. She secretly feared the house might not even exist. Three months had passed since closing. It had taken six weeks for the wire with the down payment to go through, and then after stay-at-home orders were issued she had sat tight in Berlin. Maybe she was about to run into a roadblock, and they'd send her back to the city. Or she'd get to Bracken, only to find the lot at the village's edge completely empty. Maybe she'd imagined the whole thing. These thoughts made Dora break out into a sweat. But there was no roadblock. And when she got to Bracken, the old estate manager's house and its yard were right there, just like the first time.

Dora leapt out of the van and then just stood and stared. She had to rub her eyes, not because she couldn't believe it, but because she was welling up. It was so beautiful. Back in late autumn the tree's thinning crowns had been ablaze with color. Now they were sprinkled in a tender spring green, as if spritzed by Mother Nature. Below the trees stood the house, just as she remembered it, set far back from the road, built with reassuring symmetry. The left and right sides had three windows each, with a double-doored entryway between. Both windows and doors were framed by engaged stucco columns topped by triangular lintels. It had a raised ground floor, and a stair with six steps led from the main door down to a landing spacious enough to comfortably hold a table and four chairs. Like a balcony, the landing was ringed by a cast-iron balustrade. The roof sat right atop the ground floor, as if it were pulling a black hat down to cover its entire forehead. Evidently, back in the day, Bracken's estate manager didn't have enough money for another floor.

Dora learned from the realtor that, after the fall of the Wall, the house had gone to a community of co-heirs, and it had taken years for all of them to agree to sell. After that, a young couple had bought it and launched headlong into renovations, but then they had a falling out and called it quits. Before Dora showed up, the house had stood empty for quite some time. Exactly how long the realtor wouldn't say. He called it a "gem with endless possibilities," which was another way of saying "wretched dump."

Dora doesn't care. She immediately intuited that the place was perfect for her. It somehow seems too small for its plot of land and its roof. But it defiantly asserts its own dignity like some funny old guy who clings to outmoded codes of conduct. The triangular lintels over the windows look like raised eyebrows. Clearly the house needs to be surrounded by a good swathe of space. The right-hand neighbor's wobbly-looking wall, which must be at least six feet tall, is a stone's throw away. As a kid, Dora would've pointed at the landing in front of the door and exclaimed, "Lookie, the house is sticking its tongue out!"

The old estate manager's house started out as a dream. Now it's the logical conclusion. A refuge. But Dora still finds it hard to believe that it's possible to own something so big. As she looks at the house today, it still seems to be asking her, "Who here owns whom?"

3

Goth

The back of the house has no stucco. From behind it just looks like an old box. The grey exterior wall looks pockmarked, and the upper half is covered with lichen spots. Dora sits out back and surveys the yard. A woman and her plot of land. Lots of room to breathe. If you can pause your thoughts for even a minute, your ears fill with birdsong. Common redstarts dart in and out of the shed, so intent on nest building that they don't even notice Dora on the lawn chair nearby. A starling on the highest branch of a locust tree belts out a tune far louder and more beautiful than one might expect from its proletarian plumage.

There isn't a soul in sight, and only occasionally can a car be heard roaring by. No TV screens blaring CNN's breaking news, either. No smartphones streaming the voices of podcasters and YouTubers prattling on about how they spend their days working from home. Dora left her phone in the house; there's no cell service in the yard anyway. In Bracken, Covid seems nonexistent. The air smells clean, and each day has its own aroma.

Dora indulges the thought that everything might, just might, be completely fine. Things are going well. She got lucky. Since she can't go to Sus-Y HQ anyway, she can work just as well from Bracken as from Berlin. Especially if she doesn't have a ton to do. Under normal circumstances she puts in ten-hour days at the agency, makes a few more work calls on the way home, and takes care of the last few emails just before heading to bed. Once a consultant has sent a client Dora's latest tagline options, another consultant is already knocking on the door with the brief for another client's Mother's Day ad, while off in the wings a bunch of junior-level consultants eagerly await with still other tasks. But now Covid has changed everything, even advertising. Clients are pausing projects and freezing budgets. Longstanding campaign launches are being nixed. Sus-Y has reduced everyone's hours, which means they'll receive short-term government compensation instead of being laid off. So Dora only has two projects to juggle, which means she feels virtually unemployed. One is a short brochure for the organic craft brewery, which she can easily crank out. The other is an ad-campaign launch for a sustainable textile company called FAIRapparel.

None of it provides any reason to panic. Dora's salary is still almost what it was before. WiFi not only works, it's a fiber optic connection—perhaps the only functioning infrastructure in all of Bracken. And she might even be able to set up a proper desk and workstation soon. If not, she can always just work from her laptop, on the kitchen table or even from bed, just propping her back up against the wall, or even out here in the yard on a lawn chair. No problem. This place will eventually grow on Jay, too. One day the yard will look sightlier. Dora just needs to finish setting up a couple of things in the house, it won't take much, she's nearly there. The wood-burning stove is the only heating, but winter is still far off, and who knows if she'll still be here by then. Maybe everything will return to normal before that. Maybe Covid will vanish, and Robert will return to being his old self, the guy it was so easy to talk to, laugh with, and think about. In hindsight, this escape to Bracken could easily look like nothing more than a minor break from life in the big city, a small-town sabbatical made possible by the societal upheaval brought on by a pandemic. Dora could return to the office, put her nose back to the grindstone, climb the corporate ladder, aim to win an international industry award or two over the next couple of years, finally be promoted to Creative Director, and enjoy sustainably fished sushi or organic vegan pizza with her coworkers on the night shift, all paid for by Sus-Y HQ. She'd live in Berlin, spending Monday to Friday in the old Kreuzberg apartment, while enjoying weekends with Robert out here in Bracken. They'd putter about the house and savor the simple life in the countryside, the dream of so many city dwellers. Two happy people in a normal world.

A mere ten minutes have passed. Dora committed to a half hour of doing nothing. Twenty more minutes before she can get back to digging.

"Is that your dog?"

Startled, she looks around. The voice is male, powerful, and deep, and it's coming out of nowhere. Even when she stands up, Dora doesn't see anyone. But she doesn't see Jay-the-Ray, either. Just a second ago, Jay had been lying in a patch of sun between the young maples. Hadn't she? When was the last time

Dora really noticed her presence? When Jay had howled at the blackbirds. And then?

"Hey! Is that your fucking mutt?"

Finally she can locate where the voice is coming from. The man is standing on the other side of the high cinderblock wall separating their properties. A round, close-shorn head is peeking out over the wall, peering right at her. It looks like a dome precariously perched on the edge. The guy has to be at least eight feet tall.

In Dora's mind, being neighbors is akin to being in an arranged marriage of sorts. You can achieve a degree of contentedness with one another, but the likelihood isn't very high. Over the last two weeks she hasn't noticed anybody next door. Which led her to conclude that the neighboring property was uninhabited. From her house only the upper half of the neighboring house is visible. It's built much closer to the road, and its front yard is also enclosed by a high wall with a broad, hefty-looking wooden door that is always locked tight. A window on the second floor of the house is boarded shut with plywood, making it look as though the house is blind in one eye. At one point Dora had climbed up on a stool to peek over the wall. Surprisingly, the yard next door wasn't overgrown as she'd expected, but looked well-tended. Far from being a plot of land, it was a veritable garden, complete with manicured lawn. No garbage, not a single bit of scrap. There was a trailer with a quaint paint job in dark green and white, propped up on jacks, its entryway adorned with geranium planters. And an old white pickup truck tidily parked next to the house.

Dora figured someone from Berlin must use the trailer as a holiday hut every now and then. A fellow city-dweller who occasionally escapes, tends the garden, mows the lawn, and goes for Sunday drives in the old pickup. And they must not be able to come for a bit because of Covid. Folks here in Brandenburg are pushing to keep people from Berlin out. Maybe the guy's a creative type, from Friedrichshain. Maybe it's somebody she'd get along with. Although, admittedly, getting-along-with is the second-best option when it comes to being neighbors. Never-being-there is far better.

The shaved head presently propped atop the wall doesn't strike her as that of a creative type from Friedrichshain. Dora hesitantly walks in his direction. As she reaches the wall, she has to tilt her head all the way back. Hopefully this guy is standing on a crate or something.

"You deaf?" He scratches his bald noggin. "I'm talking to you."

Before Dora can reply that she understood his question, only didn't respond because her answer would depend on exactly what dog he was referring to, Jay-the-Ray comes flying through the air. She spreads all four legs out wide, as if the skin stretched between her limbs might help her catch the wind and parasail to safety. Dora almost manages to catch her pet, but then Jay's slim frame slips through her hands and lands on the ground, where the dog does a half-somersault as if she were some kind of comic-strip character. Then she euphorically jumps up and down, pawing at Dora as if the two hadn't seen one another in years.

"Are you out of your mind?" Dora yells, patting Jay's legs even though it's evident her little pet is completely unscathed. When anything hurts Jay, she howls like a diva.

"Your mutt was messing with my potatoes."

Indeed, Jay looks like she's donned dark socks, and Dora is moved by the sight of damp earth clinging to her fur. Not once in her entire life has Jay dug around in the dirt. She hadn't had the opportunity until now, because where she lived only offered up tree pits and sidewalks and fenced-in dog parks. Gravel paths and flowerbeds. Leash laws and plastic bags and curb-your-dog signs veritably scolding owners to pick up their pets' poop. Perhaps some predatory instinct lingered deep in Jay's heart after all, even if her forebears couldn't possibly have included any long-legged, streamlined hounds.

"Sorry about your potatoes," Dora said, straightening up and placing her hands on her hips. "But you could've broken Jay's legs!"

"Not my fault you can't catch," the neighbor shot back.

Jay seems pleased by all the commotion. Gazing upward, panting excitedly, her thin tail lightly thumps the ground as her eyes encourage Dora to defend her. Go on! Fight for me! The two humans look down at Jay for a little while, Dora on one side of the wall, the neighbor on the other.

"Pretty hideous looking, wouldn't you say?" he finally adds.

His assessment can't readily be dismissed. Far from purebred, Jay could easily have been the descendant of a pug, a French bulldog, maybe even a

Chihuahua, and who knows what else. Her scraggly, yellowish-white fur is neither long nor short. Her body is stocky, her legs stumpy. Her face is goggle-eyed, her ears fold over, and she's got such an exaggerated underbite that you have to wonder whether she'd even be capable of biting someone, although it admittedly seems unlikely she'd ever even attempt such a thing. Surprisingly, despite all these flaws, most people who meet Jay dissolve into a puddle, cooing at her funny-looking cuteness. Dora thinks Jay looks like something dreamt up by some Japanese toy-industry designer. Something that, at the push of a button, starts flashing, wriggling around, and emitting a little ditty. But that makes no difference. Dora loves Jay for her laconic moodiness, the way her frequent pouts are punctuated by sudden outbursts of joy. Dora feels no need to find her dog adorable.

"Yeah, he's hideous alright," the neighbor repeats, as if he hadn't made himself clear the first time.

"He's a she," Dora corrects in a dignified tone.

"I thought his name was Jay."

Dora shrugs. "I just found it funny, I guess. Besides, the name can go either way."

"You city folk can be so fucking predictable."

Dora's seized by an impulse to ask him just why he thinks she's from the big city. Why he's so presumptuous, assuming her dog is male and she's from Berlin. Sure, that might be where she lived most recently, and before that it was Hamburg, but she grew up in a suburb of Münster, a place you'd be hard-pressed to call a "city." Then again, viewed from Bracken probably any grouping of buildings worthy of its own name would fall under the category of "city," and the fact that Dora isn't from these parts is glaringly obvious.

"Super predictable. Especially in times like these," Dora adds, going out of her way to lighten the city folk/country folk divide with an ironic wink.

But her neighbor doesn't seem to pick up on the joke. Maybe he hasn't even heard about Covid, or knows nothing about Berlin, or couldn't care less about either. They size one another up in silence, him scanning her from head to toe, her examining him from the neck up while the rest of his body remains hidden behind the wall. His head is shaved bald, shiny as a bowling ball, but the bottom half of his face is stubbly. He's got bags under his eyes and a wishy-washy expression. Dora could've readily redirected the "pretty hideous" compliment right back at him. It's hard to say exactly how old he is. Maybe in his mid forties, which would make him about ten years her senior.

"Goth," the neighbor says.

Annoyed, Dora glances toward the road to see if he might be referring to somebody or something headed their way.

"Goth," the neighbor emphatically repeats, as if Dora were hard of hearing or otherwise slow on the uptake. Apparently he's stating a name, although whether it's his first or last name remains unclear.

"Visigoth or Ostrogoth?" Dora retorts.

Now it's the neighbor's turn to be annoyed. An index finger appears above the wall and points to his right temple.

"Goth," he says again, "as in Gottfried."

This exchange feels a bit like the communication between Robinson Crusoe and Friday, but without any indication of who's Robinson and who's Friday. So Dora raises her hand and points to herself.

"Dora," she says, "as in my dog's a-DORA-ble."

That just popped into her head. Sometimes her ad-writing brain comes up with stuff like that. The neighbor ignores the pun. He's busy making a strange series of movements, standing up straight, nodding and then bending over to one side, nearly losing his balance and then catching it again, until finally his right shoulder and then his entire right arm appear above the wall. He gingerly extends his hand to Dora, taking care not to disturb the top row of wobbly-looking cinderblocks. Apparently people in Brandenburg don't take the new social-distancing guidelines very strictly. Nobody back in Berlin dares to shake hands anymore. It'd probably be easier to deny Swabians their stringent communal house-keeping traditions than to prevent hearty hand-shakes between the people of Brandenburg. Dora decides not to be a spoilsport, strolls straight up to the wall, stretches her own hand up, and quickly shakes Goth's hand so he can stop his elaborate ma-neuvering. She can't help but wonder what Robert would make of such an encounter, and almost bursts out laughing.

"Pleased to meet you," Goth says. "I'm the village Nazi."

Back at the ad agency, they came up with these kinds of scenes all the time. The script would read: A young woman has just moved to the countryside. She's a bit unsure in her new surroundings, but determined to find everything just peachy. She meets her new neighbor. "Pleased to meet you, I'm the village Nazi," aaand—*freeze*. The action stops, the camera slowly zooms in on the dumbfounded face of the starring actress, whose shock has turned her into waxwork. Atop this image, Dora's tagline appears in bold type, set diagonally: *New Challenge—New Chill*. For an iced tea brand. Or maybe cough drops.

Unfortunately this isn't one of Dora's own ads. She's nowhere near a pot of tea. She doesn't even have a pack of cigarettes on her. And if she ever needed to light up, now would be the time.

"You gotta fix the fence." Goth points to the back of the yard, where the wall ends and a chain-link fence continues the barrier. Several fence posts have half fallen over.

Fence breakin' in Bracken, the tagline-writing tool in Dora's brain kicks in.

"If your mutt digs up even one more potato, I'll kick his head in," her new neighbor says.

Dora considers herself quick-witted, with a riposte always at the ready. But now she's just staring at Goth like an idiot, utterly dumbfounded. The words her father said, after she told him she was moving to the countryside, come to mind.

"To Prignitz? What do you plan to do out there among all those right-wing nutjobs?"

Making sure Jojo isn't right is one of Dora's most important motivations in life. She majored in communications because he considered medicine and law the only valid courses of study. She dropped out because he said completing one's degree is essential.

She loves working in advertising, while he considers the entire field unnecessary. Thank god Jojo actually liked Robert, otherwise she'd have been forced to stick with him forever.

Her next task is to prove to him that Bracken was the best idea ever. An ideal exile. Even better if she could prove it's one-hundred percent Nazi-free. At the moment, that last part is looking a bit iffy.

She'll have to say something eventually. And since it already seems she's unwittingly entered into an arranged marriage with a neo-Nazi, she'd best immediately signal that she won't put up with any BS.

"Fix it yourself," she finally says, sounding imperious.

"Nope." Goth snarls, an expression that Dora figures is supposed to look like a grin, or maybe a sneer. "I'm on the right."

"I'll bet." Dora mentally chalks up another point on her quick-wittedness scoreboard, even though Goth is unaware there's even a game going on. He stares at her, and his expression implies he's wondering whether city dwellers' heads are outfitted with brains.

"Looking at our properties from the road, you live on the left, I live on the right. Got it? And the neighbor on the left is always responsible for the fence to the right." He thinks it over a bit more. "So, actually, you're responsible for every side of your property-line fence, since there's nobody to your left."

With that, Goth's face vanishes from above the wall like a puppet from a Punch and Judy show.

"At the edge of the village," the listing had said. Dora had pictured a beautifully bucolic, calm place.

And, indeed, vast fields stretch out just past the fence on the left side of her property. But for the last several days tractors have droned back and forth through those fields towing plows, harrows, and combine seeders. And "at the edge of the village" also means living at the city-limit sign—or, in this case, village-limit sign—which means traffic from Plausitz roars by the house going a solid 60 miles per hour. And nobody even thinks of hitting the breaks, at best they just coast down to 30 mph by the time they're in the middle of town.

Dora turns, whistles to summon Jay, and trudges toward the house. It's high time for coffee.

4

Garbage Island

The back door of the house leads to a little vestibule where Dora shakes off her sneakers. One stairway leads down to the basement, and another leads up to the raised ground floor and main living space. The kitchen is behind the first door on the left.

Of all the rooms, the kitchen is Dora's favorite. She loves the ornate old tile floor with its light-green tendrils and pink petals. The realtor said that collectors have been known to pay a fortune for even one such tile. With the tile floor the kitchen looks completely finished, especially since it's more fully furnished than the rest of the house. Dora found a small table and two scuffed-up wooden chairs in the shed, which she's placed under the window. The sink, a rickety buffet cabinet with bull's-eye windowpanes, and an old fridge came with the house. With a little effort, the table, chairs, and buffet cabinet could all be transformed into veritable vintage gems. That would be just one of a thousand projects Dora could drive herself mad with, had she not up and decided to quit such pursuits.

While moving out of the rental apartment she'd shared with Robert back in Kreuzberg, she found an old crate down in the basement storage unit with a bunch of stuff from her student days. It turned out to be a blessing of sorts. Thanks to that crate, Dora now has a plethora of plates and cups in all different colors and sizes which she's neatly arranged behind the bull's-eye windows of the buffet. She's also got a bunch of glasses that don't match, a casserole dish, and a ton of flatware she's placed in the buffet drawers.

Relishing a newfound feeling of freedom, she goes to the cabinet, takes out the big blue mug her student-era self chugged coffee from, and adds two heady spoonfuls of black grounds. Using all these old things again is such a pleasure. Closing your eyes, smelling the coffee, and taking joy in simply having this mug is such a pleasure. Above all, Dora notices how good it feels to possess only the bare necessities.

There's one carton of UHT milk left in the fridge. She's placed all the other provisions and supplies in the lower section of the buffet, next to the starter-set of pans and a stack of assorted big bowls and serving dishes that will come in handy for storing fruit, feeding Jay, and presoaking laundry.

The newer things are from a shopping center just outside Berlin. The day Dora moved, she popped in before leaving the city for good. She wheeled through the aisles nervously filling a cart with canned foods, bags of noodles, coffee, wine, shower gel, cleaning supplies, dog food, and shrink-wrapped wholegrain bread, fretting all the while that someone might accuse her of hoarding. She even snatched two packs of toilet paper. On the way to checkout, the home supplies aisle gave her the great idea of also grabbing a broom and mop, the set of pans, and a camping stove. From behind her Plexiglas shield, the check-out lady watched, thoroughly bored, as Dora rolled up with her tower of stuff and emptied the cart onto the belt. The lady then inspected her fingernails as Dora stuck her debit card into the slot, and didn't bother saying a word about hoarding or anything else. Sometimes the people of Brandenburg are better than people from Berlin expect.

Dora fills a pot from the faucet, places it on the camping stove, and waits for the water to boil. Past experience tells her it'll take a while. As she leans against the buffet, her thoughts run wild through the house like hounds sniffing for something to usefully fill the next few minutes. Maybe she should clear the windowsills of dead flies? Or quickly check her email? Jot down a few ideas for the FAIRapparel campaign launch? Or watch another YouTube tutorial on how to start a vegetable patch?

Pause—stop. Don't think. No multitasking. She's got to quit, give it a rest already. Multitasking is really just a lack of any ability to concentrate. And anyway, it's not like she has too little time, she actually has too much time on her hands. Even if she keeps busy tending to home and garden, she still runs the risk of having nothing to do come evening. It's high time she learned to just make a cup of coffee and enjoy it, full stop. Without doing ten other things at the same time. Novels are full of people just sitting by the window and drinking a cup of tea, doing nothing but staring out said window. It can't be that hard.

Dora forces herself to stay put, right where she is, leaning against the buffet and staring into the pot, where the first few air bubbles are starting to appear. The same thing is happening inside her body. Little bubbles are beginning to prickle the pit of her stomach, floating up through her throat all the way to her brain, where they burst, leaving behind a lingering irritation that can easily turn into a headache. This prickly unease has been with her for a while now. Especially when she has nothing to do. Especially at night. Sometimes she spends hours on end just lying there on her back, unable to sleep because her body is so agitated. It's like a snowballing nervousness that comes out of nowhere, a wholly unfounded stage fright. When the turmoil is too much to take, she gets up. On nights like that back in Berlin she'd go out to the balcony. Here in Bracken she goes out to the landing at the bottom of the front stairs. She smokes a cigarette, tilts her head back, and stares up at the stars. She imagines flying into space. Tries to picture what it would be like to float, free of gravity, surrounded by darkness, cold, silence. At night, Dora wants out. Not just out into exile from her life with Robert, or out into the countryside, but *out* out, once and for all. She wants to be fundamentally gone. Maybe she wants to die. Or maybe she wants out into outer space, alongside Alexander Gerst, the astronaut you still read about in the papers every now and then, back before Covid became the only news.

She still remembers the first time she felt this prickly unease. Robert was in high spirits, and had just come back from SMILE, the Summer Meeting in Lausanne Europe organized by Fridays for Future, where he'd briefly spoken to Greta. He was generally in a good mood back then, as was Dora. Working with a new agency felt great, and the people at Sus-Y were all nice and chill, thanks in part to HR's wellness setup. Staff were free to take as many days off as they needed, which everybody loved, even though it meant everybody took less vacation than they would have otherwise. Every day there was fresh fruit, there was free yoga once a week, and endless opportunities for continuing education. The concept of sustainability helped slightly temper the sheer banality of working in the ad world. Robert was pleased because Dora switching agencies had been his idea in the first place. And now they had more time to lounge out on the balcony together drinking a truly delicious wine Robert got from an organic vintner in France.

On this particular evening following his return from the Fridays for Future meeting, Robert told Dora about the Great Pacific Garbage Patch as she listened, stunned. Between Russia and America there's a huge, floating island of plastic trash that's already as large as Europe. Within decades, there will be more plastic in the world's oceans than fish.

The sixth continent is an island of garbage. The spitting image of modern civilization. Dora detected the first few bubbles prickling their way up through her innards. She got ahold of herself by lifting one hand to her head and placing the other over her glass, to keep Robert from refilling it.

Not long after, while cleaning the kitchen one day, she came across a stash of reusable cotton tote bags. They were from bookstores and organic farmers' markets, city festivals and professional conferences, Dora's ad-agency clients and the companies that advertised with Robert's online magazine. Some were even from EDEKA, the supermarket Dora would buy totes from only when she'd forgotten to bring her own bags. They held on to all these totes because they were reusable. Theoretically, at least. Just like returnable deposit bottles, tote bags signaled a rejection of consumer culture and throwaway society. A small contribution to help shrink that garbage patch. The stash in their kitchen cabinet was a veritable mountain of totes, scrunched up and nested, stuffed one inside another, at least thirty total.

Dora had heard on the radio that it takes a lot more energy to produce a cotton tote bag than a plastic bag. You'd have to use one cotton tote at least 130 times for it to be more eco-friendly than a single-use plastic bag.

She stood in front of the cabinet doing calculations. Thirty cotton totes times 130 trips to the store meant another 3,900 shopping trips total before she could say she'd done something to save the environment. At an average of three trips to the store each week, that would only take 25 years. Presuming not one more tote was added to their stash.

The prickling bubbles flustered Dora's stomach and floated up to burst in her head. She felt dizzy, as if standing at the edge of an abyss. The abyss was the futility of it all. Robert wanted to save the planet, but it made no difference, the planet simply didn't care. The planet expected them to make 3,900 shopping trips, otherwise they'd be ensuring its destruction. The dizziness was dreadful. Even more dreadful was the fact that Robert was now strolling over, laying his arm around her shoulder, asking what was wrong. He didn't even seem to have noticed the gaping abyss.

Dora spent that night on the balcony, smoking a half pack of cigarettes. She'd read somewhere that a single cigarette produces more particulate matter than an unfiltered Diesel engine running nonstop for an hour.

Sometimes Dora's convinced that there are people who simply aren't cut out for living. They lack the knack, or aren't sufficiently skilled. Just like there are people who aren't great at soccer, or playing the piano. Some people just don't have a talent for living, and maybe Dora falls into that category, too. For everything she notices or that occurs to her, she can always find a counterargument. Inspected closely enough, every valid argument crumbles, and every idea undoes itself. Her skeptical eye saw contradictions, absurdities, logical errors everywhere. It transformed her collaborative instinct, her desire to go along with things, into stubborn resistance and refusal. Which Dora suspects not only makes you unable to act but, in the long run, also makes you lonely. Maybe she just doesn't really have a place within the overarching conceptual framework of human existence.

The water is boiling. She takes the pot off the stove and carefully fills the mug. She once read that it was inadvisable to put the coffee grounds straight into the cup and add boiling water, the way Turkish coffee is made. Apparently it's unhealthy to drink the dregs. But that's just how she likes it. And she'd like to hear more about Alexander Gerst for once, too.

Maybe he's up in space again. Her cup filled almost to the brim, she takes a seat at the table. Her very first sip goes down the wrong pipe, irritating her throat so badly she has to stand up, cough, and, bending over the sink, spit. After that she doesn't even want coffee. Her thoughts are running wild again, and she has to calm them down. No matter how many hundreds of times Dora orders her mind to shape up, her thoughts always slip away, grab onto their favorite fixations, and wreak utter havoc in her head.

She takes the reusable to-go mug emblazoned with the Suz-Y logo from the buffet cabinet, forbids herself from trying to calculate how many more times she'll have to use it in order to justify its existence, pours her coffee in, and calls Jay. The dog is curled up on a piece of cardboard that shields her small body from the chill of the floor tiles. Her leopard-print faux-fur doggy bed is back in the office. As Dora walks over to the door, Jay reluctantly follows.

"Really? Another walk already?" her accusatory glower seems to say. "Can't we just go back to Berlin, where you can just carry me up and down the stairs? Where all we have to do is go around the block?"

5

Gustav

Dora's first job started as an internship. Between semesters she interned at a boutique agency in Münster, and because her work got results she was taken on as a junior copywriter. She dropped out of school, moved out of her parents' house, and rented a tiny place in town. She subsequently spent a year studying at the Texterschmiede Hamburg, before its rebrand as the Hamburg School of Ideas, and got to know all the major ad agencies while getting her certificate. So even though she was still technically considered an intern, that one-year experience gave her enough of a network to snag a job at Notter & Friends, one of the top German agencies. Around this time she also met her first real boyfriend, Philipp, a young sociology professor from Frankfurt. They had a happy long-distance relationship until she discovered he was cheating on her.

Dora stayed single for a while, and got a puppy. She worked like mad. She took on every night shift. She was the only one who happily took on pitches, even when they fell under other teams' domains. She got a thrill voting on taglines at two in the morning alongside the creative director, then letting a cab whisk her home through the empty city streets. Not because she had anything to prove, but because staying busy kept her calmer than remaining idle.

She always got to the office early, and had no problem if someone called her back in again at midnight. She never let an email sit in her inbox more than five minutes without replying, regardless of whether she was in a meeting, on the subway, or in the bathroom. When she was brought on to the team handling a major insurance account, she came up with an ad and knocked it out of the park. Her ultra-short clip showed two doves building a nest that kept falling from the trees but invariably landed in a padded suitcase. The tree type and suitcase shape changed, but the tagline stayed the same: "Just in case." It went viral and became a ubiquitous meme.

For a while after that, Dora was among the agency's most sought-after copywriters. She got a good offer from Berlin, the only downside being that she had to start immediately. For the first few weeks, she and Jay camped out in a hotel. Then she moved into a shared apartment that didn't officially allow any pets.

It was a rough landing in the capital city, and had Dora not been so overworked she'd have had to admit she was miserable. She felt like a stranger, completely out of place. The city was too strident for her taste. Sometimes she felt like the only person in town who went to work, while everybody else was busy bustling around or freaking out. Her misery was partially due to her stressful job, but also partially a result of her inner resistance, and the fact that for several weeks she'd failed to file the necessary paperwork to officially become a resident of Berlin.

One autumn morning she finally managed to take a couple of hours off. She left Jay with a coworker at the agency, hopped on the brand-new Schindel-hauer bike she'd already nicknamed Gustav, and sped over to the local residents' registration office in Pankow. The mere sight of the overflowing bike racks out front made her blood pressure spike. If it was as full inside as it looked out here, the process would take hours. Dora scanned the racks of fancy treadmill-style scooters, bike shares parked askew, and bike trailers for kids, in search of a safe spot to lock up Gustav. He had a belt drive and luggage rack mounted above the front wheel. In his impeccable, glossy, mint-green coat of paint he was practically begging to be stolen. Finally Dora found a spot, secured him with her Kryptonite chain lock, walked into the registry office, and took a number.

The waiting room chairs were full, and there were people sitting on the floor and standing along the wall. Dora broke into a sweat. After an hour and a half she emailed work to say she'd be later than expected, but still planned to be back in time for her two o'clock meeting. She knew she should probably just get up, go back to work, and try again another day. But when? And would it be any emptier then? And what about the time she'd already spent waiting?

That was the sunk-cost fallacy in action. The compulsion to continue down the wrong path only because you've already come so far. Dora knew precisely how the sunk-cost fallacy functioned. She'd even taken a coaching course for freelancers to protect herself from falling for it. Ever since, she hasn't wasted time finishing a bad book solely because she'd already started reading it. She wouldn't spend the rest of her life playing Farmville only because she'd already invested so much time building her virtual farm. Nor did she pursue any lavish ad-campaign ideas if she already intuited that the tone didn't perfectly match the client. Dora had mastered the culture of failure and cost-benefit calculation.

But she stayed seated in the waiting room anyway. She resisted capitulation. She resisted her tendency to always be too damn clever. She had no desire to give in or to let Berlin win.

When they finally called her number, she'd been waiting for over two hours. She left the registry office feeling aggressive enough to lash out at the next person who got in her way. It was quarter to two. If she pedaled like a pro, she'd still be late, but only by a few minutes.

She crossed the forecourt at a jog, heading for the bike racks. And then she spotted a man bending down over Gustav. Dora knew she could trust her eyes; it wasn't just her imagination. The bike rack had significantly cleared out in the meantime. Gustav was new, his glossy green coat was eye-catching, and he'd cost well over 1,000 euros. The man was fumbling around, messing with Dora's combination lock.

Without even thinking, she sped up. While running, she extended the hand that was holding her leather waist pack. She wasn't aware of the momentum gathering as she ran. Nor did she think about the fairly thick novel inside. She reached the man and hit him square over the head with it. It made a horrific thump on impact.

The man immediately let go of Gustav and pressed both hands to his temples. His back was to Dora, and he was stumbling so hard she thought he might keel over. She actually hoped he'd keel over, to be precise. As she watched him stagger, she was overcome by a deep satisfaction. As if her misguided excursion to Pankow had been worth it, after all. The guy had to be about six feet tall. And yet she had managed to nail him. She'd protected Gustav. She hadn't let Berlin and all its crazies get to her.

The man didn't keel over. As he turned, Dora realized he couldn't have been any older than her. He looked totally normal, not like some junkie, some nutjob, some bicycle thief. He had stylishly mussed-up hair and a neatly trimmed ten-day-old beard. Chinos and sneakers. But then again, who's to say what a bicycle thief looks like? She wound her arm back up, threatening another blow. He had to scram. If he got out of there now, she wouldn't file a complaint. She had triumphed—against the guy, the day, the whole city. That was enough.

But the dude didn't scram. Instead he took two huge strides toward Dora and screamed in her face.

"What the fuck is wrong with you?"

She was so taken aback that for a moment she didn't know how to respond. Maybe this guy is crazy, after all. Maybe he's dangerous. Maybe she's the one who should've run away. But that was out of the question. She was still feeling aggressive enough to answer him.

"That's my bike!" she bellowed.

"Oh yeah?" he bellowed back.

"Fuck off already, you fucker!"

That seemed to confuse him. He sized her up, head to toe, inspecting her clothes, clearly trying to place her, categorize her. Just like him, she was wearing the big-city uniform, albeit in luxury form. Pricey jeans, cropped business jacket, and fluorescent yellow Giesswein merino runners. Sans socks. Loose ponytail, just a touch of makeup.

"You almost bashed my head in," he said, now sounding somewhat calmer.

"You almost nabbed my bike," she confidently shot back.

Suddenly he burst into laughter. He was laughing so hard that he was literally holding his belly. Dora extracted the pack of cigarettes from her waist pack and lit one up.

"You're …" the guy stepped forward, guffawing, "you're such a numbskull!"

It'd been ages since anyone had called her a *numbskull*. The word smacked of childhood, of provincialism, of West Germany. Of the late eighties. Dora couldn't help but laugh, too. The guy glanced at his watch.

"Shit," he said, "I have an editorial meeting. At two. I can't miss it, but now I'll be late."

"I have a meeting, too," Dora said. "At two."

Her own words struck Dora as those of someone who wasn't exactly all there. But it was definitely he, not she, who was off. Even if he actually looked just fine. Nice, even.

"I've been waiting for you for an hour," he explained. "I even went back inside to ask around. But the place is just too big."

Dora took another deep drag and tossed the cigarette butt to the ground. It was time to end the charade.

"You still haven't caught on, huh?" the guy asked. He pointed to Gustav. "You looped your fucking chain around my bike, too."

The flash of recognition hit her like a slow-motion slap. Dora was in the hot seat. The current jolted her from one universe into another. She wagered a few ginger steps in Gustav's direction. She leaned down over her one-hundred-percent-foolproof chain lock. The guy's voice seemed to reach her from a great distance.

"I tried to guess your combination. Some people only turn one disc on the dial."

The chain secured not just Gustav's frame and seat, but also the frame of a fairly beat-up-looking men's bike. Dora felt the blood rushing to her cheeks.

"Okay," she said. "Lunch on me?"

Over the next few weeks they went out for several meals, both lunch and dinner, to the local Japanese place or to vegetarian restaurants, since even back then Robert was avoiding meat. On weekends they went for walks in the woods, and once they even went clubbing, ending the night at Berghain. They went to flea markets and to bed together, which was so much lovelier than it had ever been with Philipp. Not only that, but Dora felt like she and Robert could converse forever. They talked about books, TV shows, the state of the world. When Robert suggested they move in together, Dora concurred. He'd been looking for a new place for a while already, and she desperately needed out of her shared apartment. They found their dream place, a veritable palace: a vast-feeling, 850-square-foot, recently renovated apartment in a beautiful historic building in the heart of Kreuzberg. Complete with balcony. The rent was within reach, and since they'd be splitting, it was even twice as affordable.

They hadn't known each other so long at that point. At first Dora felt like their gorgeous apartment was the backdrop for a shared performance, each reciting their respective role in a play titled *Adult Relationship*. At some point it became reality. With Philipp she had constantly fought, whereas with Robert things were smooth, they had almost no differences of opinion. Robert was about her age and, like her, had grown up in a mid-sized West German city. His father wasn't a doctor like hers, but he was a district court judge. Robert had a sister he didn't really get along with, just like Dora and Axel. When she came home from the office each night, she could hear his fingers on the keyboard the moment she stepped into the entryway. She liked his fervent dedication. She liked their nighttime talks out on the balcony, staying up far past bedtime. They always had something to talk about. Neither of them lived in their own head, she never felt alone with her thoughts.

The first minor irritation surfaced as people around them started having kids. All of a sudden Robert's friends and circle of acquaintances found it harder and harder to meet up at the bar. Robert lamented the fact that now people expected him to meet up over breakfast at some family-friendly café or other. When one of his buddies asked him to hang out at the playground, he took it as an imposition. He complained about old friends who'd suddenly metamorphosed into mommies and daddies. Apparently they'd become animals driven by instinct, incapable of behaving like adult humans with brains. Conversations became monologues centered on the ins and outs of daycare, the phases of early infant development, and little else. He got all riled up about new parents' notorious inability to focus. Above all, he detested their pitying glances, which seemed to insinuate that, sure, he might have more leisure time, but he hadn't a clue as to what real life was really like. For the first time, Dora realized that Robert actually felt provoked by other people's life choices when the subject of children came up.

She herself didn't know whether she wanted to have kids or not. She'd lost her mother relatively young, so couldn't imagine becoming one herself. But Robert's tirades frightened her. He claimed you had to be crazy to bring children into this overpopulated planet in the middle of a climate crisis that was only going to get worse.

Despite all that, Dora found their life together virtually perfect. There was nothing she wanted to change. Their evenings out on the balcony were still lovely, and they could still talk on and on and on, bringing clarity to their shared world. She liked Robert, Jay, and their Kreuzberg apartment. She had enough money, and a job she enjoyed. She wanted for nothing, and nothing annoyed her. Until Greta Thunberg came on the scene.

6

Deposit Bottles

Dora follows the sandy road leading between the edge of the woods and the field. This is the farthest she's ventured outside Bracken on foot. Why go for walks when you have your own property? Her fellow villagers seem to feel the same. The only footprints in the sand are hers. But the road is also speckled by a beautiful pattern of sunlight streaming through leaves lightly trembling in the breeze.

Dora has always adored the woods. She considers them one massive, breathing entity, full of life, teeming with activity while also emanating an unflappable calm. The woods ask nothing of her, have no expectations. They don't need her support, or anyone else's. They take care of themselves, and quite successfully at that. Among trees far larger and older than any human being, Dora feels fantastically insignificant, and it comes as a relief. She loves the silence, the stillness, which the insects' buzzing only intensifies rather than ruins. The silvery, quaking leaves and sweet scent of pine needles. The birds' enthusiastic whooping and chirping as they go about their springtime business in the broad treetops. Even Jay has shed her bad mood, perkily running on ahead. When something suddenly rustles in the tall grass along the roadside, she launches into a funny jump.

The air is cool, and Dora has to maintain a steady clip just to keep warm. The sand softens her foot strike. Off to the right, the field slopes gently upward, freshly plowed, dark brown, spread out smooth as a broad cloth. A couple of cranes strut about, perhaps in search of potatoes.

The road turns, leaving the edge of the field and leading into the woods. Tractors and logging vehicles have left deep ruts in the ground. The screech of a Eurasian jay warns of Dora's approach. She stops in her tracks and scans the treetops in search of the bird.

Years ago, her mother would often call her to the kitchen window to point out special birds. A common wood pigeon, a northern wren, and sometimes a yellowhammer.

"Isn't that incredible?" her mother would whisper. "We get to see as many birds here as we would living in the middle of the forest."

Her mother liked every kind of bird except magpies. She'd shoo them away by clapping. But the Eurasian jay was her favorite. Whenever one showed up in the yard, both kids were immediately summoned to the window to admire its reddish plumage with bright blue and black patterning on the upper wing. Its role as guardian of the forest. And because Dora loved her mother, whenever anyone asked the girl what her favorite animal was, she replied, "the Eurasian jay," or sometimes just "jay."

In the last few weeks of Dora's mother's life, Jojo pushed her sickbed so it faced at an angle out the glass door leading onto the terrace, so she could look out and admire the birds right up to the very end. If the deceased do come back to watch over their still-living loved ones, Dora's sure her mother returns in the form of a Eurasian jay.

Dora eventually spots the beautiful bird in the branches of a beech, and cautiously raises her hand to wave hello. The jay casts a skeptical glance her way before flitting off into the forest, swiftly vanishing.

Robert loved the woods, too. Long before they met, he had spent months living in a hut in the Spree Forest Reserve. It was part of his high school thesis project, which involved measuring the temperature of the forest floor about 2.5 feet below the surface. He even took Dora to his old research area a few times. He viewed the forest as an open book with thousands of stories to tell, if only you knew how to read it. He knew all the trees by both their common names and scientific binomials, and could explain beetle behavior in great detail. He showed Dora the tracks of rabbits and foxes, and decoded the puzzling hustle and bustle of an anthill for her. At moments like that she felt especially close to him.

So it hurt when he no longer had time to take strolls together. It didn't inflict acute pain, it was more like a latent pressure, so subtle that even Dora hardly noticed it at first. Robert's passion for protecting the planet was intensifying, but that was the case for lots of people since Greta Thunberg had started carrying her message around the globe. When she was on TV, Robert stared at the girl as if she were an apparition. Her round face, her lips pressed tight together, her long braid.

Robert attended every climate rally, not just as a reporter, but as an activist. Whenever Greta planned an appearance within reach, he'd travel there, even when it meant flying. Every encounter seemed to stoke his engine, motivating him to take it to the next level. He had become single-mindedly focused. Over their nightly glass of red wine he'd go on and on about rising temperatures, rising sea levels, desertification, floods, storms growing stronger and stronger, and other natural disasters. He described how entire species were going extinct, and discussed coming waves of climate refugees in such foreboding detail that Dora envisioned death marches and horrific slum scenes straight out of some Roland Emmerich epic. Civil wars would inevitably ensue, and humankind would start destroying itself well before Mother Nature dealt the final blow.

Dora listened to him, as she always had. But his apocalyptic scenarios got her down. According to the World Bank, within the next 30 years there would be over 140 million climate refugees. The numbers paralyzed her. On that scale, saving the planet was impossible. Unlikely for humans, at least. And sometimes she just wanted to talk about other things. Like her current project, or the book she was reading. Even Trump, Brexit, or the AfD, if necessary. Robert said all that was secondary. "It's five past midnight, and nobody's even noticed," he pronounced, although Dora found the word *nobody* a bit of an exaggeration considering how Greta was broadcasting her opinions to the entire world on an almost daily basis.

Dora increasingly felt the urge to contradict him. Not because she fundamentally disagreed. She, too, wanted the depletion and exploitation of the planet's resources to stop. But she couldn't follow the logic underpinning all these demands. Sipping Coca-Cola through macaroni struck her as absurd when countries with populations in the billions were trying to catch up with industrialization. How much sense does it make to leave your Diesel car parked in the garage when countless gargantuan container ships cruise the oceans? And where exactly did those crystal-clear facts Robert always cited come from? Wasn't it feasible that a commuter driving his suv to and from the office every day, where he'd be fed alongside his coworkers in a communally heated and lit space, had a lower carbon footprint than a freelancer in Berlin-Kreuzberg who, although he only got around by bike, still prepared three meals daily on the stove, streaming music from dawn to dusk, in a space lit up and heated solely for him? Is cotton really so much better than plastic? Who's more carbon-neutral, an activist crisscrossing Europe to attend rallies, or a stubborn grandma who doesn't bother with recycling but has also never set foot on a plane? What happened to the old certainty that there are no absolute certainties, which is why everything needs to be doubted, debated, and fought about? Dora couldn't understand how Robert could feel so completely certain his lifestyle was so superior. She just didn't follow.

Sus-Y had recently banned plastic bottles, so staff were expected to bring their mineral water to the office in stainless-steel bottles instead. At the company meeting where this had been decided, Dora had asked on what basis they were presuming stainless-steel bottles were more eco-friendly than PET-plastic bottles, which were just as refillable. Her coworkers stared at her, some with pity, others with disapproval in their eyes, as if Dora had some kind of cognitive impairment that prevented her from understanding the issue at hand.

She'd have liked to share experiences like that with Robert, but Robert no longer had any interest in her experiences. He'd gotten in the habit of just raising an eyebrow. Which meant: "What, now you're a climate denier, too?"

Robert had catapulted, and was now several rankings higher in his newspaper's pecking order. He was publishing more articles than ever before, had the final word in all their editorial meetings, and was being sent to the federal environmental agency's press conferences, where he contributed lengthy diatribes in the guise of "uncomfortable questions" in hopes of getting to the "inconvenient truth." His already non-stop working hours seemed to almost double.

Even though things were going well for Robert, he was sleeping poorly at night. Dora realized his fear was for real. His obsession wasn't just a politically expeditious pose. It stemmed from his conviction that the world really was coming to an end. "I decided to panic," Greta had said, and Robert had, too. Dora tried to relate to Robert's worldview, to see it from his perspective. Everywhere he looked, he saw cars, trucks, planes, and ships spewing Diesel. Plastic, disposable toys, throwaway furniture, fast fashion, cheap everything, everywhere. Every single day centered on the principle of producing and consuming, a.k.a. squandering it all. Dora could only guess how Robert got through life if behind every plastic bag he saw a blustering storm, behind every light-bulb a flash flood, behind every suv a civil war.

But at least he knew what sparked his fear. Dora was worried, too, but her fear was more diffuse. It was too nebulous to be pinned down, turned into a slogan, into action, into political engagement. Even worse: She feared that the real problem just might be the sheer degree of global panic. That the only rules governing the fight over who's right, who can say what, were nonsense, the rules of insanity. Donald Trump, Björn Höcke, and all the Brexiteers were totally nuts, that was clear. But if even Robert had become incapable of levelheaded dialogue, unwilling to consider the facts from all sides, refusing to question every purported Absolute Truth, well, where did that leave the two of them? What remained was a one-woman worldview, one that Dora couldn't share with anyone. One that felt increasingly insane.

Dora still liked Robert, but it was getting harder and harder to live with him. The world they had previously shared morphed into a suffocating corset of rigid rules. They would only buy certain products and eat specific foods. No more taxis, and vacations involving travel were out of the question. As soon as dark fell, Robert ran around the apartment turning off the lights Dora had turned on. He handed her a list of acceptable boutiques where she was still allowed to buy clothes, and implored her to limit herself to one pair of winter boots. When Dora turned the heat up, he turned it back down. November came, and the apartment was cold. Dora started staying later and later at the office. She hardly even wanted to go home anymore.

And then the whole deposit-bottle thing started. The first time was just an accident. Dora heard a report on the radio about tractors blockading Berlin and was so distracted by it that she inadvertently tossed a returnable bottle into the trash. When she noticed what she'd done, she felt curiously liberated. It felt so good that she did it again. When the European Parliament declared a climate emergency, she disposed of a glass bottle in the bathroom trash can. When an attacker stabbed multiple people on London Bridge, Dora stuffed multiple liter-sized plastic bottles emptied of their organic lemonade into the wastepaper basket in their home office. When the AfD held a party rally in Braunschweig, of all places, a glass yogurt container ended up in the yellow bag designated solely for plastic, metal, and composites.

When Robert found out, he nearly lost it. He immediately started checking every trash can in their apartment multiple times a day. He even checked the collection bins down in the courtyard, which were for the entire building. He begged Dora to cut it out. She tried to control herself. But the deposit-bottle thing had become an obsession. She was hooked. When Norbert Walter-Borjans and Saskia Esken were elected co-chairs of the SPD, she tossed a wine bottle into the blue bag designated solely for paper and cardboard. When the United States assassinated General Qasem Soleimani in Baghdad, when Iran accidentally shot down a Ukrainian passenger plane, and as Australia burned, Dora hid beer bottles in the compost bin. Robert's confrontations grew louder. He threatened to kick Dora out of the apartment. Dora's final infraction of the recycling rules took place the morning before she first drove out to Bracken. Once she'd seen the old estate manager's house, she was able to quit. From then on, not a single deposit bottle landed in the wrong bin. The domestic tension subsided.

And then came the virus. Robert went from climate activist to epidemiologist, and the world turned upside down. People were saying the good old days were over. Life would never be the same again. Virologists became media stars. Newspapers started asking prominent people what they were praying for. The massive, widespread suffering was overpowering.

Suddenly Dora was annoyed by how Robert's eyes always popped wide as he bit into a slice of buttered bread. Even the noises he made while eating drove her crazy. She half expected to find the sound of her own chewing unbearable soon, too, so that she'd be forced to go on a liquid diet. She constantly imagined she could hear insects buzzing about. She'd get up in the middle of the night to scan the bedroom for flies, and then neither of them could get back to sleep.

When Robert said that to some extent Covid was a blessing in disguise, because it would save the planet from the carbon emissions of human transit, Dora knew she had to leave. When he forbade her from taking walks with Jay, she left. Her entire thirty-six years of existence fit into a rented moving van. Only Gustav, her belt-driven bicycle, had to stay behind in Berlin.

Deeper into the forest, the sandy road peters out into a broad footpath. The trampled earth is covered in moss and dry pine needles. Dora has to watch out, lest she trip over tree roots. The crowns of the trees close in, forming a solid canopy. Tender shoots of grass are growing down below, a promise of eternal renewal. Jay's enthusiasm gives way to resentment that their walk doesn't end the very second she detects the first feelings of exhaustion. Tongue hanging out, she slowly creeps along at Dora's heels, preparing to put on her finest act, a number affectionately known as "Dying Dog." She'll plop down, sink into the grass, lie flat on her stomach with her back legs splayed out, and refuse to take another step.

As the path comes to a T-junction, Dora is stopped in her tracks by a wondrous sight. Just past the junction there's a bench. It's quite basic, just two blocks of wood with a board nailed on top. It has no back, no arms, and is completely unsanded and unvarnished. Somebody built this bench in just a few simple steps. Somebody who knows how to make things. Not on commission, or with EU funding, or a grant from the local tourism office—probably for no pay at all. Nothing whatsoever is noteworthy about this bench. But it does beg the question: what's she looking for here? As far as Dora can tell, nobody in Bracken goes for walks. The village dogs, all of which are some sort of German Shepherd mix, and are probably all related, run up and down their fences all day, barking whenever a cat appears or a person deigns to move around without driving a car. They probably wouldn't even understand the proposition of going for a walk with their owners. Taking walks is something that belongs solely in the big-city inhabitant's fantasy of country living. Bracken's residents venture into the woods only once a year, to gather mushrooms or firewood.

But there's a bench here anyway. Whoever made it must've been a truly happy person. On a whim, they just put together a few pieces of wood and created a place to sit down. An opportunity to pause that hadn't previously been there. And they situated it at this intersection in the woods. Dora would just love to be capable of doing something like that. Just making something. No questions asked, no doubts. Just because it can be done.

Not that the bench is all that comfortable. The main board is narrow and uneven. You can't lean back. Nevertheless, Dora declares this intersection her new favorite place. And Jay seems to concur. She's found a moss-padded spot and is basking in the April sunshine. Dora tilts her head back and gazes up at the canopy of shimmering leaves. Too bad she left her cigarettes at home.

All around her spring is having its way with things, pushing every living organism toward growth and abundance. It forces life itself to give its all, coerces every creature to go forth and multiply. No judgement, no waste. Everything is put to good use. What dies gets repurposed. When one species goes extinct, another fills in. Death and birth are neither drama nor trauma, rather they're the very hinges existence pivots on. Just part of life's mechanics. Human panic plays no role here. No one could care less than a coal tit whether humans die out or not.

Aside from strains of virus, nobody needs us, Dora thinks. And because that's a dark thought, she pushes it back inside.

A sudden movement behind her, slightly off to the side, causes her to flinch. A rustle, a cracking sound. Jay jumps up, too. Something's there, definitely. Something big, and now it's rushing to retreat, shielded behind the pines. Maybe a wild boar, or a roebuck.

But Dora's almost certain she saw a flash of brightly colored fabric.

7

R2-D2

The scythe falls, and on the other side of the road R2-D2 steps out his front door.

At the very last minute, Dora pulls her foot back. After watching a few DIY tutorials on YouTube she's getting better at sharpening the blade. Although that only increases her risk of injury.

But Dora's quite pleased with herself nevertheless. The sharpened scythe makes it much easier to clear the front yard of all those young maples. She's been at it since early morning, and she's making headway. Rather surprisingly, she's also managed to finish preparing the back-yard vegetable beds over the last few days. She now knows that muscle cramps really can feel like a lethal malady. But the payoff is that all that tough ground now lies perfectly tilled within the neat rectangle she cordoned off, exactly as she'd planned, with precise right angles and an even surface. The sight of it fills her with pride, despite the mounds of trash piled up along the sides. A bunch of detritus and scraps have surfaced, as have still more pots and pans, doll heads, ragged old teddy bears, and a few small, surprisingly unscathed metal matchbox cars. As she worked the ground, Dora periodically worried the blade of her spade might run into the skeleton of a long-dead baby.

Even more distressing than the mounds of trash is the fact that the earth she's tilled is already beginning to dry out. The slightest breeze triggers a dust cloud. Dora's beginning to suspect gardening has something to do with watering. And probably manure, unless she opted for chemical fertilizer. Or front loaders, to cart off the spent soil and replace it with fresher, more fertile topsoil.

Unfortunately Dora doesn't have an adequate outdoor water supply, nor a good garden hose. Not to mention a front loader. Nor does she have a car, so she can't even drive herself to the hardware store. She's got to figure out the public transit options, immediately. Bracken doesn't have any stores, not even a bakery, nor an inn. There are still a few bags of noodles and some stale bread left from her first shopping trip on the way out here from Berlin, but if she doesn't get to a supermarket a.s.a.p., her vegetable-bed project won't be the only thing that dies. She'll have to be buried with it.

But she's not about to let that kind of fretting spoil her day. The first swath of slain maples are already strewn across the ground. The vegetable beds are already thoroughly *brackened*. And things are going fairly well career-wise, too. Her current client, FAIRapparel, is a Berlin fashion startup launching a new line of sustainably produced jeans. While everybody else in the fashion industry is freezing their budgets because shops are closed and sales are plummeting, the founders of FAIRapparel want to persist. They're determined to make it big in the post-Covid era by flooding all the right channels with their product debut. Dora knows she's lucky.

Her happiness is well-founded, especially since more than a few of her coworkers are worried about job security. If Sus-Y loses a major account, ten or even twenty people might end up unemployed. And if that happens at a bunch of agencies, all at the same time, then the job market gets flooded with high-caliber talent and supply far exceeds demand. Normally, senior copywriters are hard to come by, so they have their pick of the best in-house positions. But when people are being fired left and right, the rules change faster than you can reboot your MacBook Air. Luckily, at the beginning of every Zoom meeting, Susanne reiterates the fact that Sus-Y values sustainability before all else. And that includes its team. Dora's job is safe.

Yesterday evening she had a videoconference with her clients. While Zoom was still establishing a secure connection with the folks back in Berlin, Dora realized once again just how much responsibility people were handing to her with jobs like this one. FAIR apparel is devoting its entire marketing budget to this one model of jeans made from sustainably sourced, organic cotton, chlorine-free processing, and hardware free of any heavy metals. If anything goes awry, the whole place might have to shutter. Whether these pants come to dominate their sector of the jeans market or wind up collecting dust on neglected store shelves is entirely up to Dora. Will her brain manage to spit out the right slogan, the perfect turn of phrase, the catchword that people will remember twenty years down the road? If there's any appeal in advertising, it's this kind of opportunity: The possibility of coming up with one unique idea that then turns into a glorious triumph. Either that, or a total catastrophe.

Once the connection stabilized, Susanne gave her introductory spiel, and then Dora presented her strategy with thirty PowerPoint slides. Then they had to convince the client that sustainability can't be treated like a novelty among their target market of young urbanites. Far from an exception, it was the rule. The new normal. Totally self-confident. They had to shed the stuffy old traditional fair-trade look of sappy earth tones and faux-natural, brown-paper everything. They needed to tap into *the new style of sustainability*. Meaning *lifestyle*. At that, all anyone could do was nod.

Then Susanne took the virtual stage again to reiterate that FAIRapparel's current budget wouldn't be enough to make a splash on the national level, so in order to garner visibility they were pivoting to a digital-only campaign. In order to go viral, it would have to be bold and provocative. Social videos would constitute its core, in order to rile people up, play with their emotions. "We've got to make you the *talk of the town*," Susanne effused. Everybody nodded again, and Dora was back at bat.

The crux of the matter was coming up with the right name for these new jeans. Dora clicked through twelve slides of suggested possibilities, culminating in her favorite: GUTMENSCH, meaning DO-GOODER. Silence. Dora had expected as much. And then she explained how using a controversial term, especially one previously used dismissively, would ensure they'd not only be visible, but that people could rally behind them. It had been Duden

Dictionary's cringeworthy neologism of the year back in 2015. A big red flag of a word. Everyone would notice. And it would turn everyone who bought a pair into a staunch supporter. It'd become part of their own identity. If you really, truly believe in sustainability, be a real DO-GOODER for once, and stand proud. That's precisely what you could do by buying the right jeans, and soon you'd be able to show the world.

Finally the Berlin-based founders of FAIRapparel got it, and Dora felt like the lightbulbs clicking on over their heads cast shadows as far as Bracken. She built on their bubbly enthusiasm by moving right along to her next winning point, revealing that this brand name paved the way for every aspect of the campaign. Because of course the protagonist, the guy giving the testimonial, would also be a DO-GOODER. Not some predictably preachy moralizer, of course—no, they'd find a straightforward good guy, and we'd see him doing good things in every ad, and somehow they'd always go hilariously wrong. The DO-GOODER as antihero, presenting his own fallibility with a dash of ironic self-awareness. It's boldly original, humorous, and strikes all the right chords to resonate with the target audience of digital natives. And it takes the sustainability issue seriously enough. Tagline: GUT, MENSCH! DO IT GOOD!

It was a slam dunk, the rest took care of itself. By the time Dora explained how the chosen Do-Gooder would appear on all posters and in all print media, giving the campaign a recognizable face, the client was already on board. When she went on to explain how a subsequent campaign could be built around user-generated content, clips sent in by real people wearing their jeans and self-identifying as DO-GOODERS, everyone in all the other boxes of the Zoom room broke into applause.

Working from home really suits you, Susanne remarked after their client had left the meeting.

R2-D2 is still there. Now he's crossing the street. Dora wonders if it's just some optical illusion; maybe she's just seeing things. Maybe all the solitude, the physical exertion, and low blood sugar are causing hallucinations. But whatever it is she's seeing, it's definitely headed for her front gate. Maybe it's some Covid-crazy local, a paranoiac who's made his own protective suit? Whatever this thing is, it's at least five foot three, wearing a helmet with visor and built-in ear protection, a fluorescent safety vest that goes down to its knees, and rubber boots that also reach up to its knees. It's making such small strides that it looks more like it's waddling than walking, which only heightens the resemblance to its relative from the *Star Wars* franchise. It's toting futuristic weapons, one on each side, which are presumably laser guns or energy-shield emitters.

"Can I help you?" Dora asks as R2-D2 tries to slide, side arms and all, past her and through the gate. He doesn't respond to her question, which might be because of the earmuffs. Instead, he tussles with her for a moment until he finally makes it into the yard.

"How many Arabs does it take to mow a pasture?" R2-D2 asks, beaming and just a little too loud, like all people who can't hear a thing.

Dora's jaw drops, but not a word comes out of her mouth. It makes no difference, since R2-D2 answers himself anyway.

"None, because we can do it ourselves."

He laughs with gusto, at length, until his laugh is drowned out by the deafening noise of his first secret weapon. R2-D2 holds it with both hands, swinging it back and forth. Dora isn't needed here. R2-D2 works his way through the whole yard. The young maple trees fall over in droves, a veritable army felled by superior technology. Severed sprigs of stinging nettles and blackberry bushes fly through the air. R2-D2 leaves slightly larger saplings alone. Maybe he'll tackle them later, with his second secret weapon. A chainsaw still holstered in a case that says *Makita*.

Dora witnesses this massacre with both hands pressed to her ears. Although the past two and a half weeks have taught her to hate her plot of land, she's getting no gratification out of this. R2-D2 and his secret weapon clear an area the size of a tennis court in the same amount of time it took Dora and her scythe to clear an area the size of a ping-pong table. It's not fair. Such differences in weaponry make any trace of equity evaporate on the spot. R2-D2 doesn't duel with organic matter the way Dora did, he just carries out a heartless extermination campaign. The persistent noise drives Dora back into the house.

She puts on a kettle of water for another coffee and wonders whether, in a stroke of momentary derangement, she might've called a landscaping service and promptly forgotten all about it. Although you have to admit that, even if that were the case, it's unlikely the landscapers would be headquartered in the house just across the street. Nor would the realtor have hired such a service. The price she paid was undeniably based on the fact that this place was a real fixer-upper, and she agreed to take it as-is. Based on R2-D2's behavior thus far, one can only deduce that this must be some form of neighborly help.

When the noise finally dies down, Dora goes back out, her hand cradling the coffee mug, which R2-D2 proceeds to grab as naturally as if he'd ordered it. He leans his weapons against the fence, raises the visor from his face, drinks the first gulp, and gives an approving nod.

"I like it black," he says. "And that goes for both my coffee and my money. Hopefully the taxman won't catch on."

"Good one," Dora forces herself to laugh. It's the least she can do. The little guy has just cleared her entire front yard, in any case. And she's just as glad to be spared any more derogatory jokes about foreigners.

"But I'm still tired. I think maybe your coffee's broken," R2-D2 continues.

Dora decides to respond in kind. Maybe jokes are the only language R2-D2 is capable of conversing in.

"With the haul I just brought back from the supermarket, you'd think a packrat lived here," she ventures. "Now all I need is a cage ..."

R2-D2 stares at her, his face blank. Maybe he doesn't like jokes about how Covid's making everyone panic-shop. Or maybe, as a matter of principle, he only likes jokes he himself tells.

"I take care of my body," he finally responds. "I drink twelve cups of water every day. I just let them flow through the coffee maker first."

That last one's not so bad, Dora thinks. Maybe she'll try that one out on her brother Axel, who's always going on and on about mineral water and basically spends his days making sure he's drinking enough of the stuff. If she ever even sees her brother again. Axel takes the stay-at-home orders and all other Covid restrictions pretty seriously, as they fit so perfectly with his natural affinity for spending all day, every day at home, lounging on the couch.

"How can you make a blonde laugh on a Monday morning?" R2-D2 changes the subject and then immediately delivers the punchline: "Tell a joke on Friday night."

Blonde jokes are the worst, but they're still better than Arab jokes. Dora's not a stickler for political correctness, but she can't stand xenophobic statements, joking or not. Racism makes her go stiff. She gasps, but later is ashamed that she neither seized the opportunity for fruitful dialogue nor spoke up in support of democratic, humane values. Although, admittedly, she has no idea whether a non-racist has ever managed to convince a racist that racism is utter nonsense. Nevertheless, she feels morally obliged to try her best. But then she fails. She doesn't even know whether it's true that most right-wingers aren't open to dialogue. Because she herself isn't open to dialogue. Her tactic thus far, in all honesty, has been to steer clear of anyone espousing right-wing dogma. Avoid them at all costs.

"This coffee's so black," R2-D2 cheerfully chimes in, "it's about to start pickin' cotton."

She just might have to rethink her tactic.

8

Fugginforeignfarmhands

Of course Dora had googled it. She had a few numbers and facts on Bracken. In the last state election, the AfD won almost twenty-seven percent of the votes in this municipality. A few more percentage points than the state average.

That's what worried her the most. Not spiders, burst pipes, or the dearth of cultural offerings. Not even the threat of feeling lonely out in the countryside. No, what Dora most feared was her new neighbors' political views. Jojo's remark still echoed in her head: "What do you plan to do out there among all those right-wing nutjobs?"

In Brandenburg the AfD is more bark than bite: right-wing, leaning toward fringe. Although it wasn't just the hard right that voted AfD. A lot of wimps did, too, or so Dora thinks. For decades now, the unholy alliance between politics and mass media has specialized in speaking to the lowest common denominator, stirring up people's basest instincts: fear, envy, selfishness. So it should come as no surprise that, eventually, people end up voting for a party as self-pitying as they themselves are. That said, Bracken isn't exactly a Nazi stronghold.

At least that's what she's told herself, attempting to allay her fears.

But then what did the Ostrogoth next door say by

way of introduction? "Pleased to meet you, I'm the village Nazi." That phrase would have no meaning, semantically speaking, if everyone else in town were a Nazi, too. Although there's no telling how much Goth knows about semantics.

So, there are no real Nazis in Bracken. Just a bit of well-kempt everyday racism. Like with R2-D2.

But that's precisely what Dora takes issue with. When it comes to Nazis who look like Nazis and behave like Nazis, at least you know what you're dealing with. Everyday racists, on the other hand, have a way of coming out of nowhere and catching you unawares. You'll be having a delightful conversation and then *bam*, they drop a derogatory term like it's nothing. And then what? Do you pause the chit-chat and call them out? Or do you just keep quiet and let it slide, as if you didn't hear a thing?

Racism triggers a sudden stiffness that feels like a shock. Like a pinched nerve. Sometimes the clever riposte Dora's looking for only occurs to her three days later, after she's racked her brain.

She's often wondered what, exactly, lies behind this racism-triggered stiffness. Maybe a quandary. A series of impossible either-or decisions: Be a moralizer, or be a coward. Follow your convictions, or society's expectations—or go for a third option and follow your aversion to conflict. On top of that, embarrassment plays a role, since racism is just so damn shameful that you cringe for others' sake. It's like when you catch someone urinating in public. You want to tell the guy to zip it up and get lost, but then you take on the shame you think he should feel. So you say nothing, and look the other way.

And it's not like Dora's had a ton of practice handling the phenomenon. Luckily, in the circles she's moved in so far, no one would ever have even dreamed of cracking a derogatory joke, or poking fun at foreigners. Robert figures right-wingers are mostly climate-deniers and anti-vaxxers. Her brother Axel views right-wing populism as a proletarian vice with which no one with any taste would dare dirty their fingers. Jojo sees the AfD as a mere manifestation of widespread depression among German males, best treated with amitriptyline. And at Sus-Y, as Dora knows from an internal staff survey, almost everyone votes for the Green Party, just like her. Above all, everybody Dora knows finds the AfD atrocious. Her friends and acquaintances are all against turning Europe into a walled fortress. They're in favor of protecting the environment, support international collaboration, emphasize Germany's need to answer for its past, but they also always cut the conversation off right at the point when one would naturally have to ask what should happen if five million refugees suddenly want to come to Europe. You have to wonder whether it's even tenable to preach liberalism and love for one's fellow human beings here in the German heartland while all the surrounding German states are busy closing their international borders.

Such questions had come up already in Robert's realm, though. At some point not long after 2015 there was a phase when people in his circle of acquaintances started snapping at one another. An air of welcome gave way to the recognition that there were real problems, and the cognizance of those problems turned into a fear that Germany was losing its national identity. At the same time, the mere suspicion of racism poisoned all discourse. Within seconds a conversation about rescuing refugees from the waters of the Mediterranean could escalate into an explosive argument. Longstanding friendships turned into bitter enmity solely because one person said something the other couldn't bear. In situations like that, even Dora sensed, deep within herself, how easily aggression can well up. She noticed how, once her racism-triggered stiffness subsided, she was suddenly overcome by an intense rage. How she said things she later regretted.

At some point people's circles of friends began sorting into new constellations. You'd still meet up with some friends, but not with others. You'd unfriend certain people on Facebook, unfollow them on Instagram and Twitter, and replace them with new connections. Launching careers and having kids acted as filters, people's paths forked, and now politics was yet another filter ensuring your social life led you to encounter fewer and fewer mentalities that didn't mirror your own.

But Dora remained fully cognizant of the latent explosive force of that racism-triggered stiffness. No other topic was capable of so intensely infuriating otherwise agreeable people, regardless of what side they were on. In that respect, perhaps that racism-triggered stiffness is nothing more than a self-protective mechanism. A tripwire installed by the secret fear you could lose all self-control at any minute, offending the whole world. Or an entire village.

Just as these notions badger Dora's brain, she

chokes so hard that R2-D2 extracts a hand from his gloves in order to help out, hitting her on the back.

"And what's up with him, anyway?" Dora asks, still coughing, and pointing toward the wall.

"Huh?" R2-D2 replies. So his sole form of communication is indeed just cracking jokes. He isn't programmed to respond to even the simplest question. He's also still wearing ear protection.

"With Goth," Dora shouts, again pointing toward his place.

Following that first appearance, there's been no sign of Goth. Jay has gone off three times, and each time she's returned unscathed. At one point Dora dragged one of her patio chairs over to the wall, climbed up, and peered over. The idea that Goth's head might appear on the other side of the wall at that very same moment made her heart race. But nobody was there. The property looked all tidied up and abandoned. Dora took her time observing each and every detail. Amid the neatly mowed grass stood a white plastic table and set of chairs. Striped curtains were visible through the trailer windows. The potted geraniums on the entryway stairs were in bloom. Next to the fence stood a larger-than-life statue of a wolf, hewn from a single tree trunk. The old pickup truck was parked next to the main house. A Toyota HiLux, probably from the eighties. Dora notices the grass under the truck has grown taller than the rest. Clearly the pickup hasn't picked anything up in quite a while. Maybe it's totally kaput. Goth must have driven off in some other vehicle.

She wonders why he hasn't repaired the thing. Why he's living in the trailer while the main house just sits there, empty. On closer inspection, she notices the place doesn't look so dilapidated, despite the dirty windows. Two flags are on display out front. There's a red and white one she can't quite place, and an iconic black-red-gold German flag huge enough to hang on a government building. Even now, fourteen years after Germany won the World Cup in a "fairytale summer" coup, she's not thrilled by the sight, especially in front yards here in the east.

Maybe Goth is away on holiday. Or out working some construction job. R2-D2 doesn't seem to know either, since he just shrugs, heaves his weapons up onto his shoulders, and gets ready to leave.

Dora takes Jay into her arms and accompanies him across the street. She wants to get a glimpse at his mailbox to find out what his name is. Not least so that she isn't forced to keep calling him R2-D2 for all eternity.

A little ways down the road, three white vans pull up and park in front of a whitewashed structure that appears to be part of an old farm. Dora has noticed the place before. It's fairly large, there's the main house and two other buildings with solar panels on the roof. The drivers hop right out. They're all dark-haired young men, laughing and chatting with one another so loudly that Dora would have no problem making out what they were saying if she could understand their language. But she can't even identify what language it is. Listening in on their buoyant laughs and sing-songy voices, she's suddenly elated. How long has it been since she's heard people laugh like that, together? And how amazing would it be to discover that there's a whole handful of foreigners living right here in Bracken! She can already picture herself telling Jojo about it with a relaxed, dismissive wave of her hand: "Problems? Not here!"

R2-D2's eyes have followed her stare.

"Fugginforeignfarmhands," he remarks apologetically.

"Huh?" says Dora.

"They farm for Tom and Steffen."

It's his first non-joke. Dora's ad-writing brain starts chanting "For-eign-farm-hands here-on-our-land." She'd better watch out, lest it get stuck in her head. She decides to have a little talk with R2-D2. Like a little training session against racism-triggered stiffness. R2-D2 strikes her as the perfect teaching partner. His expression is so friendly, he's beaming below that orange helmet. Dora doesn't know if it's possible to deploy a derogatory term for foreigners without meaning it in a mean way, but if anyone were capable of such a thing, it'd be R2-D2. She gingerly reaches out, takes a hold of his left earmuff, and pushes it a few inches back as if he were a little kid.

"What are fugginforeignfarmhands?"

"Fugginforeigners who farm for Tom and Steffen."

Dora had read newspaper articles about problems with the asparagus harvest. Apparently, in spite of Covid, Romanians were coming to Germany to help with the harvest because Germans were too unskilled to pluck it from the earth themselves. This in the land where asparagus season is so beloved it might as well have its own national holiday. Especially the white kind. She draws courage from R2-D2's friendly demeanor, and tries her luck.

"That's a bit cruel, don't you think?"

"Huh?"

"Fugginforeigners. I mean, it's just mean."

"Everybody says it."

"Well, it could be pretty offensive."

"How so?" R2-D2 takes his helmet off and scratches his head. He's older than Dora thought. Late fifties, for sure. But he has a full head of hair that's still more pepper than salt. "They can't even understand."

He shifts from one leg to the other, obviously eager to just go home. No wonder, either. Wearing all that gear and hauling those secret weapons around can't be fun in this sun. And now Dora's asking all these stressful questions, abruptly cutting off his joke supply. Even Jay is uncomfortable, wriggling in Dora's arms, trying to jump down. But Dora can't stop, the training session is in full swing, and she's actually stoked at her newfound ability to converse.

"Where are they from?"

"Dunno, but definitely not from here."

"And that's an issue?"

"They farm for Tom and Steffen."

Repeating it this third time, R2-D2 carefully enunciates every last syllable, as if Dora were somehow slow on the uptake. Apparently everybody on the planet knows who Tom and Steffen are, and why there are never any issues there. Not even with a bunch of fugginforeignfarmhands.

And that's that. R2-D2 bids her farewell with a nod and turns to go. As he maneuvers all his gear through his gate, which is even narrower than Dora's, she glances at his mailbox. It's labeled HEINRICH.

9

Flashlight

Come evening, Dora carries a lawn chair onto the landing at the bottom of the front stair. It's like sitting out on a balcony, with a view of the road. Looking straight ahead, Dora sees Mr. Heinrich's house. Turning her head, she sees the wall and, behind it, her neighbor's house, where nothing stirs. Her puffy jacket protects her from the coolness of day's end. Propping her computer on her lap, it's an ideal spot to work. She hasn't gotten any runtime error messages for some time now. Maybe the fresh country air does her laptop good. Jay-the-Ray is the only one who insists on staying inside.

When her feet start tingling, Dora gets up and circles the house. Thanks to Mr. Heinrich's special operations, the yard now looks a lot more suitable for her agricultural aspirations. At least if you imagine the heaps of uprooted saplings aren't still there. Dora has no idea how to deal with those. Should she load them into the pickup truck she doesn't have and drive them to the probably equally non-existent municipal composting and tree mulching center? Or turn them into a burn pile and make herself the kind of bonfire people light to celebrate Saint Martin's Day? Or maybe the local practice is to just toss the trimmings over the wall? She can't help but grin at the idea. Just imagine the expression on Goth's face when he comes back. She actually thought she heard some sounds coming from over there recently. But when she gets up on the chair to spy over the wall there's nothing. A Nazi neighbor who's never there is almost as good as a neighbor who isn't a Nazi.

What she really does hear from time to time are the voices of the dark-haired men just a little way off, as they work the grounds of the property that, if she understood Mr. Heinrich correctly, belongs to Tom and Steffen. Maybe it's some kind of farm. Images of asparagus and boiled potatoes with melted butter automatically come to mind. When she can't hold out any longer, she prepares a serving of noodles, coating them in her last pat of butter and some extra dashes of salt. Sitting back down out front, she polishes the entire plate off in minutes.

As darkness falls, a nightingale in the back yard starts to sing. It's quite loud, and quite psychedelic sounding. Rather less Romantic than all those poets have claimed. More like ornithological noise pollution. Dora wonders if the weird tune will keep her from getting to sleep. She's been feeling that prickly unease in the pit of her stomach for some time now. The mere thought of yet another sleepless night releases the bubbles from her belly and they go straight to her head. She quickly bends back over the bluish light of her laptop screen. As night descends on Bracken, Dora diligently works, full steam ahead, on the campaign. Once she finds her flow state, the ads write themselves. Two hours later she's got five ads finished, in both twenty-second versions and their snappier seven-second clips.

Her favorite is the one where DO-GOODER is

riding a packed bus. He decides to offer his seat to an elderly passenger, so stands up and taps the bald man, who's standing in front of him but facing the other way, on the shoulder. As the guy turns around, we see that he isn't elderly at all, he's actually a tough-looking skinhead who immediately makes a menacing fist. His tattooed knuckles read HATE. DO-GOODER recoils in horror. The skinhead takes a seat and his eyes cast a disdainful look at our hero's jeans, where he spots the DO-GOODER label. "Classic do-gooder," the skinhead says with scorn. A cheerful voiceover says: "Wear what you are—and make the world a better place."

Nazis are probably the most taboo thing imaginable in German advertising. But maybe it's time for a change. The script is flawless, no grounds for reproach there. What's reproachful is the reality it depicts. Which, ultimately, touches on what the client is really after: changing the world.

Dora stands up, leans against the cast-iron balustrade, and stretches her back. She tilts her head all the way back and looks up at the sky. So many stars! The spot that looks like a streak of cloud must be the Milky Way. Could Alexander Gerst be up there at this very moment? Dora would love to share a cigarette with him right about now. Even if he definitely doesn't smoke. Maybe he'd just puff at it, out of niceness. She'd heard on the radio once that astronauts are the nicest people in the world. It's no coincidence, nor is it a result of their line of work. It's the other way around, that's actually why they're chosen. It's essentially in their job description, because they have to be able to withstand spending months at a time with a handful of colleagues in super-tight quarters. Basically quarantine, but in outer space. It only works when everyone involved is an impeccable Mr. Nice Guy by profession.

Dora tries to recall the last time she met a truly nice person. At Sus-Y HQ everybody's nice, but that's just the manifestation of their mutual interpersonal service–oriented mentality. Most of her coworkers devote more energy to their social media profiles than to their actual, real-world friendships. They tirelessly present their children, their dogs, their houses, their breakfast spreads. At work they advertise their clients' brands, and in their free time they advertise themselves. It's not all that different outside the advertising realm. Everyone's busy being interesting and important. And successful, of course, in both their professional and their personal lives. It's a rat race of conformists outcompeting one another to come across as something special, someone different. Maybe if you want to meet a truly nice person you'd have to rocket into outer space.

Dora's no better than anyone else in this regard, she's just a little lonelier. She shifts her gaze from the stars to her immediate surroundings. The empty road. The village-limit sign. And, behind it, the fields stretching out beyond the last street lamps, plummeting outward into darkness.

All at once she realizes all the things that aren't here. It's incredible how many things simply don't exist in this world. Almost everything. No boundless seas of buildings. No chaotic traffic. No bicyclists, no pedestrians. No elevated train tracks, no billboards, no neon lights. Just a few houses, a few trees, and endless stretches of grass.

Dora sucks the cigarette smoke deep into her lungs and then slowly blows it out into evocative clouds that linger in the still night air. She wonders whether she's really lonely. For her, aside from elevated train tracks and pedestrians and all that, there are a few other things absent here. No companion awaiting her in bed. No coworkers she'll cross paths with tomorrow morning in the office. No family she could drop by to check in on. No best friend expecting a nighttime call from her. No dance class, no book group. All she really has is what's right there next to her: Jay, an unfurnished fixer-upper, and a partially finished pack of cigarettes. Plus Goth and Mr. Heinrich. Conference calls and Zoom meetings. Surprisingly enough, she doesn't find that frightening in the least. What does frighten her is the fact that she can't actually say whether she truly misses all that. Right now, really, she only misses Alexander Gerst.

She lights another cigarette. Inside, in a deep slumber, Jay yawns. Dora envies her dog's ability to fall asleep anytime, anywhere. Sometimes she thinks sleeping is the most important ability of all. Anyone who can't sleep has already lost. Anyone who can is safe and sound. What must it be like to just lie down each night and disappear? What wonderful things could happen? What would it be like if every morning offered up a brand-new day ahead? If it filled you with promise, instead of dread?

Suddenly her thoughts stop in their tracks. Something's distracted her, caught her eye. There. Over at

Goth's place. A beam of light is moving around, she can see it through the windows on the upper floor of the main house. She stares. The light gets stronger, brighter, it dances across the interior walls, disappears, then reappears. It's not just her imagination. Someone's definitely wandering around that house with a flashlight.

Should she call the police? Does Bracken even have a police force?

The light vanishes. Whoever's wandering around over there has either turned the flashlight off, or gone down to the ground floor, which the wall hides from Dora's eyes. She stands up on the tips of her toes, bracing both hands on the railing. There's no car in front of Goth's property, no van with the hatchback down. If it's a burglar who's broken in, he'll have to carry his booty out by foot. And what's there to steal at Goth's place, anyway? Potatoes? A couple more German flags?

Dora waits. Nothing makes a peep, nobody leaves the house. The road remains deserted. Even the nightingale has fallen silent. Dora empties all the air from her lungs and tries to relax. It must be Goth himself wandering around the house with a flashlight. Maybe he hasn't paid the electricity bill? And now he's looking for something in the dark. When did he get back, anyway? She tosses her cigarette butt and decides it's time for bed. Whatever's going on over there, it's definitely none of her business.

10

Bus

Aside from a half-stick of butter, the fridge contains nothing edible. There's an almost-empty jar of jam on the sideboard. Dora's run out of bread, the milk has gone sour, she's even low on coffee grounds. She spoons out the very last bit, makes a cup so black and so strong that Mr. Heinrich would almost certainly come up with a couple more jokes, and takes a seat at the table. *Nearest shopping center: 18 km*, the real-estate listing had said. Today, she'd find out what, exactly, that refers to.

Searching Google Maps for nearby shopping, Dora finds something called Elbe-Center just outside Plausitz. Apparently it has a hardware and home-improvement store, a hair salon, a few boutiques, and a REWE supermarket. And there's a bus line connecting Bracken and Plausitz: Bus 42.

Dora goes to look for a couple of cotton totes and gets distracted by the number 3,900, a number she immediately tries to suppress. She gives Jay a pat on the head, leaves the house, and heads for the bus stop.

In front of the firehouse she sees five men in dark-blue uniforms with reflective yellow stripes on the sleeves and trousers. They're standing evenly spaced, about six feet apart, and each has a cigarette between his fingers. As Dora walks by on the other side of the street four heads slowly turn to track her movement, while one looks the other way. All five men then lift a hand to their mouths, take a drag on their cigarettes, and then lower the hand to their side again. It looks like an installation from Documenta. The men are all tall, with broad shoulders. Every single one of them could easily hoist Dora into the air. She mentally calculates how many of them must've voted for the AfD, and comes up with 1.35. One says something to the other four, whereupon they all shrug their shoulders as the corners of their mouths turn slightly downward. Dora figures it has to be about her. Taken aback, she suddenly wonders if it's Sunday. No, today is Saturday, she's in luck. She picks up the pace and only relaxes a bit once the firehouse is out of sight.

The bus stop has a sun-bleached Plexiglas panel bearing text that's almost as terse as a fortune cookie and just about as decipherable. It's like a note renouncing the very concept of local public transit, turned into a nominal timetable. Apparently it's Easter break, even though all the schools are closed because of Covid. On holidays it says there's a bus that runs morning, midday, and evening. The route to Plausitz, which Google Maps says really is exactly 18 kilometers away, takes 40 minutes.

Dora's too late for "morning," but too early for midday. But at least now she knows what the firemen must've said to one another: "Look, poor city girl—she actually believes that here in Germany you can just catch a bus to the supermarket."

She realizes she has no desire to walk past those guys again. She can already picture their grins. But as she approaches the firehouse on the way back, the firefighters are gone. Without a trace, without a sound. Show over, exhibition closed, the installation is back in storage.

Back home, Dora stares at the script, both head and stomach completely empty. She tries to forget how hungry she is. She has to adapt the DO-GOODER ads for radio, too, which turns out to be a real challenge. You can't see the DO-GOODER doing good on the radio, and Dora doesn't want to just have a voice actor narrating the action from the video scripts she's already drafted. There must be another solution, she's just not coming up with it.

As Dora leaves the house for the second time, Jay flashes an accusatory glance in her direction, turns over, curls back up on her scrap of cardboard, and doesn't even bother accompanying Dora to the door. "You human beings might be clueless when it comes to contentment," her eyes seem to say, "but you could at least be better organized."

Dora figures this attempt might be as futile as the last. She'll stand at the bus stop for minutes, then hours, then hours and days, until time ceases to have any meaning, until the village vanishes, the houses cave in, and the only things left are Dora and the bus stop, smack in the middle of a vast, flat, dusty expanse, frozen stiff and portrayed in a surrealist painting titled *End Times*.

But the bus finally comes, and its front display reads 42. Dora wonders if she needs to put on a mask, and momentarily panics when, through the windshield, she sees the driver has one hanging from one ear. She should board through the back door, since she has no mask and no ticket. The driver gives a dismissive wave when she asks about the mask. She's not sure where she should sit. The bus is empty.

When she finally sits, she realizes she's forgotten to bring her tote bags.

The bus smells like disinfectant, and isn't just empty in the sense that there are no other passengers. Its emptiness is somehow definitive, quintessential, existential. It's carrying Dora through abandoned landscapes, not another human being in sight. Maybe this area is infested, emptied by an outbreak, the corpses already completely decomposed. She and the driver are the only survivors. They do the only thing a bus, a driver, and a passenger can do: drive the route in an endless loop, every day, over and over.

Power lines, wind turbines, the low hangars of agricultural businesses that have long since closed down. Then almost endless fields of asparagus. Perfectly parallel furrows covered in reflective plastic sheets. A rippled, cubist sea.

A couple of houses, a patch of woods. A jaybird between the branches. Dora sees her mother, her broad smile, her blonde hair. She wants to grab her phone and give her a call. "Isn't this just an incredible spring?" her mother would say. She'd tell her about all the latest bird sightings. She'd dismiss the Covid pandemic with a hearty laugh. "People's fears never have been based on statistical probability, you know."

Her mother's death was extremely improbable, statistically speaking. Dora presses the heels of her hands against her eyes. This just happens some-times. She knows all she can do is wait until it passes.

The bus comes to a stop at the edge of the road, nary a bus stop in sight. The driver puts his mask on, gets out, and helps an elderly woman board the bus. She, too, is masked. As they pull into the shop-ping center parking lot, Dora's still wondering if the driver only carries a mask for this old lady. If maybe she's the only reason he's still driving this route.

11

Shopping

In the shopping arcades of the Elbe-Center, every other storefront is empty, but the place is busy nevertheless. At the bakery and pharmacy, staff work behind panes of Plexiglas. Customers maintain distance from one another while waiting in line. Much like a theatrical stage, the floors are marked with strips of tape indicating where to stand. There's foot traffic. Not a trace of the state of emergency that's so palpable back in the big city. Maybe it's a stroke of poetic justice: while higher-earning city folk are going crazy cooped up in their apartments, the oft-mocked country folk are out digging in their gardens, contentedly waiting for rain. Dora just stands there for a while, watching normal people going about their normal lives. It feels good. The banality of everyday life. Until now, she had no idea how important it was.

At the entrance to REWE there's a newspaper and magazine display rack. Just a few weeks ago Donald Trump and Greta Thunberg dominated every front page, every cover. Now they've been replaced by a reddish massage ball with a crown of rubbery spikes sticking out everywhere, on every newspaper, every magazine. Dora feels a few bubbles prickling the pit of her stomach. She forgot to grab a shopping cart, so has to go back out to the parking lot. Then she's so bombarded by stimuli in the home-goods aisle that she can't even remember what she came here to buy. It's as if, after a mere two and a half weeks of country living, she's unlearned how to be a consumer.

She pulls herself together. Fruit and vegetables. Bread, butter, cheese, wine. She mustn't buy more than she can carry. Coffee, milk. Nor should she buy too little, lest it not have been worth the long bus trip. Ten packs of noodles and rice. The supermarket is playing a radio station. Chancellor Merkel refuses to discuss loosening the lockdown. Shower gel, kitchen and bath cleaners. According to some experts a vaccine will soon be found, while other experts say a vaccine is still years away. Dog food. Two packages of toilet paper. Schools should absolutely remain closed until summer vacation, or they should absolutely reopen as soon as possible.

At checkout, Dora lays four new tote bags on the belt. The girl behind Plexiglas expects almost 150 euros total. Dora gulps. Clearly underdeveloped backwaters function according to principles she has yet to comprehend.

With one package of toilet paper under each arm, Dora feels like a caricature of the typical Covid-era German citizen. But, on the plus side, the toilet paper acts as a buffer, so the bulging shopping bags don't bop too hard against her knees with each step. She's sufficiently laden down that it's hard to walk, but she heads over to the home improvement store anyway.

Walking in, she gapes like a kid in a candy store. Garden hoses, garden benches, garden lanterns.

Equipment to help you turn even the densest thicket into a veritable paradise. Sacks of soil, mulch, fertilizer, all sorts of splendors—and you not only have to pay for it, but you have to haul it all home, too. Seed potatoes are sold out.

After a frustrating loop through the garden department, Dora picks out a few seed packets from a display rack. Lettuce, various herbs, cucumbers. No matter what, something will grow. At least she already has two watering cans.

On the way to checkout, a handcart piled high with sacks of potting soil rams into her. The towering piles wobble and start to slip, Dora's bulging tote bags crash to the floor, and a few apples roll under the drawers full of screws. She's now relieved to realize she forgot eggs. As the person in charge of the handcart tries to gather Dora's purchases while simultaneously trying to prevent his towers from completely tumbling over, he apologizes over and over again. He has a mellifluous voice, like a dubbing actor who's always cast as the good guy. Once they've mutually agreed it was a no-fault mishap with no tragic consequences, Dora gets a chance to look at the guy. He's at least fifty, not especially tall, but bulky. His gray hair is gathered into a ponytail. He's wearing cargo shorts and, despite the mild temperature, a Norwegian sweater whose worn-out neckline exposes bits of bare skin below, making her suspect he's not wearing an undershirt. The hair on Dora's lower arms stands on end.

"No hard feelings," he says, heading toward checkout with the heavy handcart.

Weird guy, Dora thinks. He seems out of place

somehow. In Berlin she'd have said he was some upper-management type who'd taken early retirement, gone off to find himself, and just bought a wine store.

She almost wants to run after the bulky guy and hug him from behind, like a tree trunk you're trying to see whether you can get your arms all the way around. He could definitely hoist her into the air. Apparently she's developed a hopefully passing yet nevertheless intense interest in being hoisted into the air. Robert couldn't lift her up. Dora isn't particularly thin, nor particularly petite. Sometimes Robert behaved so tentatively, like he wasn't sure it was such a good idea that they even touch each other. But Dora actually liked that about him. He never put on a show. With a guy like him, you never felt threatened.

What's he up to now? Probably sitting in his home office, at his computer, typing up a storm. Does he miss her? Somehow she's sorry about the whole situation. They didn't even officially break up. They're just taking a break. He still doesn't even know where she is. He hasn't sent her a single WhatsApp. Dora keeps thinking about calling him, but she has no idea what she'd say.

On the way back to the bus, her arms almost drag the heavy bags. It feels like she might've dislocated her shoulders. But she can still use her big hands. She manages to get all the way to the bus stop, pausing a few times en route. Once there, she heaves a sigh of relief and leans the bags up against the pole, the only thing designating this particular bus stop. Why there's no bench, no shelter, and why it's so far from the shopping center entrance are three more backwater riddles she has yet to solve.

No shelter means no shade. Dora wipes the sweat from her forehead and studies the schedule. Her face goes pale. With a naivete bordering on idiocy, she'd somehow presumed different rules would apply for her return journey. But the next bus will come at 5:35 p.m. It's now shortly before three. Dora's starting to see why some proposals to curb climate change don't go over so well with everyone.

12

Axel

She decides not to panic. There is always a solution. Take a taxi, make the trek on foot, or hitchhike. As she pulls out her smartphone, it dings. She thinks: *Robert*. But it's Axel.

Papa+Sibylle wanna meet.

Her brother is in the habit of distilling his text messages as if they still lived in a world limited to 160 characters. Or as if they worked for the military's telecom division, where strict discipline reigns supreme. Or as if digital type were a precious resource, best used as sparingly as possible.

But he's actually quite good at saying a lot with just a few keystrokes. And because Dora has time on her hands, she delves into a closer analysis of Axel's message. *Papa+Sibylle wanna meet.* Neither she nor Axel have ever called Jojo *Papa*. She can't really say why. Maybe Jojo himself disliked the word, and repeated the "Jo-" sound instead of the "Pa-" sound back when they were babies lying on the changing table. If he ever even set foot near the changing table. And *Papa* doesn't really fit him, anyway. It doesn't stick, it just slides right off. Mama was Mama, Jojo is Jojo. But since Axel's had kids he's used the word *Papa* every now and then. Now that he's given his father grandkids, Axel wants to establish a tighter bond with him. For a long time, Dora was the better child. The diligent, reliable daughter. She did well in school. After Mama's death Axel was spent, hardly present, whereas Dora did her best to take care of everything and everyone. She kept Jojo from hiring a nanny. She didn't want a replacement mommy. The only help she allowed was from a neighbor lady, who came by to cook lunch and lend a hand with house chores for a couple of hours. Dora was the boss: she's Jojo's daughter, 100 percent. But Axel is Jojo's son and heir. He's the one who procreated, who's passing on Jojo's genes. So now he's "Papa's" son. And he's making sure Dora knows it.

Papa+Sibylle wanna meet. But of course Sibylle's true designation is "Jojo's new companion," even if Jojo's been with her for over fifteen years now. Maybe even longer. He introduced the kids to Sibylle shortly after Dora moved out of the house. Dora's got nothing against Sibylle, she just avoids saying her name, as if that somehow softens her existence a bit, effectively undermining it. And Axel had always done the same. Was he just playing along all this time? By writing *Papa+Sibylle* instead of *Jojo and his new companion*, it must mean Axel is angling for change. He wants to move, but not to a new home, rather to another planet altogether. He wants to leave Dora-and-Axel world behind and settle into the universe known as Adult-Male-with-Family. Dora gets it. But it still makes her sad.

Wanna meet is also loaded with meaning. More precisely, it translates to: "Despite Covid, Jojo is coming to Berlin this week to operate on patients at the Charité Clinic, and even though he's in a high-risk group and family gatherings are forbidden, he insists that we still go to his place in Charlottenburg for dinner as usual. I find it both irresponsible and inappropriate, but I don't have the courage to say as much to Jojo, so I'll be there anyway, just without Christine and the kids."

Dora cracks a knowing smile. She's so used to understanding her brother that this brief, cryptic text message is an open book. She types back: *When?*

And Axel answers: *Thursday.*

Their father, a.k.a. Jojo, a.k.a. Herr Professor Doctor Joachim Korfmacher, is one of Germany's most renowned neurosurgeons. As such, he is also above the everyday strife against the pandemic. Doctor Korfmacher's surgeries aren't elective, they're existential. Once a fortnight he comes to operate on patients at Berlin's Charité Clinic, hence his second home in Charlottenburg. If Doctor Korfmacher decides his new companion will accompany him to Berlin, and that they will meet with his children, then it will happen, regardless of whatever whims might pop into the government's mind regarding Covid lockdowns. And, anyhow, as lead physician he possesses secret medical knowledge that places him above and beyond the average discourse and mass agitation. Insisting on a small family reunion is his way of displaying his contempt for the virus.

Dora realizes she actually looks forward to seeing her father. Even if his arrogance can be annoying sometimes, it can be really good to talk to him. Especially in times of crisis. As always, they'll enjoy a first-rate red wine, head out to the balcony overlooking Savignyplatz for the occasional cigarette, and bask in the secure knowledge that they possess far

more style than all those wusses down below. Jojo
will delve into how the real pandemic Germany
faces is *entitlement*. It's one of his favorite topics.
People's feeling they should always have more and
more rights. More safety, more comfort, fewer dis-
turbances, fewer things left to fate. Entitlement
leads people to feel as though they're always in crisis. Because they never get what they want. Because
desires like that can never be satisfied. And a lasting
crisis leads people to suspect the apocalypse is nigh.
The era of endless self-pity and constant complaining, Jojo will say. When everyone is always offended,
afraid, and feels like they're in the right. What a
combination.

At Jojo's side, current events can be taken in from
a bird's eye view. Dora doesn't know anyone who
hovers as high above it all as Jojo. After all, life and
death are his closest associates.

They'll talk about books and films. And Dora will
tell him about R2-D2. They'll marvel at things together, and laugh together. Jojo's new companion
will be in good spirits and spend most of her time in
the kitchen, cooking up something unassailably
healthy, something involving quinoa or tofu,
whereupon Jojo will crack his usual joke, "We having gummicubes with gravy again?" His new companion will answer the taunt with a silent, loving
smile that shows how thoroughly she has Jojo
wrapped around her finger. There are few women
indeed who'd be able to deal with Doctor Korfmacher so skillfully. Some time ago, Jojo's new companion gave up her job as a nurse. Having completed
some additional training, she now works as a yoga

teacher and nutritionist, and earns good money. Thanks to Covid, she's moved her yoga classes and nutritional coaching sessions to video conference. Her stressed-out clients are so grateful that business is doing better than ever.

Just to tease Axel, Dora texts him a joke: *We country bumpkins are prepared to get face masks, but first we need to know: where can we get this "public transit" thing you keep talking about?*

Axel texts back three question marks. He doesn't like Covid jokes. Nor does he like the fact that Dora has left Berlin. End of conversation. The waters are placid.

As far as Axel is concerned, Dora should be a good auntie who lives around the corner, dotes on his twin girls, and is always there to babysit. Dora has nothing against the twins, but she's not exactly into children. She works a lot, often straight through the weekend. Axel can't understand. In his worldview, other people are there to take care of him. Especially Dora. After their mother died, Axel's M.O. became complete and total passivity. First it was a life raft, then an attitude, and, finally, a prison. The passivity principle Axel subscribes to says that all important things happen by themselves anyway, so it's pointless to struggle. This motto has made it possible for Axel to just lie on the couch for years while Dora struggled through life, fists drawn, teeth clenched. He only finished his high school degree because at some point Dora's nagging became more of a nuisance than the effort of actually going to his exams. When she moved to Berlin, he followed her, but continued just playing video games all day and clubbing all night instead of studying or looking for a job. Jojo's willingness to continue supporting him always amazed Dora. And then along came Christine, proving Axel's passivity principle one-hundred-percent correct. She took on the task of providing for Axel's every need while also transforming him into a househusband and full-time father, a role he performs with pride. He probably even enjoys being cooped up in their spacious apartment in Berlin-Mitte with their five-year-old twins Fenna and Signe while his Powerfrau spends her days performing her essential work at a major law firm.

13

Tom

Then the bus comes. Or something Dora initially takes to be a bus. A shadow falls over her. It's cast by a large van, maybe some kind of shuttle substituting the usual public transit. But Dora hasn't been waiting two and a half hours, as the schedule implied. She's only been here ten minutes. And the van has no windows in back. The thing pulling up next to her as she waits at the roadside is a Mercedes-Benz Sprinter, all white, no decals. The kidnapper's classic. Who knows how many women and children were last seen getting into this van. There's probably a stash of zip ties and chloroform inside. Dora takes a few steps back, so the driver has to lean far over the seat for her to make out what he says.

"You can forget about it," he shouts through the rolled-down passenger window. "Nary a bus for the rest of the afternoon."

She recognizes the gray ponytail and the sonorous voice. The man points to an outdated election poster on the trunk of a linden tree behind Dora. Just two words in white on a bright blue background: *Save Diesel!* And the AfD logo in the bottom corner. If the right-wing populists are posting slogans like this next to bus stops on purpose, they must have a pretty good agency. Dora thinks she'd have advised exactly this tactic if it had been her account. The thought frightens her. Of course she'd never work for them. No one she knows, in the entire ad industry, would. But whoever did this job certainly knows a thing or two. If not creatively, then strategically. The major parties only ever put up posters portraying top candidates, their faces frozen into a smile, which underpaid junior ADs have touched up. These oddly rejuvenated-looking masks are usually accompanied by a line or two of text, almost always containing the words *Germany* and *Future*. Unless you know the parties' colors, it's hard to tell which party such ads are promoting. A bunch of small posters on lampposts and trees are far better. You literally can't miss them. Go where it hurts. Like this bus stop, for example. Every minute the bus doesn't come is a minute gained for the right-wing populists. The people in power can't even get local public transit up and running, and now they want to abolish diesel?! That's how anger turns into rage. And rage turns into hate.

"There's more than six feet here," says ponytail guy, chuckling as he pats the seat beside him, a bench that stretches across the entire front cabin, so you actually can sit with adequate social distancing. Dora wonders whether she should climb into a van with a stranger. And then she wonders whether maybe, once you've met at the hardware store, you're no longer strangers. In Berlin, accepting an invitation of the sort would be suicide. Out here, it might well be suicide to stand at a fictitious bus stop for two and a half hours with a week's worth of groceries. And no bus shelter. She saw this guy buy bags of potting soil, which must be in back now. Surely there's some crime statistic that says rapists never buy potting soil.

"You're headed to Bracken, aren't you?"

Dora nods in surprise. "You know who I am?"

"I know where you live."

Presumably this isn't meant to sound threatening either, he's just conveying neutral information. Exactly when and where did people start being so afraid of each other?

The man doesn't wait for Dora's internal debate to wrap up. He gets out and walks around the van to the side she's on.

"Tom."

Instead of offering her his hand, he extends his elbow, and Dora bumps hers against it. The man loads her groceries into the footwell of the passenger seat. He lifts the heavy bags as if they were full of featherweight foam. He probably stowed the hundredweight bags of potting soil just as easily. Observing the process is fascinating. Apparently there are people who not only are a little stronger than Dora, but ten times stronger. When Tom bends over and the worn-out Norwegian sweater hangs down, Dora can see the fuzzy gray chest hair goes all the way down to his belly button. Somehow it feels okay to stare at Tom. His belly is substantial, but not fat. His arms and shoulders work like a machine. Human bodies come in such different forms. This one looks like it's made of a different material than hers. Well, everything except her hands, maybe. Her hands are a bit like Tom's. This Tom-type body stands on its feet as if it were firmly planted on the ground. Even though he's wearing flip-flops.

"Shall we?" Tom says, and Dora obediently climbs into the cab alongside her bags.

"Dora," she says.

"Suits you," says Tom.

Dora enjoys the ride. Sitting so high up, she can see far into the countryside. Tom keeps a steady clip and maneuvers the steering wheel, pedals, and gearshift as if he'd grown up driving. Life must really be something with a vehicle like this. You could buy half the hardware store and schlepp it home. You could move house whenever you wanted, and take all your worldly possessions with you. You could live in the car. Escape with the whole family, even, if it came to that.

Behind a patch of woods Dora sees dark clouds rising, so big they're darkening much of the sky. Startled, she points in that direction.

"Is that a fire?"

Tom smiles an oh-you-city-folk smile.

"It's dust, due to the drought."

As they exit the patch of woods and the next field comes into view, Dora sees some kind of agricultural machine. The huge dust clouds loom behind it. The machine crawls through the furrows of an asparagus field, unspooling an endless strip of black plastic from its rear. Men and women with dark hair run after it, securing the plastic sheets to mounds of earth that stretch for miles.

Dora's careful to shop with cotton totes while agribusiness covers half the state with plastic. She waits for the prickling sensation. It doesn't come. For a moment, she sees the scene as a freeze-frame. Angular, pressed mounds of earth wrapped in black film. An insectlike machine. The dark silhouettes of stooped people. All that's missing is a bit of piano music. A dash of anachronistic Futurism. Machines overseeing the enslavement of human beings. Tom's voice startles her out of her thoughts.

"Our people are out there, too."

Dora almost hears the lightbulb slowly click on over her head. Then her mind presents what should be an obvious conclusion: the new subject of her human-body-type study is part of "Tom and Steffen."

"Fugginforeignfarmhands." It just slips out of her mouth.

Tom grins. "You catch on quick."

"You all … in the asparagus business?"

"God forbid." Tom briefly raises both hands from the steering wheel. "Asparagus is mobbed up. They control all the supermarkets. You can't break in as a small business owner. It's like everything else: the big guys go boom, the little guys go bust. And because of this latest hoax, business is so bad we have to lend our people out."

Even though Dora thinks it's absurd to call a virus a hoax, it's a relief to talk to someone who's concerned less with principle, more with business.

"I feel sorry for the striplings," Tom says. "Their backs get mighty sore."

Dora tries to recall the last time she heard the word *striplings*. Suddenly the next lightbulb pops on. She sits there, riveted, and feels a slight blush rise in her cheeks. Tom and Steffen. The subject of her study is with a man. She notices Tom watching her from the side. He's already donned another oh-you-city-folk smile.

So you really believe, his expression seems to sneer, homosexuals only live in hip big-city neighborhoods?

Dora is already looking forward to telling Jojo and Axel about this on Thursday. Not only does Bracken have migrants, it's got homosexual couples, too, and it's not an issue for anybody, everything's totally chill. And you're still trying to claim this dump of a village is full of right-wing nutjobs?

"Got any seed potatoes?" she asks good-humoredly.

"You want to be a potato farmer?"

"I've built a vegetable bed. Turned out a bit big."

She says it so casually. Who cares how sore her muscles were? What counts is the result. Dora straightens up a bit. She might be a woman, she might not have R2-D2's special weapons, and her body, except for her hands, might not be made of the same special material Tom's is. But not only has she built a vegetable bed, it's turned out a bit big.

"You were just at the hardware store, weren't you?"

"Seed potatoes were sold out."

"And so you figured the guy with the pigtail getting ten hundredweight bags of potting soil was growing potatoes? Oh, you city folk."

It sounds more affectionate than contemptuous. Maybe Tom isn't from here either. Maybe he himself was once a big-city boy.

"Ask your neighbor," Tom suggests.

"Goth?"

"He's the potato man around here."

"I know," Dora says, "but he's not around. Haven't seen him in days."

Tom turns his head to the side and looks out the

window, as if there were something interesting out there, anything besides asparagus and alfalfa. Finally, he clears his throat.

"Oh, he's there, I'll bet. Just wait a little longer."

When the van suddenly brakes, it takes Dora a few seconds to realize they're stopping in front of her own house. Clearly Tom knows where she lives better than she herself does. He gets out, grabs all the grocery bags at once, and carries them up the front stair to the main door.

"If you need anything, just stop by." He points down the street to the big white house, and has already hopped back in and driven off before Dora gets a chance to thank him.

PART TWO

Seed Potatoes

14

AfD

The whole undertaking had to be planned with military precision. First, Dora looked for her dog backpack carrier, the indispensable piece of equipment that exactly fit Jay's body. It was the only means by which Jay could be carried long distances without suffocating, falling out, or being scared to death. Dora just cannot understand why she has to spend so long looking for something so important. She's on the brink of calling Robert, or simply losing her mind, when she finally spots the backpack hanging from a hook high up the bedroom wall. She can't remember how it got there. Inside, she finds a few T-shirts and several pairs of socks that've been missing since the move. Dora removes the clothes, places Jay into the pack, and takes her for a practice run, circling the house a few times. Their most recent outing with the pack was last autumn. Luckily it still works. Jay gazes up over Dora's shoulder and seems happy enough to be carried. Now all Dora needs is a bike. Too bad Gustav isn't here.

As she steps out the door, a machine suddenly revs up, loud enough that Dora flinches. She stays put, listening. The noise is coming from Goth's yard. It sounds like some kind of grinding. Dora's body can almost feel the abrading plates as they work their way across a wooden surface. Matter battling matter, one material against another. She goes over to the wall and climbs up on the chair. There's a stack of wooden pallets in front of the trailer. The camping table is covered in various tools. A partially coiled orange power cable leads her eye to the back of the house. Where she spots Goth. He'd disappeared for days, and now suddenly he's back, raising a racket. He's bent over one of the pallets, both hands gripping an orbital sander whose buzzing grows louder when he increases the pressure.

Dora climbs down from the chair before he even sees her, leaves the yard, and walks along the road until she reaches Tom's place. His yard isn't fenced in. Dora goes toward the door of the main house and looks for the doorbell. There isn't one. No nameplate either. On the mailbox, where you'd usually find a name, there's a bright blue AfD sticker. Dora tries knocking. Nothing happens, so she hits the door even harder, and then nearly falls into the hallway when someone suddenly opens the door.

"Is the sky falling down?" Tom asks, his strong hands bringing her back to her feet.

"How should I know?" she replies.

"You need seed potatoes that urgently?"

"Can you guys loan me a bike?"

She could've just asked him if he'd give her a lift to the nearest train station later that afternoon. But Dora's determined to do things on her own. She needs a day-to-day existence where she's in charge. Being able to get to Berlin is part of that. Take away the possibility of escape, and every refuge turns into a prison. *Berlin* was a key part of the realtor's vocabulary, and hence had become the strategic keyword Dora used to convince herself the move was doable. Translation: "It's a bit isolated, but you can always escape to the city." Dora had shared that sentiment with the realtor, and it's the exact phrase she plans to say to Jojo and Axel, just to make it extra clear that she doesn't miss a damn thing. The realtor had looked a bit skeptical, but was professional enough not to disagree.

"Steffen!" Tom's voice thundered through the house.

Not a moment later, a second man appeared at the door. He, too, had a ponytail, but otherwise was completely different: significantly younger and quite lean, with long red tresses more suited to a pretty woman than this otherwise fairly average-looking man. He was wearing a loose linen shirt, chinos, and Windsor eyeglasses with tinted lenses that turned him into a caricaturesque intellectual.

"This is Dora, our new neighbor," Tom says. "She needs a pair of wheels."

"Nowadays, good deals are hard to come by," Steffen replies.

"A pair of *wheels*," Tom repeats, slowly, as if speaking to a little kid. "A bike. We got one to spare?"

Steffen chuckles to himself and silently vanishes, slinking off barefoot. He clearly gets a kick out of kidding his boyfriend around, especially when Tom isn't even aware of it. Dora stays at the door with Tom and can't come up with anything to talk about. She'd love to tell him about her latest discovery: that there are hobgoblins in her yard. Or maybe they're brownies, or little earth spirits. That morning, still cradling her cup of coffee, she and Jay wandered around the yard. She was sure she'd left her spade at the edge of the vegetable patch. But now it was leaning against the trunk of a beech. And two old buckets from the shed, which she hadn't laid a finger on, were now lying out on the lawn. The lawn chair by the cinderblock wall had moved too. And the maple saplings Mr. Heinrich had cut were now grouped into handy, orderly little piles.

But she doesn't want Tom to think she's crazy. It's bad enough that she can't stand a bit of silence. He seems totally unfazed by it. He's just standing there, narrowed eyes gazing skyward, whistling to himself. Maybe Dora could talk about birds. There are two wood pigeons cooing in one of their linden trees and, despite being in broad daylight, a nightingale is improvising from their lilac hedge. Farther away, she hears a cuckoo. It almost sounds excessive, like some souped-up fairytale soundtrack. Dora's pretty sure Tom isn't interested in birdsong. Why is it so hard to just stand there together in silence? She finds it unbearable. Embarrassing. Almost more excruciating than her famous racism-triggered stiffness.

"You guys vote for them?" she suddenly says, pointing to the AfD sticker.

That's actually the last thing she wants to talk about. Birdsong or even hobgoblins would've been far better. But Tom seems as unfazed by this question as he was by the preceding silence.

"As if there's any other option." He turns around and uses his stageworthy voice to yell down the hall. "Nuno! Don't forget the cornflowers in the drying chamber!" Then he fishes a pouch of tobacco from his pocket and starts rolling a cigarette. Suddenly Dora wants to smoke so badly her mouth is watering. "Those higher-ups treat us like total idiots."

"Who're the 'higher-ups'?" Dora asks.

"The leadership. In Berlin."

Tom manages to make air quotes while still holding the open tobacco pouch and a rolling paper pinched between his fingers, although it's not clear whether they're meant to go with "the leadership" or "Berlin." Or maybe both.

"They sing the praises of agriculture while bankrupting farmers with new regulations restricting the use of fertilizers. They blather on about education while letting the schools go to rot. And when retirees are on the brink of starvation, all of a sudden they proclaim solidarity with the old folks. Just ask the village grannies whether they'd like better benefits or lockdowns instead." Tom pauses to lick the rolling paper. "Covid has made it beyond evident. It's like everyone in power has completely lost their mind."

That last sentence sounded like something Robert would've said. *Everyone in politics has lost their mind!* Said in that same *how-dare-you* tone, of course. The only difference being that Robert was the polar opposite of an AfD voter.

"Half of Bracken works in geriatric care," Tom went on, searching his pockets for a lighter. "Visiting nurse services, meals on wheels, old-age homes. Lousy hours, piss-poor pay, damn hard work. You think any of 'em got any extra training for Covid? They're just doing their jobs as usual. They've got no other choice. Without any special hygiene protocol, not to mention no personal protective equipment or regular Covid testing. They drive from house to house, from one high-risk patient to the next. Because that's all they can do. And, all the while, all those self-important politicians preen and prance around, destroying the national economy, devastating average folks' everyday existence. They sit there on TV, mask-free, and drivel on about how dangerous the pandemic is."

Dora then remembers she has a lighter, and feels newfound self-confidence as she holds it out to him. It's no Makita, but at least it's something.

"The preventive measures aren't the problem," Tom says. "The real problem is that people feel like they're being jerked around."

"And by 'people' you mean you guys?"

"Obviously. Who else?" Tom lights his freshly rolled cigarette and hands the lighter back. "Here in Bracken you're a person among people. It's not so easy to feel like you're so far above everybody else. It'll take you some getting used to."

Again, Dora can't help but think of Robert. She'd once accused him of acting as if he were above everyone else. As if he considered himself a superman. Maybe not exactly in the Nietzschean sense, but still ... he definitely acted like someone who thought he knew more, could do more, and therefore was entitled to more freedom than others. Because he possessed Absolute Truth. Robert grew livid. He said he only wanted the best for people. And he just couldn't understand why Dora considered that, in itself, a problem.

"And the AfD is idiot-free?"

"Of course not. But at least they admit as much."

Dora has to laugh, despite herself. The racism-triggered stiffness response seems to be malfunctioning today. She's already posed three questions, and laughed at the joke of an AfD voter. What was it Tom had said when he gave her a lift? "You catch on quick." She'd better watch out, lest she catch on too quick. Then again, Tom surely can't be a racist. He wears Norwegian sweaters, rolls his own cigarettes, and gathers his grey hair into a ponytail: it all adds up to the unmistakable outfit of an erstwhile GDR–civil-rights campaigner or anti-nuclear activist. But then there was that AfD sticker. When did everything go so totally haywire? Dora would love to know what Tom and Steffen were up to. Cornflowers. Drying chamber. The big building nearby, with all those solar panels. Maybe they're running a massive cannabis plantation? And keeping it hidden from the higher-ups, from the lamestream media, from ultra-corporate Deutschland Inc. His cigarette smells good. Dora does her best to catch some first-rate second-hand smoke, sucking the fumes out of the air and deep into her lungs. Tom hands her the cigarette.

"Here, the rest is yours."

The butt is moist from his lips. It could be teeming with billions of virus bits, but at this moment Dora couldn't care less. She takes a long drag and savors the light buzz. She'd love to snap a selfie and send it to Robert. Caption: *Just sharing a smoke with this Covid-denying, hash-growing, AfD-voting dude. Greetings from the parallel universe of rural Brandenburg.*

Luckily, Steffen saves her from carrying that idea

to fruition when he reappears in the driveway, pushing a dusty bike her way. It's a large men's bike, and doesn't appear to fit their back-to-the-land, German-Buddhist aesthetic. They must've bought it at the hardware store eons ago and then forgotten it. Still-barefoot Steffen pushes it across the gravel driveway without so much as a wince.

"I had to search a bit," he says. "Will this boneshaker fill the bill?"

Dora hadn't heard the word *boneshaker* in ages. It had been almost as long since she'd heard *fill the bill*. It's nice to come across such turns of phrase again, like running into old acquaintances you'd lost track of. She offers her profuse thanks, puts real effort into swinging her leg over its tall frame, and zig-zags her way back home.

15

Jojo

Getting to the nearest train station means going to Kochlitz, which is just over four miles from Bracken. With a bike, it's not that far. But because the frame and seat on this bike are so high, Dora can only pedal standing up, which hurts her thighs and makes Jay bounce up and down in the backpack. Dora longs for Gustav. If Steffen's bike were to have a name, it'd be Ronny, at best.

The train station is nothing more than a concrete platform with a clock, a bike rack, and a digital display streaming meaningless messages from right to left. There isn't even a ticket machine. The train is punctual and almost empty. There doesn't even seem to be a conductor. Dora spends half the ride buying a ticket on her smartphone. After an hour and fifteen minutes, the train pulls into Berlin's main station. As Dora takes one escalator after another to reach the city trains, Jay panting over her shoulder, she feels dazed. So *that's* how fast and easy it is to cross the border between provincial backwater and bustling metropolis. The regional train she took must've been a teleporter in disguise. Or this capital is a stage set. In which case the budget for bit players has clearly been cut. A lot of the shops are closed and there are only a few travelers, which gives the large glass-covered station a ghostly aura.

All of a sudden, Dora feels her presence is somehow illegal. She's terrified someone will ask her what she's doing here.

Once she gets to Savignyplatz she checks the time. It took three hours for Alexander Gerst to return to Earth from the International Space Station. One and a half hours is all it took Dora to get from Bracken to Charlottenburg. The effect is similar. Her leg muscles feel weak as an astronaut's, and she feels the urge to keep her eyes and ears shut tight. Jay, on the other hand, catapults into high spirits the second she's freed from the carrier. She runs from tree to tree, elatedly greeting each urban inch of ground, sniffing in the millions of messages the big city is sending her. Dora gives her time to soak it all in. Welcome home, Laika. As Dora observes her dog she realizes that the so-called Clash of Civilizations really does exist. But it's not between East and West. It's between Berlin and Bracken. Between metropolis and province, center and perimeter, city and outskirts.

She'd like to tell Robert all about it. He's into formulaic worldviews, and he'd love this one. They could discuss it out on the balcony, over a bottle of red wine. But then she remembers the old Robert who enjoyed long talks out on the balcony doesn't exist anymore. All that's left is a breakup bike named Gustav, which maybe she'll be able to take home on the train later tonight. And red wine, of course. Above all, a rich Cabernet Sauvignon called Montes, which Jojo could spend the rest of his life drinking. Montes gives Dora a headache as soon as the bottle is uncorked.

"Heya. Cool, c'mon in."

Axel opens the door as if this were his place, and Dora knows him well enough to know he loves this charade. She was about to give him a big hug, even though his mask and apron make him look like an insect dressed up as a maid, but then he takes a step back, brings his palms together at his solar plexus, and bows like a sensei. Dora sighs. Avoiding physical contact is totally fine, but Axel's theatrical bow makes her innards begin prickling again.

The absence of background noise in the apartment confirms that Axel didn't bring Fenna and Signe along. No Grampa-Grampa shouts, no toys clattering all over the floor. Which means no Christine either. Every downside has an upside. Dora likes her nieces, and her sister-in-law, too. But when Christine and the girls are present, every conversation revolves around the granddaughters, which means every gathering devolves into a celebration of granddaughters, whereby the main activity becomes doting on the kids in all their marvelous kidness. As Dora sees it, the girls are rather poorly behaved, which in Christine's language translates as "highly gifted." The moment the little ones sense they're not the center of everyone's attention, they raise hell until the adults break off whatever they're doing and go back to doting on the granddaughters.

Jojo and his new companion—who, since becoming a yoga teacher, has taken to calling adults "manifestations of the present" and children "gateways to the soul"—are wholly indifferent to the girls' behavior. In the end, after just a few hours, the kids are always whisked back into their own world, leaving little lasting damage in their wake aside from a few new grease stains on the sofa. If Dora pauses to recall the stormy scolding she endured as a child when she so much as inadvertently spilled a glass of water, she has to admit she finds Jojo's grandfatherly forbearance downright distressing.

Dora figures Fenna and Signe are completely normal, it's just that their father can't be bothered to set any boundaries, and their mother is too busy to do so. As a tax lawyer, Christine is a certified Powerfrau who puts in serious hours, earns serious money, and probably brought her adorable daughters into the world simply so she could check that item off her to-do list with serious efficiency. After a few irksome weeks spent nursing, she was glad to get right back to work, and within days Axel completed his transformation from couch philosopher to loving stay-at-home dad. Ever since, he's been the son who could do no wrong. In Jojo's eyes, marrying and bearing offspring with a successful lawyer is evidently just as valid a life choice as having passed the bar exams for yourself, whereas Dora's less-than-professional path—studying communications but then dropping out, working in advertising, starting a failed relationship with a climate activist, and finally making the perplexing move to a rural backwater—seems increasingly problematic in comparison.

The Montes has already been decanted and now sits on the table, breathing. Piano music in the style of Erik Satie plays in the background, perhaps as a compromise between Sibylle's meditation CDs and Jojo's Bruckner symphonies. Jojo stands up and kisses the air to the right and left sides of Dora's face. Jay happily prances from one family member to the next as Axel openly speculates on the likelihood that petting a dog might transmit virus particles. Jojo's new companion walks in from the kitchen, her sleeves rolled high, waves at Dora, and lifts her wet hands above her head to underscore the fact that she's literally up to her elbows preparing dinner.

"Sibylle, shall I give you a hand in the kitchen?" Axel proffers.

Dora doesn't hide her amazement: Axel is such a suck-up. But even she can't deny that's where his real talent lies. He must've used the same ploy to catch Christine. Nowadays maybe all a guy needs to bring to the table is a ton of time and a willingness to serve, then he'll have his pick of the Powerfraus. And apparently such women will find such a guy more alluring than even the most successful macho man in the finest custom-tailored suit.

"Have a seat."

Jay-the-Ray follows orders, leaping up to occupy one of the free seats at the dining room table. Jojo laughs and scratches her forehead, so she scrambles over the armrest and makes herself at home on his lap. She might be bow-legged, but that doesn't stop her from being nimble as a squirrel when need be.

Dora takes a seat next to Jojo and accepts a glass of Montes. Satie plays on, heartrending, somehow both melancholic and merry at once. The sound of clanging pots and muffled laughter makes it through the kitchen door, which Axel and Sibylle have closed in order to protect the rest of the rooms from all the steam. It's a rare moment of privacy between father and daughter. When was the last time they did anything together, just the two of them? Whenever Jojo's in Berlin, he gladly convenes his beloved "Savigny-soirées," which means his friends and acquaintances often join his family at the table. Maybe he figures it's more efficient to see a bunch of people simultaneously. Or maybe that's his way of ensuring the talk doesn't get too personal.

When Dora was little, sometimes Jojo would come to her room, take a seat at the desk, and strike up a conversation. About a book, about school, or about whether or not outer space was endless. He spoke to her as he would with an adult. Then her mother fell ill, and Jojo stopped knocking on Dora's door. Maybe she should go visit him in Münster again. But if she's honest with herself, she's avoided setting foot in the house she grew up in. Sure, Jojo and his new companion have entirely remodeled the place, but the view from the kitchen window remains unchanged.

Dora takes a deep gulp of the Montes, which courses warm through her veins. She's out of practice when it comes to drinking, since Robert and their balcony went out of the equation. As for conversing, well, she's even more out of practice there. She absolutely wants to tell Jojo about her new life. About the old estate manager's house and its striking, albeit somewhat scruffy, stucco facade. She wants to tell him how it's really, truly hers—hers alone—and how unbelievably amazing it feels to own a piece of this planet. About her Sisyphean yardwork, about Mr. Heinrich, about Tom and

Steffen, and about how, when it comes to Bracken, she still can't quite make head nor tail of the place.

She's still pondering where to start when the kitchen door opens, filling the dining room with the billowing scents and sounds of dinnertime. The aroma of asparagus, the low roar of the range hood. Axel and Jojo's new companion waltz in with the first course: blood-red beet carpaccio and home-baked nut bread with cilantro-lime butter.

Dora would never say she came from a family where the men spoke and the women merely listened. But that turns out to be the case. Throughout the meal, Jojo and Axel are the only ones conversing. Actually, to put it more accurately, the two of them take turns talking at each other. Axel has doffed his mask and is swearing like a sailor about the government's overly lax policies, complaining about the whiners who want stay-at-home orders to be lifted. Jojo is going on about doctors playing skat in empty hospitals while patients in dire need of vital care stay home because they don't dare go to the doctor anymore.

"People are totally intimidated," Jojo says.

"People don't get how serious the situation is," Axel says, and they both take another bite of their beet Carpaccio.

As Dora listens to her brother, once again, she can't help but think of Robert. He and Axel are about the same age. Maybe these not-exactly-young-anymore men are the most vulnerable to being seized by a virus-fighter mentality. They get sucked in, viewing it as an all-or-nothing battle against the unthinkable alternative: complete loss of control. A declaration of war against the impertinent future, which insists on making you older by the day, and doing whatever else it fancies with your fate. Dora doesn't know a single woman who spreads panic like that. Then again, she doesn't know many people in general. But one thing's for sure: being a hardliner is a luxury both Axel and Robert can afford. One is totally taken care of by his wife, the other is making a killing off the media circus surrounding the pandemic.

"It's utterly irresponsible for people to say schools should reopen." Axel continues his rant.

"It's utterly irresponsible for the people influencing public opinion in this country to not even know the difference between infection rates and mortality rates," Jojo counters.

"Oh, come now," Jojo's new companion chimes in. Neither political provocation nor bad table manners sit well with her, so she stealthily shuts things down by handing her man the bread basket.

Remarkably, Jojo keeps his cool. Normally he has a short fuse and explodes whenever anyone dismisses his opinion. Especially when it comes to the field of medicine, where he's so much more knowledgeable than everyone else. Now he's just sitting and chewing his nut bread like a good boy, while Axel's busy reciting the latest infection rates. Maybe Jojo's ego is already set for the rest of the evening, satisfied because he's managed to bring his family together despite the ban on gatherings.

As Sibylle clears the first-course dishes from the table and disappears into the kitchen to check on the asparagus, Jojo tells the story of one particular patient. "This was a woman in the prime of life, two kids and all," but she'd spent weeks hiding out at home, suffering a steadily increasing mass effect, because her husband didn't want to risk going to the hospital.

Even as a little girl, Dora was aware that "mass effect" was another way of saying *tumor*. And by her mid-twenties, when a popular video game titled *Mass Effect* came out, the first thing those words brought to mind was still the secondary pathological symptoms such a growth creates. She had always been aware that Jojo's life work involved cutting those masses out of people's heads. Like all little girls, she was infinitely proud of her father, and listened closely each time he recounted one of his miraculous lifesaving procedures. But as the years passed, she noticed she could no longer stand hearing his stories. As he begins describing this patient's symptoms in detail—"she could no longer speak or even see, but *he* was afraid of *Covid!*"—the prickling bubbles return with such a vengeance that Dora nearly retches on her red beets.

She flees from dinner table to balcony and lights up. The cigarette tastes delightful, its smoke hovering like a sculpture in the still air. Berlin can be beautiful, or at least it can overlooking Savigny-platz at twilight, especially when you're standing on the tastefully greenscaped third-floor balcony of an art nouveau apartment building. The streets are a bit livelier here. People are taking their dogs for a leisurely evening walk, or calmly carrying groceries home. There are taxis, delivery vehicles, teens and twentysomethings vaping, men with bike straps at their ankles. Dora's relieved to note, yet again, that

Robert and Axel are wrong. The virus is real, there is a pandemic, but the sky isn't falling. It's not the end of the world. Normalcy is powerful, a force of nature. It makes inroads wherever it can.

Dora fishes her phone from her pocket and texts Robert, with maximum concision:

Getting Gustav.

When? comes the rapid reply.

Dora estimates how long it'll take her to get to Kreuzberg, and when she'll need to be back at the main station to catch the last regional train home.

In an hour and a half.

It's in the main hallway.

Of course. He doesn't want her in the apartment. He doesn't even want to see her. He'd probably say he's just following the social distancing recommendations, or the ban on gatherings. Dora decides to cancel, that very evening, the automatic draft that's still regularly sending her half of the rent.

She goes back inside, returns to the dinner table, and lets everyone know she can't stay much longer, since she still has to pick something up from Robert and the last regional train leaves at eleven.

As she says the words "regional train," Axel's mouth curls into a mocking sneer.

Nobody asks how things are with Robert. Nobody wants to know whether she's actually living in Bracken full-time now. Or how she likes it. Whether she's lonely. Nor do they ask whether things are going okay with her job, or what she's going to pick up over in Kreuzberg. They aren't intentionally belittling her. That's just the way her family is.

"But you'll stay for dessert, right?" Jojo's new

companion asks. "We were planning to share some news with you two."

"We might as well go ahead," Jojo tersely adds, promptly standing up and tapping his glass to add an extra touch of irony. "We're getting married."

"All of us?" Dora lets slip, earning a burst of relieved giggling.

"Despite Covid?" Axel demands to know, causing Jojo to raise an irritated brow for the first time all evening.

"No party needed," Jojo's companion calmly adds. "We're just going to the city registry office, but we wanted you to know beforehand."

"Congratulations to you both," says Axel, ever the exemplar.

Sometimes Dora has to wonder whether Axel lost his mother, too. Or if she's the only one who at this very moment is picturing her emaciated face and oversized eyes, the sickbed in front of the terrace door where she lay, utterly still, staring out the window. Dora's no longer really following the dinner-table conversation. Phrases like "married filing separately," "long-term care insurance," and "joint will" fly right by her. She ponders the notion that she'll have to call Jojo's new companion "Jojo's new wife" from now on. She leaves earlier than she'd necessarily have to, and runs downstairs taking two steps at a time.

Two hours later, as the regional train pulls up in Kochlitz and she exits with Jay on her back and Gustav at her side, the sky is black. Bats flap back and forth in the light of the lamps lining the platform, looking a lot like larger versions of the tiny insects they're hunting. A nocturnal bird silently glides by.

The first crickets are chirping, and a fox barks in the distance. Animals have taken over the train station. Ronny is still there, even though Dora didn't have a lock to secure him with. She almost feels pity: being parked at a train station, unlocked, and *not* being stolen must be pretty rough rejection if you're a bike. It's surprisingly easy to settle in on Gustav's saddle and lead Ronny by the handlebars. Dora speeds through the darkness, making hardly a sound. Homeward bound, she thinks. I'm going home.

She parks both bikes in the shed, unlocks the front door of the house, walks in, and heads straight for the bedroom to call it a night. She flicks the light on and flinches. There's a bed in the room. Not just a mattress on the floor, like before, but a bona fide bed. The bedframe is built out of wooden pallets someone has sanded smooth and sealed with white varnish. The scent of fresh paint permeates the air. Its surface is large enough that the mattress is surrounded by a broad shelf, the perfect place to set your phone, books, alarm clock, a bedside lamp. Dora couldn't dream up a better bed if she tried. But that doesn't change the fact that this bed doesn't belong here. When she left, earlier today, it definitely wasn't here in this house.

She slowly walks toward the new piece of furniture. It doesn't vanish into thin air. She can even touch it. She walks to the back door of the house. It's locked. The front door was locked, too, she's absolutely certain. She goes out, stands on the front landing while bats and owls whoosh through the cool air, and casts her gaze over the cinderblock wall. It's utterly still on the other side.

16

Brandenburg

"Goth!" Dora shouts. "Goth!"

It's morning, and she's standing atop the lawn chair next to the cinderblock wall. Trailer, geraniums, wolf. The empty house. She's determined not to let him get off scot-free this time.

"Goth!"

First she had to put the chair back in the right spot. Fresh out of bed, she'd gone to glance out the kitchen window and promptly noticed all the lawn furniture had been moved. It was now further back, under the fruit trees, and arranged in a circle, as if the hobgoblins had gotten together and thrown a little tea party overnight. Thank god Gustav and Ronny were still in the shed, side by side like two trusty steeds.

"C'mon out! I know you're there."

This goes on for a while. It's only seven thirty. In Brandenburg that's considered late morning, Dora thinks with palpable disdain. Time to get up. Jay-the-Ray is noodling around the yard looking for the right spot to take care of her morning duties. Dora stands on the chair and shouts. On the other side of the wall everything is still for a while, until it isn't. The trailer door flies open, bangs against the siding and bounces back, nearly hitting Goth as he appears on the threshold, steadying himself in the doorframe with both hands. He's swaying, and lifts one hand to shade his face, as if the sun hurts his eyes. He must have a mega-hangover.

"Over here!" Dora yells.

Goth staggers down the three grate-metal steps and moves in her direction, half blind, still holding a hand up to shield his eyes. He comes to a halt just a few feet from the wall.

"What?"

"Was that you?"

"What?"

"The bed. Was that you?"

He gives it some thought. When he finally lowers his hand, Dora sees his eyes look red. His brow is so deeply furrowed, you could slide an index card into the slit and it'd stay put.

"Yup."

Of course Dora's prepared for this answer. She saw the pallets in Goth's yard, and it had to be somebody, after all. Nevertheless, his open confession leaves her feeling somewhat muddled. But she can clear the emotional air later on. For now, she needs to keep the dialogue going before Goth slinks back into his burrow.

"Why?"

Goth looks annoyed. Dora gets it. "Why?" is an irksome question every time it pops up in her life, too. More accusation than question, really. Why is she once again unable to sleep? Why is she still thinking about how Jojo and Sibylle want to get married? Why can't she just be like Axel, the guy who only ever asks one question: Will this hurt me or help me? Or like Robert, who doggedly sticks to just one thing and completely forgets about everything else. Goth clears his throat and hocks a loogie.

"You didn't have one."

This is an answer Dora would love to contemplate at length. She can envision building an intro-level philosophy course around it. Title: *The Why Question—A Quintessentially Modern Chimera?* And because she hasn't said anything, Goth once again figures she didn't get what he said.

"You didn't have a bed," he patiently explains.

"How'd you know that?"

"Eyes can see, you know."

"Wha—whe—through the window?"

"Yup."

"You come into my yard and look through my windows?"

"Every Friday."

She needs time to swallow this bit of news, let alone digest it. Same goes for the fact that she now spots Jay on the wrong side of the wall, right behind Goth, who hasn't noticed the infraction. The happily panting dog casts Dora a friendly glance before heading for the potato bed. Dora doesn't dare call out to her, lest she betray her presence. She diverts her attention back to her neighbor.

"So, every Friday you come and look through my windows."

Goth doesn't answer. Of course it was a statement, not a question, strictly speaking. And she'd basically just repeated what he'd already said.

"And why did you move all my lawn furniture?" she follows up.

Again, no answer. The conversation seems to be

stressing him out. He keeps pinching the bridge of his nose and then massaging his temples.

"Goth! I don't get why you had to rearrange my lawn chairs."

"Dammit!" he shouts. "They're your chairs, what do I care?"

"Somebody rearranged them overnight."

"Wasn't me."

"Who, then?"

"How should I know, man?!"

Making him angry won't help.

"Okay," Dora shifts her weight on the rickety chair, takes a deep breath, and goes out of her way to strike a friendlier tone. "Look, Goth, the bed is nice, really. But I don't want you nosing around over here."

He raises his head and looks squarely at Dora for the first time.

"I've always looked after that house."

"My house?"

"It was here before you."

"You mean, when the house was empty, you came by every now and then to make sure everything was okay?"

"Somebody had to."

"So you have a set of keys?"

Goth nods, and another riddle is solved.

"But now," Dora's tone grows even gentler, "now I live here."

Goth shrugs, "You're alone. You're a girl. And you can't even swing a scythe right."

"You nuts? I've mastered that scythe!"

"I told Heini to buzz by with his Hilti trimmer every now and then."

Suddenly another tiny lightbulb clicks on over her head. Heini. Hilti. Heinrich.

"You're the one who told Mr. Heinrich to clear my yard?"

"Who?"

"R2-D2—I mean, Heini."

Goth fumbles around in his pockets, pulls out a squashed pack of cigarettes, and walks up to the wall to offer her one. He smokes nasty Eastern European knock-offs, contraband filter-tip cancer sticks. First thing in the morning, no less. No effing way, Reason says, as her right arm is already reaching across the top of the wall. In order for Goth's lighter to reach her, she has to stand on her tippy-toes and lean out, propping herself on the wall, which makes the rickety chair wobble and causes the cinderblocks to sway.

Diplomacy calls for sacrifice, Reason relents, as Dora inhales with gusto.

"Are you really from Poland?" she asks, just so the conversation doesn't peter out.

Now Goth looks at her as if she really has lost her mind.

"'Cause of that flag," she gestures toward the main house on his property, "out front."

"That's the German flag."

"The other one! The red-and-white one."

"Brandenburg."

Dora feels her face turn red. If there were a prize for stupidest city-slicker cliché, she just won it.

"I'm no Polack," Goth clarifies, just in case she still hadn't caught on.

Polacks in the boondocks, the tagline tool in Dora's

brain fires up again. She's got to switch the subject, stat.

"Haven't seen you for quite a while. Work take you out of town?"

"Wasn't doing so great," Goth mumbles.

After that they just smoke in silence, and are almost perfectly synchronized as each flicks the spent butt onto the other's side of the wall.

"We're all clear, then," Dora wraps it up. "Thanks again for the bed. But I'd like you to hand over your set of keys now."

Without paying her any heed, Goth walks toward his trailer. His footsteps seem steadier now.

"Goth? You're getting the keys, right?"

The trailer door slams shut behind him.

17

Steffen

Dora spends the morning writing new treatments, just to be sure there's a large enough selection for the next presentation. DO-GOODER at the zoo—he frees a lion from its far-too-small enclosure, only then the animal tries to eat him alive. DO-GOODER helps a guy switch out his flat tire, only to discover the man is a bank robber on the run. DO-GOODER offers his guest room to a stranger, only to find, come morning, all the furniture is gone.

The more time Dora spends with DO-GOODER and his mishaps, the more she likes him. She herself is a lot like DO-GOODER. Everybody she knows is. Except maybe Goth, but even he makes furniture for his new neighbor, for free. Everyone, in their own way, is doing their best to come to terms with this merciless world. To do something positive, to add a bit of meaning to all the mess. Everyone feels an instinctive need to help others, however strong or stunted their motive might be in each particular case. DO-GOODER is an ironic caricature of the zeitgeist, a present-day parody aimed at selling as many sustainably produced jeans as possible. But he's also an icon standing in for the profoundly human desire to make the world a better place. Despite the inherent futility of it all. It's funny, it's tragic, and above all it's existential.

When she's done, she shuts her laptop. The dull roar of its cooling fan dies down. A leaden silence envelops the house. Every sound—putting a pencil down, putting a mug away, opening and closing a door—suddenly seems unnaturally loud. Dora's stomach starts prickling. Next, her drafts will be sent to the client. Then she'll wait for feedback. Maybe a few days, maybe even weeks. Under normal circumstances, Dora would get the next brief right away. But nothing's normal right now. She's an engine forced into idle. From one moment to the next, she finds herself with nothing to do.

She takes a shower, has a second breakfast, and takes Jay out for a walk. Eleven thirty. She gathers the cut saplings in the back yard into a huge pile that can eventually be burnt. She takes a second shower and cooks up some eggs for lunch. She bought them from the butcher van, and she cracks open two for herself, one for Jay. She eats as slowly as possible, stifling the urge to doomscroll. Despite her heightened state of mindfulness, she finishes her meal in just twenty minutes. One thirty.

One thirty is the worst time in the world. One thirty means the day is just halfway done. Dora sits at the kitchen table and mops the last bit of liquid yolk from her plate with a bit of bread, while her body prickles as if her blood were carbonated. There's so much she could be doing: Answering emails, tidying up her hard drive, updating her cv and résumé. She could get active on social media, and seriously think about setting up her own homepage. But she immediately intuits she won't be able to devote her attention to such things. Under stress she's able to take care of five things simultaneously. But this forced inactivity gobbles up all her energy. Besides, it'd almost be hypocritical to start coming up with her own tasks to feed the never-ending cycle of projects. A cycle that's currently gone dormant.

Of course she could try reading a book. She could clean the bath, and take a bunch more walks. But none of that would really kill time. Every empty hour heralds yet another. Dora tries telling herself she's just got a few days of vacation ahead. Something normal people would be thrilled to hear. Unfortunately for her, free time is only a gift when it isn't really free, but rather when it's filled to the gills with activities. Outings, sports, family gatherings. Writing a novel, or tending to little kids' needs. Truly free time is terrifying. It expands in all directions, endless as a battlefield with nary a nemesis in sight. Just a mute, threatening mood. Running away is as wrong as staying put.

Dora gets up from the table and lets a fly out the window. The insect has been banging against the glass for quite some time and clumsily reels out into the open with an oddly hopeless air, as if the notion of freedom is nice only so long as there's an invisible windowpane restraining you.

At least the buzzing has stopped. The distinct advantage of this particular fly was that she hadn't just imagined it, unlike the ones that used to plague the bedroom she shared with Robert. It's been a while now since Dora found herself hunting down nonexistent insects. That's progress. Maybe one day she'll manage to read the newspaper without getting a stomachache. Maybe someday she'll manage to quit thinking about herself all the time. Just do something because it can be done. Like that person who made that bench in the woods. But she still needs a project for the days coming up. Procuring and planting seed potatoes. Painting the walls. She'll come up with something. What's important is that she be able to do it on her own. She doesn't want to ask anyone for help. She refuses to believe she's incapable of spending a few days in her own company. Even if she already feels that emptiness gnawing at her, and how her body's growing blurry at the edges. She needs out.

For starters, she can do something meaningful: return Ronny. She gets him from the shed and pushes him along the shoulder of the road. As she passes Goth's place, a light breeze stirs, briefly billowing the flags, and for a fleeting moment Dora can make out the eagle on the Brandenburg flag.

This time Steffen opens the door. His long red tresses hang loose, framing his bespectacled face like curtains that could be drawn shut when the show is over.

"Whatcha want this time?" he asks.

"I'm returning Ronny."

"Who's Ronny?"

Dora points at the huge men's bike, which she's leaned against one of their lampposts.

"You baptized the boneshaker?"

Dora shrugs. "He just looked like a Ronny."

"And you still don't want to keep him?"

"No, I just thought—I mean, I figured you—"

"You got a problem with this bike?"

"No, not at all, it's just that in the meantime I

finally got my own back, from Berlin. It was pretty expensive."

"And just because it was expensive, it's better?"

"No, it's just—"

"Ronny wasn't exactly cheap, y'know."

"Of course, but Ronny's way too big for me, and—"

"Or is it just because your other one's from *Berlin*?"

"No, but Gustav is—"

"Gustav!" Steffen's eyes flash with fury behind his glasses. "So you're choosing a Gustav over our dear Ronny?"

Dora feels like she's in the wrong movie. "Did you guys think I wanted to buy Ronny? Is that why you're so riled up?"

"*Buy* him?!" Now Steffen's rankled mood turns into real rage. "All you city folk can think about is buying things! You're so hell-bent on having. Possessing. Have you ever tried appreciating anything without wondering who it belongs to?"

"I didn't mean it like that," Dora tries once more, "I just—"

But Steffen won't let her get a word in edgewise.

"Here we were, just trying to do you a favor, entrusting you with this shiny new bike, maybe as a welcoming gesture, maybe just because we like to help people out, maybe we let you borrow it, maybe we meant it as a gift, what's the difference? Ronny is one helluva beautiful boneshaker, and you could've used him as long as you wanted, but no, you're calling it quits, you're turning him away, rejecting him!"

Dora just stands there, stunned, speechless. She stares at Steffen, his narrow face, his furious expression, his round glasses and red hair, and then she notices how his bizarre rant is still lingering in the air somehow, like some verbal sculpture, a bit of acoustic installation art—maybe it's titled *Gustav & Ronny*, or *City-Slicker out in The Sticks*. And now Steffen actually appears to be collapsing, as if he were a marionette whose strings somebody just cut; his long hair falls forward, he carries out some strange kind of bow, and when he stands up again Dora notices he's laughing. He's laughing at her. Maybe he's high. Even if his eyes look crystal clear.

"You should've seen your face," he smirks. Then he brings his hands together like the Dalai Lama. "C'mon in," he says, suddenly sounding friendly. "Your dog's already here."

18

Mon Chéri

Jay-the-Ray doesn't appear to be in the hallway. She's probably off searching for a bowl of cat food, a plate of cookies, or the kind of snacks you usually find on coffee tables. Once she's polished off every last edible morsel she'll reappear again, in a state of annoyed boredom, punctuated by her trademark can-we-go-already whimper.

"Keep straight, all the way back," Steffen instructs, leading Dora down the narrow hall and out to the rear. "I'm guessing you want to see the cannabis plantation, right?"

Dora wonders whether he can read minds. Or whether people from the city are really so predictable. As they walk down the hall she nosily peeks through every open door. A bright, ultra-modern kitchen with stainless-steel appliances. A living room with low-lying furniture and a flat-screen TV. A bathroom in which she's pretty sure she spots a jacuzzi. The plant business seems to be going well.

Jay slips through a door left ajar, which Dora presumes leads to a bedroom. The dog is gnawing on something, but she doesn't want to know what.

"This way."

Steffen opens a back door. Jay darts right past him so she can call dibs on these new hunting grounds. Unexpectedly it leads not to the courtyard, but into one of the outbuildings, a long flat-roofed structure. The sweet, slightly repelling scent of cut flowers wafts toward them. Long workbenches line the walls, strewn with piles of plant material, most of it gathered into bundles. Ferns, grasses, blossoms, stems—most dried, some fresh. Off in a corner, Dora sees the finished products: fresh floral sprays, funeral wreaths, and countless little dried-flower arrangements, in small baskets or glazed ceramic vessels, adorably arrayed and petite enough to fit on the tiniest shelf, or even a medicine cabinet mirror.

"Around these parts people occasionally get married, they frequently pass away, but, more often than anything else, they decorate," Steffen declares.

It sounds like one of their catchphrases. Dora can imagine Tom's droning voice saying the same words. She goes to one of the workbenches so she can get a closer look. Every arrangement is unique. Some feature colorful little pebbles or splashes of red rose hips, others are more minimalist, little rock gardens with various types of decorative grasses.

"We do most of our business by the side of the road. Our people divvy up the points of sale across the entire region. Take an old sewing-machine table from a junk shop, put a lace doily on top, write a sign by hand, and set a mason jar there as a till, and you've got yourself an honor-system flower stand. It oozes countryside authenticity, and the tourists from Berlin can't resist. They picture a little old lady in a plaid apron tying a bow on every single arrangement. They buy these things like there's no tomorrow, and pay an average of fifteen euros per piece. Our people drive their routes, stock the tables, and empty the tills. On a good weekend we sell a few hundred arrangements."

"They're quite cute, really," Dora lifts one up. This one's a miniature forest with tiny evergreens and deciduous trees and teensy, colorful glass beads perched like birds in the greenery.

"We grow most of the flowers and grasses in our greenhouses," Steffen says. "But I also go into the woods to gather some stuff."

Somehow it suits him, this combo of wiccan herb-woman and lifestyle designer. Much as he indulges his love of irony, his tone betrays the pride of a true artist.

"Normally we also sell a lot through florists, and at county fairs and seasonal markets. But now everyone's on lockdown. Stupidly we'd just invested in a new drying chamber. We're running up quite a tab. But we're fighters. We'll eat our own flowers before we accept so much as one eurocent from the government."

Jay seems to have taken that first part as a command, since she's lying flat on her stomach, chewing on a stem of something or other.

"In addition to the roadside sales, Tom built our online shop, which is still expanding. It's going pretty well. Times like these, people are all too happy to put a little piece of nature on their kitchen table."

Dora imagines what it'd be like to still be living back in Kreuzberg, in that old apartment, Robert always on the phone, yelling. She pictures herself there, staring at one of Steffen's arrangements long enough that she starts to hear birds singing.

"Your people," she asks, "are they refugees?"

Steffen gives a weighty nod.

"They're boat people from Aleppo. Their plight works to our advantage, insofar as they're cheap labor."

"Dumb question, dumb answer?"

Steffen resumes his weighty nodding.

"So—what's the actual answer?" Dora asks.

"Every year we hire two or three Erasmus-program students from Portugal. They study in the city, and earn some extra cash working with us. They wanted out of Berlin because of Covid, but they didn't want to go back to Lisbon. So they're living here and lending a hand harvesting asparagus."

"And there's no trouble?"

"With the tax bureau?"

"With the villagers."

"Bracken's full of left-wing liberals. A veritable bastion of open-mindedness. We welcome everyone."

Dora can't stifle a smirk. "So—what did you used to do? I mean, before you became a little old lady in a plaid apron?"

Steffen rolls his eyes skyward, as if digging deep into ancient memory.

"Back in prehistoric times I just *might* have studied at the Ernst Busch School."

Dora's smirk turns into a grin. The Ernst Busch School specializes in performing arts, and is famous for its puppeteering program.

"What about Goth, is he a left-wing liberal, too?"

"Goth. Yeah. Well—" Steffen ties his hair back into a ponytail. Apparently the tour is over. "Goth's actually calmed down a bit recently, praise be to Thor."

"What about before?"

Steffen strides along the workbenches and starts picking out materials for the next arrangement. Pampas grass, birch sprigs, baby's-breath, a couple of glass marbles.

"He'd come over every now and then and get all rowdy out front. He'd pace up and down, shouting, *Bumfuckers, fugginforeigners, I'm gonna beat the shit outta you.* Stuff like that."

"Oh my god." Dora goes pale. "Does he drink?"

"You asking whether someone has to be an alcoholic in order to be a Nazi?"

"That's not what I meant."

"At some point, anyway, Tom cleared it all up. He explained the situation, plain and simple."

"What situation?"

"That we'd round up a few folks and pound him to a pulp if he so much as once bothers us ever again."

"Oh my god," Dora repeats, sounding like a teenage girl.

"That's the only language Goth understands."

Steffen's fingers deftly organize the foliage, securing everything on a styrofoam ball covered in moss. He holds the blue marbles up to the light before placing them among the grasses.

"Did that help?"

"A bit." Steffen shrugs. "Then again, maybe Goth and his friends are just too busy with other things. Like taping death-threats to people's front doors, squeezing ketchup into people's mailboxes, planting black wooden crosses in people's front yards. Being a citizen of the Reich is a full-time job."

"People do that stuff here?"

"Don't you read the papers?"

Dora gulps. She's landed in a warzone. She can already hear how Axel will gloat the next time she seeks asylum at his place: "Where'd you think you were moving? Some idyllic, bucolic, woodsy wonderland?"

Dora doesn't have anybody to round up and pound anyone to a pulp. All she can do is hope Goth never develops even a tiny grudge against her.

"You okay?"

Apparently she's gone even paler. She nods, clears her throat, and pushes her hair back with both hands.

"I just don't get how, in a situation like this, you guys can vote AfD."

Steffen's expression closes down, as if he's shut some internal door tight.

"I don't vote," he says. "Voting isn't spiritual."

Dora glances at him to see whether he's making fun of her again. But his face remains inscrutable.

"Tom votes," she says.

"Then you'll have to ask Tom."

"He told me."

"Well, then, it sounds like the two of you are already fast friends."

Steffen sets the styrofoam ball in a perfectly sized basket and examines it, eyes narrowed. Then he places two empty snail shells next to the marbles, and sets the piece down in front of Dora. She has no desire to fawn over it. She's annoyed by his whole I-don't-vote shtick. She almost prefers Tom's misguided protest vote.

"I'll tell you a little something about Goth," Steffen

says. "His wife cheated on him. For months. With a delivery guy. Goth became the village laughingstock. He put up with it, then one day she up and left, taking their young daughter with her. Now she's living in Berlin and here he sits, all alone in his trailer."

"And he's a foreigner?"

"Goth?"

"No, the delivery guy!"

"He's from Plausitz, I think."

"Then why'd he become a Nazi?"

"The delivery guy?"

"No, Goth!" Dora shouts, fed up.

"He was a Nazi long before that," Steffen says with equanimity.

"Well, what's the goddamned connection then?"

Steffen smirks. "You like things strictly black and white, huh?"

Dora wants to tell him off, but a little voice in her head informs her that perhaps he isn't entirely off base in this case.

"Because you want everything crystal clear, you're always finding fault with the world. That's why you're so restless."

"I'm not restless."

"You can't keep your hands still, and you're wiggling your left foot."

As inconspicuously as possible, Dora slowly sets down a spool of string she's been fidgeting with for a while, and shifts her weight so she can keep her left foot in check.

"Y'know what people learn out here?"

Suddenly Steffen's voice sounds serious yet friendly, free of all irony. Dora shakes her head.

"It's not a matter of resolving conflict or contradiction," he says, "it's a matter of tolerating them."

Dora's not into fortune-cookie wisdom. Her lips draw tight.

"Some things really are clear-cut, plain and simple," she maintains. "Right-wing populists, for example. They even win elections with their stupendous simplicity."

"What's so simple about right-wing populists?"

"You're either a racist or you're not."

"I beg to differ."

"You hate foreigners?"

"Obviously. Totally."

"Well then, you're racist."

"But I hate Germans just as much."

Dora lets out a laugh despite herself. Steffen is brazen, and slippery as an eel, which is both annoying and disarming.

"Me included?"

"You *especially*."

"What if I buy one of your arrangements?"

"Well, that changes everything."

Dora points to the piece Steffen just completed. The blue marbles make it look like a little lakeside scene framed with reeds and trees.

"Twenty euros. For you, nineteen."

Dora fishes her phone out of her bag. She always keeps a couple of bills in her phone case.

"I'll give you thirty."

"Thank you, Ms. Big-City Moneybags."

Steffen hands her the arrangement. "Watch out for Goth, okay?"

"Why?"

He lifts his hands in yet another shrug. "It's just a feeling I get. Nazi or not, something's off about that guy."

Before Dora can say anything else, Steffen points to the corner where the large floral sprays are.

"You'd best leave now. Your dog has devoured the Mon Chéri in every last gift basket."

19

Franzi

When Dora was little, hobgoblins and elves were everywhere. Gnomes made their homes between tree roots, sylphs brought about every breeze, and little fairies tended to beetles and ladybugs. And then, of course, there was the Easter Bunny, Father Christmas, and a guardian angel protecting every child. Dora and Axel were surrounded by invisible beings who took care of them and made the world a more wonderful place. As long as their little universe was permeated by love, which brought about ever greater touches of magic, nothing bad could happen. When one of her elementary school classmates dared question the Easter Bunny's existence, Dora slapped her, and remained unfazed throughout the teacher's scolding. It seemed only logical that she'd stand up for the beings that protected her.

Then their mother died, and all the magical beings died along with her. Truth assailed her like a merciless psychopath. The only thing Dora was left with was her childlike weaknesses and a mountain of misunderstandings. By then, the notions of warmth, security, and safety were history. They seemed about as real as the Easter Bunny.

Now she's returned to the bench at the junction in the woods, and even though it's only her second time sitting here, it's already one of her usual spots. Even Jay has plopped down on the same mossy patch as before. Sunlight tickles Dora's nose as a light breeze plays with her hair. Daylight streams diagonally down onto the pines, and a raptor silently sails between the boughs. The woods whisper, a mellifluous murmur. Perhaps this is home to magical beings. And the Eurasian jay is back, too.

"Hi, Mom," Dora says, and the bird lets out a warning call. "You could've raised us with a more grounded sense of reality, y'know. It doesn't feel so great when everyone takes you for a fool." The Eurasian jay ruffles its feathers in a way that looks a lot like a shrug. "I even fall for the charades of people like Steffen, or a little rustling in the bushes."

Dora actually does get the feeling there's something lurking in the brambles behind her, watching. Something larger than a fairy. Maybe an elf, or a hobgoblin. The Eurasian jay plumps up its plumage again, then vanishes into the woods.

"Taking the easy way out, eh? Well, you didn't have to dart off like that."

Now Dora thinks she's heard a giggle. She slowly turns around, then jumps up, and takes three big bounds into the underbrush. She grabs at the noise, and catches the corner of a yellow T-shirt. There's a girl inside, fairly young still, maybe eight or nine. The little one puts up a fight. Her long braid whips through the air as if fighting its own battle, while the girl thrashes about with her fists. Finally Dora gets a hold of the girl's wrists, grips her tight, and hugs her close until she calms down.

"Take it easy, now!" Dora says in as friendly a tone as possible. She feels the little kid's warm body briefly shake. At first she thinks the girl is crying. But then she hears the giggle again.

"You talked to a birdie."

"You've tailed me before, haven't you? Are you spying on me?"

"You called the birdie 'Mom'!"

The giggle grows into a guffaw. The girl's voice sounds artificially high, like a falsetto, as if she's playing the role of a little kid. Even the word *birdie* seems like an affectation, and her laugher isn't a real belly laugh.

"That was a Eurasian jay."

"A jay? How d'you know? Did it say hey-I'm-jay?" The girl guffaws even more insistently. "Everybody knows birds can't talk!"

"Oh, but I talk to birds. I even talk to my dog," Dora says as calmly as she can manage.

Upon hearing the word *dog*, all tension drains from the girl's limbs. Neither the tussling nor the Eurasian jay interest her anymore. She turns her head, scanning for the dog. Jay-the-Ray is lounging on her bed of moss, watching the commotion without the slightest stir. Maybe she's waiting to see who wins, so she can join the victor's team.

"Oh, he's sooo sweet. Can I pet him?"

"If I can ask you a few more questions."

"Okay."

"Promise? You won't run away?"

"Promise."

Dora lets go of the girl. She bounds out of the underbrush and kneels before Jay-the-Ray.

"Aww, good boy," she says softly, petting the dog's head. Jay rolls over onto her back, spreads her legs wide, and offers up her pink tummy.

"He likes me!" the girl waxes enthusiastic as Jay exposes her private parts to the whole wide woods. Dora wonders whether the girl doesn't even know how to tell the difference between a male and a female.

"He's a she."

Dora carefully picks the burrs and brambles from her jeans, stomps out of the underbrush, and sits back down on the bench. Her arms are all scratched up, not just from the blackberry bushes, but also from the girl's fingernails. She's lucky the little beast didn't bite her.

Dora inspects her more closely. Maybe she is ten already. If it weren't up in a braid, her hair would clearly reach down past her hips. The braid is messy, more knotted than neatly plaited. Her arms and legs are filthy, and even her cut-offs look like they haven't been washed in weeks. The girl's feet are bare except for a pair of rubber sandals that, once upon a time, must've been pink. Hysterical as she was just a moment ago, the girl is now entirely absorbed, petting Jay's throat, the inside of her thighs, the tender, lightly fuzzy skin of her armpits. The caresses have rendered Jay comatose. Her limp ears fall to the forest floor. Her mouth is open wide, her tongue flops out between her teeth.

Dora's never really taken much of an interest in children. But the subject is impossible to avoid. Mass media are full of parenting columns, psychologists being interviewed, and war correspondents reporting from German public schools. As if there were nothing more important in the world. Much like the mining industry, the modern family receives perpetual promotion and support. The fate of humanity hangs in the balance, and apparently it depends on early-childhood English classes and child-friendly hobbies. If she's honest, Dora has to admit she reads a lot of those kinds of articles. She doesn't really know why. Maybe because there's nothing more relaxing than observing other people's problems. In any case, she now knows both the criteria for being deemed gifted and talented as well as the symptoms of ADHD. She's familiar with the phenomenon known as regretting motherhood, as well as the book that named it. And she's heard of regressive behavior, whereby people act in a younger or needier way, oftentimes in unconscious response to neglect or stress. Like a ten-year-old speaking with a baby-like voice because her parents have split up. For example.

"What's your name?"

"Franzi. What's your dog's name?"

"Jay."

"I thought it was a she."

"You're right, it's an unusual name for a girl dog. I named her Jay-the-Ray because her body makes a diamond shape when she lies on her tummy."

The girl silently furrows her brow while leaning even closer toward the dog.

"Do you know what a ray is?"

Franzi shakes her head without looking up. Dora tries to keep a neutral tone.

"Rays are huge fish. They're really flat, and they

look like they have wings, like they're flying through the water."

"Cool." All of a sudden, Franzi's voice doesn't sound at all baby-like. It sounds sad. "I'd love to see that."

"I could show you. On YouTube."

"Yeah! Show me!" Franzi sticks both arms up and immediately reverts to her little-girl act. "Please, pretty-please? You promise?"

Dora already regrets having offered. Even if she's on pause between projects, that's no reason to invite aggravation over for a visit. Bored children can easily turn into stalkers. And maybe Franzi already knows where Dora lives.

"You live in Bracken?" Dora asks.

"Only because of Covid."

Another exile, thinks Dora. "Where, exactly?"

"Huh?"

"Where, exactly, do you live?"

"With my daddy."

"And who's your daddy?"

Franzi thinks it over for a moment. "My daddy, duh!"

"What's he do?"

"My daddy's a carpenter. But lately he just lies in bed a lot."

Jobless dad, Dora thinks. Hefty case of welfare-induced depression.

"And where's your Mommy?"

"Back in Berlin. Working."

"Why are you following me?"

The girl's head sinks lower, as if she were about to start checking Jay's fur for lice.

"Franzi! Why are you following me?"

"Your dog is sooo sweet." The baby voice is back. "Can I keep her?"

Dora gets the urge to grab the girl and shake her by the shoulders. Talk normal! Don't act like that! And look at me when I'm talking to you, goddammit!

"I don't want you spying on me. Understood?"

Franzi nods, and Dora's irritation evaporates on the spot.

"Can I ... can I take Jay out for a walk sometime?"

"Jay doesn't love going for walks. She's not like other dogs there."

"Can I ... can I maybe come visit Jay sometime? Just to pet her?"

Dora doesn't want this girl coming over to visit. Not to watch YouTube videos, not to pet Jay. But when Franzi finally lifts her head, there are tears in her eyes. That's why she was looking down before, trying to hide her face. Dora clears her throat.

"We'll see."

"Okay."

Franzi bolts to her feet, brushes the dirt from her knees, and extends her hand to Dora. A real Brandenburg girl, Dora thinks as they shake hands. Her long braid loops through the air as the girl turns away and, with a hop, skip, and jump, disappears into the underbrush.

20

Horst Wessel

Once again something has changed. Maybe it's time she gets used to it. There are four chairs on the front-stair landing. They aren't lawn chairs, they're kitchen chairs with wide backs and woven seats. Someone sanded them and painted them white. Out here, the chairs could be part of a modern sculpture garden, a work of art titled *Absence*. Dora sits down to try one out. Comfy, stable. They'll look great in the kitchen, turning it from dingy into shabby chic, showing that everything here is intentional.

Dora doesn't want Goth to give her any more furniture, but she does want these chairs. And this time he left them outside. It's a sign: he's respecting her privacy. He heard her, and will do what she says. She leans back. Dora's the only flesh-and-blood guest in this group of four chairs. The free spots are taken by invisible beings. Mother, father, brother. Or three close friends. Or a husband and two kids. Jay is visiting with invisible beings, too. She's in the front yard, battling with some ghost, barking, jumping to and fro, and flinging twigs into the air. Even Goth isn't alone this evening. There are two cars parked in front of his place. Dora hears male voices coming from the other side of the wall. They probably aren't ghosts. Either way, it's the perfect pretext to postpone her next conversation with him.

She'll thank him while at the same time making it clear that she doesn't want any more gifts. That she feels perfectly fine in her empty house, even if that isn't exactly true. Dora doesn't want to be indebted to anyone, especially not the village Nazi.

Since her invisible guests turn out to be rather boring conversation partners, Dora takes out her phone. Over the last few years she's downloaded a bunch of novels that people spoke highly of, but so far she hasn't actually read a single one. So many books come out. So many get praised or panned. Staying on top of contemporary literature is too much to ask. Yet another task that's impossible for mere mortals. Yet another task she instinctively resists.

But now Dora has time. And chairs. She can set her resistance aside and work her way through her entire smartphone library. Reading can be her new hobby. It sounds good when you tell others about it, too. "Ever since I moved to the countryside, I read so much it's unbelievable." She can become a contemporary literature expert and even start posting reviews on Amazon.

Luckily, the first book she clicks on is described as "a crystal-clear confrontation with the contemporary world, as well as a poetic analysis of the present-day human condition."

The novel's very first page opens with alarm clocks ringing on the nightstands of women across the United States at the exact same time. Shrill ringing, beeping, buzzing, bursting out into some favorite song or the local radio station's peppy morning show. In fancy bedrooms and run-down bedrooms, in big-city penthouses and modest suburban houses, in sumptuous historic buildings and cramped tenements. A countrywide concert, as if every alarm clock were connected by some invisible wire. Women everywhere, alarm clocks everywhere. This is what this novel describes. And it just doesn't stop. An alarm-clock lamentation, page after page after page.

Dora lowers her arm, her phone sinking onto her lap. The woman who wrote this novel appears unaware of the fact that there's more than one time zone in the United States. But that isn't the real issue. Dora takes issue with the message the lines of this novel herald: What a scandal! All these women have to get up early. They have to go to work, or take care of their families, or both. They're all in the same boat. It's an unbearably deplorable state of affairs. A radically blessed lifestyle that, all of a sudden, looks like hell on Earth. If that's the human condition, what's left to attain? If even the mass-scale luxury of our present day, unheard of at any point in history, doesn't result in a reasonable degree of wellbeing, what's left of progress? What more can it hope to accomplish? If life is an imposition, and the fact that a woman has to get up in the morning is considered a disgrace, why should people bother, what should they strive for, as individuals and as a society? If all it takes is a ringing alarm clock to threaten human happiness, Dora thinks, we might as well throw in the towel.

The tragedy of our times, Jojo is always wont to observe, is that people take their personal disaffection for a political problem—or mistake, as the case may be.

Maybe that isn't just a typical Jojo-ism. Maybe it's the truth. Maybe it's not even a case of mistaking one thing for another. People's personal disaffection *is* a political problem, and a huge one at that. Disaffection is capable of causing entire societies to explode. All you need is a little fuel for the fire, refugees or Covid, and the whole thing threatens to fall apart, because nobody ever really believed in the blessings of freedom and prosperity anyway.

Dora closes her eBook app and opens a video of Alexander Gerst. His cute face and puppy-dog eyes stare at the camera, exuding friendliness, as his ultrafit body slips into a boxy white spacesuit. He looks like an overgrown child playing dress-up for an adventurous game. He even says as much: Outer-space exploration is a way of extending childhood—out into the universe. For a curious child, first the yard is too small, then the local woods, then the country and, finally, the planet. Curiosity knows no bounds. Astronauts are probably the last people left on Earth who have a real goal. After the first video, YouTube recommends another, then another. Dora keeps watching.

But even the best chairs start to get uncomfortable after a while. Your legs get stiff, your back hurts. Dora goes into the kitchen, fills Jay's bowl, then makes herself a plate of little cheese sandwiches. While doing all that, she also watches as Gerst and Wiseman wind their way around inside the International Space Station, a many-winged dragonfly swiftly orbiting through outer space. In the background, the blue marble that is planet

Earth. It really is a marble, a ball—a big ball of rock and water—on whose surface nearly eight billion people are roaming around. Only a small handful of astronauts have ever seen it with their own eyes. Only they know the key to the ultimate riddle of existence, which is that this whole thing actually exists. This whole mess really is here. That's why perennial, endless curiosity has a goal. That's why ringing alarm clocks hold no interest whatsoever. That's why astronauts aren't just the nicest people in the world, they're also the happiest. And these astronauts are so happy they seem to be singing. At the top of their lungs. Some sort of folk song.

Dora opens the window. The singing isn't coming from outer space, it's coming from the neighbor's yard. And it's no folk song.

"Raise the flag, close the ranks ..."

"The Internationale," says Dora's bewildered brain. I had no idea people were still into that here.

"Storm troopers step up, marching boldly onward!"

Dora slams the window shut and sets her bread-knife on the counter. Her hunger has vanished. *I'll take it!* Jay's envious eyes seem to say as she gazes longingly at the plate of bread. But Dora pays her no heed. She just stands there, immobile. Ringing alarm clocks, curious astronauts, singing Nazis. With the window closed the voices are fainter, and she can't make out the words. Maybe now she can just ignore the singing. Dora tries to convince herself to make some tea. To give the cheese sandwiches another chance. To watch a few more documentaries on outer space. But her legs carry her toward the front door. As Jay tries to squeeze past her and run outside, Dora's foot pushes the dog back inside. "You're staying here!" She quietly closes the door.

"Millions fill with hope as they gaze upon the swastika."

Now the voices are really loud. Dora doesn't know what she's about to do. Nothing, really. She just wants to have a look. It's as if there were some huge, exotic beast lurking on the other side of the wall, so weird and worrisome that you can't help but take a peek.

"Hitler's flag waves valiantly o'er every street."

Dora goes over to the wall and steps up on the chair. There are four men singing, including Goth.

They're sitting at the camping table in front of the trailer, an entire battery of beer bottles between them, plus a family-size bottle of Nordhäuser Doppelkorn. Two of the men seem to have come from the same production line as Goth: large, round heads atop bulky shoulders, camo cargo shorts, ratty T-shirts. One has a beard so dark and full that you could easily take him for a jihadist. The other is covered in tattoos, the ink spreading from his arms to his shoulders and up to the edges of his face.

The fourth man, on the other hand, doesn't fit in with the others. He's short and thin and wears his straight hair a little too long, so it constantly falls over his forehead and he has to keep pushing it out of his face. His slim legs are in loose jeans and his slender upper body is clad in an autumnal-looking brown corduroy jacket. Although he looks like a kid next to Goth and the others, he emanates an unsettling energy. He's the chorus leader, waving his finger in the air and rising in his chair so that by the end of the song he's half standing.

"Our days of servitude near their end!"

The song is over, and the four men clink their beer bottles together.

Which is when a rather basic realization dawns on Dora: if she can see the men, they can see her, too. She should get back to her cheese sandwiches. Now.

Dora recalls having read a book about the Third Reich once, and finding a description of how, in societies on the brink, fear steps to the fore early on and soon steers everyone's every move. How, almost unnoticeably, new criteria slink in to alter people's everyday decision-making. What you can still say to whom. When you should leave a given restaurant or take a different route to work. The brain grows accustomed to fear and its instructions, it becomes an integral part of your thinking, and erases its own tracks. You don't endure fear—you practice it. You don't suffer through it—you unwittingly put it into action. You change to fit the changing circumstances, until you painlessly blend into the background.

This mechanism means that horrors are continuously repeated. They're self-perpetuating. There's only one cure: fight. But it's not evil you have to fight, it's your own cowardice.

Shut up, says a voice deep in Dora's head. Go back inside and watch another Gerst video.

But she stays put. She wants to be a good citizen, and is pondering what to do. Call the police, perhaps. If she isn't mistaken, singing the Horst Wessel song is forbidden by law. On top of that, this definitely constitutes the kind of party that's illegal during Covid. But would the authorities even bother getting into their car on account of a few backwater beer-quaffers? And would that make her a good citizen, or would it just make her a nosy know-it-all who denounces her neighbors?

Yeah, she'd better just go back inside, eat her cheese sandwiches, and mind her own business.

But it's also entirely plausible that, right there next door, the new National Socialist Underground is taking shape. Beer and schnapps on camping chairs, and a massive weapons stockpile in the main house.

But Goth isn't that kind of guy. Not at all. No, he's the kind of guy who gives bedframes and chairs to his neighbors.

And that's when Goth raises his head as if he's heard someone call his name. He squints, focuses his eyes, and nods at her before she has a chance to duck behind the wall.

He struggles to his feet and holds on to the table-top for a moment so his body has time to find the right vertical positioning in space. Then he sets himself in motion, swerving like a sailor after months at sea.

It's too late to retreat. Goth is coming right toward her. The nape of Dora's neck starts to prickle. This time it isn't bubbles starting to rise, it's real fear.

He come right up to the wall and then stands still, without getting up on the crate. That would probably be too much, in his condition. Even at this distance he reeks so strongly of Doppelkorn that he might as well have bathed in it.

"I didn't go into your house," he says.

The prickling on Dora's nape begins to let up.

"I know," she says.

"I didn't even look through the windows."

She nods.

"And I'm gonna give you your keys back, one of these days." He looks straight at her, a trusting gaze from bloodshot eyes. "You like the chairs?"

"They're great. But, Goth …"

"I'm glad." His mouth hints at a grin. He turns around. He clearly doesn't expect any thanks.

"Wait!" Dora searches for the right words. "The chairs are lovely, but I don't want any more furniture from you."

It's clear from Goth's expression that he doesn't get what this is all about.

"Why not?" he asks, just as Dora simultaneously says, "On principle."

He looks at her for a while before shrugging his shoulders and going back to his friends.

Dora tries to muster up some pride. She stood her ground, that's something. Not on the internet, not in the comments section, not over a few glasses of wine with likeminded friends. She spoke her mind to a Nazi. A guy who, just minutes ago, was belting out something about swastikas and Hitler flags. That's certainly more than ninety percent of Berlin's left-leaning liberals could say for themselves. Even if, strictly speaking, the thing she stood her ground about was just a bunch of chairs.

"I don't need any furniture," Dora calls over. "The walls aren't even painted!"

Goth doesn't turn around anymore. But now the other three Nazis are staring at her, and the tattooed guy is leaning so far to the side he almost falls off his chair. The guy in the jacket furrows his brow. He doesn't seem as drunk as the others.

Dora feels the urge to grab Gustav and Jay, ride over to Kochlitz, hop on the regional train, and hole up in Jojo's Charlottenburg apartment.

"What's up, Goth?" she hears the corduroy guy ask.

"Nothin', Krisse," Goth replies.

Dora hops down from her chair and runs into the house. Jay greets her as if they hadn't seen one another in months. Dora wants to call someone. But not the police. Still standing in the hallway, she dials Robert's number. He picks up right away.

"Hey, how are things?"

His voice sounds unbelievably normal. As if everything were the same as ever. As if there were no problem whatsoever between the two of them. As if Dora were just away on vacation, getting a little distance from things. She clears her throat.

"Pretty good, actually."

"What's going on out in the countryside?" Dora wonders how Robert knows where she is, but then he answers without her even having to ask. "Axel told me where you're hiding out. What's the name of the village again?"

"Bracken."

"Funny. When're you coming back?"

"I don't know."

"Take all the time you need."

Now she hears it in his happy-sounding tone: sarcasm. Robert is restraining himself. He doesn't want to reveal how hurt he is. Maybe out of pride. Or he thinks she'll come back sooner if he pretends everything is normal.

"And how're things where you are?"

"Ugh, well, you know—all this ecstatic talk of re-opening is really getting to me."

At first Dora has no idea what he means. Then she remembers hearing how Angela Merkel has said she won't entertain any debates about loosening current Covid restrictions. That's how distant Dora is, already, from societal discourse. Whatever calls the tune back in the capital is only faint background music here.

"Stay-at-home orders absolutely have to be maintained," Robert adds.

"There are four Nazis singing the Horst Wessel song in the yard next door," says Dora.

Robert remains silent for a moment, taking in what she's just said, processing it. Dora expects a gloating retort. Anything from "What'd you expect?" to "You're the one who moved there" would be in keeping with his character. But he surprises her.

"Maybe that's just part of the bargain."

His tone isn't gloating in the least. Not even gleeful. It's more like he's trying to comfort her. She counts that in his favor.

"I feel a little afraid."

"Of the Nazis?"

"Maybe just of the fact that I'm not sure what I should do."

"I'm afraid of the second wave," Robert says. "It's going to be bad."

After a few minutes the conversations ends. Dora goes to the front door and pauses to listen. It's quiet. No singing, no bawling out, no laughter. She goes out and over to the wall. She doesn't hear a thing. A magpie flies through the treetops. Its nest must be nearby. The word *nest* makes the Horst Wessel song echo through her head once again, and her ad-writing brain connects the dots: *Horst* is both a name as well as another word for *nest*.

Curiosity compels her to step back up on the chair. She carefully raises her head and peeks over the wall. Nothing. The yard next door is empty. Even the bottles are gone. Dora was only inside ten minutes, max. That means this undeniably qualifies as a hasty departure. Who here is afraid of whom? she wonders.

Whether this speedy disappearance is a good or a bad sign remains to be seen.

21

Rays

Two hours later, Dora has watched three more documentaries about Alexander Gerst. She now knows the trip to the International Space Station is just barely longer than taking a flight from Germany to the Canary Islands, that people in space get osteoporosis and, despite all that, there's still nothing more meaningful than having seen the Earth from outer space.

She'd love to be able to see herself from outside, for once, too. Board a rocket, leave her body behind, break through the gravitational field of the self and ascend into the impersonal realm. Maybe then she'd finally grasp the fact that she actually exists. That the copywriter with the little dog is just as present as this landing below the front stairs, the lampposts lining the road, and the village of Bracken. A slice of life, of the common, shared state of *being*, rather than just another babbling voice in some incoherent film.

Dora remembers how, as a child, she experienced moments of immense clarity. While at play, the perpetually narrating voice in her head would suddenly fall silent. Like a glitch in the operating system, or when your screen freezes. *Runtime error 0x0.* It felt as if someone had yanked back the veil concealing the true nature of things. As if she were staring, astonished, at the source text behind it all. All at once,

Dora was neither storyteller nor listener. Rather ... while at play, she was able to pause, lift her head, and look at everything around her through new eyes. The desk with her partially finished homework, the dresser with two drawers, T-shirts on the right, socks on the left. She thought something along the lines of: *How crazy—I exist. As much as the desk and the dresser.* Then the feeling faded away, and she went right back to playing, as if nothing had happened.

YouTube recommends the next video, but she sets her tablet down. It's late. For hours now she's been perched on one of the new chairs out front. Goth and his friends haven't come back out.

She's in the bathroom, just about to brush her teeth, when Jay starts raising a riot in the hallway. Whining, barking, scratching at the old floor tiles. Did somebody knock? It's almost midnight. Maybe Goth is bringing over some more furniture. Or he's come to tell her that he'll beat her to a pulp if she peeks over the wall ever again. Or Heini's come to saw down a locust tree. Dora quickly rinses her mouth out. As she walks into the hallway, it sounds like somebody is hitting the front door with the palm of their hand. It's a creepy noise. Especially since she doesn't see anyone on the other side of the door's two windowpanes. Hobgoblins, she thinks. Then she yanks the door open.

"Hello," says Franzi.

She's so short that her blonde head doesn't even reach as high as the windows. She's wearing the same clothes as earlier that afternoon: yellow T-shirt, denim cut-offs, rubber sandals. Her long braid looks like it might be even more disheveled than before. Jay leaps up at her, jumping for joy, as if she'd been waiting all night for this visit.

"It's the middle of the night," Dora says. "What're you doing here?"

"You said you'd show me the ray videos."

"I can't imagine your dad actually lets you run around town at this hour."

"Daddy lets me do whatever I want. Mommy doesn't."

Such freedom—or neglect, thinks Dora. But that's not what she says.

"Go home."

"Pleeease!" Dora can't stand the way she draws out the *e*. It's almost as bad as fingernails on a chalkboard. "Pleeease!"

She takes a breath, in preparation for telling Franzi yet again to go home. But then she sees the imploring expression in the girl's eyes, the lips pursed tight as if to stifle a sob. Dora sighs.

"Fine, but only for a few minutes." She figures it'll be her last cigarette break of the day.

When Dora points to the chairs, Franzi adamantly shakes her head. She wants to sit down on the landing. Jay lies halfway across her lap and lets the girl pet her. Dora opens YouTube. A second later, two huge manta rays glide through the Indian Ocean. The motion of their fins is slow and majestic, their wide-open mouths slightly unsettling. The rays circle as if in slow motion, unfazed by the divers filming them. They look like some kind of crazy flying machine straight out of a sci-fi flick. Watching them, Dora senses the grandeur of all creation. Nature's immense intelligence. Suddenly, even without climbing into a rocket, she grasps that she, too, is a part of it all. She belongs. Humans, huge manta rays, miniscule microbes—they're all varieties of the self-same *being*. She's so enthralled that she forgets her cigarette entirely. Even Franzi's jaw has dropped, eyes glued to the screen.

The next video shows a manta seeking out the company of divers so they might free it from the fishing line that's cut deep into its fin. Clearly the manta has intuited that there's an overarching *us*, uniting all creatures above and beyond the dividing lines separating the species. Exterminating and saving. Cooperating and fighting. Destruction and care. They're all aspects of the same relationship, and that—thinks Dora—is what you just might call *home*.

"That's it for tonight," she says to Franzi.

"One more," the girl begs, and they watch one last manta ray video. This time Dora does smoke, as Franzi's hands keep petting Jay, who's already fallen asleep.

"That was sooo nice," says Franzi as the video ends.

Surprisingly, Dora feels the same. It's nice to sit down right next to each other on the landing in the middle of the night, as bats and owls go hunting and a hedgehog rustles through the grass, huffing and puffing like a tiny wild boar. Dora puts her arm over Franzi's shoulders and gives her a quick little hug.

"Time for bed," she says. "Where exactly do you live, anyway?"

Franzi stares at her like she doesn't understand the question.

"With my daddy," she says slowly and emphatically.

"What I mean is, which house do you live in?"

Franzi shakes her head, perhaps imitating a school teacher shaking her head because her students are so dumb.

"Those chairs," she says.

"What about them?"

"I used to sit on them. With three cushions."

While Dora's mind declines the opportunity to connect the dots, Franzi keeps talking. "Daddy got them from the house specially for you. Normally he never goes in there."

Franzi pushes Jay off her lap and stands up. The dog is befuddled, and shakes her folded-over ears as the girl runs down the stairs and across the front yard. Toward the wall, not the front gate.

Daddy. The chairs. The empty house. The flashlight through the windows of the upper floor. The hobgoblins in Dora's yard.

Franzi clambers up onto the lawn chair, jumps up and heaves herself over the top of the wall, swings her legs over, and raises a hand to wave goodbye before leaping down and disappearing on the other side. Dora hears a dull thud on the grass.

22

Krisse

On this particular night, Dora forgives herself for remaining sleepless. The Nazi's daughter. It almost sounds like the title of a novel, the kind of pulp you'd buy at the gas station. Dora lies on the bed—its new frame still carries a faint whiff of fresh paint—and surfs the internet.

Countryside Covid Deniers: Nazis Stage Online Protest.

A journalist based in Berlin reports on how Nazis in rural eastern Germany, banned by Covid restrictions from holding their usual rallies in the market squares of small cities, are intensifying their online social-media campaigns. There's Christian G., for example: a former elementary school teacher from Plausitz who's so far to the right he calls Björn Höcke a "softie." Christian G. has just started a YouTube channel called "LUP," which stands for "Liberty, Unity, Purity." Conveniently, it can also stand for "Land Use Plan." He seriously believes Covid was created by Angela Merkel, and is convinced that the exodus of rural Germans to big cities is part of a secret plan linked to the so-called Great Replacement: rural infrastructure is dismantled in order to depopulate entire regions of the country so they can then be repopulated by Muslims.

The journalist writes that Christian G. writes that this is a blatant violation of the German Constitution, hence the people must rise up and avail themselves of the right to resist, which is guaranteed by article 20, paragraph 3, line 4 of said constitution. The newspaper article includes screenshots of the relevant twitter posts. Christian G. and his allies cite the historic notion of *Umvolkung*, the supposed "ethnic inversion" whereby Germans were "de-Germanified," which they plan to confront with what they call an "Ethnic Mass Effect." At all costs—no matter what it takes.

Dora could've laughed out loud. Ethnic mass effect! She should send Jojo a screenshot. Caption: *The Tumor of Racism.*

But she leaves it be and reads on. She tries to get all worked up about how big-city journalists only look to Brandenburg when they want to rent a houseboat or ogle at Nazis. But her feelings of attachment to her adopted home town aren't enough to truly get her riled up. She's stalling, trying to delay the inevitable: she knows she'll eventually click on Christian G.'s YouTube channel. She's already seen a picture of him. It was low-res, but definitely him. The slight frame, the longish hair. Even the corduroy jacket.

When Dora finally goes to his channel, all doubt evaporates. That's Krisse, alright. He's got a surprisingly thin voice for a teacher, it matches his thin arms. He sits at a desk like some bank clerk, staring straight into the smartphone video camera, blathering on about population exchange, ethnic inversion, and ethnic mass effect. All the talk of *das Volk* makes Dora's head spin. She turns her tablet off and closes her eyes. Just hours ago this same Christian G. was sitting in her neighbor's yard, singing the Horst Wessel song. Maybe they were celebrating the successful launch of his YouTube channel. Not to mention the fact that all you have to do is claim that Covid was created by Angela Merkel and voilà, online news platforms will cover anything you do, meaning you get free publicity.

Now Dora thinks she has to make a change. Change her life. Get out. Out of this town, maybe out of Germany. She needs a new job, some friends, a car. That much is clear. This isn't some fleeting, sleep-deprived, nocturnal fantasy—it's absolute fact. In the morning she'll get cracking. She'll strike camp and start all over again, from scratch. Somewhere. Anywhere.

23

Hydrangeas

When she wakes up, sunlight pours through the windows. The old wood floor glows in rich golden tones, and dust dances in the light, sparkling. There's a gentle snoring at the foot of the bed. Jay-the-Ray is sprawled out on her back, deep in slumber. Maybe they can give Bracken another go, at least for a little while longer.

Something woke Dora up. A piercing horn, a honking more horrific than any alarm clock. There it is again. A beep, then more beeps. An impatient honking in increasingly rapid succession. Dora expects neither deliveries nor visitors. The honking horn gets her out of bed anyway. She has to see what going on out on the road. Yell at the idiot, if need be, for disturbing the peace at this early hour. She glances at her phone. It's not all that early, actually. She hasn't slept this long in ages.

There's a pickup truck in front of the house. A dingy white Toyota HiLux with an angular hood. Maybe it's a bona fide classic. Dora assumed the old thing didn't run anymore. Goth is at the wheel, honking the horn. The moment he sees Dora, he leans across the passenger seat.

"Let's go!"

She's standing in the sun, with bedhead, wearing nothing but an old T-shirt and underpants. But Goth doesn't seem to care.

"Your feet stuck?"

"Wha—? Huh?"

"Shopping time!" Goth shouts. "Get a move on."

Dora obeys. She runs back into the house, pulls a pair of jeans on, heaves Jay onto her arm and, without a moment's hesitation, heads right back out and hops into Goth's pickup as if it were the most normal thing in the world. She's barely closed the passenger-side door as he floors it.

Her stomach rebels. It reels against the rapid acceleration, but even more against the question of just what, exactly, she's doing here. Next to her sits a guy who, just last night, was belting out Nazi songs alongside a few other riled-up, seditious rabble-rousers. He stares at the road ahead, both hands firmly gripping the wheel. Maybe he's driving to the nearest quarry, where he'll take care of his nuisance of a neighbor. Even the odors wafting off him make her stomach churn. Cigarettes, schnapps, unwashed man. The smell is a provocation. She surreptitiously sizes Goth up from the side. For the first time, there's no wall between them. He's truly huge, six two if not taller, and at least two hundred pounds. *Homo brackensis giganteus.* He squints now and again, as if he can't clearly make out the road. He probably has a .02 percent blood-alcohol level.

Why did she even consider getting into this vehicle? Feet stuck, get a move on. She wants to go home. Even if all she'd do there is wonder what to do with the rest of her day, and why she moved to this no-man's-land if she finds her own company so utterly unedifying. Seen from that perspective, it's entirely possible that she's in better hands sitting on the passenger seat of a neo-Nazi's pickup.

Dora holds Jay on her lap, certain the dog must really have to pee by now. After ten minutes, she can't stand the silence anymore.

"How's Franzi?"

"Good."

"What's she up to?"

"Sleeping."

"She came to my place last night."

Goth doesn't respond. His expression doesn't betray whether he thinks that's good or bad.

"Where're we headed?"

"The home-improvement store."

"Isn't it Sunday?"

"It's open because of Covid."

"How's that make any sense?"

"Beats me. Starting tomorrow you gotta mask up."

This is what panic shopping looks like in Bracken, Dora thinks. Lawn fertilizer and drill drivers instead of pasta and toilet paper. Wearing a mask is far beneath the dignity of the *Homo brackensis*. Dora's still waiting for an explanation of why she had to come along for the ride, but it isn't forthcoming. Nor does she hear any remarks about how Angela Merkel and Bill Gates plan to inject a microchip into everyone on Earth. Or that the virus is just another form of natural selection, clearing the ethnic body politic of all weaklings. Goth silently stares at the road ahead.

"How old is Franzi, actually?" Dora resumes the conversation.

"Can you be quiet? I'm driving."

If ever she needs a teacher to guide her battle against multitasking, Goth is her guy. Hold the steering wheel. Hit the gas. Nothing more.

Since Goth bolts down the road to Plausitz at a steady 75-mile-an-hour clip, coasting down to 50 mph only in the few areas with a handful of buildings, the Elbe-Center soon appears on the horizon. Goth parks and heads straight for the revolving door without so much as waiting for his passenger to climb out. Dora sets Jay down on the dry dirt of the parking lot's floral border, where the dog promptly has her morning pee before running off after Goth, who's since disappeared inside the store. When they get to the huge revolving door they have to wait a moment as people steer their carts in one by one. Nobody seems annoyed, everyone is patient. The mood inside is just as calm as the last time she was here.

Dora follows Goth's broad back through the aisles and wonders whether other customers think they're a married couple. On this particular morning they really do look like a perfect match: both are wearing stained T-shirts, neither has showered, and in Dora's case she's neither combed her hair nor had breakfast. The way Goth doesn't bother checking whether Dora's following him also fits with the dynamic of a longstanding marriage. The notion sparks a weird excitement. Another life. The heady rush of freedom that comes after you've decided you no longer give a shit about anything.

When Goth comes to a halt, she nearly runs into him. They're in an aisle of the paint department. As Goth examines the shelves, he furrows his brow as if making a mental calculation. Finally, he grabs six big cans of paint. White, for interiors, middling quality. He turns to face her.

"How's this—you want a different color?"

Dora shakes her head, taken aback. She doesn't want any paint, of any color. She doesn't want any of whatever this is. But Goth has already walked off again, heading for the checkout counter. If she tries to pry the cans of paint from his hands now, she'll make a scene. What was it she'd shouted at him yesterday? "I don't need any furniture. The walls aren't even painted!" The mental math—Goth was calculating the surface area of her walls. He's got three two-and-a-half-gallon paint cans in each hand. Dora pats the back pocket of her jeans. Thank god she brought her wallet.

When Goth stops again just before checkout, she actually does run into him. It feels like crashing into a well-upholstered wall. She nearly tramples Jay in the process. And it's almost the same exact spot where she recently ran into Tom. Goth doesn't even budge.

"Those're nice." He motions toward a pyramidal display of marked-down flower pots. Most are hydrangeas, their petals in various pastel-toned poufs.

"Deep discount," he says. "Grab two."

Horst Wessel and hydrangeas. It could be the opening line of some Dadaist poem. Of course there's no law stating that neo-Nazis can't appreciate hydrangeas. But it's a jarring notion nevertheless. It poses a threat to the life-affirming yet mistaken idea that good and evil can easily be distinguished from one another.

"Those are the best." Without setting the cans of paint down, Goth points with his foot at two specific flowerpots. "Those'll go on your front stairs."

Dora lifts the flowerpots and brings them to the cashier. She wants to ask whether seed potatoes are back in stock. But Goth is already heaving the paint cans off the checkout counter. Dora's turn to pay.

24

Soldiers

When they get to Dora's front gate, Goth hits the brakes so hard her upper body is thrusted forward. He leaves the engine running, unloads the cans of paint, and carries them up the outer stair, setting them down between the kitchen chairs up on the landing, which is gradually filling up. He doesn't say a word about how Dora hasn't taken the chairs inside yet. He lights a cigarette and watches as Dora sets the potted hydrangeas to the right and left of the stairs, wiggling them into symmetry. They look great.

"Give 'em lots of water," Goth instructs, offering her a cigarette. They smoke in silence, their eyes following Jay as she darts around the yard. Dora glances at her phone. Eleven thirty. She nearly asks: *What's our plan for the afternoon?*

They toss their butts out over the railing, perfectly synchronized.

Goth says: "Lemme show you something."

He opens the front door, steps into the house, and shoots straight up the stairs to the attic, surefooted as a man who knows his way around. Dora's only been up to the attic a couple of times. The upper floor isn't finished, and is a bit creepy, the kind of space you'd find in a scary movie for kids. It's its own world of raw beams, cobwebs, dust, and faint light coming through the small dormer windows. The floor is covered in dried-out flies and butterfly corpses.

Goth's purposeful gait takes him clear across the large central space. His boots leave tracks in the dust. Because of the slanted roof, he has to duck as he gets toward the back. It looks like he's searching for a specific spot on the floor. He kneels down and brushes a bunch of dead insects away with his bare hands.

"What're you doing?"

"This used to be the nursery school," he says.

"You mean—here? In my house?"

"The village nursery school." Goth slaps a supporting beam with his palm as if patting a trusty old steed on the rump. "Since forever, until it closed for good."

A film reminiscent of *The Children of Golzow* flashes before Dora's eyes. It's in black and white, the frame unsteady. Children in uniform wave at the camera, go up the front stairs two by two, and disappear into the old estate manager's house, all under the strict eye of a stern schoolmistress.

"Were you here, too? When you were little?"

"Of course."

"Heini, too?"

"Everybody was."

So Goth isn't the only one who knows her house inside and out. Everyone in Bracken does. Dora's new neighbors spent their early childhood in the rooms of this house, and maybe even still have a few vivid memories of it. The shape of the doorknobs or the caulked lines between the kitchen floor tiles.

The knotty spots on the floorboards, which in some places look like animal eyes. The musty scent of the basement, like the building's humid breath. Dora thinks back to the broken toy she found in her vegetable patch. She had no idea she was living in a bunch of strangers' long-lost childhoods.

She goes over to Goth and kneels down next to him. His fingers are feeling at the floorboards. Finally he finds what he's looking for. A hole left by a big knot in the wood, into which a darker knob of wood has been jammed. Goth slips the nail of his index finger into the gap and pries the darker piece of wood out. Then he tries to fish something out of the hole, but his fingers don't really fit far enough through.

"I can't reach," he says, surprised. "You try."

Dora balks, and almost says that surely her hands are also too big, but then she actually succeeds in slipping her pointer and middle fingers through the opening. She feels around underneath the floorboards with her fingertips until they run into something. She carefully pinches a corner of whatever it is between her fingers and pulls it up.

"There should be another one."

She manages to fish that one out, too. She sets both of them on her open palm, gets up, walks out of the cramped corner, and goes to stand under a skylight. They're tin soldiers, brightly painted down to the tiniest detail, and surprisingly heavy for their size. One is lunging forward with his weapon, the other is standing to attention. Goth has walked over and is now next to Dora, leaning down, inspecting the contents of her hand and smiling.

"Are they—I mean, did you hide them here?" she asks. "When you were a little boy?"

He nods, "They were too precious to play with. I didn't want anybody to take them from me."

All of a sudden Dora could cry. She strokes the soldiers' tiny tummies with her fingertip. Goth stands up straight.

"They're yours now."

Before she can say a peep, he's turned and is thumping back down the stairs. Once again, he hasn't returned the keys.

25

Email

Dora carries the chairs into the house and sets them around the kitchen table. Then she gets Steffen's arrangement with the blue glass marble. She places both tin soldiers among the grasses, so it looks as if they're lurking on the reedy edges of a swamp, waiting to ambush the enemy. She sits at the table for quite some time, observing the results. Steffen's design and Goth's past have melded to form a miniature world. A tiny work of art. It fits in here, Dora thinks. The entire house now seems structured around this centerpiece. Patterned tiles, wooden floor planks, hydrangeas, pallet bedframe—all of it. Now that the arrangement is here on the table, Dora feels even more that she inhabits a provisional place. Everything's changing. Maybe she could scrounge a couple of crates from Tom and Steffen's workshop and stack them up as bookshelves, the kind of thing featured in lifestyle magazines. Towers of old wooden crates with faded logos on the sides, with just a few carefully curated, completely useless objects inside. Two books casually placed at an angle, a lamp that casts light on nothing but itself, one lone apple in a bowl. Then this would look exactly the way you'd picture the home of a creative type in Berlin, and Dora could start issuing her oh-it's-so-nice-here invitations. She gives herself a pat on the back. Bringing one's self-image into accordance with reality is the highest achievement a modern-day person can hope for.

She thinks about who she could invite, even though she already knows she has no circle of acquaintances to draw on, and she also knows that merely thinking about it won't make one materialize. She thinks back. She remembers gatherings with Robert and his friends. How they'd all meet up, occupying entire tables at Berlin bars, each with a glass of wine or beer in hand, each with a brain in their head, each ceaselessly bent on creating its own sense of self. How they'd talk and laugh. For a few hours they morphed into a multi-headed, self-satisfied being. Such a nice image, too bad it's a total illusion. Not because the Covid crisis has shut down all the bars, but rather because Dora knows how that image feels from the inside. She sits there among everyone else, chatting and laughing and feeling like a fish out of water. She keeps hearing the same discussions over and over: the latest Netflix series, the government's latest misguided policies, the rents always going up. She knows some parts of these conversations by heart, and can already tell you who'll say what, when. Later in the evening the focus shifts to relationships. Invariably, at some point, everyone expresses pity for the friends missing from the table because they're now young parents and have to stay home taking care of the kids. Somebody asks the group which fully automatic espresso machine makes the best *crema*. Somebody else announces that, from now on, he's making all his vacations domestic, staying close to home here in Germany. The whole time, Dora sits there thinking up an excuse to leave early, but ends up staying till the very end anyway.

It's dumb to sit and yearn for something you don't even really want. But it's also totally human. She takes out her phone and sends Jojo a WhatsApp message.

Got chairs. You can come visit now.

She tops it off with a beaming smiley face emoji, just to make it clear that she's in no way desperate.

A few seconds later, her phone dings with a reply.

What do you mean by chairs? Xo, Sibylle.

Dora stares at the screen, perplexed. Apparently Jojo's phone is no longer a way to reach just him, it now reaches his future wife, too.

The things you sit on, she texts back.

The current situation precludes traveling to Brandenburg, Sibylle writes back.

Dora's frown betrays her disgust. Wasn't it just last week that they all got together in Charlottenburg for an asparagus dinner? And wasn't Sibylle Jojo's accomplice as he thumbed his nose at all the Covid restrictions?

Meanwhile, apparently Sibylle herself has realized that Dora's repelled, because she follows up with a string of smiley faces and writes, *Joachim's stressed with work, but I'll ask him when I get the chance.*

There is no Joachim, Dora wants to text back. It's Jojo, you dum-dum. Whoever your Joachim is, he's just a figment of your imagination.

Instead, she opens a news app. Greta Thunberg views the Covid crisis as a blueprint for the climate crisis. Angela Merkel's already warning people about an imminent second wave. Berlin's main airport should reopen soon. A famous theatrical director doesn't want to be forced to wash his hands, and has no problem whatsoever with death.

The bubbles begin to prickle and rise. Dora lays a hand on her stomach.

In Canada, a man dressed up as a police officer shot twenty-two people because he was furious at his ex-girlfriend. Donald Trump suggests injecting a disinfectant.

The bubbles are rising so quickly that Dora tosses her tablet facedown onto the kitchen table and pushes it away. She extends a finger and touches the tip of the lunging tin soldier's weapon. It pricks her. It feels good. Dora pricks her finger again, and again. She thinks about Goth. About the little boy who chose to hide his toys instead of playing with them. Who crawled across the attic floor to admire his treasures. Maybe he, too, liked to prick his fingertips with them. The longer she thinks about it, the fewer bubbles there are. All of a sudden it's easy to just sit here.

Later on, Franzi appears at the door asking if Jay can come out to play. All afternoon Dora hears the girl's cheerful laughter, punctuated every now and then by the dog's barking. Come evening, she cooks up some spaghetti. Franzi plops down on one of her childhood chairs and inhales three servings. After that she wants to draw. Dora grabs some paper from her printer, hands Franzi some pencils, and goes out for a smoke. When she comes back, there are two rainbow-colored hearts adorning her kitchen window. Franzi's working on a drawing of Jay, which is coming out quite well. Dora gives her another half hour, then tells her time's up. Franzi gives a good-girl nod and takes off without objection.

For the first time in weeks, Dora puts some music on. During the last phase of her Berlin life she hadn't been able to stand music. It was just another voice demanding something of her—thoughts, feelings, an opinion. Now she realizes music has something to give her. She listens to Ludovico Einaudi's lovely piano pieces, pours herself a glass of wine, and sits down on the bed, becoming a part of the picture. A world in miniature, made up of wine, windows, and thoughts.

When her phone dings, she assumes it's Jojo writing back to say he'll come by soon. But it's an email from her boss, Susanne. On a Sunday evening, late. It'd be best to just not open it. It's dark out. The light from the kitchen is reflected in her bedroom windows, so cozy. Dora opens the email anyway, and reads the first couple of lines.

Dear Dora, I'm regrettably writing today to inform you …

She doesn't need to read any further. She already knows what comes next.

26

Paint

"I heard there's something for nothing to be had here today," Heini says. "Meaning work."

Dora lets out a hearty laugh, whereupon Heini's face lights up. He looks like a little astronaut today, dressed as if he's setting off to give the heavens a fresh coat of paint. His entire body is hidden beneath a white protective suit, and there's a white cap on his head. Next to him is a big bucket filled with paintbrushes, masking tape, and drop cloths. He's carrying a few rollers on long handles under his arm. The scene is extra strange because Heini is standing in the shade of a huge, large-leafed tropical plant. It must've grown on Dora's front landing overnight. Although upon closer inspection she sees it's actually growing out of a big pot inside an even bigger ornamental wood planter. It's massive, with outstretched limbs and finger-like leaves. A sponge has left tracks where someone dusted them off.

"This weed grows quicker by the day," Heini says, looking at the palm tree.

If Dora complains to Goth, he'll doubtless point out that a plant doesn't count as furniture.

Heini gets right to it. They open up the second half of the front door and drag the monstrous plant down the hall into the study, where it stretches its limbs out every which way and looks absolutely fabulous. The leaves glow in the morning light.

Dora notices that when people and things suddenly pop up at her place she no longer finds it as disturbing as before. She goes to the kitchen and puts on a big pot of coffee while Heini dives in without a word, masking off the base boards in the study.

Half an hour later, he's downed three cups of coffee and painted a half wall. Franzi walks in, asks "What's up?" and Heini answers wordlessly, handing her a paintbrush. "So you're here now, too?" she says to the palm tree, then gets to work painting the corners where the walls meet.

Goth turns up around twelve, pays Dora no heed, nods to the palm tree, and grabs the roller with the longest handle.

With so many people the work proceeds quickly. Dora makes more coffee, and brings Franzi a glass of water. Everybody's sweating. Heini's telling jokes from his inexhaustible repertoire, and periodically making sure the drop cloths are staying put.

Once they've finished the study and bedroom and start in on the hallway, Goth begins whistling. He's a virtuoso, trilling and vibrato and all, like someone who's deeply musical but never learned to play an instrument. Dora recognizes "She'll Be Coming 'round the Mountain," and Franzi chimes in with such gusto Dora figures they must've sung it together in the car on family trips. Heini warbles along with the chorus at the top of his lungs, and by the third time they're through the first stanza Dora decides it's safe to start chipping in with her own lyrics. *"She'll be wieldin' six white paint cans when she comes ..."* and when the rest have the lines down they all sing together, moving their brushes and rollers to the tune. Next up, Heini starts singing "Eisgekühlter Bommerlunder," a punk drinking song that's even more of an earworm. For Dora, it conjures up memories of school field trips to the West German countryside, where the best part of the trip was always the bus ride. That was the last time Dora had sung alongside others. Fun as this singalong is, Dora's worried they'll eventually start singing the Horst Wessel song. But then she realizes her fears are unfounded when Franzi suggests "Who Stole the Cookie from the Cookie Jar?" Then they launch into a bunch of old East German songs—"Bolle reiste jüngst zu Pfingsten," mocking the city slickers of Berlin, and "Es geht um die Erde ein rotes Band," a communist song. Dora and Franzi have to sit that last one out, as the guys belt out every last line, almost shouting the finale, *"It's a word we all trust, in all sincerity, and that word is: solidarity!"* and they all start laughing uncontrollably.

Then, tired of singing, they all just keep painting in silence. The email from the previous night pops back into Dora's thoughts, although she had managed to suppress it for a while.

Dear Dora, I'm regrettably writing today to inform you that FAIRapparel has decided to hit the pause button, and won't be proceeding with the campaign for the time being. They're still impressed by the DO-GOODER proposals, it's just that there's too much uncertainty, given the current situation, and they can't risk so much of their budget.

Should things start looking up over the next year, they'd like to continue with the campaign in 2021.

Over the next few lines, Susanne officially dismisses Dora, albeit with friendly words, and expressing her deep regret. That's just how it goes, and Dora knows. When a project falls though, people are sent packing. It's already happened to many, and soon it'll be happening to even more. Still, she's shocked. Apparently she thought she was among the indispensables. She thought she belonged among the ones who'd be spared by fate.

The worst part is the closing, where Susanne yet again reiterates that Sus-Y values solidarity and sustainability above all else, but that "times like these" leave no other choice. She expresses her hope that in the future, if the situation stabilizes, they'll be able to count on Dora rejoining the team. Sincerely, Susanne.

Dora was so irritated, she hadn't even stopped to consider what this really meant. In concrete terms. But now, while she's making calm brushstrokes up and down the wall, the thoughts rush in. She's just bought a house. She sunk all her savings into it. She has monthly payments to make. Of course she already knows what all her colleagues would advise right about now: go freelance. Stat. Put together a portfolio of your best work from the last few years, set up your own website, and hang your shingle out as an independent copywriter. Let ad agencies all over Germany hire you on a daily or weekly basis, to fill in when their in-house staff are sick, go on parental leave, or are just overloaded. Freelancing is, hands down, better, say the freelancers. Work less, earn more. Day rates between 700 and 800 euros. As Dora's former coworker Oli put it: *Money's always being tossed out the window anyway, you just have to go out there and get it.*

But that's not really an option for Dora. She's not sure that money's still flying out the windows nowadays the way it was before Covid. But that's not even the crux of it. Dora's worked with enough freelancers in her day to know how freelancing really works. Freelancers are first-rate networkers, and as impervious to stress as elite soldiers. They're the special ops of the ad world. They received their brief at 11 a.m., and by 5 p.m. they need to deliver ideas worth 700 to 800 euros. Every gig is a test, and they put their entire reputation on the line with every proposal. In-house staff lie in wait, looking for freelancers to make the tiniest mistake, like amateur soccer players who cheer every time a pro player botches a shot in the national league tournament. It means living in a pressure cooker. Working under merciless micromanagers. Dora bristles at the very idea. At the same time, she has no desire to chase daydreams, and she needs an ulcer like a hole in the head. She doesn't want to sue Sus-Y for unlawful dismissal, nor does she really feel like dealing with employment centers or temp agencies. She's just as unwilling to fill her empty hours by cleaning the windows or catching up on email. Strictly speaking, she has no idea what she feels like doing. She'd kind of like things to just go back to the way they were two years ago. Secure job, a life full of certainties, Robert and her out on the balcony. But she also knows she wouldn't go back, even if she could. She knows something's changed.

She's come so far with her reflections when Goth suddenly appears next to her, sticks a finger into the can of paint, and dabs the tip of Franzi's nose. The girl squeals and runs off, her nose white, so Goth turns to Dora and is about to do the same to her when she darts off, running through the study, the bedroom, the hallway, the kitchen, the bathroom, treating all of it as her personal racecourse, looping round and around again. Goth is surprisingly fast, but Dora's more agile. Only when he suddenly reverses course is he able to catch her in the kitchen, grab her tight, and flick little white droplets of paint all over her face. Dora laughs so hard she can barely breathe, and suddenly all the email in the world fades into the distance, becoming nothing more than messages in a bottle from some faraway land that can safely be ignored.

Heini disappears, and moments later there's a loud rattling sound outside the house. Dora looks out the kitchen window just as Heini rounds the corner. He's pulling something behind him, it looks like a mini space station on wheels. He's shed his protective gear, and is now wearing an apron that reads *Achtung: Serial Griller*. He positions the stainless-steel grill beneath the kitchen window, and in no time at all the house is filled with the aroma of charred sausages. Heini picks each link off the grill with tongs and hands it through the window, where Dora piles them on a platter. She eats three, no bread, Goth downs five, and Franzi eats two and a half. All the while, Heini jokingly repeats

"Hot *dawg*!" and Franzi replies "Her name's *Jay* dawg, not Hot dawg," and collapses in laughter every time.

When they're done eating, Heini drinks his umpteenth coffee while Dora and Goth hang by the windowsill having a smoke. Sincerely, Susanne. Dora allows herself a second cigarette. Out in the yard, swallows are running reconnaissance flights, preemptively trying to fend off a magpie who's just strutting through the grass, wholly uninterested in the nest of strangers.

Come evening, everyone's gone. They painted a bunch more rooms, ate tons more sausage, and sang several more songs. Goth asked Dora if she needed a real desk, and she adamantly shook her head no. Heini said he'd come back soon with his electrical gear, to install a few lights.

Dora didn't want them all to go. She nearly asked Heini if they could dive in and install the lights right away, but then held her tongue. Ever since the door shut behind them, the silence they left behind has been booming in her ears. She lies on the bed and can feel every muscle. Everything around her looks shiny and new. The place smells like wet paint. She desperately needs a shower, but can't muster up the strength. Even Jay-the-Ray seems completely beat, even though all she did was lie around all day and wasn't forced to take even a single walk. Maybe she scarfed down the last few sausages when no one was looking. It was a good day. Heini. She'll Be Coming 'round the Mountain When She Comes. Everybody was so relaxed. Franzi. The girl laughed so sweetly, and worked so diligently.

Dora tries to let it sink in: The woman lying on this bed is now officially unemployed. This person has nothing to do, nobody who needs them. She just can't process it.

Once, quite some time ago, Jojo had said that in the future health would be the center of every aspect of humans' everyday lives.

"Health will supersede politics, in terms of people's focus. There will be doctors, and lawyers to battle the doctors in court. There will be journalists to report on the courtroom battles between doctors and lawyers. Pick one of those professions."

And that's Dora's problem: She isn't an essential worker. The system works just fine without her. Jojo is essential, she is not. Not even a website or booking freelance gigs will change that. Sincerely, Susanne.

27

Sadie

The next morning someone's at the door again. This time they're ringing the bell, so Dora has time to tie her hair back and put on a pair of pants. She slept terribly, and feels like she won't be able to stand a thing today—not even herself, and certainly not a visitor.

The person at the door is a woman she's never seen before. She's slightly younger than Dora, and is heavily made-up. Short, bleach-blonde hair, pierced lips, countless tattoos covering her arms. On her left shoulder Dora spots the kind of busty mermaid you'd expect to see on a man.

"G'morning, Sadie," the woman says.

Since Dora's name isn't Sadie, she deduces it's this visitor's name.

"Seed potatoes," Sadie continues, holding up a bulbous bag that weighs at least twenty pounds. Does everyone here drink magic potion? Dora wonders how the woman knows she needs seed potatoes. But the question is probably moot, since she's sure the answer is simple: the village grapevine. "Coffee?" Sadie asks, pushing Dora aside and walking down the hall toward the kitchen.

Yet another grown-up from the old nursery school who still feels right at home here. When Dora gets to the kitchen, Sadie's already seated at the table. At least she hasn't started making coffee yet. Dora sees to it, since she could use a cup, too.

"Black," Sadie says, before the water even boils. "No milk, no sugar," she adds, as if otherwise Dora might think *black* refers to her favorite color. Or some political party affiliation.

"You flee from Berlin?"

Dora feels the need to explain that she's from Münster, but doesn't get the chance.

"Lot of people have," Sadie says. "City sucks. Now more than ever."

Dora's about to say the pandemic actually could spark a rural renaissance, since working from home is feasible even in no-man's-land, and somehow life is just freer out here, it's almost like the virus doesn't even exist, really. It feels like it's just some overblown urban-dweller's nightmare. But Sadie doesn't need a second person to talk to. Before Dora's brain has finished a single sentence, Sadie's already off and running on her own.

"This used to be the nursery school."

Dora nods and gives up trying to say a word. Monosyllabic speech from a chatterbox isn't a contradiction here in Bracken. She decides to focus on making coffee.

"Then it closed down, like everything. Now the only daycare's in Kochlitz. I drive Audrey there and back. André's already at school." Because she says "Oh-drey" and "An-drey," it takes Dora a minute to realize they're names. "In Plausitz. School's there. An hour bus ride. Comes at seven. Three hours after I get back from work."

Dora wonders if she's understood correctly that

Sadie, despite having children, gets off work at four in the morning. But she doesn't have to bother asking. Sadie's monologue is on autopilot.

"Take the big guy to Plausitz, the little one to Kochlitz, then clean house and snag a nap before picking up the little one again. I can only swing six hours of childcare, that's all I can afford. I'm a single mom, my ex doesn't pay a cent. Sometimes it's a bit complex."

Dora puts two full cups on the table and sits down. Sadie takes a sip and nods.

"Good stuff."

Her fingers start fiddling, spinning the coffee mug on the tabletop. Then she really gets going.

"Now daycare and school are both closed 'cause of Covid. But my boss doesn't get it. So I still have to work. Lockdown's destroying us. The higher-ups in Berlin don't even notice."

Dora could point out that the "higher-ups in Berlin" are just as non-existent as the "lowly folk in Bracken," and that stay-at-home orders are set by each state capital, not the federal government. But instead she says:

"I just lost my job."

Apparently you can utter a sentence like that without the sky falling, without anything at all happening. The words sound almost like a declaration of membership in some club. Dora lost her job, so now she belongs. She's a local. Next she'll try "I'm unemployed," but that'll take some time yet.

"That sucks," Sadie says, and goes on to tell her story. As she talks, she keeps stroking her short hair and tugging at her lip piercings. Dora pours more coffee. She's beginning to find Sadie's chatter interesting.

She works at a foundry on the western edge of Berlin, where she operates the overhead crane. It's a full night shift, an hour's drive away. Even though Dora doesn't really know what an overhead crane is, she can picture this petite woman in the middle of the night, perched in machinery up near the ceiling of a sprawling factory hall, operating levers that pull huge vats full of red-hot molten metal out of the blast furnaces and then bring them to the molds for casting.

At half past five in the evening, Sadie puts food on the table for the kids and usually has to leave before they've finished eating. Ten-year-old André puts his little sister to bed and spends half the night on the internet, which Sadie has no power to stop, although she does call every half hour, telling him to go to bed. She gets home around four in the morning and dozes on the couch for a couple hours, usually too stressed to sleep. She starts preparing breakfast at six.

"At first, they wouldn't give me emergency-care help, since I'm home all day—ha," Sadie laughs. "Meantime, I got a few hours of after-school care. But, even with Covid, I still only sleep on weekends. Can only hope the company holds out. If they cut back my hours, we'll be underwater." She holds her cup out to Dora, completely emptied again.

"André wants a mountain bike. I've been saving up for six months." She rubs her face, careful not to smudge her eye makeup. "On weekends, my mom sometimes takes the kids. That's when I stay in bed twelve hours straight." She smiles and falls silent, as if the mere thought of bed caused her to nod off momentarily.

Dora asks if she heard right that the kids are home alone every night.

Sadie comes to with a start and says, yup, they sure are. Her job at the foundry is the only full-time work she can manage. The night shift is the sole solution that lets her be there for the kids during the daytime.

What would all the mothers back in Prenzlauer Berg say to two small children who have to put each other to bed every night? Dora tries to imagine what it would be like to work all night, every night, and then tend to household and kids during the day. How life would consist solely of exhaustion and stress: worrying about the kids, worrying about the finances, worrying how long she could keep it up.

But she can't. Sadie's story is unimaginable to Dora. Instead, she thinks of things she herself used to worry about. Imaginary flies in the bedroom. Nervous stomach pains that feel like rising bubbles. A significant other who's terrified of Covid.

At least now she's lost her job. Maybe that's the first step toward normalcy. It's catapulting her out of the filter bubbles, out of the echo chambers, and into real life. Into the kind of reality Sadie inhabits, where real things are at stake, things nobody in Prenzlauer Berg has the slightest clue about. Maybe she should be thankful to Sus-Y for dismissing her. Sincerely, Susanne.

"I try really hard, but I just can't keep up, I never get everything done," Sadie says.

In the past semester, she says, she's been called in to school several times a week to discuss André's bad behavior and plummeting grades. Most recently, she says, he set a garbage can in the schoolyard on fire. Sometimes he doesn't come home after school, so she drives around all afternoon looking for him. When she tries to talk to him, he calls her a slut and blames her for driving daddy away, too.

"Then I start bawling, and, well, so much for talking." Sadie laughs. "My son's no dummy." She holds the coffee cup out again for Dora to fill. "In that sense, Covid's a blessing. They were about to kick André out of school. Now he gets a break, and then maybe he'll get a second chance." With a nod, she thanks Dora for the fresh coffee and immediately chugs half the cup. "There's an upside to everything, y'know?"

If she's honest, Dora has to admit she's always seen it the other way around. Everything has its downside, too. Jobs, apartments, cities, life partners, friends, political parties, vacation destinations. It's always a matter of finding the faults, considering them, discussing them, and, if possible, eradicating them. She furtively watches Sadie, who's having another lapse and is staring blankly, straight ahead. She's so young, perhaps not even thirty. She sits at the table, slumping, super pale, the dark circles under her eyes masked under makeup. Dora's in awe of the young woman. It's an old-fashioned feeling she hasn't had in a long time, but she recognizes it immediately. She's also astonished. It's like she's seeing Germany's secret underside. It's hard to believe such a filthy-rich country allows itself to have entire regions where there's nothing. No doctors, no pharmacies, no sports clubs, no buses, no pubs, no nursery schools, no schools at all. No greengrocers, no bakers, no butchers. Regions where retirees can't live on their pensions and young women have to work day and night to provide for their children. Then, in those same areas, you plop down a bunch of massive wind turbines, ban commuters from using diesel, auction off farmers' fields to the highest bidder, try to take wood-burning stoves away from the people who can least afford natural gas, and then you think out loud about banning barbecues and campfires as well, the last bastions of leisurely, sociable enjoyment. And everyone's just expected to keep going without complaint. Keep suiting up, functioning efficiently. Anyone who rebels is dismissed out of hand, called a stupid peasant, a whatever-denier, even an enemy of democracy.

Somehow, Dora thinks, Germany must've manifested the AfD. Her country asked, and the universe delivered.

But Sadie doesn't complain, not even once. She thinks everything has its upside. Dora would love to get up and take the young woman into her arms. But she doesn't dare.

Sadie must've sensed the impulse anyway, because she lifts her head and looks Dora directly in the eyes for the first time.

"It's so nice to just sit here, drink coffee, chat a bit. Haven't done this in ages."

They clink their coffee cups together. It makes a muffled clunk.

"Sometimes I feel like I'm not even here," Sadie

says. "It's so weird. It's like, one day you'll be gone, but you weren't even really here in the first place."

When she was first in college, Dora had a lecturer who tried to teach the basic principles of dramaturgy. He explained that there's a point in every story where the main character has a realization that changes their life. Most of the time, he said, the realization is sparked by a small detail. An offhand observation or seemingly incidental piece of information. Or in a sentence said by some minor character. Dora remembers what the lecturer called this process: receiving the elixir. She looks at Sadie. The bearer of the elixir. "Sometimes I feel like I'm not even really here." Actually, I always feel like that, Dora thinks. She thinks back to that fleeting feeling she had as a child: *How crazy—I exist. Error oxo.* It didn't scare her as a child. It was more like: Ooh, so *this* is the here and now. Her chattering mind fell silent for a moment, then babbled on. Dora considers telling Sadie about it, asking her if it sounds familiar.

But just now she's looking out the window.

"Ooh, there goes the little Proksch." She points toward the yard. "What's she doing here?"

Outside, Franzi frolics across the lawn, turning on a dime, followed by Jay, who's trying to catch the girl. When she finally does, both dog and child roll through the grass before jumping back up and running another lap.

"Nadine's daughter." Sadie looks at Dora. "You looking after her now?"

Proksch, Nadine, looking after. It takes Dora a few tries, but she finally connects the dots.

"Franzi's with her father because of Covid. She likes playing with my dog."

Sadie nods. "She used to love playing with André. He was sad when Naddy took off with her. I didn't think she'd let Franzi come here ever again."

"Why? She cheated on Goth, didn't she?"

"What?" Sadie laughs.

"With the delivery guy."

"You're kidding me." Sadie laughs even louder. "Somebody's been spinning you a yarn." She places her hands flat on the table. Her fingernails are long, pointed, and powder blue. "I knew her pretty well. Naddy was basically a single parent, too—just with a husband. But then Gottfried really messed up, and Naddy left."

"Messed up how?"

Dora's afraid of the answer, but also desperately wants to know. She opens the window, sets a saucer on the table as an ashtray, and hands Sadie her pack of cigarettes.

"Sweet." Sadie helps herself to one and hands it back. They take a few drags in silence. Then Sadie says:

"Attempted manslaughter, aggravated assault."

Dora doesn't bother hiding her horror.

"Refugees?"

"Leftists."

The bubbles are back, prickling worse than ever.

"In Plausitz, three years ago. Gottfried and two other guys."

Sadie looks at the clock and her eyes grow wide. She takes such a deep drag that a third of her the cigarette goes up in smoke. "They started an argument with a couple, then threatened the woman and stabbed the man."

Dora stubs out her cigarette. Too much coffee on an empty stomach. She feels like lying down. Or going for a long walk. Sadie has to go, too. Break's over, back onto the hamster wheel. But there's one more thing Dora still needs to know.

"How's Goth not behind bars?"

"That's how things are here in our fine country." Sadie grins. "Do a little time, spend the rest on probation."

Dora figures it couldn't have been that bad, then. Extenuating circumstances. Maybe even self-defense. The village grapevine has embellished the story.

But at the same time, Dora knows exactly what her own mind is up to. It's looking for reasons not to believe Sadie. She justifies Goth's actions because she doesn't want to live next door to a violent criminal. That's exactly how alternative facts are born.

"Look, I can't stand the hippie-dippie multi-culti crowd either." Sadie stands up and stubs out her cigarette. "I work my ass off, and all these foreigners don't have to lift a finger. But knives aren't the solution. In my humble opinion." She shrugs and turns to go. "Thanks for the coffee."

Dora doesn't have time for the old racism-triggered stiffness, nor to wonder whether Sadie's a bad person for using that xenophobic catchphrase or a good person for rejecting violence. She has to rush and accompany her visitor to the front door, and Sadie is already marching down the hall.

"Thanks for the potatoes," Dora yells, but by then

Sadie is already outside, climbing into a bright-yellow Clio parked outside the front gate.

Dora pauses on the threshold and keeps looking at the road, where the occasional car roars by, speeding. Between passing cars it's quiet. Unusually quiet. The silence comes bearing a message for her: Franzi and Jay are no longer there. They're gone.

28

Museum

Dora rides Gustav down every street in the village, even the little lanes, which would be fun if she weren't so angry. She tries to calm down. Where could Franzi and Jay have got to? It's unlikely they hitchhiked to Kochlitz and escaped to Berlin on the regional train. If she catches Franzi, she'll read her the riot act. How dare she just disappear with Jay! And how dare Jay go with Franzi, without leash and collar, especially since both are hanging on the hook right next to the door back home.

She passes a bunch of yards, knowing their owners have even more time to mow the lawn than usual. Lots of people are out and about, but nobody has seen a girl with a small beige dog. Dora rides past the edge of the village. When the path gets sandy, Gustav starts to waver. They reach the forest and then the bench at the crossroads. Nothing. Dora calls out for Jay, but as her voice travels off into the trees it fades away. Not even a jay is anywhere in sight. She'd like to call her mother right about now. The whole world is going digital, but there still isn't a phone for dialing the afterlife. "Oh, sweetie!" her mother would say. "What's the worst that could've happened?"

You've got to be kidding. That's what a more proper person would say. Anything can happen. Jay could decide to walk home and get hit by a car on the main road back to Bracken.

"Everything'll be fine," says her mother, and Dora slams the imaginary telephone back onto its nonexistent receiver.

She rides back into town, getting drenched in sweat and covered in dust. What's she supposed to do now? She can't just sit in the kitchen and wait for Jay to reappear if and when she feels like it. It occurs to her she might never see the little dog again, and she's suddenly seized with a despair so deep it surprises even her. Nothing and no one should disappear anymore. Enough has already disappeared, especially lately. On a whim, Dora decides not to go home. Instead, she hits the brakes in front of Goth's wall and tries the gate. It's unlocked. Attempted manslaughter. Aggravated assault. On the other hand, he gave her his treasured tin soldiers. They played tag and flicked each other with wall paint. He won't kill her just because she's on his property. But she's still uncomfortable.

She pushes Gustav through the gate and looks around. So far she has only ever seen Goth's realm from over on the other side of the wall. It's bigger than she thought. The area between the house and the trailer is as big as a tennis court. Tidy and well trimmed. The camping chairs are folded up against the table. The geraniums in front of the trailer are in full bloom. A fruit crate stands against the wall to Dora's property. His counterpart to her lawn chair. The only item Goth never puts away.

She parks Gustav and walks over to the trailer. The grass is soft under her soles. His yard isn't a stubble field like hers. The wolf next to the trailer steps is sitting on its hind legs, mouth slightly open so its teeth and tongue are visible. His expression is friendlier than she suspected from afar. So lifelike, he might wink at her any minute now. His wooden fur is crafted with great artistry, covering his entire figure in slightly wavy strands. Whoever carved this has serious talent.

Dora steps onto his grate-metal front steps and knocks on the trailer door. Nothing. Obviously Goth is out again, even though his pickup is parked in its usual spot. Maybe he's out for coffee with some violent criminal friends. She pushes the image out of her mind and circles the trailer. His potato field extends to the very back of his property. She enviously eyes the well-watered soil and green plants. Her own plot is still just a stretch of dirt and dust. She also discovers traces of Jay's digging expeditions, but no dog beaten to a pulp by the border. She gradually admits to herself that she doesn't know where to look anymore. But there's only one possibility left. She turns around, and walks across the lawn toward the main house.

The entrance is on the side. Before even thinking about it, Dora turns the handle. It's unlocked.

The familiar smell of long-empty house hits her nose. The smell of damp walls, of the past. She enters a vestibule that serves as a coatroom. Jackets on the wall, shoes on the floor, carelessly flung off people's feet as they entered. Men's boots, women's sandals, a toddler's slippers. Everything looks like a family has just come home, except the jackets and shoes exude a musty smell. Dora shudders. She crosses the vestibule, opens the door to the hallway, and turns right into the kitchen, where she encounters a bizarre tableau. On the table there's a booklet open to the local TV schedule dated September 22, 2017. Next to it lies a coffee cup, the mold inside long since morphed into a black goo. The sink is filled with encrusted dishes. There's half a loaf of bread on the sideboard, hard as stone. The kitchen-table chairs are all missing.

Feeling a mixture of revulsion and fascination, Dora walks through the remaining rooms. In the bedroom, the double bed is unmade. The doors of the closet are open, the drawers sticking out as if someone had hurriedly grabbed only the essentials. In the living room, a large flat-screen TV veiled in dust. A sloppily folded blanket on the couch. You might plausibly think someone had just been sitting here a moment ago. Except, in this case, that "moment ago" must have been September 22, 2017. Dora's standing in an almost three-year-old snapshot. A slice of the past, preserved like a freeze frame. A museum exhibiting someone's swift escape.

On the carpet she spots a circular imprint, cleaner than the rest of the floor. This must have been where the large plant now adorning her study stood. There are three healthy-looking smaller palms on a low table nearby. Apparently Goth comes by to water them occasionally. Dora steps up to the window and is surprised to see her own house. It looks strange from this perspective, half-hidden behind a wall and a bunch of black locust trees. As if it didn't belong to her. As if it belonged to no one. Dora gets the feeling she shouldn't be here. Suddenly something happens. A veil lifts. The room changes shape. Everything inside takes on sharper contours, more intense colors. She looks around, awestruck. It's all real, her mind says, then shuts back up. It lets her just stand there and contemplate. Around her is Goth's house, earth below, sky above. Eight billion people on a chunk of rock orbiting through space. Dora can feel it—an ancient, speechless knowledge. Knowledge of the difference between something and nothing.

oxo, she thinks. Then something falls over.

A thud from above. A rustling.

"Jay!"

She runs down the hall and up the stairs. She immediately notices that, unlike the rest of the house, the stairs are being used. The layer of dust is worn off in the middle of the steps. There are footprints on the landing, not particularly large, like those of a child.

Upstairs, she follows the footprints down the hall. The doors are open. She fleetingly registers that the rooms aren't fully built. There's a half-finished bathroom, a bedroom probably meant for future guests. It's still a construction site, fallen quiet: drywall panels and drop cloths. All the doors are open except the last one on the left. She opens without knocking.

It takes her a minute to process what she's seeing. Clearly this is a child's room. Just as clearly, she sees it is inhabited. But the degree of neglect is breathtaking. The floor is covered in broken things—toddler toys, toddler books, toddler clothes—all carelessly tossed aside and being trampled to bits. The desk is a craft-supply cemetery: yellowed paper, dried-up tubes of glue, felt-tip pens without caps.

The blankets and pillows on the tike-sized bed look like a homeless encampment. A row of stuffed animals sits against the wall, looking slumped and sad. Dora sees empty bags of chips on the floor and a flashlight on the nightstand. Apparently there's no electricity, probably no water either.

So this is where Franzi lives, all alone in a mummified house. Amid the rotting relics of her own childhood.

Dora can't imagine Nadine Proksch is aware of her daughter's living conditions. She probably thinks the child is living here with her dad, in their former family home, exactly as she remembers it. Dora's task now is to track down Nadine and have Franzi picked up. Or call the office of child protective services right away.

Franzi sits on the floor and doesn't make a move while Dora surveys what looks like a battlefield. The girl is holding Jay on her lap, and the dog's coat is covered in chip crumbs. That explains what she's doing here. Food first, ethics last, if ever.

"So *here* you two are."

Dora's sharp enough not to let on how horrified she is, so is careful to behave as if everything were fine, completely normal. What she sees breaks her heart. But Franzi mustn't catch on. She shouldn't be made to think there's anything wrong with her or her situation.

"My room," the girl says with forced pride. There it is again—she's back in toddler mode. Dora keeps her poker face. She shoves her hands in her pockets as she looks around, paying exaggerated attention.

"Nice place you got here," she says.

As Franzi beams, Dora's heart seizes up again.

"I've got everything I need," Franzi says in her baby voice, gesturing to the chaos all around her.

"Ever heard of Pippi Longstocking?" asks Dora.

"Of course!"

"She lives alone in a big house, too. With all her animals."

"Exactly!" Franzi jumps up, causing Jay to tumble off her lap. "I'm Pippi Longstocking, and this is Mr. Nilsson!" She points at Jay, calls out a few more times, "Mr. Nilsson, Mr. Nilsson!" and begins a silly dance, swaying her upper body from side to side. She starts singing with a lisp, *"Add two plus two and you're bound to get three, but give me a rabbit and I'll make him pee! It's a fact that one seed can grow several flowers, but days are made up of just forty-two hours!"*

Her lyrics are off.

"Okay, Franzi," says Dora. "Everything's okay."

The girl immediately falls silent, plops down on the edge of the bed, and hangs her head as if she's done something wrong. Dora doesn't say a word and just waits.

"Don't tell my mommy, okay?" Franzi finally says, her voice normal again.

"Do you like staying at your daddy's?"

Franzi emphatically nods.

"Why don't you sleep in the trailer?"

"He doesn't want me to. Too cramped. It's better here." She turns on the baby voice again: "Like Pippi in Villa Villekulla!"

"Is your daddy at work right now?"

"I dunno. Maybe he's going beddy-bye. He goes beddy-bye a lot."

"You mean he lies in bed all day?"

"Sometimes." She thinks it over. "A lot more, lately." Then she waves her hands around again. "He's still the best daddy in the whole wide world!"

"Absolutely."

"You won't tell anybody, right?" begs Franzi.

And suddenly Dora knows exactly what she'll do: nothing. Goth might not be one of those fathers who show up at school every week trying to convince the principal their child is a genius. And he's definitely not one to have a nervous breakdown in the organic section of the supermarket because the spelt cookies are sold out. Indeed, Goth is physically violent, verbally abusive, and has a drinking problem. But Franzi loves him. And he loves her back, in his own way. What the girl needs is a little support. What she doesn't need is someone trying to take control.

"Listen, Franzi—"

Just fifteen minutes ago, Dora wanted to tell the girl to stay away from her and Jay in the future. She doesn't run a summer camp, especially not for little kids who kidnap dogs and have Nazi ex-cons for fathers. But that was fifteen minutes ago.

"When you play with Jay, you're not allowed to leave my yard. Not without telling me. Got it?"

"Got it." Franzi nods, suddenly very serious. "I won't do it again."

"And—" Dora sighs, then squares her shoulders. "Why don't you come over for a meal more often, if you want? I'd like that."

29

Knife

All day long Dora's been indulging the debate team in her head. Part of her says she should sit down at the computer and catch up on email. She even has a bright idea: she could specialize in radio advertising, preferably for regional clients. Less money, less competition, less stress. Dora is certain radio's potential is far from exhausted. She knows a sound engineer she could contact right away, suggesting they team up. Maybe with the idea of then starting their own small agency.

But then another part of her says it's best to wait until the world goes back to normal again. It'd be utterly idiotic to start your own business during Covid! As long as budgets are frozen solid, there's no point in Dora going out to find new clients. Besides, she's got to get the seed potatoes into the ground.

Under normal conditions, the debate team would've lost to the next deadline. Now, the debate team wins. Specifically, the part of the team that's anti-computer, pro-gardening.

Dora loosens the soil in the vegetable patch and sows the potatoes Sadie brought her, properly distanced, per the tutorial she watched on YouTube. Social distancing for vegetables. She heaps the soil above each potato into a little mound, imagining she's burying the eggs of an alien queen. This sparks a little daydream: During a trip into outer space with Alexander Gerst, Dora was abducted by aliens who implanted a chip in her brain. This allows them to control her remotely. The chip forces her to walk back to the house sixteen times and haul thirty-two filled-to-the-brim watering cans to the flower bed. The cans are heavy, hitting her thighs and soaking her pants. Dora doesn't stop until the dusty sand has turned to mud. Her back protests, her arms and legs ache, but it's a meaningful pain—at least, as long as you don't ask what's supposed to be meaningful about a clutch of alien egg pods. Or homegrown potatoes.

After dinner, she sits down at the kitchen table with her laptop. Googling is a bad idea. She should contact the sound engineer instead, or at least draft an outline of her future website and portfolio. But the debate team in her head wants to know. Dora types *Gottfried Proksch* and *knife* into the search field and thinks about clicking *I'm feeling lucky*, but then opts for a regular search.

The list of results is so long it gives her pause. She's startled. Apparently she was still secretly hoping Sadie was lying.

Knife attack after exchange of insults: man hospitalized.

Wife of Plausitz attack victim: "I'm traumatized."

Mike B. shows little remorse in court.

Verdict after knife attack: Regional court charges attempted manslaughter.

How far right is Prignitz?

Each new link is like a slap in the face. Nevertheless, page after page, she can't stop clicking through. She reads the headlines as avidly as an addled hypochondriac googling their latest symptoms.

Case of Mike B., Gottfried P. and Denis S.: Victim-support association criticizes lenient sentence.

Lawyer for joint plaintiffs files appeal.

Plausitz: Police monitoring 50 violent neo-Nazis.

The longer Dora reads, the more befuddled her imaginary headlines become. Friendly neighbor builds furniture for newcomer. Villagers help renovate old nursery school. Franzi P.: Happy childhood or case for the Office of Child Protective Services? Everything swirls around like pieces of a jigsaw puzzle someone has wantonly tossed up in the air. Dora can't get a clear picture. She lacks perspective. Without perspective, there's no order to things. Without perspective, the world is chaotic and incomprehensible, which hurts so bad she can hardly bear it. So she does what all confused people do in confusing times: She looks for the truth in information. Data. Cold hard facts.

The facts are clear. Plausitz, September 20, 2017. On a beautiful, late-summer afternoon, a forty-year-old couple strolls through the local market square. Karen M., an office clerk, and Jonas F., a web designer, are both from the region and have lived in the small town in the East Prignitz area for a long time. Out of nowhere they're mobbed by a group of men drinking beer on a bench in front of the local arts center.

"They shouted 'Scram, you leeches!'" reports Karen M. "They called me a 'leftist cunt.'"

By his own account, Jonas F. used to be a member of the local Antifa.

"It's a small town in a sparsely populated part of the country," he tells the local newspaper. "Everybody knows everybody here."

He confirms he's known two of the three perpetrators, Mike B. and Denis S., since elementary school.

"No one ever did anything about the Nazis here," he says. "Only Antifa. The police just stood by, watching."

A heated exchange develops in the middle of the town square. Karen M. tries to pull her boyfriend aside. When the men get physical, she goes off to get help.

"In the nineties, there was a fight almost every day," says Jonas F. "Clashes were normal."

According to witnesses, Mike B. pulls out the knife. Jonas F. is unprepared. The blade penetrates between his ribs. Miraculously, his lungs are unharmed.

"People even died, y'know?" Jonas F. says outside the courthouse. "The public didn't care. In that sense, I was lucky. I hope my case will be a wake-up call for the authorities."

Dora shuts her laptop. It wasn't Gottfried P. who wielded the knife. That's important information. But is information—are facts—the same as truth? In images from the trial, the defendants hide their faces. Dora recognizes them anyway. Mike B. has the full beard and Denis S. is the tattooed one. Goth is Goth. All three have since been released. The truth is that it doesn't matter who had the knife. They're all to blame.

Jonas F. and Karen M. could've just as easily been Dora K. and Robert D. from Berlin. Leftist leeches on a stroll through the quaint, small town. Insulted and accosted by Nazis, solely because of their political stance. Because of their belief in democracy. Welcome to Germany in the twenty-first century.

Jay-the-Ray snores on the tile floor, beyond the reach of all the Google hits in the world. Dora squats down next to her dog and puts a hand on her warm body. They have to get out of here. She's known that all along, really. But where to? She's bought a house and lost her job. She's not in a great place. She could ask Jojo for help. Or make up with Robert. Accept his rules and let him keep her fed and housed. The mere thought of it brings her old need to resist back to the fore, fiercer than it's been in a long time. Maybe just some other village. Maybe through a house swap.

But then Dora thinks: What if her new neighbor is also a Nazi? Maybe not right next door, but just a few houses down? How much distance does a left-wing liberal need from the nearest neo-Nazi to be able to live in peace? Does the whole village have to be Nazi-free, or even the community? The region? Or even the whole country?

Dora buries her face in her hands. Maybe the alien queen could have her picked up. Then she could just live in space, tending to clutches of alien egg pods. Occasionally Alexander Gerst would stop by, and they'd have space coffee together. The nicest two people in the world, who always say and do the exact right thing.

You can think all that and more. You can twist and turn the endless stream of information. But the truth remains the same. The truth is that whether Dora stays or goes doesn't matter in the least, for one simple reason. Nazis don't cease to exist just because you no longer live right next door to them.

30

About People

It's just past nine in the evening and already almost dark when Dora decides to go over to Tom and Steffen's. She wants to confront Steffen about his tall tale with the delivery man. Or maybe she just wants to talk to someone. After all, it's local custom to show up at other people's doors unannounced. Jay has to stay home because of the Mon Chéri incident, and because Dora is still annoyed she ran off with Franzi.

She hears Steffen before she sees him. More precisely, she hears his voice. She's still all the way out on the street. He's singing, loud, with long, drawn-out vowels and a hefty dose of vibrato. It's a famous 1970s folksong by Reinhard Mey, but with different lyrics. The original title said something about being sky-high, above the clouds.

"Concerned citizens / your ignorance must be boundless."

The lines float through the air. Dora listens. How strange to find Bracken filled with song at twilight. There's no musical accompaniment, it's all a cappella. Dora wouldn't have thought Steffen could sing. Somehow he doesn't look like a vocalist.

"Your fears, your worries / will ..."

Dora tries to locate the voice.

"... dull into hatred / and the day after tomorrow / what burns ..."

She crosses the lawn, walking up to the house. There's a pot of bushy rosemary on the windowsill that provides a little cover. The ground-floor windows are low enough that she can easily see into the house. She just has to shield the reflection in the windowpanes with her hands.

"... will be another home for refugees / And everyone asks: How can it be?"

Steffen is seated in the middle of the room, his side to the window, on a bar stool. The only light is a single floor lamp, aimed directly at him like the spotlight on a theatrical stage. The rest of the room is cloaked in darkness. Still, Dora recognizes it as the living room she saw on her first visit. All the furniture is squat. Low armchairs, low couch, low table. Low sideboard with shallow decorative bowls. The bar stool must be from the kitchen. Among all these short-legged furnishings, he looks like a giraffe amid a pack of dachshunds turned to stare at him in wonder.

Steffen lifts an arm as he sings the refrain.

"Concerned citizens / your freedom shall be boundless ..." He holds his right hand as if he's the Statue of Liberty carrying an invisible torch.

Then he stretches his arm diagonally, hand flat, palm down: the Hitler salute. Next, he brings his hand to the front of his shoulder, elbow down, and clenches his fingers into a socialist fist. Then again Statue of Liberty. Hitler salute. Socialist fist. He continues to sing the melody in scat, la-la-la, higher and higher in tone, louder and louder in volume. The vibrato morphs into a tremolo, he becomes the parody of a theatrical vocalist, and repeats his gestures, torch, Hitler, socialist fist. He holds the last note almost indefinitely, then suddenly breaks off. A cloud of smoke or vapor rises to envelop him, looking impenetrable in the spotlight. Dora tries to locate the fog machine. Then she spots the vape pen between Steffen's fingers. He takes deep drags, as if he wants to completely hide behind a thick cloud. Dora is certain he doesn't usually smoke. And he looks different than normal too. Hair in a bun, no glasses, legs lasciviously crossed. A freaky male Marilyn. He starts singing again, this time softly, to the tune of "Happy Birthday."

"*Neo-Nazi, boo-hoo / neo-Nazi, boo-hoo.*"

Between lines he shakes his head, laughing softly, as if thinking things he himself can't believe.

"*So much fffffear / so much worry ...*"

Dora pulls out her phone and starts googling with one hand. She realizes she doesn't even know his last name. She tries *Steffen, Berlin, theater, Ernst Busch.* Then she adds *Bracken.*

"*Neo-Nazi, boo-hoo.*"

The very first link is a Wikipedia page. *Steffen A. Schaber, born in 1979 in the Lower Rhine region, is a German cabaret artist.*

The scant amount of text that follows indicates his big breakthrough is yet to come. Dora clicks on the second link and sees, onscreen, the exact same image now before her very eyes on the other side of the windowpane: bar stool, smoke, male Marilyn. The online image is a promotional shot announcing an event, on the homepage of a club called Endless Fun. Steffen Schaber, debut program: Über Menschen— About People, premiering April 28, 2020, 9 p.m.

April 28 is today, 9 p.m. is now. Dora puts her phone away and looks through the window again, but not before noticing another announcement on the webpage, set diagonally, in red:

Cancelled due to Covid.

Steffen, done singing, is now puffing away on his bar stool, occasionally taking a deep breath as if he were about to say something, but then keeping it to himself, since talking in times like these makes no sense anyway. Then he seems to get a hold of himself after all, raises his head, and looks directly into the flat-screen TV as if his audience were sitting there, or perhaps he sees his own reflection in the black glass. The monitor is off.

"Funny, isn't it? Downright hilarious, isn't it? I mean, isn't it uproarious, so hilarious you could cry, so hilarious you could die? Yes! It is hilarious! *You all* are hilarious! So hilarious, *I* could die!"

He turns off the vape pen and puts it away. He's a man on a mission, launching into a lecture.

"Do you all still remember? It wasn't so long ago. A mere seventy, eighty years back. You were supermen, quintessential *Übermenschen*. You were the master race. Blond stallions on your way to world domination. Philosophers described you, composers sang about you, foreign countries trembled in their boots before you, and the people, das Volk, trailed behind you. And today?" Steffen's eyes widen. "Today you're at the camping table, lounging. Trailer behind you, warm beer before you. You smoke Polish cigarettes, make the Hitler salute before the flag of the Reich, and manufacture your own IDs. *Übermenschen* in *Unterhemden*—Supermen in undershirts ... or would you prefer I say *wifebeat-ers?*" Steffen feigns a fit of laughter. "You're not saving Germany. You're saving the fine-ribbed textile industry." He laughs even harder, so hard he can barely go on. "Scum is what you are. Have you noticed that yet? You are the scum you always wanted to exterminate. Nobody likes you, nobody needs you. You sleep the days away, drink the nights away. You believe every bit of bullshit you see on the internet and plant potatoes for the apocalypse."

Dora is mesmerized. Steffen is talking about Goth, it's crystal clear. It's a reckoning. It's ballsy. Are people really allowed to talk like that? Scum. Did she just let out a laugh by mistake? Is Goth scum? A superhuman battling relegation? Isn't Goth just ... The sentence remains unfinished. Steffen should stop. Somehow he's right, but somehow she doesn't want him talking that way. But she can't stop listening. He's a performer in front of an imaginary audience. A cabaret artist making his premiere in a completely empty room.

"And you know who's perched up in the Palaces of the Republic? People with bike straps at their ankles, talking about third toilets for the third sex! The twenty-first century is here, getting right up in your face, wiggling its ass so you can lick it. Every woman in the armed forces, every married gay couple, every immigrant, every new climate accord, they're all sticking their asses right up in your face!"

Now he's almost shouting. Dora braces herself against the windowsill in order to see better. She wants to yell something in, but doesn't know what. If there were an audience, there would certainly be commotion. Grumbling, laughter, cheering, jeering, maybe even heckling. All these reactions are now taking place within Dora. She's a stand-in for everyone.

"There's a selection going on, and you dim-witted know-it-alls are out. Rejected. It's survival of the fittest, folks, and that's not you. The *Übermensch* is *Unterschicht*—superman sucks, man. Newsflash: you're the underclass. If that's not history having a little *esprit d'escalier,* I don't know what is! Go on, laugh! You are hi-la-ri-ous, so funny I could kill you, you're those shooting-gallery figures, targets on your chests, targeted for retirement, rendered obsolete by the new era. Chug your cans o' beer while you're waiting to get picked up—by the garbage truck of history!"

Suddenly something crashes to the ground. Dora has accidentally knocked the pot of rosemary off the sill. Steffen wheels around on his stool, nearly tipping over, unsure what's going on until his gaze meets Dora's as she gives him a guilty wave. He makes a few frantic arm movements to shoo her away, his face masked in fury, until he gives up, jumps off the stool, and runs out of the room. Not a moment later, the front door flies open.

"What the fuck?!"

Dora walks gingerly toward him. She's sorry about the rosemary and for interrupting, but she doesn't see why it's such a catastrophe. Didn't he want someone to see his show? It's a performance, after all. Dora's his audience.

"You ruined my goddamned recording!"

Now she's blushing. So he wasn't just talking to

the turned-off TV. There must be another device she didn't see, a camera, a tablet, maybe just a cell phone.

"Are you livestreaming?" she asks.

"Nah." He runs his hand down over his face, already a little calmer. "Just recording for YouTube. Thanks to you, now I take it from the top."

"Sorry, I had no idea."

"Whatcha want, anyway? Got another bike to return?"

Dora knows why she came, but no longer understands her own logic. She's embarrassed by it. But she can't think of anything better than the truth.

"Because of the delivery-guy story," she says.

"The delivery guy—and Goth."

"Oh, gosh. Someone told you what really happened?"

"Sadie."

"Well, now you know what kind of guy Goth is."

"Why did you lie to me?"

"Seemed like the nicer story."

Again, Steffen runs a hand down over his face. In the light of the street lamps he looks like a ghost. Pale skin, rings under his eyes. Dora wonders whether he's ill, or just in a bad state. She wonders what it means for a stage performer when there's no open stage to perform on.

"I just got laid off," she says.

"Good for you. Now you can spend all your time just thinking."

"I will." She tries to smile. "Why're you talking about him like that?"

"Come again?"

"About Goth. Y'know, in your show."

"Hmm ..." Steffen feigns perplexity. "Let's see, why might that be, lemme think a sec ..."

"The greatest risk of war is that you start to resemble your enemy more and more."

"What's that—a pearl of wisdom scrawled on a bathroom stall?"

"I think it's from *Batman*."

"Know what? You can go fuck yourself. If I see you at the window ever again ..."

"You'll round up a few folks and beat the living daylights out of me?"

"That's right."

The front door slams shut.

PART THREE

Mass Effect

31

Au Revoir

Hiding your face behind a piece of cloth isn't all that unpleasant, after all. Dora made herself a mask with an old T-shirt, two rubber bands, and a pipe cleaner. Jojo has promised to send professional-grade masks from the hospital. He considers masks the "official membership cards of law-abiding citizens," and wonders whether the requirement that people wear face coverings will lead to greater tolerance of niqab wearers in Germany. In any case, the package hasn't arrived yet, which could be because Dora still doesn't have a mailbox.

The T-shirt mask Dora has fashioned is no masterpiece, and keeps slipping down, but the upside is that it means you can't immediately see how tired she is. She slept badly. In the middle of the night she got a second email from Susanne. Her now former boss wrote to inquire whether she could stop by the office when she gets a chance—ideally as soon as possible but preferably after 6 p.m.—and clear out her desk, since the whole "shop" has to be remodeled. Making it Covid-compatible means installing plexiglass panes, increasing the amount of space between workstations, and creating special Zoom-friendly conference rooms. Stay healthy and so on and so forth. Sincerely, Susanne.

Even though Dora's desk might as well already

have been gone, news of the office being remodeled triggered the initial reaction she expected but didn't experience after her actual termination: she started feeling anxious. Instead of sleeping, she got out of bed, pulled up her bank statements online, and calculated how long her money could last if she didn't go to the office, didn't talk to Susanne, and didn't buy anything except food. She researched the possibility of suspending her home-loan repayments, and what conditions would make her eligible for a job-transition loan. As a precaution, she increased her withdrawal limit, and looked up when the first early potatoes would be ready to harvest.

The results were sobering. However Dora tries to spin it, she needs to start earning money again. As soon as possible. From home. In Bracken.

As she changes trains at Berlin's main station, her eyes fall on a digital display: May 7, 2020, 5:35 p.m. How little dates and times mean to her now. She has to think for a minute to figure out what day of the week it is. Thursday. Maybe Jojo is in Berlin. She walks past the windows of a magazine store and notices that the massage-ball-shaped virus is not only depicted in red and purple on magazine covers, but now also in green, which could be considered a signal that diversity of opinion lives on, even in these circumstances. Since she's been out of work, she's been reading news on the internet again, which doesn't sit well with her.

She leaves the magazine store behind her and continues her way through the bowels of the main station. A retiree yells at a young man who got too close to him while walking by. A homeless man hunts for deposit bottles in trash cans, coughing all the while.

Mothers pull playing children apart. On the Intercity Express platforms, individuals in suits wait for long-distance trains, speaking into their phones like the high-powered laborers they are. The category of "essential worker" appears rather flexible. Exhortations to wash your hands and respect the social-distancing guidelines run across digital screens normally filled with ads. On the platforms for the city trains, people either demonstratively keep their distance or form defiant crowds. The question of where you stand has literally become a political statement. At least the trains are pleasantly empty.

Dora gets off in Prenzlauer Berg and takes her usual route through the neighborhood. The streets are almost deserted, cafés and restaurants closed, playgrounds cordoned off by red-and-white striped tape. The only people gathered in front of the Spätis are the usual untouchables, but you'd probably find them standing there even in the middle of a nuclear war.

Dora can still recall the feeling of having to spend day and night with Robert in their shared apartment. She imagines being cooped up with two small children and a husband whose work hours have been cut back. Behind countless windows on endless streets, frightened people hunker down and keep Covid diaries. Because they're no longer allowed to go anywhere, their internal thoughts and feelings have become deafening. They ponder the meaning of life and suicide. Meanwhile, Dora strolls through the forest outside Bracken, spends all day in the garden, and worries about the Nazi on the other side of the wall. Covid has redistributed various privileges. A short trip to Berlin makes that eminently clear.

Dora sees a uniformed man and half expects him to ask her what she's doing out on the street. She couldn't take Jay along for cover because her back pack will be full on the way home. She read on some blog that in France armed policemen check if there are really only "essential" products in people's shopping bags as they leave the store. She thanks heaven she lives in Germany. She reaches her destination without being stopped by anyone.

Sus-Y is located on the upper floors of an ornate old building. Dora knows the code for the door by heart. As always, she prefers to take the stairs rather than the elevator because she loves the colorful Art Nouveau windows on the landings. On the fourth floor, she enters the code one last time and realizes she also loves the *buzz* of the door opening and the professional *click* as the door locks. Almost reverently, she steps onto the wide, gleaming wooden floorboards that must've cost a fortune to restore back in the day.

The rooms smell of disinfectant and desertedness. Large, flat packages lean against the walls. Those must be the Plexiglas barriers. On a flip chart, someone has drawn hasty circles in red Sharpie, labeled "Optimal Performance types," "Hedonists," and "Adaptive Pragmatic types." A target group analysis for vegan fruit chews. Apparently it's for the sweets-4all brand, which Dora has never heard of.

She turns away and looks at the open-plan office space. Although she often worked until late at night, she's never seen the place so deserted. Last year's *Happy Birthday* paper chain hangs above Sven's workstation. Loretta's monitor is still framed by photos of horses. At Vera's, empty coffee cups are piled up. Two desks have already been cleared: Simon's and Gloria's. Obviously other colleagues have also been given notice. The desks look naked, just standing there, waiting to be picked up by the garbage truck of history. The sight frightens her. She'll probably never see Gloria or Simon ever again.

Jay's furry faux-leopard-print doggy bed is still under her desk. Every morning, the little dog would run around the agency greeting everyone. Suddenly, Dora misses all the noise that used to get on her nerves. Employees would stand and shoot the breeze by the coffee machine, or lean against a colleague's desk to share some news. Chattering voices, clattering keyboards, ringing phones. Almost a kind of music. And then there was the aroma of coffee, stronger each time the big machine hummed into action.

All that's over and gone. Unceremoniously, a phase of life is sinking into the past, and only now does Dora realize how much it meant to her. No matter how the situation develops, she can't go back to Sus-Y. After *Sincerely, Susanne*, it would feel like living a lie. She knows herself well enough to know it wouldn't work.

During the trip home, she consoles herself with the thought of how happy Jay will be to get her bed back. She can still picture the sterile rooms of Sus-Y HQ, but they're already out of step with her daily life. They're pictures, nothing more. Just a series of snapshots titled "The Day After" or "Au revoir," a photo-essay about how humanity disinfects everything one last time before disappearing from the face of the Earth. Dora feels calmer. She still doesn't know how things will go, but at least she knows how they can't go, and perhaps that's all a person ever can know.

32

Sculpture

When she steps off the regional train at Kochlitz station, it's nine o'clock in the evening and almost dark. The backpack with her office supplies is on her shoulders as she straps the doggy bed onto Gustav's front rack. The lights on her bike have sensors, and automatically switch on. She carefully steers over the bumpy streets of Kochlitz until she reaches the road to Bracken and the smooth, well-paved bike path that parallels it. She pedals hard. She feels guilty about leaving Jay alone for so long. At the same time, she's enjoying the fast ride. The fields stretch far into the distance, the forest is a patch of black on the horizon. Chirping crickets fill the air with tension. Even though the day is through, you can still feel the warmth of spring on the light breeze.

Dora thinks everything is quite simple, really. The answer to all questions lies right before her eyes. It's hidden in the landscape, in silence, in darkness. The secret is to keep still. Watch life take place. She'll break off contact with Goth, making sure to be friendly yet firm. She'll take care of Franzi for a bit, keeping her distance until the girl disappears again into her city life. As for her job, everything will work out once Covid is over. In the meantime, she can sell Gustav. Out here, she can get by on so little that the proceeds will last her two months. No problem at all. Steffen was wrong. It's not time to start thinking, it's time to stop. Time to pursue peaceful coexistence with everything as it is.

It's a nice thought, but it suddenly vanishes into thin air in light of what Dora sees next. There's something sticking up in the air. Something big. A black shadow in the moonlight, then a silhouette, finally the sharp outline of a vehicle. More precisely, the rear part of a vehicle. The front part is stuck in the ditch at the edge of the field, like the vehicle is doing a crooked headstand.

As she approaches, Dora slows down to give herself time to process the sight. The vehicle is a pickup truck, an older model, maybe from the eighties. In this position it looks huge, a bizarre sheet-metal sculpture like something out of a mystery series, *Tales from the Loop*, maybe, where strange things start happening because the village is on top of a particle accelerator. Next, the pickup truck will lift off from the ditch and begin hovering.

At a safe distance, she stops and dismounts. To get to the driver's door, she has to push Gustav across the road a bit because the back of the pickup is blocking the bike path. It's quiet and yet so chaotic. *En-tro-py*, her thoughts chant. The vehicle's wheels aren't moving. The engine is off. A special sort of silence surrounds the scene. Dora wonders how long the truck has been in this position. How long has no one come by? Or do the denizens of Bracken not even notice when a truck is stuck in the ditch? Peaceful coexistence with everything as it is, and no one cares about entropy?

She listens out into the darkness. No engine sounds. No airplanes, either. No human voices, not even an animal, unless you count the overzealous crickets. Dora considers the possibility that she's dreaming. Usually her dreams are less about whimsical sculptures, and more about annoying, everyday events like missed trains and botched presentations. It seems more likely that this pickup truck is not a dream, but so-called reality. But then where are the police, fire department, ambulance, road barriers, and gawkers that normally accompany such accidents? If it just happened, why didn't the driver get out and gaze at his towering car, all confused? Why didn't Dora hear anything on the way over? Or do such accidents barely make a sound? She realizes she has no experience with accidents at all. Who does anymore, in this blissfully accident-free era that everyone claims is drawing to a close? The most plausible scenario is that time has stopped. Yes, that must be it, time has stopped. Dora finishes walking around the truck and also comes to a stop.

She can tell by how jumpy her thoughts are that she's slightly in shock. Her brain braces itself for what she's about to find when she finally approaches the driver's cab. It's so quiet, you'd think the driver wasn't even there, that he's just gotten out and gone home to sleep it off. But no, unfortunately, Dora can see his back.

Car, road, trees, moon. The latter hangs high above the field, round and white, providing faint light. Dora just stands there, holding her bike by the handlebars, next to the towering pickup truck in the moonlight. It's quite the picture, actually. The emptiness of the landscape is reminiscent of the American West, as is the pickup. If Dora took a step back, she could leave the picture, look at it in peace, and think about how masterfully executed it is, how many stories it tells, a series of dramatic events condensed into one frozen moment. Then she could saunter on to the next painting, of a couple of people sitting in a bar at night.

But she can't. There's no stepping out of this. She's part of the picture, along with the moonlight, the backpack, the furry dog bed on the front rack of her bike. Someone else is standing in front of this particular picture, looking at Dora, wondering what will happen next.

She sets Gustav down and steps up to the driver's door. The man has followed the tilting motion of his truck, and is lying slumped over the steering wheel. He doesn't move. Dora knows she has to call someone. Police, ambulance, fire department. This sort of entropy has to be left to professionals. They're the ones with the tools: Jaws of Life, emergency stretchers, helicopters. But before any of that, she has to find out if the driver is responsive. The driver's window is down. The man has been driving with the window open, maybe to keep from falling asleep, maybe because it's a balmy spring night.

Of course, in truth, she's known all along. She recognized the pickup truck, and she recognizes the driver too. Shaved skull. Broad shoulders, washed-out T-shirt. He's got his hands on the top of the steering wheel and his head nestled between his arms. It looks comfortable. Because he's looking to the other side, Dora can't see his face. If he still has one. She's terrified his face might be gone. But there's no blood anywhere. No stains on the T-shirt, no splatter on the windshield.

And then she sees something else. His back is moving. His shoulders rise, his chest expands rhythmically with each steady breath. Dora slides a hand through the window and places it between the man's shoulder blades. Warm. Alive. She's so relieved she could cry. Attempted manslaughter, aggravated assault. All of a sudden, it doesn't matter anymore. Here lies a human being, and Dora is glad he's breathing. She strokes his Nazi back, pats his Nazi head, and finally gives his Nazi cheeks a couple of gentle smacks.

"Goth?"

She smacks him a little harder, and shakes his shoulder.

"Goth? Goth!"

The massive torso suddenly expands with a deep breath. Goth's arms twitch. Then he tries to sit up.

"Stay put. You have to stay still."

He lets his upper body slump back onto the steering wheel, but turns his head, trying to locate her voice.

"It's me, Dora. Your neighbor."

His eyes are closed. He looks like a newborn looking for its mother. Dora puts a hand on his forehead. Dry. Cool. She has never been so close to him. She's rarely this close to other people in general. She's never liked how friends and acquaintances are constantly hugging and kissing. Good thing Covid is putting an end to all that now. She runs her hand

over Goth's shoulder, which is surprisingly volumi-
nous, at least twice as built as Robert's. This here is
a different kind of creature, plummeted to Earth
from outer space in this rusty spacecraft. Crashin'
in Bracken.

"Hey," Dora says, sounding so affectionate she has
to clear her throat. "Recognize me?"

Goth opens his eyes. His expression is blank and
flat, as if he's seeing for the very first time. He nods,
but Dora is almost certain he can't see her. He braces
his hands against the steering wheel and partially
sits up, propping himself on his arms to keep himself straight.

"You should stay put, leave your head down. You
could be injured."

"Nah. I'm okay."

Dora notices he's not wearing a seat belt. She notices something else that seems important, but
can't quite put a finger on it.

"I'm calling the police now."

"No!"

His gaze clears. He looks directly at Dora and tries
to say something, but has trouble finding the right
words. Even so, Dora knows what it's all about.
There's no other person in sight who could've been
involved in the accident, nor is there any large animal carcass lying on the side of the road. Goth drove
into the ditch all by himself. He can't see properly,
can't speak properly. His blood alcohol is probably
through the roof. He's on probation. If the police
find him in this state, he'll most likely be put behind bars for quite some time. She hears Franzi's sad
voice: he's the best daddy in the whole wide world.

"Can your truck make it out of this ditch?"

"Four-wheel drive," Goth says. "Think so."

"You need to get in the passenger seat," Dora says.

He nods. Amazingly nimble, he manages to maneuver his massive body over the gearshift and handbrake to the other side, bracing himself against the glove compartment so he can sit upright in the forward-tilting car. Dora pulls the handle and the door opens. She throws her backpack onto the flatbed, where it immediately slides into the front-most corner. Getting in isn't easy, but it's not too hard, either. She has to move the seat forward a bit to reach the pedals, which she's almost standing on. The key is in the ignition. The engine starts. Even the lights work.

Once again Goth tries to explain something, and finally gestures to show her how to engage the differential lock. She has to give it a good throttle and slowly engage the clutch. The engine howls, the front tires find their footing. A jolt goes through the vehicle, it rocks back, the front wheels lose contact with the ground, then it tilts forward again, where it picks up the next thrust. Holding his hands flat, Goth makes a see-sawing motion in the air. Dora feels like she's at an amusement park. She feels how powerfully the wheels hit the ground. She steps on the accelerator even harder. Suddenly the pickup truck takes a mighty leap backward, and lands with all four wheels on solid ground, half on the bike path, half on the road.

Goth nods appreciatively, fumbles a pack of cigarettes out of his pocket, lights two and gives Dora one. Rarely has a cigarette tasted so good. Rarely has smoke looked better in the moonlight.

Dora jumps out of the car, pushes Gustav to the back of the pickup, opens the hatch, and heaves him onto the flatbed, cigarette dangling from the corner of her mouth. She gets back in, buckles up, and shifts into reverse with a crash. Goth rolls down the passenger window and puts his elbow over the door.

They drive off through the night, as wind swirls through the car. The truck is loud, and reeks of diesel. It's fun to drive. Dora wouldn't mind driving like this until dawn.

After ten minutes, the trip is over. They stop in front of Goth's house, and he gets out to open the gate. Relieved, she watches how effortlessly he moves. She slowly steers the pickup onto the lot and parks next to the house. Goth is already on his way to the trailer, so she has to run to catch up with him.

"Goth!" He turns around. "Are you sick?"

He shakes his head.

"Do you have a headache?"

He hesitates for a moment and shakes his head again.

"You want to go to the hospital?"

He grins and taps his forehead, as if to say: You're nuts.

"You can't drink that much anymore, Goth, you hear me? Especially not when you're driving. You could have gotten yourself killed. Or someone else."

He salutes her—military style, not Hitler style—and she decides to let it slide. Just to be on the safe side, she walks him to the trailer. He stoops low to push the key into the lock. When he's done, he straightens up.

"Dora—thanks." He's never used her name before. "G'night, Goth."

His cigarette-and-sweat scent is strangely familiar to her by now. He disappears into the trailer and locks it from the inside.

That's the moment she realizes what seemed so strange this whole time. One detail didn't fit into the broader picture. Now she's put her finger on it: Goth smells strong—as he always does, really. But he doesn't smell one bit like alcohol.

33

Father, Daughter

It's still Thursday, May 7, 11:30 p.m. Dora did the math yet again. The first Thursday of the month is Charité Day. So Jojo is in Berlin. She hates asking favors of him. She's not like Axel, who long ago decided to let other people take care of him. But this isn't about her. She just has to do something. Or maybe she should stay out of it. She's been lying in bed for an hour, tossing and turning. Falling asleep is out of the question. Jay's plush doggy bed is right next to her bed. The little dog is sleeping on her back and looks so happy, like she'd never want to leave this spot ever again. Gustav is resting out in the shed. On the other side of the wall, Goth is lying in his trailer. Everything is fine. If only it weren't for the alcohol—the key element Goth definitely didn't smell of.

Dora was never a fan of Jojo's neurology monologues, but she listened anyway. She knows the symptoms and what they mean. The only question is whether it's any of her business. And whether she wants to get any closer to that specific world of words. When certain terminology comes up, everything falls apart. She knows from experience, and it's an experience she doesn't want to relive, ever. The alternative is peaceful coexistence with whatever happens. After all, Goth is just a neighbor. A pretty impossible one at that. Scum, as Steffen says.

Jojo is probably already asleep. It would be ridiculous to wake him up now. Whatever the problem is, it can wait until tomorrow. Or next week.

Steffen's video has been available on YouTube for a week now, with lots of laughing smiley faces and ultra-aggressive comments. Scum in an undershirt.

She can't do it. She can't simply sit and do nothing. She has to talk to Jojo, at least. Ask a few questions. The dial tone sounds. She imagines the ringing on the other end of the connection resounding through his quiet Berlin apartment. Echoing through his spacious, sparsely furnished rooms. Long shadows cast by the streetlights pouring in from outside. Walnut shelves, leather couch, armchair, television set. A few carefully chosen pictures on the walls. Colorful Kemal carpets on the floor.

Ring, ring …

No dust bunnies, filthy crumbs, or pet hair anywhere. Jojo and his future wife maintain a level of order completely foreign to the world Dora inhabits. Its scent is that of cigarettes, shower gel, aftershave, and a general cleanliness bordering on godliness.

Ring, ring …

The prints in the living room above Savignyplatz are of paintings by Edward Hopper. No *Nighthawks*. Just a woman at the window, a man on the balcony.

Dora hangs up and tries his cell phone. Sometimes Jojo isn't even home at this hour. But she suspects he's lying in bed and just doesn't feel like answering the phone. Dora knows he, too, often can't sleep. Unlike her, he doesn't always expect rest. Which is why, for him, not sleeping results in exhaustion, at most, but not abject despair.

"Oh, it's you."

He recognized her number on his smartphone and answered right away. For a moment, Dora feels love for him.

"Hello, Jojo. You in bed already?"

"Almost. I'm sitting in my armchair, reading a fantastic novel by Ian McEwan. That man can describe a squash match as dramatically as the Battle of Verdun."

Of course he not only saves lives, drinks fine wines, and listens to modern classical music—in his ample leisure time he also enjoys international contemporary literature. It's like his entire life unfolds in the illustrious House of History, in an annex devoted to the Department of Civility and Humanism. He's a living memorial to the art of paying attention, and heralds a powerful message for Dora's generation, which has lost the ability to focus on anything for more than five minutes. Dora envies him, but still wouldn't want to trade places with him. Maybe someday she'll understand why.

"Out with it, then," he says, sounding quaintly old-fashioned, as if they were characters in a sitcom from the eighties.

Dora talks. Because she doesn't know where to start, she just tells him everything. About Heini and Goth, about Franzi and Jay, about the new furniture and the cleared yard, about the trip to the home-improvement store and the painting party. Jojo doesn't interrupt, he just listens. He grumbles in occasional agreement and sometimes utters little sounds of amazement. It feels so good to talk that Dora goes deeper and deeper in detail. She embellishes, loses herself in minutiae, makes characters and scenes come alive. Jojo shows no signs of impatience. Dora no longer understands whatever it is that sometimes comes between them. Why she often has the feeling that he's not the least bit interested in her. They've always been a team, one has always known what the other was thinking, no matter how much or how little they had to do with each other. Father and daughter, a story as old as mankind.

She tells him about the Horst Wessel song incident, and about Goth's friends. The bearded man, the tattooed man, and jacket man.

"Go on," says Jojo. "I'm just stepping out to the balcony for a smoke."

Dora, too, steps just outside the door and lights up. She hears the rattle of Jojo's lighter. Apparently Nazis and leading neurosurgeons are the sole remaining people you can still enjoy a cigarette with.

For a while they blow smoke silently into the nighttime spring air, one in Bracken, the other in Berlin.

Then Dora gets to the Plausitz knife attack. She realizes that she's ashamed. As if somehow she's to blame for what happened. Jojo doesn't say a word. No "Figures," no "See," no "I told you provincial Brandenburg wasn't the best idea." He just listens and keeps his mouth shut, which in his case is a form of extreme athletic endurance.

As she pauses, she hears him tap the next filterless cigarette from the soft pack. It's an authoritative sound, befitting a leading neurosurgeon, matter-of-fact and calm. Dora feels how it soothes her. Jojo has always been the kind of person whose mood can affect an entire room. Back when Dora and Axel were children, when he came home from work, they always listened for the sound of his footsteps. By the way he walked across the hall, they could tell if it was going to be a good or bad evening. If Jojo was stressed, everyone was stressed. If he was cheerful, everyone became cheerful. Dora's mother was the only one who could counter his moods. If he was gloomy, she'd laugh and say, "Oh, just go take a shower." Then, one way or another, she'd ensure the rest of the evening was pleasant.

As Dora drags out each detail, Jojo smokes his second cigarette in silence. Then he finally asks:

"The real reason you called is yet to come, isn't it?"

That's when she squares her shoulders, takes a deep breath, and tells him about how she found Goth and the pickup truck in the ditch. How she didn't call the police or the fire department to spare Goth any trouble with the authorities. How she single-handedly steered the truck out of the ditch instead.

Jojo doesn't ask if she's lost her mind. He says:

"That was pretty smart of you. His parole could be revoked for something like that."

"He couldn't speak," Dora says.

Jojo is silent for a moment. Then he says, "He must've been drunk as a skunk."

"I'm pretty sure he was sober," Dora replies. Jojo doesn't ask how she knows. He thinks it over.

"THC?" he asks.

"I don't think it's that, either."

She hears Jojo take one last drag and flick the cigarette off the balcony.

"I'm on my way over, then," he says.

The connection drops. This is probably the moment where books usually say, "suddenly everything happened so fast." Dora imagines a film playing in her head. It shows Jojo crossing his Charlottenburg apartment. In the hallway, he opens the coat closet and takes out a ready-packed, cognac-colored leather bag with brass clasps. He grabs a sports jacket from the hook and steps out the door. He runs down the stairs two steps at a time, and follows his own shadow across Savignyplatz, which is empty. He has no dog, but nevertheless has no curfew, either. He's a man on a mission. He takes long strides and quickly reaches the parking garage in the Stilwerk Building, where he rents a space for his car. Minutes later, he's gliding through the city in his Jaguar, perfectly air-conditioned, violin sounds streaming from the sound system, while the outside world silently passes by in the windows. On the highway, he hits the gas, and Dora can almost feel the acceleration like a large hand at her back, powerfully pushing her forward. The Violin Concerto is by Khachaturian, one of Jojo's favorite recordings, a little too lively for Dora's taste, but fitting for this drive in its sudden, churning drama.

Jojo drives, and Dora sits beside him in her thoughts. When they reach the interstate, he turns down the music and looks at her from the side.

"It's nice to be able to do something for you," he says.

Out of sheer surprise, Dora almost forgets that these words are only a figment of her imagination. They seem like a logical continuation of the phone call.

"You've been like this since you were a kid," Jojo says. "When you were three, you wanted to tie your own shoes every morning. Sat outside the door for half an hour, fighting with the laces. And you hissed like a cat when we tried to help you." With a quick glance over his shoulder, he changes lanes to pass a truck. "I always thought that was great. Your striving for autonomy. Axel is completely different. He probably still lets Christine tie his laces."

Jojo laughs, and Dora laughs along.

"Sometimes people hardly dare ask you how you're doing. You didn't even tell us about your move to the countryside."

"I thought you weren't interested," Dora whispers into the night.

"That's all right," Jojo says. "You and I are alike that way. I respect that." Still in the realm of fantasy, he leans over to pat her arm. "Anyway, I'm glad I can finally help you out."

34

Mr. Proksch

As the Jaguar drives up, the moon is even higher in the sky. Its silvery glow outshines the light of the stars, except for the evening star, which beams so brightly it could be mistaken for an approaching airplane. Jojo gets out, stretches his back, and looks around. Dora tries to see Bracken through his eyes. Featureless houses along a country road at night. The scent of manure and sand. It would be impossible to explain why she likes it to a man like Jojo. For him "city" is the only conceivable way of life, and "countryside" is just another word for being in a coma, or dead. He isn't here to be convinced otherwise.

Dora opens the gate and lets an impatiently whining Jay out. The dog greets Jojo on the grassy strip at the side of the road, euphorically wagging her entire rear end. After she's done rejoicing, she circles the yard, repeatedly lowering her angular body into the grass, stretching out, and getting up again, as if to extend the outer boundaries of her territory.

Dora takes the scene in. The lonely road. The shiny sedan in the light of the street lamps. Next to it, her perfectly poised father with silver at his temples, wearing a casual jacket and black jeans, and toting a leather bag, a complete stranger in this environment. A walking portal to another world.

She walks over and wants to hug him, but he

extends his elbow to her in greeting, grinning ironically, as if making fun of the rules rather than playing by them. Dora returns the gesture and says, just as ironically, "Welcome to Bracken!" Then she points out the surrounding houses now hunkered down for the night behind fences and walls.

"Me, Heini, Goth. There's even a cabaret artist just over there."

She adds that Steffen is gay and lives with a florist, as if to prove that Bracken has a few normal inhabitants, too, considering what someone like Jojo would consider normal. At the same time, she's ashamed of her words and ironic tone. She feels like a traitor.

"It's quite nice here," Jojo lies. "Where is he?"

Dora walks Jojo over to Goth's gate, the same gate she walked through just three hours ago with Gustav. It's still unlocked. She opens it a crack and lets her father enter.

The scene they walk into seems like another Hopper painting. A white plastic chair is overturned on the dark lawn. The table has been pulled up to the trailer window. There's a girl standing on the table. Her blonde hair hangs loose, reaching almost to the back of her knees. Both her hands are on the window, and she's pressing her face against the glass, trying to see inside. She's softly calling out, "Daddy, Daddy!" and gently knocking on the glass, which makes the most pitiful sound in the world.

Dora and Jojo stand, transfixed, until suddenly Jay-the-Ray shoots past them, dances around the table the girl is standing on, and doesn't give up until the little girl jumps down and takes the dog in her arms. Jay licks her face. Dora sees she's been crying.

"That's Franzi," she says, half to Jojo, half to herself.

Dora goes to the trailer, climbs up on the table herself, and shields the window glass with her hands. Inside, a dim light glows. It takes a while before Dora can make out anything. The trailer looks more spacious than she expected. It's furnished in light wood, and has a table with a sitting area, a kitchenette, and a cupboard with lots of doors and a small built-in TV. Everything looks clean and tidy. The inside windowsill is a narrow ledge covered in small carved wooden figurines. Several wolves, some lying down, some standing. A few human figures, too—a woman, a man, a child—but compared to the wolves, they're not as artfully crafted.

The bed is against the end wall of the trailer, shaded in darkness. There's a dark mound on it. Maybe it's a pile of blankets. Or a human body.

Dora climbs off the table and squats next to Franzi, who's sitting in the grass whispering baby words into Jay's ears.

"Franzi, is your father in there?"

The girl shrugs without looking up. "I dunno. It's dark."

Dora glances at Jojo, who's discreetly lingering in the background.

"Listen, Franzi. I need you to do me a favor." She shakes the girl lightly by the shoulder until she looks at her.

"Jay hasn't had dinner yet. She's really hungry. Can

you go over with her and feed her? You know where everything is."

Franzi's expression brightens. She nimbly pops up, takes Dora's house key, and runs off, barefoot as usual.

"Stay with her and keep her company, okay? I'll join you in a minute. You can help yourself to some food from the fridge, too."

Franzi nods eagerly and walks ahead, patting her thigh for Jay to follow. They don't go to the road, but further back, along the potato patch and deeper into the yard, to some secret Franzi-and-Jay loophole. The potato plants are only dimly visible, but look like they need watering.

Just to be thorough, Dora tries the handle of the trailer door. It's locked. Jojo has already started searching the property for the right tools. After a few minutes, he comes back with a rusty metal fence pole, which he must have pulled out of a bush.

If you only ever saw Jojo in his apartment at Savignyplatz, it would be easy to forget how practical he is. Dora's parents' house used to have a workshop in the basement where they tinkered together, making stilts, birdhouses, and once even a wooden climbing wall. Dora sanded the blocks of wood, worked the vise, and covered her ears when Jojo used the drill. They had their own lingo, and she was proud to know what "pass me the sixteener" meant.

Jojo deftly forces the pointed end of the bar into the crack and pries open the door. It swings around and hits the wall. Dora and Jojo flinch like unskilled burglars. They listen for any sound from the dark interior. Not a peep from the trailer. All around, the crickets continue their nocturnal concert. Jojo picks up his bag.

"What's his last name?"

"Proksch."

"Mr. Proksch, don't be alarmed," Jojo loudly announces. "I'm coming in to see you now." He enters. "Mr. Proksch?—He's here," he says, turning to Dora. Then he takes a few more steps. "Mr. Proksch?"

There's a grunt, followed immediately by Goth's voice, clear and distinct: "I'll bash your face in!"

Dora is so relieved she could almost cry. Goth is alive, that's for sure.

"Get out!"

"Mr. Proksch, I'm a doctor," Jojo says, unflappable. Dora marvels at his courage. "I'm going to do some tests with you. Can you tell me what day it is?"

The trailer door is pulled shut from the inside—Jojo knows how to respect his patients' privacy. Dora goes over to the wall separating their yards, turns Goth's fruit crate so it's on the taller end, and climbs up. She observes her house from a foreign perspective yet again. The kitchen light is on. Franzi's head isn't visible; she's probably squatting on the floor, sharing a bowl of dog food with Jay. So far, so good. Dora leaves her wobbly perch, shoves her hands in her pockets, and paces back and forth in Goth's yard, waiting. When doctors step in there's always a lot of waiting. With each step, she feels the ground beneath her feet. The turf, the earth beneath, layers of rock on an unimaginable scale, the whole, vast planet. It feels like she's spinning the globe with her walking, the way a circus bear spins its ball. Waiting compresses time, and ultimately dissolves it. How long has it been since she removed the remnants of her old life in Sus-Y's abandoned headquarters? Dora remembers it like an episode from the distant past. Something that once seemed exciting and has since lost all meaning. Now is now. Her father is with Goth. Jay is with Franzi. She herself is running back and forth to keep the planet spinning, because if it stops, everything will falter. Everything must remain as usual. Dora doesn't want anything to change. Not yet—not again.

The trailer door opens, and Jojo steps out, bag in hand.

"Mr. Proksch is just packing up a few things," he says formally.

Typical Jojo. Whenever he's in the vicinity of a patient, he transforms into lead physician Herr Professor Doctor Korfmacher, who inhabits a medical universe in which there are no people, only cases. Dora wouldn't be surprised if he started addressing her with the kind of formality usually reserved for people you're just meeting either.

"I'm taking Mr. Proksch in to the Charité for some more tests."

Herr Professor Doctor Korfmacher doesn't say "clinic," he says "Charité." And he doesn't go to just any Charité, he goes to the Charité, as if it were some mysterious place of worship.

"Right now?"

"Right now. You want to come along?" He stands stiffly erect in front of her, the leather bag firmly in his hand. He radiates impatience. Goth is rummaging around in the trailer.

"I have to stay with Franzi."

Jojo nods. It's all the same to him. There are no daughters in Doctorworld. People are always in a hurry and only think about the task at hand. Goth appears on the grate-metal steps, an almost empty-looking plastic bag in his hand. He stares at Jojo as if assessing whether this person might have a plug that can be pulled out. Jojo gestures, prompting Goth forward, and walks to the gate, his stride long and serious as ever. Dora hears him opening the trunk of the Jaguar at the roadside. The trunk slams shut again.

"Mr. Proksch!" Jojo shouts through the dark night.

Goth starts to move. As he passes Dora, he looks at her blankly. He follows Jojo's call like a dog follows its master. In Doctorworld, the lead physician is the boss. Not even someone like Goth can refuse his orders.

"I'll lock up here," says Dora. "And keep an eye on Franzi."

If Goth understands her, he doesn't let on. He disappears through the gate, the Jaguar's engine already humming. Two car doors slam shut, the car makes a two-point turn, accelerates, and drives off. The engine noise remains audible for a while before fading away down the country road.

Goth is gone. Someone has picked him up, as Steffen predicted, even if Jojo isn't exactly the garbage truck of history. Maybe this is worse than that. Dora knows from experience that in Doctorworld, it's never a good sign when someone's being taken somewhere.

35

Mass Effect

When the phone rings, it takes Dora a minute to get her bearings. It's still dark, and she feels body parts in her bed that don't belong to her or Jay. Arms, legs, and a whole bunch of hair. Franzi. Dora remembers finding the girl asleep, Jay in her arms, and that she herself also fell asleep surprisingly quickly, although she doesn't really like it when anyone is lying right next to her. Hastily, she answers the call before its ringing wakes Franzi up.

"Hold on a sec, Jojo."

She slips into jeans and a sweatshirt and heads out the door. A bright glow appears on the eastern horizon. The birds are chirping away, so eager you might think they were tasked with bringing the new day about solely through the power of song. There are still a few isolated stars here and there in the sky. It will be sunny once more, cloudless, as if the question of weather had been settled once and for all, and will never change again. The hydrangeas need water. Not to mention the potatoes. Today Dora will get right on it. Not just the potatoes. Everything.

"Almost there ..."

She clamps her cell phone between her shoulder and ear, and extracts a pack of cigarettes from her pants pocket. If she keeps this up, she'll become a chain smoker. But she can deal with her nicotine addiction some other time. In all probability, what comes next can only be endured while smoking.

She recognizes Khachaturian's violins in the background. So Jojo is back on the road yet again, at the crack of dawn, en route from Berlin to Münster, where he'll presumably give a lecture, sit in on some important meeting, or perform an emergency operation in three hours. Dora tries to calculate whether he slept at all. Out of the question. Maybe he didn't even go back by his apartment. Straight from the Charité to the highway.

"Ready?" He still seems a bit formal, but is no longer fully in Doctorworld. Actually, it sounds like he's in a pretty good mood. It's crazy, Dora thinks, what people are capable of achieving when they truly believe in what they are doing.

"Okay, I'm ready. How'd it go?"

"Good question." Jojo laughs. "During the drive to Berlin, your gym buddy didn't say a word."

"He's not my gym buddy."

"Even on the ward, he was very quiet at first. Things were calm, there's not much going on at the moment."

Jojo has told this story several times before: Because of the Covid-crisis curfew, there isn't much activity in the emergency rooms. On top of that, forty percent of the beds are empty because everyone is postponing examinations and operations. If we manage to save people from Covid, he's taken to saying, they'll start dropping like flies from heart attacks and strokes.

"Luckily for us, that means all the equipment was open." Jojo takes a drink. He probably bought a large coffee at the gas station. "And, you know, my team at the Charité is always at the ready. Even in the middle of the night. All it takes is one phone call and the machine is up and running."

That's Jojo's favorite topic: loyalty, team spirit, unconditional devotion to duty, and the fact that he presides over this well-oiled machine staffed by superlative humans. It's like he's some kind of admiral, or general—a medical general instead of a military one. Everyone heeds his command, from the senior officers to the lowly infantry who empty the bedpans and mop the hallways. Even at three in the morning.

"Dr. Bindumaalini took it upon herself to come in personally. She's my best radiologist, a veritable MRI prophet. Unfortunately, when your gym buddy saw her, he kind of freaked out."

"He's not my …"

"He called Dr. Bindumaalini a fucking foreigner, and basically insisted she be deported right then and there."

"Oh my God."

Dora is so ashamed on Goth's behalf that it hurts. Jojo laughs. Embarrassing her, just a tiny bit, is a mood booster for him. Buoyed, he goes on.

"Dr. Bindumaalini explained to him the examination she was about to perform, and he explained to her that she wouldn't survive it. It took four orderlies to subdue him. Your gym buddy really is strong, I'll give him that."

Jojo's teasing is the price she pays for having made him pull an all-nighter. Humoring him is the least Dora can do. So she lets out an agonized groan.

"Then, when he knocked a coat rack over, Dr. Bindumaalini withdrew for the time being. The blond X-ray technician managed to calm him down quite easily."

"Oh. My. God."

"We gave him a tranquilizer before the scan. Otherwise he'd never have held still."

Dora realizes that this thoroughly unpleasant report was probably the more pleasant part of the still-evolving conversation. She decides to light another cigarette.

"And?"

"And then they took him to a room so he could sleep it off. I had to leave, I have a couple of appointments in Münster at nine. Dr. Bindumaalini just called me."

"And?"

"Your gym buddy won't talk to anyone."

Every time Jojo says "gym buddy," it creates a little more distance between her and Goth. A gym buddy isn't a real person, it's more of a situation. Dora begins to suspect Jojo isn't just out to annoy her. Deep in his medical-general chest beats a very human heart that would rather deal with gym buddies than living creatures.

"What do you mean? He won't let anyone talk to him?"

"Dr. Bindumaalini failed to tell him the results. He's been covering his ears and yelling at her to leave him alone. He said he didn't want to know a thing."

"Ugh."

"Y'know, everyone has a right to *not* know. If he's uncooperative, there's nothing we can do. It's his choice."

"And?"

"And so he's sleeping again. Like a baby. When he was done yelling at Dr. Bindumaalini, he just fell asleep. Can you believe that?"

"And?"

"And—there's another problem. Your gym buddy doesn't seem to have health insurance."

This news throws Dora for a moment, but Jojo keeps talking.

"Don't worry about last night's assessment, we'll take care of that internally. But, going forward, Mr. Proksch isn't really in a position to seek medical attention."

"What does that mean, exactly?"

"It might not mean a thing. There's not much that can be done, medically speaking, anyway."

"Geez, Jojo!" Dora can't take it anymore. "Just tell me what the goddamned MRI showed!"

"The MRI isn't a damnation, it's a blessing to humankind." Jojo yawns. "And I'm sworn to secrecy." He takes another drink. Dora imagines a giant latte in a to-go cup. "I'm not supposed to give you any more information. Really."

Dora really doesn't want any more information, either. In fact, the whole thing was a terrible idea anyway. What was she thinking, dragging Jojo into this? Goth's BS is none of her business. If he doesn't want to know anything, then she certainly doesn't. She wants to end the conversation, go back to bed, and forget all about it. Sorry, made a mistake, how dumb of me. Let's move on. Just keep going.

"Okay, Jojo. Well then, I'd just like to thank you very much, and—"

He immediately interrupts her.

"On the other hand, I've also taken the Hippocratic Oath. And that's sometimes better served by not being overly strict about things."

"I'd say we should definitely stick to the rules," Dora says. "This is already way too complicated as it is."

"Your gym buddy is going to need support."

"He's not my gym buddy!" Dora reiterates. "He isn't even a friend!" Now she's almost shouting. "He's my neighbor. I was just trying to help. If he doesn't want it, he doesn't want it. That's that. It's all good, really, no problem."

"That's not how this works." Jojo's raising his voice now, too. "This isn't some game you can just back out of. You wanted me to come, now you're in it. I'm doing my job, and I'm doing it the best I can. Understood?"

In fact, Dora understood that even as a child. He might as well have added: the best I can, and at all costs. She doesn't say a word. She doesn't have the strength to argue with Jojo. Not at six in the morning, not after such a night.

"I'll send you the necessary information, prescriptions, and behavioral instructions. The rest is up to you. Got it?"

She nods, though of course he can't see it. She realizes what comes next. One of those words. She's always loathed those words. Words are capable of creating disease. Disease words are like germs. Her childhood home was completely contaminated by disease words. Glioma, blastoma, carcinoma, astrocytoma. The words stuck to all the walls, piled up in all the corners. That's what made her mother sick. Neuroendocrine tumor. Another one of those words. Such words rob you of everything and everyone you hold dear. No one should ever use them. No one should ever say them out loud, or even think them. No one should ever have to hear them. Dora understands why Goth covered his ears. She'd like to do the same.

"The brain scan reveals that Mr. Proksch has a tumor occupying significant space. You have already noticed the resulting mass effect."

A third cigarette before breakfast is definitely a bad idea. So, in the grand scheme of things, it's perfectly called for in this situation.

"My assessment is that it is a glioblastoma."

Glioblastoma is the shittiest word of all shitty words. A dark warlord cloaked in the form of twelve little letters. The Darth Vader of medical parlance. He's invariably accompanied by his aides-de-camp, who are named Inoperable, Incurable, and Palliative. Immediately, Dora decides to take a shortcut. Getting in Darth Vader's way is utterly pointless.

"How much longer does he have?"

"The prognosis is poor. Of course, in some cases ..." It's not often that Jojo doesn't finish a sentence. "Oh, what the hell—you ask, so I'll tell you. Mr. Proksch has symptoms of massive failure. You know what that means."

"I want to know how long he has."

"A few months at most. If that."

A question creeps into Dora's mind: Was it the same with her mother, back when she was a little girl and felt like the world was ending? Did someone say "at most" then, too? Right after saying "neuro-endocrine"? Dora has to stop these thoughts. An abyss opens up inside her, so profound that not even bubbles rise from its depths. Is it possible to collapse in on yourself and just disappear? What would be left? A black hole?

"What's next?" Her system is kicking into coping mode. Jojo joins in. The question of what comes next is his lifeblood.

"When Mr. Proksch wakes up, we'll send him home by ambulance. Before that, he gets a starting dose of steroids and something for the pain." Dora nods to herself. That sounds reasonable. It's a plan. "I'll send all the paperwork—doctor's letter, prescriptions, a schedule for his medications—by courier. Everything has to be taken strictly as directed."

"Do I have to inform his wife? And what about—?" She was about to say "Franzi," but can't bring herself to say her name.

"That's up to you," Jojo says. "But please keep in mind, I've broken confidentiality."

Dora understands. Officially, she knows nothing. It's a protection, not just for Jojo, but for herself. It offers her some breathing room. It's the shadow she'll operate in going forward.

"The most important thing is that he not be allowed to drive anymore. Do you hear me, Dora? Under no circumstances should he get behind the wheel. He's not only endangering himself, but others as well."

"And just how am I supposed to stop that, huh?" Dora hears her voice grow shrill. Her coping mode is failing again. "Am I his guardian, or what? Damn it, Jojo, I barely know the guy! What the hell am I supposed to do?"

"Have some coffee first." Jojo takes another sip as well. The Khachaturian spirals up toward its finale. "You asked me for help, and that means something. I don't know what it means, but you'll figure that out." In the background, the audience applauds. "Good luck, my dear. Call me if you have any questions. I have to get on the highway now."

As soon as Jojo hangs up, Dora opens the browser on her phone and searches for a specific YouTube channel. She clicks on LUP and on the first video posted. There's Krisse. Maybe she should send the "paperwork" Jojo was talking about to him. With best regards from the scales of justice—blind justice, who balances everything in the end. Three minutes and 42 seconds into the video, she finds the spot she's looking for. Counter the population exchange with an Ethnic Mass Effect. She replays it, over and over. Ethnic Mass Effect, Ethnic Mass Effect. Finally she manages to laugh, and once she starts, she can't stop. She laughs until her stomach hurts. She succumbs to total hysteria. Then she goes to the kitchen and brews up the strongest coffee ever.

36

First Early Potatoes

"Can we harvest these already?"

Instead of answering, Franzi shrugs. Dora sighs. She's standing in Goth's potato patch, spraying coarse dirt off her hands with the garden hose and rubbing the cool water on her face. She's exhausted and sweaty, having spent the last few hours laboring like a madwoman. She swept all the rooms of her house, did the laundry, and cleaned the kitchen. Then she watered the hydrangeas and the vegetable garden, weeded, and pulled up several square yards of nettles. Ever since Franzi got up, Dora has had an annoying assistant. The girl doesn't leave her side, following her everywhere like a little shadow, trying to help but invariably getting in the way. They've rehearsed their new dialogue a hundred times by now: "When's Daddy coming back?" "Soon."

To get rid of Franzi, Dora sent her over to Goth's place, even though he isn't there. Instructions: clean your room. Twenty minutes later the little girl was back. Dora took pity on her, so she followed Franzi up the dusty stairs of the main house in order to praise her progress. Since she was already there, she decided she might as well move the bed, air the room out, clean the windows, mop the newly cleared floor and, finally, decorate the walls with the pictures Franzi painted. Afterwards, the room looked so warm and welcoming that Franzi clung to her arm and exclaimed, "Thank you, thank you, thank you!"

Unfortunately, the room-cleaning campaign only increased Franzi's attachment, so that every step Dora took now landed on a child's foot or a dog's paw. Once again she sent both child and dog out to the field, to see if there were enough early blooming plants to pick a wildflower bouquet for Goth's return. Dora took advantage of the lull to finally search the trailer. She did it hastily, her jaw clenched, as if she could somehow lock the discomfort away behind her teeth. Thank God she quickly found what she was looking for: one pair of keys on the hook next to the door, a second in the table drawer, both for Goth's pickup. She also found another bunch, which she recognized as her own front door keys. She took the opportunity to shake out his blankets, dust, and clean the almost empty refrigerator. Relieved, she left the trailer and began watering Goth's potatoes, which were as thirsty as her own. Dora read on the internet that early potatoes are harvested while the cabbage is still green, about sixty days after sowing. She calculates. When she moved to Bracken, Goth's seed potatoes were already in the ground. Perhaps because of the mild winter, he planted them as early as the beginning of March.

The water cools her palms and forehead, which feels wonderful. Franzi picked a large bouquet of clover, dandelion, speedwell, and bittercress, and set it on the table in the trailer. Now she wants to cool off, too. Dora holds the hose out to her, and the girl washes her hands, arms, and face. Dora finally takes a deep breath for the first time all day. The weight of Goth's keys rests heavily in her pants pocket. It's a reassuring feeling.

Strictly speaking, nothing at all has changed. It's still early May, a totally normal Friday. Spring is entering its height, it no longer cools down as much at night, and the days are already getting quite warm. The fruit trees in Dora's yard are in bloom, which makes it look as if they're covered in white foam. She's even seen a few bees, although according to recent reports there aren't really any bees anymore. Everything is as it should be. Only now an additional phrase has entered her vocabulary. *Mass effect.* At least it sounds friendlier than *glioblastoma.* Still Darth Vader, but dressed in spring-green camo. Because of that word, Dora has been struggling since the wee hours of the morning to regain control of everything. Now she realizes she might as well just let go and take it all in: the keys are heavy, the sky is blue, and tractors are abuzz all around the village. Everything that has wings and a voice is in the air and singing. On the wall, an orange tabby walks by and looks down at them contemptuously. You are so embarrassing, you and your whole species, the cat's eyes seem to say.

Indeed, they look rather roughed up. Dora is still wearing the T-shirt she slept in. Jay's underside is muddy from digging. Franzi ostensibly washed herself up, but what she really did was just turn the dirt into mud and spread it all over her arms and face. The cat settles down to diligently clean her right paw. As she does so, she pretends not to notice the two redstarts scolding her in an attempt to lure her away from her nest.

"When's Daddy coming back?"

"Soon."

Dora slips her left hand into her pocket and grips the keys tightly.

"Why's he in the hospital?"

"Told you already, they did some tests."

"'Cause of his headaches?"

"That's right."

"But he doesn't have anything bad?"

Dora steps away to turn off the water.

"Can you show me how to harvest potatoes?" she asks.

"Of course!"

Franzi sprints off and returns immediately with a tool that looks like a large bird's claw. Dora wonders if Goth will beat all three of them to a pulp for tampering with his potato patch. But then again it doesn't really matter anymore. They're already goners. Franzi reaches into the soil with her claw and loosens the soil around a plant until she gets hold of the stalk, which she steadily pulls on. What comes to light actually does look like a clutch of alien eggs. A nest of dirt-smeared eggs in a tangle of white veins. Slightly disgusted, Dora watches as Franzi picks the eggs out, wipes them with her hands, and throws them into the grass. She forbids herself from thinking about glioblastomas again.

"Still pretty small," Franzi says.

"We can cook 'em anyway," says Dora.

"Daddy, Daddy, Daddy!"

Dora didn't hear the sound of the engine or the

gate opening. But here he comes, big steps, plastic bag in hand. He looks as if he's flickering a bit around the edges, as if he's been sloppily cut out and pasted into this picture. Dora runs toward him.

"Goth!"

He doesn't dignify her with a glance. Instead, he shoos Jay away with his foot, pushes Franzi aside when she tries to hug his legs as he walks, and storms straight toward the trailer. He yanks open the door, disappears inside, and the door slams shut. Then it swings open again, and the jar with Franzi's wildflower bouquet flies through the air. It makes a high arc, then lands in the grass. Jay yelps, the cat on the wall yawns, and Franzi bursts into tears.

Asshole, thinks Dora. Why don't you just die already, as fast as you can? Free the world from your presence. It'd be the best thing for everybody, not to mention a boon to the local political balance.

She'd have liked to indulge that train of thought for a while, but she has to concentrate on Franzi, who's now sobbing in her arms. Dora gently shushes her, says something about Daddy just being a little stressed, and wishes she were far, far away. If only Alexander Gerst could beam her up to the International Space Station.

After a late lunch, with the pretext that Jay-the-Ray urgently needs to go for a walk, she sends both dog and girl off into the woods, connected by a leash. She needs some breathing room to make further preparations. She hides the keys to the pickup in the planter of the big palm tree. UPS delivers a thick envelope from Charité Berlin. She works through the documents and then reads a whole lot of disturbing medical details on the internet that she doesn't really want to know. She relieves a screw box of its contents and labels the empty compartments with days of the week. She calls the Elbe-Center pharmacy and places a bulk order. Because she's still full of nervous energy afterwards, she writes a shopping list, cleans her fridge, and starts to worry because Franzi and Jay aren't back from the woods yet.

A fat fly bumps into the kitchen window with a loud buzz. Dora sits at the table and experiences the crystal-clear feeling of not wanting to live anymore. What's the point? She's just buzzing around like that fly, bumping up against the glass, a swirl of prickling bubbles brewing in her body. She'd gladly trade places with Goth. Then he can go shopping for her while she waits for it all to end.

Dora does what she's taken to doing lately when she feels stuck: she goes to the wall, climbs up on the lawn chair, and looks over. She wants to see if Franzi and Jay have come back. When she sees Goth sitting at the camp table in front of the trailer, she recoils. He's smoking and watching his fingers drum a slow rhythm on the tabletop. He's no longer flickering around the edges. He looks the same as ever.

"Goth!"

He immediately raises his head, as if he'd just been waiting to hear her voice. He comes over to the wall and climbs onto the fruit crate.

"Hey," he says. "How's it going?"

"Okay," Dora says hesitantly. "You?"

"Good."

They look at each other, heads almost level, he on his box, she on her chair, a wall of hollow cinder-blocks between them. Goth's upper body lightly leans against the wall, so their faces are fairly close.

"My father sent some prescriptions for you," she says.

"For the headaches."

"You have to take the pills regularly."

"I will."

Dora looks into his eyes, her gaze intent, like she's trying to see inside his head. For the first time she notices he has green eyes and light eyelashes. The whites of his eyes have a yellowish sheen interspersed with fine red veins. The bags underneath are swollen as always. They aren't pretty eyes. But they're so trusting that Dora's heart clenches up a bit. Somewhere in there something is growing. Like a first early potato. She wonders if Goth knows. She searches his eyes for a hint of horror. Doesn't a head have to know what's going on inside it? There must be different kinds of knowing. Knowing and not knowing can probably coexist without interfering with one another in the slightest.

"I have to tell you something else, Goth."

"You took the keys."

Say what you will, he isn't slow on the uptake.

"My dad says you absolutely must not drive."

"Must be cool to have a dad like that."

She quickly checks his expression; there isn't a hint of irony in it.

"No," she says, "not really." She thinks for a moment. "Sometimes I'd have preferred to have a father who did something normal. A bricklayer or carpenter or auto mechanic."

"I'm a carpenter."

Dora raises her brows in surprise. "You do stuff with wood?"

"I do stuff with wood." He laughs. "I always thought the city was full of smart people. But you really are dumber than all of them put together."

"Maybe that's why I moved here." Dora grins. "You still working as a carpenter?"

"Haven't for a while now."

"Why not?"

He shrugs. "Been sick too often, I guess."

"You get government assistance?"

"I'm not stupid."

"What do you mean?"

"Nobody likes to be treated like a piece of shit."

Dora wonders if she will soon be the piece of shit seated in front of a job counselor. But somehow, for now, it doesn't matter. She's glad Goth isn't angry with her. Apparently he accepts that she sicked Jojo on him. Maybe, in his own way, he's even grateful that she did.

"How do you make ends meet?"

"Something always comes up, things just work out. I don't need much."

They've never talked like this before. He smells different too. Apparently he showered at the hospital. He's also wearing a T-shirt she hasn't seen before, dark blue and not so heavily worn. On the chest it says *Criminal Worldwide*. Dora decides that now is not the time to laugh about it. Instead, it's time to broach a difficult subject.

"Listen, Goth. I need your pickup."

"Huh?"

"Grocery shopping, hardware store, pharmacy. You're not allowed behind the wheel." She almost added *ever again*, but thought better of it. "If you ever need to go somewhere, I'll drive you."

"So now you're my mommy?"

"Just a little neighborly helping hand. You do the same, y'know."

"That's different."

"Why? Because I'm a woman?"

"The truck's mine."

"You can't drive it, Goth."

"Touch my pickup and I'll break every bone in your body."

That went well. Goth raises a huge hand. Dora has big hands, too, but Goth's look more like an action figure's hands than a mere mortal's. He slides his arm over the wall, too slow for a slap. He awkwardly strokes her tousled hair.

"Fine." He steps off the fruit crate and moves away.

A little later, Dora peeks over again. She expected to find the yard deserted, the trailer barricaded, Goth hunkered down in his den like a wounded animal. Instead, he's sitting at the camping table, upright and with healthy color to his cheeks. Franzi is with him, the cheerful chatter echoing all the way to the wall, dishing the cooked first early potatoes onto two plates. They eat together, father and daughter, passing each other salt and mayonnaise. In the middle of the table sits a bouquet of wildflowers in a jar.

37

Unicorn

At seven in the morning, she can be sure Goth is still asleep. As quietly as possible, she opens the gate and curses under her breath as the hinges squeak. There's the pickup. She fleetingly registers that one headlight is cracked and the front license plate is missing, surely a result of that dive into the ditch. But she has no time for trivialities. Gaining momentum, she tosses Jay onto the passenger seat and starts the engine. Now it's no longer about being quiet, it's about being fast. The engine roars, Dora backs out of the driveway and onto the road. She feels like a thief about to get caught. She thinks she hears Goth's voice, rising with anger. As she pulls away, she glances at the side mirror to see if he might be following her along the side of the road like in a DO-GOODER clip.

A few miles outside Bracken, her heart begins to calm down. She tempers her speed, opens the window, and enjoys how the breeze carries the smell of the forest. A small woman in a big truck. Bonnie and Clyde rolled into one. What would Robert say if he saw her in this beast of a machine? "You've sure changed, Dora."

The Elbe-Center parking lot is almost empty. The stores don't open for another half hour. Dora goes to the bakery for coffee and a croissant, then sits cross-legged on the flatbed with them. Pickup picnic. Back in Berlin people would turn to stare, especially in Kreuzberg. Here, no one pays her any attention. The guy in the chicken truck, who has a cigarillo dangling from the corner of his mouth and is just getting the grill going, hasn't looked at her even once.

Dora imagines what it would be like to get a makeover so that her look matched that of this pickup. She'd need a textured hairstyle with blonde highlights instead of a brunette ponytail. Heavy boots, counterfeit cigarettes, and a Nazi-chic Thor Steinar sweatshirt. And a raw pork mincemeat sandwich instead of a croissant.

It must be nice. Relaxing, even. The calm after the surrender. For years, Dora has worried about democracy in general and Europe in particular. She has put up with Farage, Kaczyński, Strache, Höcke, Le Pen, Orbán, and Salvini. Watched the AfD's triumphant advance. Watched the media treat every violation of political correctness as a crime, while simultaneously eroding all limits on what can or cannot be said on talk shows and in online comments. She has begun wondering who other people vote for. What goes on behind the closed doors of their brains while they pick up their kids or go shopping. The sole certainty is that everyone is afraid, and everyone thinks their own fear is justified. Some are afraid of foreign infiltration, others of climate catastrophe. Some are afraid of pandemics, others of healthcare-based dictatorships. Dora fears that all these conflicting fears will be democracy's downfall. And, just like everyone else, she believes everyone else has gone crazy.

It's so damn exhausting. It'd be so much easier to just pick a side. Robert did, but she couldn't. Maybe she'd find it easier with the opposing team. Throw on a Thor Steinar sweatshirt and shout about how Europe was a shitty idea from the get-go. Suddenly everything would be logical, everything would make sense. Goth would be just a neighbor and the AfD would be just another party with alternative ideas. The songs she's heard by the band Frei.Wild aren't actually all that bad. Bye-bye brooding skepticism, hello carefree narrow-mindedness. Surely Nazis aren't plagued by insomnia or prickling bubbles. Surely they don't worry their hands are too big.

As a child, Dora sometimes lay down on the carpet in the living room and imagined the ceiling was the floor, so her back was actually glued to the ceiling. The chandelier stood like a statue in the middle of the room, the windows started just above the floor and had handles that were way too high, and if you wanted to walk through a door you'd have to climb over a very high threshold. In her mind, Dora wandered through this strange room, delighting in its crazy setup. She remembers how easy it was to flip the switch in her mind. Make the tiniest effort, and reality follows new laws. Just choose a new perspective.

Maybe the local REWE sells Thor Steinar sweatshirts.

When she pushes the shopping cart out to the truck an hour later, she doesn't have a new sweatshirt, but she does have a bunch of bulging paper bags. It's dreamy to just load everything onto the flatbed instead of hauling everything to the bus stop, sweating. She shudders to think what the pharmacy trip cost. Because of Goth's health insurance issue, Jojo wrote private prescriptions. The total blows all her calculations out of the water. How long will her money last? Ha.

On the way back to Bracken, her heart starts racing again. She feels like taking another little joyride, but that wouldn't solve the problem, it would only postpone it. On the one hand, she doesn't think Goth will do anything rash. Surely he wouldn't hurt her just because she took the pickup. She can't picture him dragging her out of the cab, throwing her to the ground, kicking the shit out of her. On the other hand, she probably should expect a reaction like that. Given the scene with Dr. Bindumaalini, it's clear he tends to snap. Besides, Steffen already warned her—although Goth has behaved reasonably in Dora's presence so far.

As she lets up on the accelerator and passes the town sign, she sees the yellow arm of a wheel loader looming behind Goth's wall. The vehicle's bucket is up in the air, and it's backing out from his yard. Dora stops and turns on the hazard lights to make it easier for the wheel loader to maneuver. The behemoth carefully creeps onto the road, thanks her with a flash of its headlights, and roars past her at astonishing speed. She takes advantage of the open gate to make a sweeping turn into Goth's driveway.

Next to the main house there's a brownish rectangle in the grass where the pickup is always parked. It's as if a picture had been taken off the wall. Dora maneuvers the truck right onto its outline and turns off the engine. In a single bound, Jay-the-Ray leaps from the passenger seat onto her lap and from there out through the open driver-side window to pounce on Franzi, who is sitting on the ground next to the camping table, examining something. Dora is always amazed at how athletic the little dog can be when it counts.

She stays at the wheel for a while, pretending to read something on her phone, and waits to see what happens. Like a kid with a bad report card goofing off in the street instead of going home.

But no one seems to care what she's up to. Nobody even notices her return. Goth stands in the middle of the yard, contentedly admiring a huge piece of tree trunk lying in the grass in front of him, which is obviously what the wheel loader just delivered. He walks around it, examining the colossus from all sides, while merrily whistling to himself. Thankfully, it's not the Horst Wessel song. It's a children's song that Dora has heard on the radio: "I'm a unicorn, that's how I was born." It's a dreadful earworm. She gets out and stands next to him. Together they look at the wood as if it were a famous landmark. Which, in a way, it is.

"Cool, huh?" asks Goth.

"Impressive," nods Dora.

The log is twelve feet long and so thick that even a giant like Goth can't hug it. Its gleaming bark is greenish-gray and soft as skin, the cut surfaces are a shiny yellow and intensely fragrant. Its annual rings are clearly visible. The tree must've been over a hundred years old.

"Maple," Goth says. "There's nothing better for carving."

Dora shudders as her imagination revs up again. She pictures a farmer planting the little sapling in the yard behind his house shortly after World War I, perhaps to commemorate the fact that his wife had given birth to a son, or because the war was over and everything was going to be better from then on. By the time the maple's trunk is as thick as a thigh, World War II is sweeping across the planet. The farmer's son refuses to serve in the army and is shot, and part of the family flees to the West after the Nazis surrender. The farmer stays behind, the new socialist regime expropriates everything, and he hangs himself. The maple continues to grow. The maple is now in the GDR. It sees the farmhouse decay and the yard go wild. After reunification, it's over sixty feet tall. Each spring, armies of bees buzz in its enormous crown. Every autumn it releases its seeds, which float to the ground like helicopters touching down. Around it, vast numbers of its sprouts grow all over the property. The maple greets the new homeowners with the peaceful rustle of its leaves—after all, it's the real reason they bought the house. The grand maple makes the dilapidated estate look stately. It doesn't hold it against the new owners when they uproot all the saplings and turn the wilderness back into a yard. The maple now stands in the midst of globalized turbo-capitalism, just as it has stood in all other systems. Nazism, socialism, waves of refugees and expulsions have done it no harm.

What finally brings it down is the twenty-first century's mania for optimization, in the form of an over-eager landscaper who tells the homeowners that the roots of the huge tree will one day attack the foundations of the house. Besides, disposing of its leaves each fall is a lot of work, and if a branch comes crashing down in a storm, it could kill someone. The husband gets a permit. The wife cries when the tree falls.

"It was a steal," Goth says. "It pays to have good buddies."

Dora pulls out two small cardboard boxes and pries the pills out through the foil. High-dose cortisone and a powerful painkiller. Goth reaches out, she places the pills on his palm, he tosses them in his mouth, and swallows without water. It's as if they've done nothing but pass pills to each other all their lives.

"Be careful with the paring knives, they're sharp!"

Now Dora realizes what Franzi's up to. There's a leather case containing various tools on the ground next to her. Carving knives of all sizes, various chisels, even a couple of small axes.

"I've always wanted to make a second one," Goth says.

Dora's gaze wanders to the wooden sculpture sitting next to the trailer steps. The wolf looks at them, expectantly.

"I wanna carve something, too," Franzi says.

"Just a sec. I'll get you some wood scraps."

Goth walks to the back entrance of the main house and enters like it's no big deal. He returns carrying a chainsaw in one hand, as if it's a toy. Dora hears him sing, *I'm a maple tree, and I was born free.* She can barely stifle her laughter.

"Did you get any beef-neck steaks?" he asks. She has to think a moment, then shakes her head. "Then you can head right back out." With his free hand, he reaches into his pants pocket and pulls out a crumpled-up twenty-euro bill. "But skip the supermarket, go to the butcher in Wandow. Six pieces, in herb marinade."

He revs up the chainsaw, which howls like a wild animal.

38

Beef

The chainsaw grumbles and growls all afternoon, so insistently that Dora forgoes gardening and closes all the windows. But it's audible inside too. The sound gnaws its way into the brain like the screeching of a dentist's drill. When she decides to go for a walk, it follows her quite a ways into the woods. Throughout their excursion, Jay creeps three feet behind her, demonstratively disapproving of such a pointless enterprise. The dog is offended because Franzi has been squatting on the ground in Goth's yard for hours, engrossed in whatever it is she's carving, and using her arms to shield it from prying eyes.

Around eight o'clock in the evening, Dora goes over again. For once, she doesn't bother peeking over the wall, isn't look for her missing dog, nor is she plotting to steal Goth's pickup. Instead, she cradles a salad bowl in her arms as if she's headed to a party. She's even swapped her sneakers for sandals, despite the fact that the invitation was a mere three mumbled words: "Barbecue—c'mon by."

As she walks through the gate, Goth nods to her, barely looking up from what he's doing. Gripping a knife with both hands he peels long strips of the trunk of maple, which now stands upright, has been cleared of bark, and shaped into a rough cone.

Dora is glad the chainsaw is silent. But there is no grill in sight. She sets the salad on the table and sits down. Jay squats down next to Franzi and pouts.

Dora doesn't like waiting. It has always struck her as a supreme waste of time. It's both pointless and humiliating to boot, because for every person who waits, there's someone making them wait. But now, seated on this camping chair, she feels in tune with the world, as if she has found her new purpose. Going unnoticed is glorious. It's glorious not to know what's to come. To be the one merely watching, while everyone else busily keeps the story going.

After half an hour, Goth sets the tool aside, grasps the log with both arms, tips it over onto the grass as if it were papier-mâché, and rolls it to the edge of the fire pit, where the wood scraps are piled in a wreath of stones. Dora hadn't noticed the fire pit before. He hands her a cigarette without asking if she wants one, sets a long chip of wood on fire, lights both their cigarettes with it, and then throws it onto the pile, which hesitantly begins to burn. Franzi skips over, tossing dry twigs into the flames until they flare up. Then she fetches some thick, well-seasoned logs from somewhere, and Goth places each into the fire with a practiced hand.

The fire grows at breathtaking speed. The air gets so hot Dora has to step back. It crackles and pops. Fountains of sparks rise into the sky. Franzi cheers and brings more and more logs, which her father willingly feeds to the fire. It smells good, like smoke and freedom. Dora can't recall the last time she stood by a fire. But she distinctly recalls how her incessantly questioning brain falls silent as she's staring into the flames. Just like when she's at the seaside watching waves lap the shore.

At some point, Goth stops his daughter from fetching more logs. They let the fire grow smaller. Goth brings a three-legged stand with chains and a large grate that looks like something out of some medieval movie. He places it over the fire while Franzi brings over the soft package of meat that Dora bought in Wandow that afternoon. With his bare hands, Goth puts the steaks on the grill and uses a fork to turn them over. Dora thinks of Heini and his gas-powered space shuttle.

The steaks are fantastic, better than anything Dora has cooked lately, probably even better than what most Berlin restaurants serve. The meat is juicy, the marinade tastes of garlic and rosemary. The three of them sit on the trunk now destined to become a wolf, balancing the plates on their knees and sawing off large chunks of meat, bumping elbows with each other. In between, Goth gets up and turns the second-round steaks. There are no side dishes. The salad bowl sits untouched on the camping table. Goth helps Franzi cut her meat and tosses the fatty edges to Jay, who squats at his feet and worships him as if he were the new Messiah, just descended from heaven.

After dinner, Franzi returns to her carving while Dora and Goth linger by the fire. She clearly senses his presence next to her, beyond any epistemological doubt. She also senses Franzi and then herself, but in a calm way. Instead of feeling dizzy, as if she were on the edge of an abyss, this feels like a crystallization, an exquisite hardening of her surroundings, combined with a newfound ability to see clearly.

She once read a text by Heidegger for one of her classes. As far as she could tell, it claimed the only way one could properly comprehend the notion of Being is through fear. Maybe that's not true. Maybe Being is something you can get used to. And then *runtime error oxo* is no longer an error, it's just *oxo*. The answer to all questions. Like Douglas Adams's *The Hitchhiker's Guide to the Galaxy*—even if his supercomputer, when working on the question of life, the universe, and everything, came up with 42 instead of *oxo*.

"What's the story with Plausitz?" Dora hears herself ask.

"Huh?" Goth seems puzzled.

"The one with the knife."

"Who told you about that?"

"Sadie."

"What's she doing telling stories?"

He stares into the fire, his brows drawn tight. The peaceful atmosphere has vanished, but it's too late to back down now. Dora might as well get on with it.

"Tell me about it."

Goth sighs, stands up, and walks over to Franzi to give her some pointers on her work. Gently, he puts his hand on the girl's shoulder. When he returns, he sighs again.

"Whaddya wanna know?"

"What happened."

"It all happened pretty fast."

"Start from the beginning."

He props his elbows on his knees, hides his cigarette in the hollow of his hand as if a strong wind were blowing, and continues to gaze into the flames as he tells the story. It was a sunny September day. He went to Plausitz with Mike and Denis to listen to Krisse, who was standing on the steps of the local arts center with his mobile amplifier, ranting about Angela Merkel. How she lets millions of foreigners come to Germany while there isn't even enough money for the local fire department. The audience jeered, Goth and his pals downed a few bottles of beer. That's when this couple came strolling through the market square. They knew the guy from before, but the woman looked showy, she was wearing a skirt and colorful top, and was probably from Potsdam or Berlin.

"The woman's name is Karen and she's from Kochlitz."

"I doubt it."

"It was in the news reports."

"And whatever's in the news reports is true?"

Dora shrugs, signaling him to keep talking.

Goth and his pals didn't have any issues with the two of them, really. But as they walked past, the woman hissed, "Fucking Nazis." Not particularly loud, but just loud enough to be heard.

"The strange thing about you Nazis," Dora says, "is that you get angry when people call you Nazis."

"I'm not a Nazi."

"See?!"

"I'm just a little old-fashioned."

Dora chokes on her beer.

"I don't even have anything against foreigners," Goth asserts. "As long as they stay where they belong. I'm staying put right here, after all. Everyone should just stay right where they are."

"That means I shouldn't have moved to Bracken either."

"Maybe so."

He pulls two fresh bottles out of a crate underneath the trailer, knocks off the lids, and hands one to Dora. She briefly pauses to ponder what alcohol does when mixed with cortisone and painkillers, but realizes she has no desire to broach that particular subject right now.

"You city slickers call anyone who disagrees with you a Nazi."

" Goth, you've sung the Horst Wessel song. I heard it."

"The what song?"

"Horst Wessel." Dora quietly whistles the tune.

"Oh, I see. Well, it's just a song."

"It's a Nazi song. Singing that song is illegal, forchrissakes."

"Us sitting here is illegal, too."

He's right. Once again, she's forgotten all about the pandemic. Maybe her new feeling that she's getting used to Being is nothing more than her losing a grip on reality.

"You're just another big-city girl."

"That's not true. I chose to leave Berlin."

"The strange thing about you city slickers," Goth says, "is that you get angry when people call you city slickers."

Dora wants a cigarette. Goth reads her mind and offers her one.

"I guess we have something in common," he says, raising his beer bottle for a toast. "We're not who everyone thinks we are."

He displays no difficulty finding words. Sentences are pouring right out of him. After another sip of beer, he returns to the Plausitz story. How Denis jumped up. How Jonas stood in front of his girlfriend. How they started yelling and shoving at each other.

"Three against one," Dora says.

"I was just a bystander."

"Yeah, nah, obviously."

A beer bottle fell to the ground and shattered, and the woman started screaming. Denis yelled something about left-wing leeches and the guy yelled something about Nazi pigs, and all of a sudden a knife appeared.

"Whose knife?"

"That guy's."

"Which guy? Jonas?"

"Exactly. He had it on him."

"You're lying."

"Oh yeah?"

"It said in the newspaper that your friend Mike pulled the knife."

"Talk to the newspaper then, not me."

For a while they're stubbornly silent. Then Goth starts talking again.

"In court, they believed that Jonas guy when he said it wasn't his knife. But the thing was from Nesmuk, man. Had an olive-wood handle. Mike doesn't have anything like that."

"And you know your knives."

"Everybody knows something." Goth takes a sip before continuing. "Mike snatched it away from the guy before he could flip it open."

"And then he stabbed the left-wing leech."

"In self-defense."

"You can't seriously believe that."

"His little lady was still pepper spraying us, and then the cops came, too."

Dora could almost laugh. It's so damn tragic it's almost comic. Everyday German reality: one sunny September day a few fine German citizens go at each other with knives and pepper spray in the middle of a small-town market square. And then the cops show up.

"The knife went right between that Jonas guy's ribs."

"I suppose you read that in the newspaper, too."

"He could've died."

"I didn't do a thing, really."

Dora wonders whether he's lying to her because he doesn't want her to think badly of him, or whether he actually believes he was unjustly convicted. How many versions of reality can coexist without the very concept breaking down entirely?

"We used to do other stuff around these parts. But nobody cared. Nobody even noticed. Leftists got beat up every weekend."

"And foreigners?"

"There were hardly any here."

"I don't even want to know."

Goth grins. "Maybe some other time."

"Words cannot express," Dora says, "what an asshole you are."

She takes another cigarette from the pack lying on the log between them. Goth stokes the fire and feeds it. His movements really are totally different. Steadier than usual. Surer. More free.

"Funny, isn't it?"

"What?" asks Dora.

"Us," says Goth.

"Daddy, look!" exclaims Franzi.

He puts a hand on Dora's shoulder before going to look at what his daughter wants to show him. He lets out a burst of laughter and holds something up.

"Dora," he calls out. "Franzi carved a bone. For Jay!"

39

Pudding

Dora spends the next few days developing a new routine. The trick is to simply declare that the absence of normal is normal. Outside there's a pandemic, inside there's unemployment, on the other side of the wall there's a Nazi neighbor with glioblastoma. Everything's fine. After the little barbecue, it's *Sun.* then *Mon.* then *Tue.* The days of the week neatly fall into place, kept in order by Goth's screw-box-turned-pillbox with handwritten labels. Every morning Dora's alarm clock rings at seven sharp, as it probably does for many other women all across Germany. First thing, Dora crosses the yard and climbs onto the chair by the wall. On the other side, Goth sits at the camping table with coffee and cigarette, almost as if he were waiting for her, despite the fact that he'd never have voluntarily gotten up this early before. When she whistles he looks up, walks over, climbs onto the fruit crate, and she hands him the pills, which he swallows right away, without a word and without any water. Meanwhile, Jay-the-Ray is lying on the outside steps in the morning sun, gnawing on one of the wooden bones Franzi carved for her. The dog then pukes up the pulpy remains in the kitchen, which is why Dora secretly begins calling her "Jay-the-Boneslayer."

Dora makes coffee, showers, eats breakfast and

forces herself to read the headlines on the internet for half an hour, because that's what normal people do on a normal morning. Until a few days ago, the few pundits who called for looser Covid restrictions—in order to spare the national economy, preserve people's basic rights, and save society's collective mental health—were treated like enemies of the state and publicly shamed. Now presidents and prime ministers are trying to outdo each other with plans to phase out stay-at-home orders, and everyday citizens are busy planning for Pentecost and their summer vacations. Apparently people can still put up with school closures, bans on gatherings, work-from-home arrangements, and economic crises. But when vacation season begins, the pandemic takes a break. People who were just posting comments online telling those in favor of ending the restrictions that they could go ahead and die now want to meet up with masses of fellow vacationers on the Baltic seashore. At the same time, politicians are either threatening to abolish normality or hailing its return, depending on how you interpret the polls. The refrain is either return to normal, here's the new normal, or never normal again.

The most interesting thing about these posts is that Dora can read them. She still feels a slight tingling sensation, but it's bearable. It would seem she's no longer tasked with getting upset about absurdities. Others can. No one's commanding her to join in, there's no imperative, no order she feels compelled to resist. Dora observed the general excitement, and then she put her device down, looking away again.

After her compulsory reading, the gardening begins. Since she's been watering regularly, the vegetable patch is turning into a green oasis, while everywhere else the grass is withering and the parched soil is becoming more and more cracked. Maybe the weather has opted for non-stop blue skies until all the vegetation is destroyed. In the neighboring yard, Goth, whose property has its own well, has started up several lawn sprinklers. The rhythmic clacking and hissing is the background music of Dora's mornings.

When she needs a break, she climbs up on the chair to watch Goth work. There's a large animal trapped in the block of wood, and he's gingerly freeing it. Two pointed ears are already peeking out at the top, as well as a piece of forehead. He steps back and looks at the block in peace, over and over again as if waiting for the wood to tell him what to do next. At some point, he gets the message, chooses a tool, and gets back to work. With great care, he removes everything that doesn't look like a wolf.

At half past twelve, Dora goes inside and cooks lunch. Since she's now taking Goth's pickup to the grocery store, her refrigerator is well stocked. Her account balance, on the other hand, was supposed to last another two months but is now dwindling like snow melting in the sun. Occasionally she thinks about radio advertising, but doesn't take any action. She also puts off calling Jojo. When the oil boils in the pan and the first eggs are cracked, Franzi and Jay come running into the house. Obviously, both dog and girl have an excellent sense of smell, or an amazing sense of timing. They drop onto the cool tile floor, both overheated and covered with sawdust, and wait to gobble down large portions of Dora's lunch, carefully sorting out the vegetable portions. After eating, they sprint back over to the interesting side of the wall.

That's fine by Dora. The main thing is that everyone is doing well. She's the worker in the engine room, invisible but largely responsible for ensuring that her piece of reality functions as well as possible. And it does. Franzi is the proof. The little girl seems like a changed person. She hasn't lapsed into her baby voice for days now. When she shovels mountains of food into herself and then romps back outside with Jay, a feeling of happiness flows through Dora, almost as if the little girl were her own daughter.

Maybe Franzi is also why Dora dreams of her mother one night. Her mother is standing in the kitchen with the window open, because she likes to listen to the birds while she cooks. Dora is still a girl, maybe Franzi's age. She leans in the doorway and watches her mother toss an occasional crust of bread or chopped apple peel out the window. Blackbirds, blue tits, robins, and greenfinches flutter down from the treetops to get their tidbits. From the living room, Jojo yells that she'll attract rats if she keeps throwing kitchen scraps into the yard like that, but her mother only laughs, putting the palms of her hands to her cheeks as if she had to hold her head together to keep it from bursting apart. Dora is overcome by a deep wave of love for her mother. Such a cheerful, energetic woman.

"Know what, sweetie?" her mother says. "I'm making pudding. A big pot of it. Instead of dinner."

Pudding-instead-of-dinner happens every now and then, when mom is in a good mood and doesn't feel like "real" cooking. For Axel and Dora, it's a feast every time. They're allowed to stuff themselves silly with the chocolatey stuff, until they can't take any more. Sometimes there are hot cherries and vanilla sauce to go with it. Even in her dreams, Dora feels her mouth water. When her mother comes closer to let her taste a spoonful of the hot, still liquid pudding, Dora suddenly realizes she's no longer a child at all. The two of them are standing opposite each other, at eye level, and they're the same height. The same age. Or is she already older than her own mother? Is that even possible? Isn't that a violation of the natural order?

Her mother blows on the spoon and holds it in front of Dora's face. She dutifully opens her mouth. The pudding tastes delicious. Tongue, palate—her whole body knows this taste.

"Yummy," she says.

"Call your children in," her mother says. "Dinner will be ready in a minute."

Dora pauses. Franzi comes to mind. But Franzi isn't her daughter.

"I don't think I have any children," she says.

Now it's her mother's turn to pause. "Oh, come now."

"Really," says Dora.

"Why not?"

As Dora is thinking it over, the next spoonful of pudding appears in her face. And then another. Her mother is feeding her. It's not unpleasant, but it is a little too much, actually.

"I'm too scared," Dora says with her mouth full. "That I'll die and leave my children alone. Like you did."

Her mother snorts. She puts her hands to her temples and laughs so hard that Dora is startled. The spoon falls to the floor. Her mother doubles over and gasps for air.

"You can ..." she gasps, barely able to continue. "You can't, just because ..."

A Eurasian jay flies up, lands on the window sill, and lets out a warning screech. Dora's mother collapses on the kitchen floor.

"Just because I ..." she blurts out. Then she dissolves into thin air.

Dora wakes up in a cold sweat. She has to change her T-shirt. Thank God it's already after five, so she doesn't have to try to fall asleep again. She sits down on the outside stairs with a cup of coffee and waits for the sun to rise above the horizon. Her subconscious is an idiot. After all, it was Robert who didn't want children. Even though she herself wasn't exactly committed to fighting against his refusal. And now she has no one. Dora isn't really one of those women who pay attention to the ticking of her biological clock. Still, she's thirty-six years old already—if she meets a suitable guy today and they get right down to it, she still has a real chance. All at once, she realizes what the self-imposed solitude of living in this village means, aside from extra breathing room and callused hands: for the time being, the men in her life are Goth, Heini, Tom, and Steffen. If she's looking for anything else, she'll have to turn to Tinder.

Sometimes Goth comes to the wall in the evening, whistles, and invites her to come over for a barbecue. Sometimes there's a pot of cooked potatoes waiting for her on the wall. Before bedtime, Dora goes to the wall one last time and whistles. Goth comes over, climbs up on his fruit crate, and they smoke together in silence.

40

Peep

A week later, the money runs out.

When she goes shopping on Saturday morning, Dora grabs only the essentials from the shelves: a pile of pasta packages, stacks of canned tomato sauce. Plus milk, bread, two cases of beer. When she asks for five packs of cigarettes at checkout, she already knows she's running low. She begins to sweat. The mask makes it hard to breathe, and slips in front of her eyes when she looks down, which is why the contents of her coin purse fall to the floor when she tries to pull her debit card out of her wallet. Behind her, people patiently wait for her to get her shit together, displaying the stoicism so typical here in Brandenburg. It's the magic glue that allows everyone to *not* get along, each in their own special way. Dora holds her breath as she slips the debit card into the slot. She feels like a con artist. When the machine rejects her card, she'll yell "What's going on?" and "I don't understand!" while everyone else stares blankly into space. Just then, she's glad her face is covered. A white poker face with little blue hearts, ordered on eBay. Transaction successful. Dora exhales. With her cart half-full, she leaves the shopping center.

At home, she calls up her online bank statement: 4.34 euros in the red. She reloads the page. The number disappears and reappears. -4.34 euros. It's not a number, it's a judgment. Dora has to request a loan-payment deferral. She has to go to the job center. Or call Jojo. Not sometime, not tomorrow—right now.

Cheerful voices stream over from the neighbor's yard. Dora goes to the wall and climbs onto the chair. A soccer game is in full swing. Goth versus Franzi and Jay. The tactic of the girl-and-dog team is to clutch Goth's legs and bite his boots, respectively, to prevent him from running. Packed together, they push towards the goal, which is marked by two beer crates, with the ball playing a secondary role. Franzi's loud laughter rings through the air.

All of a sudden, Dora understands the bond between parents and children. It is a love so deep, so boundless, that it exceeds all comprehension. The flip side of this love is the fear of losing each other. Just as boundless, just as deep. Downright abysmal. It's more than a human being can bear. It's immoderate exaggeration, an accident of nature. Perhaps it's appropriate for animals that have to risk their own lives to defend their young. But not for humans. An animal has no concept of the future. It doesn't run around all the time wondering what will happen next. It can care for and protect its young without the slightest clue regarding the countless possible disasters looming in wait. But forms of life to whom evolution has given a consciousness, a sense of time, and knowledge of the transience of all existence shouldn't be endowed with such boundless feelings. It's sheer perversion. No wonder people are growing more and more neurotic.

Dora can't stand the sight of Franzi and Goth any longer, and jumps off the chair.

That's not your child, and certainly not your husband, she says to herself. You're just in charge of logistics here.

She forces herself to dial Jojo's number. He answers right away and sounds like he's in a good mood. It's late Saturday afternoon, so he's probably still sitting at the kitchen table in his robe, reading the weekend edition of the *Frankfurter Allgemeine Zeitung*, his paper of choice, embodying his ideal image of success. Of the good life. Provided no emergency calls come in. He might even have slept a few hours.

"Hey, honey, what's up?"

"Good, great."

Dora realizes too late that her answer doesn't match the question. She pictures the house Jojo is sitting in. The small kitchen of her childhood no longer exists. It's now a guest bathroom, while the dining room, living room, and parts of the hallway have all been joined to form an open-plan eat-in kitchen with a cooking island. The furniture is no longer a motley assortment, but well coordinated, black leather and silver pipes, for which Jojo has a soft spot, while colorful scarves on the walls reflect Sibylle's Buddhist-inflected taste.

"I have a request."

"Do you need money?"

Sometimes Dora wonders if they teach you to read minds in medical school. Maybe it's a secret skill reserved for neurosurgeons.

"No problem, honey." He's also correctly interpreted her silence. "After all, you're a homeowner now. And I'll bet they've cut back your hours."

"They fired me."

Jojo audibly swallows, then clears his throat.

"Well, I can't really ... I mean, that wasn't supposed to ..." There's the old Jojo Dora knows so well. He's scared he'll have to keep her fed, clothed, and housed for the next ten years. Generous gestures are part of his self-image, as long as they aren't too extravagant.

"It's not that I don't want to help. I just thought ..."

"It's okay, Jojo," Dora says quickly.

"I was thinking more of a one-time payment."

"Me too."

"I'll send you a transfer."

"Thanks, Jojo."

"It goes without saying ..."

Dora doesn't ask how much he plans to send. He won't be stingy, but he won't be particularly generous either. She'll be able to make ends meet for a while, maybe until the end of next month. The conversation has gotten a bit awkward. Jojo seems to think so too, because he changes the subject.

"How's your gym buddy doing, by the way?"

"He's playing soccer."

"You read too much into that," Jojo says.

Dora had just been about to hold up her phone so Jojo could hear the cheerful voices from the neighboring yard. But now she's furious, as if suddenly someone flipped an internal switch. An episode from her childhood comes back to mind. Dora was perhaps six or seven years old when, around Easter, she found a Playmobil horse-drawn carriage in the yard that she had wanted for a long time. Ecstatic, she ran into the house to show it to Jojo.

"Funny," he said, "the exact same carriage was in the window display at König's toy store."

Dora replied that the Easter Bunny must've gotten it there, then.

"A bunny?!" exclaimed Jojo. "At König's?! Did he pull the carriage off the shelf with his paws? Does he have pouches in his fur coat where he keeps his money?"

Dora can still feel the searing pain those words caused her. She even thinks she remembers Jojo laughing as tears welled up in her eyes.

"It's possible," she says defiantly.

"What's possible?" asks Jojo.

That the Easter Bunny shops at König's, Dora thinks.

"That Proksch is getting better," she says aloud.

"Temporarily, perhaps. At best."

"The mass effect—the tumor could've been an artifact." Artifacts are bright spots that can show up on MRI without meaning anything. Technical optical illusions. Asking Jojo if he mistook an artifact for a glioblastoma is about like doubting that a veterinarian can tell cats from dogs.

"Dora ...," Jojo begins hesitantly.

"Goth is friendly. He laughs. He's become a completely different person, you know? He's started working with wood again. You should see what a great sculptor he is."

"Dora," Jojo repeats.

She hears him light a cigarette. His new companion doesn't want him smoking in the house. Maybe he's gone into the yard without Dora noticing. Maybe he's looking at the bush she found the horse-drawn carriage behind. If that bush is even there anymore.

"We barbecue together. His little daughter is happy. Overjoyed even, really, believe me." As if Franzi's happiness proved anything. As if it were a matter of speaking so fast that Jojo wouldn't get a word in edgewise. As if Dora didn't already know what he was going to say next.

She remembers another episode. When she had outgrown the Easter Bunny, she got a parakeet named Peep. The little bird was so tame it would land on her index finger and run around her bedroom floor admiring its reflection in the metal feet of her bed. At some point, Peep stopped eating and didn't feel like leaving his cage. Jojo said Peep was sick. Dora didn't want to believe him. She claimed that Peep was just tired, or offended because she had so little time for him. She kept finding new explanations, while Jojo repeated that Peep was probably dying. A little later, she found the parakeet lying on its back on the floor of the cage. Dora was sure that Jojo was to blame. She hated him for it.

Now he takes a deep drag and audibly exhales the smoke. Don't say it, Dora thinks. Just keep your damn mouth shut.

"Edema often forms around a glioblastoma, pressing on the rest of the brain," Jojo says. "When the swelling goes down because of the cortisone, the patient initially experiences relief."

The words are hand grenades that fall to the ground all around Dora. And the word *initially* is a hydrogen bomb. She wants to run away.

"But there are cases ..." She has to cough, something catches in her throat. "I remember a patient of yours where the tumor just didn't grow. He lived with it for decades. I remember you saying how he'd pass out sometimes. In the shower. While out strolling. Everyone thought that was it, his time had come, but then he just kept going."

"There are cases like that," Jojo confirms. "But they're rare. Extremely rare. You understand?"

Dora feels the thing growing in her throat. Maybe it's a tumor, too, and she's about to choke on it. Maybe tumors are growing everywhere, randomly, uncontrollably, prolific as first early potatoes. Dora feels like screaming. She wants to rail against words like *initially* and *extremely rare*. A world that works like that is a shitty, fucked-up, fatally flawed world. People and animals getting sick and dying from one second to the next—what's that supposed to mean? If anything like this happened with a household appliance, the manufacturer would be legally required to issue an immediate recall. Totally faulty design. Exchange within fourteen days.

"You have to be careful not to take on too much responsibility," Jojo says. "Mr. Proksch is your neighbor. It's nice of you to help him. Most people would just look the other way. But you mustn't identify with him. You cannot get too close. In the end, this whole thing has nothing at all to do with you."

That sounds pretty darn right, and yet it's complete bullshit. Everything has to do with her, how could it be otherwise? After all, everyone is their own window onto the world. She barely manages to say, "Okay, Jojo, thanks again," before hanging up and then swiping to delete any trace of the call from her phone.

41

Aroar

The she-wolf grows. From top to bottom. After her ears, her forehead, and the back of her head, finally her face appears, with a slightly open, smiling snout. It's fun to watch Goth at work. He moves with such confidence, persistence, and concentration. When he strokes the she-wolf's head, it looks like he's touching a living creature.

On Wednesday, they have another barbecue. Dora chows down on the meat until she can't take another bite. When she finally sinks back with a sigh, she feels calm and heavy. The conversation with Jojo was four days ago and is about to turn into a historical anecdote. Jay chews on a bone, Goth smokes, Franzi brings over a stack of colorful playing cards and explains the rules to Dora. The game is fun. Goth opens two bottles of beer and a soda. He shuffles like a pro. They yell "Uno!" at the top of their lungs when they hold the last card. They laugh with unadulterated glee when an opponent has to draw four cards. They get ticked off when they have to draw four cards. Goth slams his fist on the table, pats Franzi's upper arms, goes and grabs another soda and two more beers.

By the time they've finally had enough, it's almost midnight. The fire has burned down to embers. The streetlight in front of Heini's house emits an orange cone of light. Dora strokes Franzi's head in farewell, shakes Goth's hand, and feels the mosquito bites on her legs begin to itch. In the heat of the moment, she got all bitten up without bothering to fight back.

She can't sleep. The insect bites turn into itchy volcanoes erupting with endlessly looping thoughts. It's too hot to sleep, anyway. When Dora gets out of bed to have a smoke out front, even Jay-the-Ray comes to the door with her.

At first it's more of a hunch than a sound. Dora thinks she hears something, then she doesn't. A distant roar. Then silence, until she thinks she's imagined it. But the next scream is so loud it's beyond doubt. She runs down the front steps, through the front yard, onto the street, and along the roadside through the slumbering village, Jay hot on her heels.

She sees him from a distance. He's standing under the lantern in front of Tom and Steffen's house. A tall, chunky figure, a black silhouette against the light, his right arm outstretched. Some kind of screwed-up Statue of Liberty, holding not a torch, but a clenched fist, which he first shakes, then stretches out flat, arm on the diagonal.

"Heyyy!" he roars. "Heyyy!"

Dora is already beside him when the front door opens. Tom steps out, barefoot, bare-chested. He's in nothing but black sweatpants, which make him look like a judoka. Everything about him seems compact, as if his stocky body harbors great strength. He crosses his arms in front of his chest and looks Goth calmly in the eyes.

"Back to this again?" he asks.

"Send your fuckin' foreigners back to where they came from, you fuckin' fairy!" Goth yells. "I'll bash your heads in!"

Unmoved, Tom watches as Dora tries to pull Goth's stretched arm down. She might as well have tried to break off the thickest branch of an oak tree. Meanwhile, Jay tries to greet Goth with a few leaps, but gives up in frustration when he ignores her.

"You fuckin' fudge packers! You and your fuckin' foreigners!"

"Take your drunken attack dog home," Tom tells Dora.

Dora fleetingly wonders if human brains actually need alcohol or tumors to produce racism. As if it's some catastrophic chemical reaction. Unfortunately, she already knows the answer. It happens in healthy heads too. Goth shakes her off, and the abrupt motion sends her hurtling to the side.

"I'll bash your brains in!" he bellows.

"If he doesn't shut up, I'm calling the police," Tom says.

"Fuck no," Dora says. "We don't need the police."

"I think we do."

"Cocksucker!" yells Goth.

"Goth!" shouts Dora. "Look at me!"

He doesn't seem to notice her at all. It's as if he's in a parallel universe. This time he reeks of alcohol, even from several feet away. If the police find him like this, they'll haul him off. They'll revoke his parole, lock him up, and if Jojo is right, he won't make it out alive. Then that raucous UNO! game will have been the last time Franzi saw her father. Dora can't let that happen. No way.

"Come on, Goth," Dora says gently. "We're going home."

For a moment he recognizes her. He looks at her, eyes narrowed slightly, as if he can't see very well. Then he shakes his head and moves a little to the side, staggering across the wide strip of grass at the edge of the road, his eyes to the ground as if he's looking for something.

"What's he doing?" asks Tom.

Dora can guess what he's doing. He's looking for a club. Or a rock.

"Get in the house and close the door," she says to Tom. "Give me a few minutes. I'll make sure he doesn't break anything."

Tom snorts through his nose. He's not one to hole up in the house while someone's raising hell outside.

"Since when are you Goth's girlfriend?"

"Since when are you one to call the police?"

Goth bends down and picks something up.

"Fuckin' foreigners, cocksuckers," he mutters.

Tom pulls his phone out of the pocket of his sweatpants.

"No!" shouts Dora, running up to Tom until she's standing right in front of him. Jay takes the opportunity to disappear into the house through the crack in the door. Dora tries to take the phone out of Tom's hand. He pushes her to the side, roughly enough that she has to grab the wall in order not to stumble. That's when Steffen comes to the door, without glasses, his long hair disheveled. He pushes Jay away with his feet.

"What's going on here?"

"Goth's making a scene again," Tom says. "And Dora's playing Nazi hostess."

Jay squeals as Steffen gives her a final shove.

Dora gets angry again. Even more furious than that awful call with Jojo. Obviously everyone is against her, the whole goddamned world: Jojo, Tom, and Steffen, Robert, Susanne, the pandemic, and the glioblastoma. Goth is such an idiot. She doesn't feel like putting up with it anymore. If there were any chance she could deck Tom, she'd try. But because she's too weak, all she can do is scream.

"Then go ahead, call the police," she yells, "and tell them about your little roadside business while you're at it. The tax authorities will be intrigued."

She doesn't really mean to say that. She doesn't want to cause trouble, threaten anyone, or sound like she's blackmailing them. But there's nothing else she can do. Shit just keeps happening, and she's out of options.

"You're such hypocrites!" she shouts. "Voting AfD and then calling the cops when a Nazi shows up at your door!"

Tom and Steffen look at her in amazement. She considers spitting on them, too. Maybe it'd earn her some respect.

"I don't understand what's going on," Tom says. "Why are you even meddling in the middle of all this?"

"Goth is sick," Dora says. "In the head."

Tom laughs. "Who'd have thought?!"

"He's dying."

"Fine by me!" Tom laughs even louder.

"Wait a minute." Steffen signals Tom to stop laughing. "I think there's something else going on here."

She can't tell anyone, especially not the stooges next door. Goth doesn't want her to, and Jojo has made her swear not to. But she has to prevent the police from coming, and that takes precedence.

"I want him to spend the rest of his time at home. With Franzi. Understood?"

Now Tom and Steffen look at each other with uncertainty. They appear downright concerned.

"What ... does he have?" asks Steffen.

"None of your damn business," says Dora. "Just start acting like human beings."

Goth suddenly groans. He stands under the lantern, pressing both hands to his head. Jay-the-Ray runs to him and sniffs his lower legs. He drops to one knee. There it is again: time stops, reality coagulates. Night, village road, lantern. A dog sniffs at the statue of The Thinker. Tom and Steffen seem to notice that something's off, too. They stand still, silently taking in the image. Goth leans down on one knee, resting his forehead in his hands. No one says a word. Roll the credits, Dora thinks. Just a few more minutes to watch and dream, then get up and leave. Instead, she has to spring back into action. She runs to Goth, gently puts a hand on his shoulder. He lifts his face and searches for her with a blind expression.

"C'mon, Goth," Dora says.

Swaying a bit, he gets to his feet and lets her lead him. His arm is heavy on her shoulders. They walk slowly, one foot in front of the other. She feels Tom's and Steffen's glances at her back. But she doesn't turn around.

42

Floyd

The next morning, Goth isn't sitting at the camping table waiting for his pills as usual. The trailer looks barricaded, the yard deserted. The finished head of the she-wolf protrudes from the cut trunk, so life-like that Dora expects the animal to turn its head and try to free the rest of its body from the wood any minute now. Only on closer inspection does Dora notice that Franzi is sitting at the back door of the main house. The little girl looks blankly in front of her. Now it's clear that something is wrong.

Dora calls Franzi over to the wall and asks her to come over and make breakfast. As soon as the girl has disappeared into the estate manager's house, she goes over to Goth's place and tries the handle on the trailer door. It's unlocked. Dora opens it a crack and sees Goth lying on his bed in the semi-darkened space, on his back, hands clasped behind his head. A peaceful image. She's wondering whether to wake him when he opens his eyes and looks at her. He tries to say something, but can't get a word out. Then he smiles. A painful smile. Almost affectionate.

If there was ever any doubt as to whether Goth was fully aware of his situation, this smile clears it away.

Dora steps over to the bed and squats down. Her sobs come out of nowhere, grabbing her by the shoulders and shaking her. She presses her lips together, but can't stop herself from audibly weeping. That's when she feels Goth's hand on her head. He strokes her hair. He pats her back as if she just choked. She gets to her feet. She has the pills in her pants pocket, and there is a glass in the sink that she fills halfway with water. She lifts his head and helps him swallow. Then she texts Jojo on WhatsApp.

"Can I increase the dose?"

She cleans up a bit and turns on the old-fashioned CD player on the small dining table. The jewel case is right next to the speakers; the band is called Wolf Parade. While Dora does the dishes, she sees the finished wooden wolf sitting by the stairs through the window. He's looking over at his girlfriend, who is still up to her shoulders in the log.

And you've decided not to die / Alright / Let's fight / Let's rage against the night.

Her stomach feels as if she's swallowed a bunch of stones. She's just putting the last plate in the drying rack when her phone dings. When Jojo isn't in surgery, he's the quickest draw in the former West.

"You can, but it won't do any good."

She'd like to hurl her phone to the floor and crush it with her heel like an insect. Goth's face still has that eerie smile. Dora goes over to him and puts a hand on his forehead.

"Lie still," she says. "Just rest a little while longer."

She suppresses the impulse to close his eyes with one hand.

After breakfast, she takes Franzi for a walk in the woods. The little girl walks silently beside her, which Dora appreciates because she's busy with her own thoughts.

She keeps an eye out for Eurasian jays or other birds who can attest to the fact that life goes on. But there are no birds. It's too hot, anyway. The temperature has been rising steeply since early morning. Around noon it'll probably reach the mid eighties. Spring has run out of steam, and wants to yield the field to summer.

When they reach the crossroads, Dora's T-shirt is stuck to her back. Exhausted, she drops onto the bench. This is where she met Franzi for the first time. Back when she was just a rustling and giggling in the undergrowth, then a little tormentor jonesing for Jay-the-Ray. To Dora, it seems like their first encounter was years ago. At the time, she was still new to Bracken and thought her failed relationship with Robert was her biggest problem.

Franzi sits down next to her on the bench and strokes the wood with both hands. Dora observes her from the side. Life will definitely go on. There are already people running around somewhere with whom Franzi will share the future. On a field in Berlin, a boy is frolicking with a soccer ball, happy the Covid restrictions are loosening up, completely unaware that one day he'll marry a young woman from Bracken with long blonde hair. Somewhere, a girl is drawing with crayons, soon to become Franzi's best friend. Maybe there's a young man on the subway wearing a mask and headphones who, thirty years from now, will involve her in a car accident that will break both her arms. Everything is already there, inscribed in the world, in preparation, just waiting for the right moment to happen. All by itself. There's no wheel to turn, no lever to pull. You just have to sit there. Dora notices how she relaxes a little.

When Franzi takes a breath to say something, she immediately tenses up again in anticipation of the dreaded baby voice. But the little girl's voice is normal.

"My daddy made that," she says.

Dora should've realized that all by herself. Of course the bench is Goth's work. The neighbor needs chairs, and the forest needs a bench. Just cobble it together and set it right there. From the beginning, even before she really knew him, Dora had been feeling his presence when she sat here.

"Look, there."

Franzi leans to the side, partially leaning on Dora's lap. She points to the inside of the wooden legs the seat is nailed to. Dora bends down. There's something carved into it, two triangles with a connecting line, like a trademark or signature of some kind.

"Are those sailboats?" she asks.

Franzi looks at her with a pitying expression that says: Seriously? Sheesh, only adults can be this dumb.

"You silly—they're ears!"

Now Dora sees it: stylized wolf ears, pointed attentively in anticipation of what's to come. Somehow, this entire place seems to be pricking up its ears and looking forward to the future.

"Back then we still lived in Bracken. Mommy, Daddy, and me. All together."

Dora senses it coming. Franzi has something in mind. Something big. A solution to all the world's problems. That's why she was so silent on the way over.

"You could marry him."

"Who?"

"My dad."

So that's it. That's what Franzi's come up with. Dora clears her throat.

"I don't think that's possible."

"Don't you like him?"

The answer is surprisingly difficult. Since Dora has been living in Bracken, life has been about a lot of things, but it's never once been about whether you like someone or not. Perhaps "liking" is something that preoccupies people in cities, more than anywhere else.

"Sure I do," she finally says. "In a certain way, sure, I like him."

"Isn't that enough?" Franzi grows louder. "What more do you want?"

Dora saw it coming, and here it is. It's moving in like a storm, lightning fast. Just a moment ago it was blue skies and sunshine, now suddenly it's big black clouds and thunder. Franzi jumps off the bench and stands up in front of Dora.

"Just do it!" she cries. "So we can be like a real family!"

"Franzi ..." As Dora reaches out, the girl swats at her. "We're already like a family, don't you think? You, your dad, Jay, and me."

"But it's not real. This is just a vacation because of Covid. I wish Covid would last forever!" Franzi stomps her feet. "I never ever wanna go back to Berlin!" she screams. "The kids at school think I'm stupid. And there aren't any animals. No rays, either."

Jay, thinking she's heard her name, runs over and leans against Franzi's lower leg. The girl sinks to her knees and wraps the dog in her arms. She cries into Jay's fur coat, and the little dog puts up with it.

"You could have a baby," Franzi sobs. "I've always wanted a little brother."

Dora sits down next to Franzi on the forest floor. Sand, pine cones, small branches, dry grass. The scent is intense as perfume.

"Or don't you want a baby?"

Surprisingly, this answer is quite easy.

"Sure, I do," Dora says. "I want to have a baby."

"See?!" Franzi lifts her face, cheeks wet, eyes puffy. "I'm sure my dad does, too."

Dora has to smile. Franzi takes that as a good sign, and smiles back.

"Should I ask him?"

"No, not yet," Dora replies. "Let me think it over a little more, first."

"Promise?"

"Promise."

Franzi stretches out her arms and gives Dora a wet kiss on the cheek. Then she wipes her face with the hem of her T-shirt and gets up.

"Come on, Jay!"

The two bound off into the woods, where they frolic among the trees, hopping over logs. Franzi shouts and laughs. Her despair evaporates as quickly as it appeared. Ah, blissful childhood, when feelings simply chase each other out the door. Dora stays seated on the ground, petting the moss and letting sand run through her fingers. From this perspective, she can see the wolf ears carved into the wood of the bench.

As they head back to town, they hear the whir of the chainsaw from far away. Franzi's face lights up, as if a dimmer switch had been turned on. She runs ahead, Jay follows at a gallop, and Dora quickens her pace, too.

Goth is standing in the yard, cigarette at the corner of his mouth, waving toward them. He shuts off the growling beast and calls out a friendly, "G'mornin'!" even though it's almost noon.

"Hey, Poodle-oodle! I cut you some scraps, in case you want to carve some more bones for Jay." At his feet is a small pile of little logs he has stripped of bark and carved into cylindrical form. Franzi pounces on it as if it were a mountain of food after a three-day fast. Dora has never heard Goth call his daughter "Poodle-oodle."

She comes closer and looks at the she-wolf. You can see the neck and even a piece of chest fur. Goth must have been very busy for the last few hours. The she-wolf is already a proud animal. She holds her head high, and captures the viewer's gaze with quiet attention. Her fur is slightly wavy, you'd think you could run your fingers through it. The finished wolf at the entrance to the trailer has also been looking at the world more cheerfully lately. He seems to be looking forward to his companion's arrival.

Over the course of the afternoon, Dora opens her laptop several times to check her bank balance. Around six o'clock, Jojo's money arrives. He's been relatively generous, as expected. And if she just manages things a little better, this cushion could last two months. That feels good, almost as if all her problems have been solved.

Because Dora is sitting in front of the screen anyway, she quickly opens a news page. Merkel meeting with prime ministers. Covid protests. The country is divided—what else is new?

Dora almost overlooks the realest news. It happened three days ago, but apparently wasn't important enough to attract the attention of reporters. They're so busy covering Covid. Stunned, she reads the brief report: In Minneapolis, a police officer knelt on a 46-year-old man's neck for over eight minutes, until he lost consciousness. The man pleaded for his life, saying "I can't breathe" several times. He died a short time later, at the hospital. Someone recorded the event with their phone. The victim is black, the perpetrator white.

Dora googles, and finds the video. She hesitates before clicking on it, but then does anyway. Over and over again, the man says "I can't breathe." He calls out for his mom. The cop kneeling on the man's neck looks like Goth. Actually, he doesn't look anything like Goth. He's got short-cropped hair and a stubbly beard, his sunglasses are pushed up on his head. He just kneels there on the man's neck, totally relaxed, hands resting on his thighs. As if it were nothing. As if nothing special were going on. Every now and then he looks up, then looks directly into the camera. Half smiling. Totally chill. A second policeman walks back and forth along the side of the road. He, too, is totally chill. In broad daylight. Passersby are present, witnessing. Nobody does anything. It's appalling. The quiet of this scene is horrific. The normality. At some point, someone feels for the victim's pulse. They drag the body onto a stretcher. There is a little commotion, but not much.

Dora lifts her eyes from the screen, looks dead ahead, and feels her hands shaking. Hands shouldn't shake. Especially not hands that are this big. For the next few hours, she can't get rid of the shaking. Again and again, she tells herself: That guy in Minneapolis was not Goth. That has nothing to do with Goth. Her mind tries outlining all the differences between German racism and American racism. But on another level, a deeper level, she doesn't care. It doesn't matter. Racism is when you think certain people are worthless. It's atrocious, and it's true all over the world. It exists everywhere.

When she goes to the wall again later in the evening, she sees Goth's massive body lying next to the camping table. And suddenly something happens inside her. The trembling disappears. Her hands are just big. Pleasantly big. Big and steady. They're hands that want to get ahold of everything, grab on to life, take care of problems. All of a sudden, Dora knows she can do it.

You don't have to be emotional about it. About anything. No anger, no fear, no horror. Everything about this insane, messed-up world suggests that you don't need emotions. They're optional. You don't need to wear a specific T-shirt, or put bumper stickers on your car, or listen to specific music. You can just do it. Goth doesn't get upset. Dora can walk up to him and kneel on his neck. For 8 minutes and 46 seconds. All the while, she could just look around a bit, or scroll through nonsense on her smartphone. Then feel for a pulse. Problem solved. Maybe it's the most sensible course of action. It would mean she had freed herself, Franzi, the village, the whole world of Goth's presence. Maybe she'd even be preventing something worse. Who knows?

But that's when Franzi comes running. She crouches down next to her father and shakes him by the shoulder. She calls his name, crying. And then something else happens. Dora's cognitive gears shift into overdrive. It's not about what you're capable of. Nor is it about who deserves what. It's not even about being for or against Nazis. The magic word is *nevertheless*. To go on in spite of it all, to be there in spite of it all, to keep showing up. Despite everything, that's a person over there. A human being.

So Dora leaps over the wall, runs to the body lying on the ground, and feels for a pulse. After a few shouts, a few hard slaps, and a half bucket of frigid water he finally comes to, and Dora helps him to his feet. She escorts him to the trailer, half propping him up, half carrying him. They make it up the three steps, although it takes them a few tries. Unable to hoist him up onto the bed, she slides the mattress and blankets onto the floor. She administers a few more pills and tells Franzi he just needs to sleep it off so he'll feel better in the morning. She even hopes that might be the case. Despite everything.

43

Blossoming Friendships

It's only half past six in the morning, but Dora can already hear Goth singing over on the other side of the wall. Not "I'm a unicorn," but the song by Wolf Parade she found on his CD player the other day. He hits the notes with a remarkably sure, pleasantly deep voice.

She stands on the chair for a while, gazing over the wall, watching him work. He's carving out the she-wolf with gusto. He's wearing a blue-and-black checkered shirt with short sleeves; she's never seen it on him before. His head is freshly shaved, and even from a distance he looks clean, as if he had showered with the garden hose after getting up. It's hard to believe that this was the man lying motion-less on the lawn the night before.

Right now he's busy perfecting the curvature of the she-wolf's back. For the first time, Dora notices there's a big bulge on the figure's right side, at ground level. Perhaps Goth forgot to cut away the excess wood in that spot. Or maybe it's a buttress of sorts, for more stability. Dora decides she'll ask him about it when she gets the chance.

She whistles, and he immediately comes to the wall and climbs up on his crate as briskly as if he were lining up for roll call. Maybe he'd stand to at-tention and salute her any minute now. Dora hands him the pill, and as he turns he actually does raise two fingers to the brim of his nonexistent cap before returning to his carving. She thinks it's probably not a great idea to work all day in the blazing sun, especially since she's never seen him drink anything but coffee or beer. On the other hand, it probably doesn't matter now anyway.

Over breakfast, she opens her browser, calls up a news page, and finds more headlines about George Floyd and, more specifically, the anti-racist protests spreading across the United States. The governor of Minnesota has mobilized the National Guard and declared a state of emergency for Minneapolis and surrounding areas. Trump spouts his usual nonsense, making threats and refusing to acknowledge the existence of structural problems in police forces nationwide. In Germany, people are stunned as usual, but Dora also gets the sense that their shock is mixed with relief, since it shifts the focus to racism happening elsewhere. For the time being, Germany's die-hard obtuseniks have set aside their mission to defend the West and are instead busy denying that Covid even exists.

She puts her phone away and starts watering her potatoes. She has to fill the watering cans in the kitchen and lug them out the back door to the vegetable patch. By trip 11 and 12, her arms already feel a few inches longer. When a white box truck brakes on the street, she's glad for the break. She leaves the watering cans and walks across the front yard to the fence. The van's engine idles as Tom and Steffen get out and approach the fence from the other side. They look solemn, standing there side by side. As if they have something to announce.

"Morning," Steffen says.

"G'mornin'," says Tom.

"It's better to water in the evening," says Steffen.

A pause ensues. Dora wonders if they come bearing bad news, since this feels like an unusual, somewhat awkward visit.

"We're going shopping," Tom says. "You need anything?"

"No, thanks," Dora says. "I've got Goth's pickup now, anyway."

"Are you his—" begins Tom.

"Shut it," says Steffen.

Another pause. Clearly something else is going on here. Tom clears his throat.

"Listen, we've been thinking about something. We want to have a party. A block party. For the whole village."

"It's allowed again now," Steffen says, "as long as you socially distance and all that."

Dora isn't sure that's true, and now it's even less clear what they want from her. What does a village block party have to do with her?

"Look," Tom says. "It's about … Goth being there."

"You could say the party's for him."

"But if we invite him, he definitely won't come. It's better if you bring him."

Slowly, yet again, Dora connects the dots. A party for Goth. "That's bold," she says, "but really nice."

"How about right after Pentecost?" asks Tom. "End of next week?"

Dora searches for a suitable phrase, but Steffen has already understood.

"We could do earlier, of course," he says. "Practically right away. How about, say—the day after tomorrow?"

Suddenly, Dora finds the two of them deeply

touching. She's moved by how they're trying, in their own way, to make things right.

"The day after tomorrow is great," she says.

"You think he'll come?"

"I'll make sure he's there."

"Fabulous. We'll all stuff our faces," Steffen says.

"There's one more thing," says Tom.

The rosemary, thinks Dora. I forgot to replace the rosemary. But then Tom drops something completely different in her lap. He offers her a job. A fair offer, on an hourly basis. He sticks his elbow over the fence, and she bumps hers against it. After that, the van drives away.

Shortly after, she's sitting on the front steps, a large mug of latte beside her, computer perched on her knees, while the watering cans languish beside the potato patch. She couldn't wait. She pounces on Tom's project like a starved woman digging into a feast. It feels so good to really put her brain to work again. Thoughts tumble around like boisterous puppies finally let out into the yard. Everything is already there, she's set. Even the name: their online presence is to be called "Blossoming Friendships." Tom told her he's in the process of moving their flower business to the internet. Due to Covid, but also going forward. Steffen's flower arrangements are selling like hot cakes. They can expand on that. The first thing to do is to reach a younger target demographic. Everyone likes flowers, but their unique floral arrangements need a hip new interpretation. Dora already has an idea: do a reboot of the old Helmut Kohl doll from the 1990s satirical show *Hurra Deutschland*. Kohl's blossoming landscapes never materialized, but Bracken's blossoming friendships are eternal. Dora's mind fills with countless hilarious clips in which the Kohl puppet gets into trouble for his promises of unifying Germany. Kohl meets with retirees, the unemployed, young mothers with full-time jobs. At the end of each clip, he gives his disgruntled interlocutor a flower arrangement. A satirical format using the classic rubber puppet of the old chancellor as spokesperson is so absurd it's bound to go viral. Dora is betting Tom won't get the idea at all, and Steffen will love it.

She spends the following day honing her campaign approach, too. Next door, Goth is whittling away at the she-wolf. The George Floyd protests are expanding. It's getting warmer, thunderstorms are forecast but don't materialize. Jojo calls to report that the highways are full of suvs towing camping trailers, boats, horses, even small aircraft. Massive groups of motorcyclists barrel down countryside roads, and the resorts on the Baltic shore are bursting at the seams.

"Imagine who's lounging in their beach chairs right about now," he says. "All those people who wrote Covid diaries, followed Covid rules, watched Covid talk shows, had endless Covid conversations, and yelled at Covid-deniers for the past few weeks. But now it's Pentecost."

He laughs. Dora can literally hear him shaking his head. She also finds the sudden mania for vacation funny, but isn't in the mood for sarcastic jokes. Jojo announces he'll come by on the Tuesday after Pentecost to "check to see everything is all *right*," having a good laugh at his own politically tinged pun, which he probably thought up before calling. Dora says thank you, hangs up, and gets back to work.

She doesn't fully realize what Jojo's call really means until that evening. She spots a Eurasian jay in the beech tree out front. It's turning its head to look at her, first to its left, then its right. She's never seen one in the yard before. But there he sits, and he has a message for her: everything will be all right. Things are past the turning point. Dora is no longer unemployed, she's about to launch a regional one-woman agency. She'll be earning a living while doing something for her new home. Tom and Steffen aren't adversaries, they're friends. The thing they're planning for Goth isn't an early funeral service, but a welcoming party for a new life.

She grasps this above all because Jojo never does anything without a reason. He has announced his upcoming visit to Bracken, and that means something. To be more precise, it can only mean one thing: he senses the possibility of recovery. When it comes to recovery, Jojo is like a bloodhound on the trail. On Tuesday, he'll discover that the tumor has stopped growing and the mass effect is subsiding, as sometimes happens in very rare cases. He won't want to get her hopes up, but he will strongly advise that Goth start therapeutic treatment. Dora will persuade her gym buddy to agree, and then she'll start drive him to his chemo appointments. A new routine will take hold. Dora will make Blossoming Friendships a success, and after that, she'll take on other small businesses in the area as clients. Eventually, school will start again, and Franzi will visit on weekends and over fall break. Maybe when Goth is completely in remission, Franzi will even move to Bracken for good. The Eurasian jay smiles. Or maybe it's a smirk? Even if both are impossible with a beak.

44

Block Party

On Sunday evening, they walk together to the village square. Goth carries a full case of beer in each hand, making them look light as a feather, of course. Dora is holding two large bags of rolls in her arms, which she picked up at the Aral gas station in Plausitz just so she wouldn't show up at the party empty-handed. On the magazine racks, for the first time in weeks, the front pages of the daily newspapers no longer showed people wearing masks, but burning cars on nighttime streets, raised fists, and the motto *Black Lives Matter*, with which more and more people, all over the world, are protesting in the wake of George Floyd's murder. Protests are happening in Berlin, too. Just hearing about it feels like opening a window in a stuffy room.

Franzi has Jay on a leash, and is hopscotching down the street singing, "We're going to a party, we're going to a party!" Jay, who has no idea what's going on but is always happy to share Franzi's joy, does a little doggy dance at her side.

Goth posed no resistance to the village block party idea. When Dora asked him if he'd go with her, he was busy polishing the she-wolf's head. He mumbled unintelligibly, like someone who's not listening and doesn't need to listen anyway because he doesn't care how he spends his evening. He walks beside

Dora, shielding her body from the traffic with his own. When she pushes a little toward the roadway, he pushes her back. Occasionally he looks down at her with a wry smile, as if mocking her for not knowing what to make of him yet again. In the era of George Floyd and Black Lives Matter, she's going to a block party with the village Nazi. She just doesn't know what to make of it, any of it. Maybe, Dora thinks, taking a stance is only right, only important as long as you're seeing things from a safe distance.

The main square is little more than a poorly mowed village green bordered by a road. It's got a few old oak trees, some crumbling benches, and two broken soccer goals. Smack in the middle, there's a fire pit with a large campfire burning. Even though they're early, there's already a lot going on. Tom and Steffen are standing at the drinks table, looking around with friendly expressions on their faces and trying to create a welcoming atmosphere by greeting everyone loudly and cheerfully as they arrive. Sadie, still downing coffee like there's no tomorrow, has changed her hair color from platinum blonde to cobalt blue, and has brought her kids along. Five firefighters clink their beer bottles together and stick close to Sadie. A couple of older women sit on the benches, giggling with one another and drinking something in small glasses that's so pink it looks like it came from another planet. More children rustle in the bushes behind the oaks.

Heini has set up his space-age grill right next to the fire. He's donned his *Serial Griller* apron and is rotating long rows of sausages, meatballs, and beef-neck steaks. By way of greeting, he says to Dora,

"You can eat those yourself," pointing his tongs at the gas station buns.

Goth pushes the cases of beer under the drinks table and makes the rounds to greet everyone, Brandenburg-style: some people touch elbows in a Covid-safe salute while others, after a moment's hesitation, decide to shake hands. Franzi does the same. Dora doesn't like parties or handshakes, yet has no choice but to follow Goth and Franzi. They curtly nod each time they greet someone, and people respond with "Hello" or "Evenin'." Nobody introduces themselves, since everybody knows everybody else. Dora is pretty sure everyone here knows her name, while she has no idea who anyone else is.

More guests arrive, and the crowd spreads out spaciously across the lawn. Dora is glad to have found a strategic spot between the grill and the drinks table where she can hunker down in a sheltered position. Goth stands next to her, holding a paper plate and eating sausages at his usual pace.

"I'm not worried about Covid," Heini says. "Won't last long. After all, it's made in China." Apparently he's settled into a new joke repertoire, and Dora starts to think maybe her spot near the grill isn't really such prime real estate.

Tom strikes up a conversation with Goth, who nods artfully to everything he says as he stoically continues to eat. The weather and the drought. Third dry summer in a row. The devastated crops, the plight of agriculture. Goth nods. More neighbors approach and form a semicircle. Apparently everyone here but Goth knows it's a Goth party. Goth nods and accepts the next sausage from Heini.

The bark beetles, the dying forest. Depleted soils that you're not allowed to fertilize.

"If you're panic shopping like a packrat, remember that packrats need to be fed, too. A packrat cannot live on hoarding alone." Heini has taken a deep dive into the world of Covid jokes. Everyone gathered gladly accepts his suggestion, digging in. Now the main topic of conversation shifts to how anybody can work when kids can't go to school or daycare. How to make ends meet when you're out of work. How important all those stay-at-home orders really were, now that suddenly everyone's going on vacation like in the before times. Goth eats and nods. If Dora is counting correctly, he's on his fourth grilled sausage. The conversation turns to how people will get to work if diesel is banned, as so many politicians have proposed.

"Then we'll all buy electric cars!" shouts a fireman, and the group laughs uproariously.

Dora gets a beer and brings one to Goth. When he pulls a cigarette out of the box, he remembers to offer her one too. Slowly she begins to relax. Nobody but she herself seems to be wondering who she really is, what she's doing here, or what her relationship to Goth is. She downs her beer in almost one gulp. She fleetingly registers that Jay and Franzi aren't nearby, then notices they're dashing through the bushes with all the other kids. Someone pushes a pink glass into her hand. The mysterious liquid tastes like strawberry gum. People are getting nicer and nicer, the party is getting funnier and funnier.

Two villages away, the last doctor's office that still did home visits has closed. It's now completely unclear where the old folks will go for their diabetes prescriptions.

"Who cares, as long as they have enough Covid tests in Bavaria," Sadie says, and everyone laughs.

Someone remarks that three inns in the area have closed down in just the last few weeks.

"That's why we have to drink outside, around campfires," says another.

"Until they ban campfires, too."

"Then we'll just stand on the side of the road and chat." Heini looks a little offended, while everyone in the group is laughing so hard that some people cover their beer bottles. Dora notices that Steffen has pulled a small notebook out of his pocket and is surreptitiously taking notes.

"But without his fugginforeignfarmhands," Goth announces, looking at Steffen. It's the first time he's said anything at all. Steffen ignores the remark. Dora elbows Goth and goes "Tsk, tsk!" as if he were a dog that had stolen a slice of ham from the table, whereupon everyone bursts into laughter yet again and starts repeating Dora's "Tsk, tsk!" until they gradually calm down again.

Dora wonders if she and Goth are friends, since it appears they're now doing a sketch comedy routine together. Maybe friendship is just something that kind of happens on its own. All the bystanders raise their bottles, and toast, including Dora, who's become part of something, even though she doesn't quite know what.

Even if Dora doesn't like parties, she has to admit that this one was a smashing success. Goth looks content, no headache, no signs of impending failure. Franzi dashes around the village green with the other kids as if she'd never left Bracken. Jay is in the middle of it all, tumbling over her own feet with excitement and making Franzi the star of the party with her adoration.

One of the firefighters brings Dora another sausage and a bottle of beer and pats her on the back as if to say: "Well done." The conversation now turns to who's made home improvements lately, paved the driveway or built a new shed, as well as how the potatoes are coming along, and what special offers there are at the hardware store. Steffen puts his notebook away and saunters over to another group.

Franzi could go to school in Plausitz. Dora and Jay could accompany her to the bus stop every morning. If she ever misses the bus, Dora would drive her into town in the pickup. Take the opportunity to go shopping. Afterwards, she'd enjoy a well-deserved coffee and work on one of her new jobs, for W. Heating Supply and F. Tailor Shop and whoever else there might be in the region. Perhaps she could branch out, developing not only advertising strategies, but becoming a consultant specialized in new business models for the post-Covid era.

Goth appears to be bolted to the bench, smoking and nodding every now and then. It's hard to believe that just a few days ago he was lying unconscious in the yard. An initial deterioration, after which things are now looking up. Heini has started a long joke about a monkey on a plane. He goes on and on, although no one's listening.

After Pentecost, Dora has an appointment with Tom to discuss the Blooming Friendships campaign.

If he's pleased with her work, he will certainly recommend her to others. Tom looks like a guy with a lot of connections. She thinks about the last time she felt the prickling bubbles and can't remember. Jojo has announced his visit for the day after tomorrow. Meanwhile, Dora is sure he has news for her. He must have looked at the MRIS again, read through the literature, talked to specialist friends. He must be coming to persuade Mr. Proksch, who doesn't want to know what's going on in his own head, to undergo therapy.

Dora listens in on a conversation about the quality of the latest robotic mowers and thinks how little polarization there really is. No east and west, down and up, left or right. Neither paradise nor apocalypse, contrary to what the media and politics often portray. Instead, it's just people, standing together. People who like each other, some more, some less. Who come together and separate again. Dora belongs, Goth belongs. Even if neither of them make a move or say hardly anything. Even though everyone knows that Goth was in prison and thinks that Dora is his new girlfriend. They're having this party to celebrate the only truth there is: They are all on this planet together, here and now. They are a community. They share this existence. Sitting or standing, silent or talking, drinking or smoking as the Earth spins, the sun sets, and the fire burns down to embers. What a fucking miracle. Seen from this perspective, the notion of any division whatsoever seems like utter delusion.

Dora wonders whether one day, after she has saved his life, Goth will wind up kneeling on the neck of a black man. Or storming into a shisha bar in Berlin to shoot people with an immigrant background. She thinks of doctors in military hospitals saving the lives of enemy soldiers. The flaw in the system isn't that lives have to be saved, it's war itself.

By the time the fire has actually burned down and the sun has finally set, most of the party guests have left. Those who linger move closer to the fire pit, peering into the puddle of embers and lowering their voices, as if convinced the night and its darkness shouldn't be disturbed. A clear liquid in small glasses makes the rounds, and Dora drinks up each time one of the shots comes to her. In the tops of the oak trees, young owls let out beckoning calls. Bats silently go on the prowl, crickets chirp in search of love. Dora sits on one of the benches she now realizes Goth probably also built. Franzi walks over and climbs onto her lap. She wraps her arms around the warm child's body, and presses it against her own. Jay drops to her feet, exhausted, and stretches her hind legs out, striking her classic ray pose. Together, all three watch sparks rise into the sky as one of the firefighters pokes at the embers.

"When the fire dies," Franzi asks, "it goes up there, right? Into the sky?"

"You could say so."

"And when people die, they do that, too?"

"Some people believe so."

"What do you believe?"

The question comes as such a surprise that Dora has to think, which isn't so easy with a head full of alcohol. She doesn't know exactly what she believes.

She doesn't believe in God. But she does believe in connection.

"I believe nothing is lost in nature. We all stay here. We just change our form."

"Into a Eurasian jay, for example," Franzi says, sounding so peaceful that Dora gives her another squeeze.

After that, they don't speak. Dora thinks the girl has fallen asleep. But when Goth comes over and says, "Let's go," Franzi immediately gets to her feet. They walk back along the side of the road, and Franzi holds Dora's hand. Jay trots along behind them. Goth again uses his body as a shield, protecting them from the traffic on the road, which at this hour is nonexistent. As they walk, Dora feels the liquor in her arms and legs. She probably drank more than Goth. If she remembers correctly, he always just passed the small glasses to the nearest person, not drinking a single one. Before she knows it, she's gone through the gate with Goth and Franzi instead of continuing to the estate manager's house—her house.

"Hold on," Goth says. "I'll put Franzi to bed."

Franzi stretches out her arms and lets him lift her. Goth carries her like a doll. With one foot, he pushes open the back door of the main house and walks in cradling the girl in his arms. His movements are so natural it's as if they do this every day. Dora stands in the yard, swaying slightly. She hears him rumble up the stairs and pictures him putting Franzi to bed, tucking her in, and planting a kiss on her forehead. She can feel the girl's contentedness in her own body.

"I want to have another smoke," Goth says when he returns.

"Sure."

"By the wall, okay?"

Dora nods, but it takes her a minute to grasp what he means. She has to get moving, leave his yard, walk along the road, and across her own lawn. At the wall, she climbs onto the lawn chair. Goth is already on the other side, standing on the fruit crate. This is how she saw him for the first time. Pleased to meet you, I'm the village Nazi. He takes two cigarettes from the pack, puts them between his lips, lights them both, and hands one to Dora. They smoke in silence. Above them the stars twinkle, some so brightly it looks as if they were about to crash to Earth. Goth is standing so close she can hear his breath and see his pulse throbbing on his neck. 0×0. No Error. Dora thinks she has a lot of things to think about. But she can't. She's too drunk. They smoke until the embers eat into the edges of the filters and they can't take even one more drag. Then they flick the butts away, perfectly synchronized.

"Okay," Goth says.

45

Schütte

She's making coffee when someone bangs on the front door. Goth is standing outside. In yet another new shirt. This one is short-sleeved and striped yellow and blue. The colors are so hideous, Dora can't help but think of carnival.

"G'mornin'."

Instead of replying, she hands him his pills. On this particular morning, she'd actually rather take them herself. A splitting headache throbs behind her temples, she can barely keep her left eye open, and it's entirely possible that she'll discover she's suffering momentary aphasia as soon as she tries speaking. She didn't realize how much she actually drank at the party. That, plus the muggy weather, and so many cigarettes. She can only remember parts of the previous night, in a complete blur. Did Goth really ask her to stand against the wall to have another smoke? And, if so, how did she manage not to fall off the lawn chair?

Goth registers her expression and shows his crooked grin. He swallows the pills casually, as if it had long since ceased to matter. Just an old habit between the two of them.

"C'mon," he says. "Bring the keys to the truck."

He waits at the door while she goes back into the house, fishes the keys out of the palm tree planter, pours her coffee into a to-go mug, and ties her hair into a ponytail while standing at the bathroom mirror. As she takes the few steps along the roadside over to Goth's place, Dora tries to chug most of her coffee, hoping it will at least clear her vision. The gate is open. Franzi is bouncing up and down next to the pickup, apparently sufficiently rested despite the short night. She barely takes the time to greet Jay, and effusively repeats, over and over, "We're going on a fieldtrip, we're going on a fieldtrip!" Dora wants to go back to bed.

Goth reaches out, palm up, for the keys.

"I'm driving."

At this particular moment, he probably poses less of a safety risk than she does. Even with her wretched hangover, Dora can tell how he's doing. Clear-eyed, relaxed expression, slightly drooping lower lip. He's in a good mood, or at least a better mood than she is.

"Where're we going?"

"You'll see."

He gets in and starts the engine. Dora climbs into the passenger seat with some difficulty, Franzi and Jay get in back. The orange tabby sits on the wall and looks down at them contemptuously. Under the cat's gaze, Dora can literally feel how awkward and inelegant the human body and its motions are.

They drive a short distance toward Kochlitz. The windows are down, a warm breeze sweeps through the pickup. Goth drives slowly and with concentration, as if he wants to be driver of the month. Before Kochlitz, he turns off. This secondary road leads through the forest. After a while Goth slows down even more, and keeps an eye on the left side of the road, apparently looking for a turnoff. When he finally finds it, he brakes, turns, and steers the pickup onto a rough dirt road leading deeper and deeper into the forest. Some time ago, heavy forestry vehicles must have churned up the ground, and then the sun baked it into a wavy landscape of bumps and dips. The pickup's snout rises and falls like that of a motorboat in a strong sea swell. Dora leans both hands on the dashboard to avoid hitting her head; in the back seat, Franzi cheers like she's on a rollercoaster. In sandy spots, the tires dig into the ground, the truck starts to fishtail, and Dora thinks they're going to get stuck every time. But Goth knows what he's doing. He finesses the clutch and throttle, turns the steering wheel at just the right moment, and brings the truck back onto solid ground.

As the road improves a bit, Dora begins to enjoy the ride. The morning sun transforms the forest into a three-dimensional painting of shadow and light. Dora breathes in the scent of warm wood and dry moss, and takes another sip of coffee. The perfect breakfast. In the rearview mirror, she sees Franzi hanging half her upper body out the open window, gazing into the passing treetops.

Finally, Goth lets the pickup roll onto a patch of meadow and turns off the engine. For a moment, Dora finds the silence deafening. Then she recognizes the sounds of the forest: the steady rustle of trees, the high-voltage buzz of insects, the cacophony of bird calls, the chatter of a busy woodpecker. For a moment they all just sit there, listening to the concert, until Franzi pushes open the door and yells "Fieldtrip, fieldtrip!"

"It's nice here," Dora says to Goth, who pretends not to have heard her.

Franzi and Jay have already disappeared into the forest. Here and there the girl's colorful T-shirt flickers between the trees. Goth lifts a basket from the flatbed and starts moving; Dora walks at his side. Although they haven't driven more than half an hour, this forest seems different from the woods around Bracken. There are no pine plantations here, but a vast variety of deciduous trees that have grown old and tall: oaks, beeches, birches. The atmosphere is somehow enchanted. It's as if no one else ever comes here. Dora sees a forgotten pile of wood, half-rotten and sinking into the ground, which no one is likely to come back for. A little further on lie overgrown coils of wire for a deer fence that no one will ever build, and an overturned hunting blind that no one will ever set upright or use ever again. The path is patterned with the paired hooves of deer. The woodpecker tirelessly keeps on tapping.

The outline of a former driveway can be seen in the grass. They follow the wheel tracks into the woods until, after a few hundred yards, a wide space opens up, not quite a clearing but a large meadow, heathy and herbaceous, with only a few shrubs here and there. In some places there are so many flowers growing that they leap at the eye like colorful puddles. Bees fly in droves, busily buzzing around wild mallow and clover. Goth pauses.

"These used to be fields." His arm motion encompasses the whole area. "There used to be stables back there. Now all that's left are the overgrown foundations."

He leads them across the meadow. A little further on, Franzi and Jay are romping in the tall grass. Dora tastes the spicy air, it smells almost like an herbal tea boutique. This just might be the most beautiful place she has ever been. A peaceful, fragrant, magical spot that belongs only to the past and to the animals.

"The main house was over there."

Dora shields her eyes with her hand and recognizes ruins of old walls now covered in weeds. Three linden trees loft their mighty crowns toward the sky. They have outlived the house they were once meant to shade.

"The buildings were gradually demolished. Once everything was empty, villagers from Bracken scavenged whatever useful material was left."

Goth points to rows of relatively low trees standing close together. Their rampant shoots have woven together into an impenetrable thicket.

"This was the orchard. Cherries, apples, plums."

The entire former plantation is covered in lichen that decorates each twig with a lacy, silvery trim. It's the perfect dwelling place for elves, dwarves, and other mythical creatures.

"Firewood storage, water well, workshop, tool shed."

Goth points to various places where there is nothing whatsoever to see. They walk a few more steps and sit down on the stump of a massive oak tree people probably used as a seat thirty years ago. Their upper arms touch. Franzi's laughter rises to the clouds, whose edges are gilt by the sun.

Meanwhile, Dora can now tell in advance when oxo is about to pounce. She can tell by the sudden certainty that she actually exists. She senses a gentle sinking in her stomach, her head feels lighter, and her vision grows clearer. The three-dimensionality of her surroundings grows more palpable. Maybe oxo is a little like dying. She had suspected it was somehow related to Goth from the very beginning. He draws in the present. It's as if he possesses some special gravitational pull. Even the most skilled storyteller would never manage to invent a character quite like him.

"You know this place well," she says.

"We used to live here."

She probably should've been able to connect those dots on her own.

He has brought her to the place he grew up. His childhood home, which no longer exists. Suddenly she sees the surroundings through different eyes, as if someone had slipped a new slide into the projector. She sees Goth as a little boy, running through a wheat field. Picking plums in the orchard. Sitting on the tractor with his father.

"Bracken's barracks, Schütte's hut. They always sang that taunt in school. Wasn't easy to get there. To school, I mean."

It takes a moment for Dora to remember the Wikipedia entry: Schütte, a now uninhabited historic settlement.

"After the fall of the Wall, we stayed for a while. Then all of a sudden they said this belongs to someone else." He performs a gesture as if trying to just push the meadows and former fields aside. "I was thirteen when we had to leave."

Now Dora spots the Eurasian jay. Somehow she's been expecting him all along. He's sitting in the branches of a young maple tree, looking over at them.

"Then we moved to Plausitz. My old man was looking for work. School was a lot closer. So we all just squatted in this tiny shack. Worse than being in the slammer. At least there you're alone for a change."

The Eurasian jay hops a little closer on the branch. Clearly, he wants to be near people.

"In the summer of '92, my father took me to Rostock. In a Barkas minibus, like tourists. I thought it was great. Finally out of the shack. Bonfires, beer, awesome evenings. It was one huge party. There's no other way to put it."

Dora doesn't immediately get what he means. Then it dawns on her, and her heart plummets. Her stomach feels as if she's been pushed off a high precipice. Rostock-Lichtenhagen, the Sunflower Tower. Germany's most violent race riots since World War II.

"It was like a resurrection. Finally, things were happening. We felt alive again."

Dora wonders whether he's trying to justify himself, showing her Schütte merely to explain why he became a Nazi. But that doesn't seem like Goth. Somehow it just doesn't fit. Besides, the point isn't what he's trying to do. The point is that she keeps drifting off. Indulging cloudy dreams of self-discovery, the whole runtime error thing, existential feelings. It's simply grand to finally comprehend the sense of Being while seated beside someone who, at the tender age of thirteen or fourteen, set fire to the shelters of Vietnamese immigrants and contract workers and called it "a resurrection."

Dora declines the cigarette he offers. She can't pretend nothing is wrong. She feels sick.

After all, he doesn't call himself a citizen of the Reich, like so many right-wing nutjobs do, she tells herself. He's not a Covid-denier or climate-denier, he doesn't believe in QAnon, doesn't belong to any armed underground, and isn't a member of the NPD. The Rostock-Lichtenhagen riots happened thirty years ago.

But somehow such thoughts don't help. She should get up and leave. Walk back to Bracken, all by herself. Get in the house, close the door, and lock it tight. If only she weren't so weak. Fucking block party. Fucking nausea. Goth's words fall like stones into her stomach.

"After Lichtenhagen we went further. We drove around, a real tour. Wismar, Güstrow, Kröpelin. We bathed in the lakes and slept in the car. In the evening we raised a riot in front of the immigrants' apartment buildings. I'll never forget the faces of the cops behind their Plexiglas shields. They were afraid of us. My father never allowed me to go all the way to the front. I wasn't allowed to throw anything either. But once I helped tip over a police car. It's easy with a few people. Get a few people together and everything's easy. That's what you all forgot."

Dora doesn't know who "you all" is supposed to be, nor does she want to find out. She keeps her eyes fixed on the Eurasian jay, which has fluttered down to the ground and is looking at her with its head tilted like a pigeon that wants to be fed.

"Why are you telling me all this?" she asks.

"I thought we were friends," Goth says.

"I don't understand all the hate."

"Everybody hates somebody. Otherwise there would be no progress."

"That's bullshit."

"You hate Nazis."

"I don't hate anyone at all."

"You think you're better than me."

Dora shoots to her feet. Suddenly she's overcome by that insane rage again. It's high time she gave Goth a piece of her mind. What is he thinking, bringing her here and pulling on her heartstrings like that? "I thought we were friends." Is she supposed to feel sorry for him? Oh you poor little village Nazi? She wants to tell him what an awful person he is. He's misanthropic, and prone to violence. She wants to tell him what an embarrassment his flags are. What unbelievably stupid stuff his friends natter on about on YouTube. She'll tell him where he can stick his hatred, alright. Best of all, she'd just love to tell him what a shitty father he is.

But then she can only think of two sentences, and she blurts them out:

"You *bet* I'm better than you! I'm a hundred times better than you!"

Goth doesn't react, but Dora realizes something. The words ring true, and it felt wonderful to shout them. "You *bet* I'm better than you." But, on second thought, those sentiments are the mother of all problems. Both on the outskirts of Bracken and on a global scale. That sense of superiority is a long-acting poison that devours all humanity from the inside.

Confused, Dora lets herself sink back onto the tree stump. Her rage has fizzled out completely. Goth takes a roll from the basket, tears it into small pieces, and tosses them to the Eurasian jay. The bird takes its time, but finally hops over and pounces on the crumbs. It almost lands on Dora's sneakers in the process.

"You don't have to yell," Goth whispers.

"I didn't know they ate bread," whispers Dora.

"Everybody eats bread."

"And hates somebody."

"I used to feed birds here. It's like they remember."

"How long does a Eurasian jay live?"

"Not long enough."

He hands her the roll. She tosses a few crumbs on the ground and then holds out a larger piece to the bird. It hops in and pulls back, turning its head, fluttering in place, wrestling with the idea of eating out of her hand. Fear versus greed.

46

Hunting Blind

"That way."

He trudges ahead, Dora follows, down a hill and diagonally across the heath. Franzi and Jay join them. They walk along the edge of the forest, then a short distance down a sandy path through the trees. Apparently there's a specific destination. When the forest opens up again, they stop.

"Another field?"

"Potato field. Before."

That sounds like the title of a book Dora wouldn't finish reading. A little ways away, a fringe of reeds betrays the existence of a small lake. Goth leads them to a long ladder leading up to a hunting blind. Before they start climbing, he takes three binoculars from the handle basket and hangs one around each of their necks. Seconds later, Franzi is darting ahead up the ladder.

"Gimme the mutt."

Dora hesitates briefly before picking Jay up off the ground and handing her to Goth. The dog licks his chin and lets him carry her without putting up any resistance. Basket in hand and Jay on his arm, Goth slowly climbs the rungs. When Dora reaches the platform on top, he raises a finger to his lips.

"Keep quiet."

They don't have to wait long. Some distance away, a pair of gray herons lands and leisurely stalks toward the reeds, looking for prey. Through binoculars, the birds seem close enough to touch. Their gray wings with dark undersides, their white necks, the black bar on their faces like the mask of a predator.

"There's a stork!" whispers Franzi.

Indeed, another bird has landed, even larger, in classic black-and-white plumage. Nodding, it searches the tall grass on its high red legs.

Next come cranes, whose sheer size amazes Dora. Their long legs, red head markings, and fluffy rumps make them look like exotic aliens. Well-fed wild geese swim across the lake, indignant mallards protest, "Quaaaack-quaaack-quaack-quack."

"Pheasants," says Goth, and three colorful males fly up, their wings flapping loud.

The birds here are all so big, Dora thinks. Especially compared to the tiny tufted titmice, robins, and wrens she used to watch through the kitchen window with her mother. Back then, she considered even magpies to be giants clad in black and white.

"There!" Goth half rises from the bench and pauses, knees bent as he presses the binoculars to his eyes and turns the focus. "I don't believe it."

"What? What?" asks Franzi, and he sternly orders her not to be so loud.

Dora follows Goth's gaze and raises her own binoculars to her eyes. She sees an inconspicuous, brown-spotted bird, smaller than a partridge. Its beak is of medium length, yet thin and straight, like a surgical instrument. Here and there, it pokes it into the meadow. Without Goth's excitement, Dora wouldn't have paid any attention to the bird. It looks dull, maybe some kind of snipe or wagtail.

"A ruff," Goth whispers. "Very rare. Maybe thirty

couples left. There's a huge reserve not far from here. I've never seen one in the wild."

"Do you come here often to watch birds?" asks Dora.

It sounds formal and forced. The earlier outburst still reverberates inside her. You *bet* I'm better than you. It's hard for her to behave normally. But, once again, Goth pretends he didn't hear her anyway. He's busy helping his daughter adjust her binoculars. When Franzi shouts "I see it, I see it!" Dora is almost certain she's lying.

When they've had enough of birdwatching, Goth lifts the basket to his knees and unpacks a picnic. He hands Dora a thermos of coffee and Franzi a bottle of orange soda. Then he presents some salty chasseur sausage and more of the semi-stale gas station rolls he must've picked up at the party. It tastes so good, Dora closes her eyes. The coffee is too sweet and the rolls are old, but it makes no difference.

"This is the best day of my life," Franzi says.

"Bullshit," snorts Goth.

Even Dora winces. Franzi swallows. Bravely, she moves closer to her father.

"Really," she insists.

Goth puts his arm around her shoulders and pulls her close. They stay like that for some time, while Dora sits by, utterly still, as if she were about to vanish into thin air. It would be the perfect moment to do so.

During the ride back, Franzi hangs halfway out the window again, squealing with delight as she's tossed back and forth on the bumpy road.

"You think people can change?" asks Dora.

"People can die," Goth replies.

"That's not what I mean."

"It's quite a change, though."

He grins to himself, and she thinks about what she really wants to ask him.

"You're always busy thinking," Goth says. "Just let the world be as it is."

Dora takes her cell phone out of her pocket and texts Jojo.

He's doing fine. No symptoms. He's philosophizing. The reply comes in the same minute. *I'll be there tomorrow around 7 p.m. With sushi.*

At three in the morning, Dora is suddenly wide awake. She steps outside. Either a film is being shot on the other side of the wall, or a UFO has landed. There's a sphere of dazzling light above Goth's yard. It highlights the treetops, so they stand out sharply against the blackness of the night. As if magically drawn in, she runs to the wall and climbs onto the chair. There's a large spotlight on the trailer steps, powerful enough to illuminate an entire construction site. Goth is busy with his she-wolf, finishing the lower back, hind legs, and tail. His upper body bobs in time with his arm movements. He's completely absorbed in his work, in a flow state where time and space no longer exist. The she-wolf looks at Dora, ears pricked, muzzle open in a half-friendly, half-furtive laugh. She'll probably leap up and run off the moment Goth frees her feet.

For a long time Dora simply watches. She can't take her eyes off it. She stands on the chair until her knees and back hurt. By the time she decides to go back to bed, it's after four, and Goth is still sculpting like a man possessed. A few feet away, the orange tabby lies on the wall, paws folded, nestled into the now.

47

Power Flower

Power Flower. These two words refuse to leave Dora's mind. It's as if they've decided she's the ideal host animal, and will now suck all the life force out of her. They circle through her head, infecting all other thoughts. The nettles she's battling are a merciless opponent. Power Flower. Dora's legs already look like she's been attacked by piranhas. Power Flower. Jojo plans to get here around seven, and right now it's only four. Power Flower.

Trying to clear the back corners of her property was such a stupid idea. Nobody needs the back corners of a plot this big. The back corners are home to butterflies and other highly important insects that treat it like a nature preserve—protected mating grounds. They're also the ideal terrain of man-sized thistles that look like monsters from outer space, with thick, spiny limbs and countless heads. The back corners belong to Dora only on paper, not in reality. This fact becomes increasingly clear to her with each attempt to yank one of these monsters out of the ground. Power Flower.

She's decided to rework Tom's campaign once again. The rubber chancellor puppet struck her as too daring, and the "Blossoming Friendships" tagline too sarcastic. Now the brand is to be called "Power Flower." She's already prepared taglines, social media concepts, and content ideas for her presentation tomorrow. She plans to pitch a newsletter to Tom, to regularly inspire customers to new creative ideas. Maybe do a few videos and have a DIY section, too. She's reserved the Power Flower domain, and has been stuck in a loop ever since.

All day she's been super nervous. She's had little sleep and little to eat, and has been trying to beat back tenacious plant adversaries under the blazing sun for far too long. Franzi and Jay fled into the woods to escape from her irritated state and haven't been seen since.

She feels like a child who's held back from running straight to the table of presents on her birthday, and is instead forced to wait until evening. The table is Jojo, and the presents are the information he's bringing her. All day long, Dora tries to convince herself that his visit might not mean anything, but her excited mood isn't fooled. Jojo isn't venturing out into the detested backwater of rural Brandenburg—"despite the current situation" and "in times like these"—just to have sushi with her. He has a plan, and that plan may well change everything. Jojo might not always have been a good father, but he has always been a superb doctor. His life-saving stats are to him what running times are to a professional marathoner. If Goth can get him a new notch on his surgeon's scalpel, he'll do anything to save him, no matter what the odds.

She slays a few more monster thistles with the scythe, and they fall to the ground in slow motion, reproachful. How frustrating to know they'll grow back anyway, since Dora isn't bothering to pull them up from the roots. She wipes the sweat from her forehead with her forearm.

Her back hurts like that first day, when she decided to turn over the ultra-hard soil of her far-too-large vegetable patch. Around five, she takes a shower and luxuriates in the cold water flowing over her body. It washes the sweat from her hair, cools her calloused fingers, and soothes the burning sensation on her scratched lower legs. Dora forms her hands into a bowl and drinks. If you've never fought nature with a scythe or a spade, you don't know what water is. She'd love to just stay in the shower until Jojo arrives. But after a while it gets too cold. Dora steps out of the shower cabin, wraps her hair in one towel and her damp body in another, and stands on the bath mat, completely still. Her nervousness suddenly becomes stronger.

By now she's intimately familiar with many forms of restlessness, fear, and excitement. She has observed, analyzed, and cataloged the various states. She is an archivist of nervousness. One day she'll open a Museum of Restlessness, where visitors can view the various genres behind glass, everything from prickling, rising bubbles to insect-like, swarming tension, to the agonizing gnawing of worry, and the destructive rage of panic attacks. What's currently spreading inside of her is nothing like her usual tingling, nor is it an unfounded panic attack. Rather, it belongs to the category of justified irritations. In other words: Something isn't right. Something's off here.

When Dora steps into the next room, where she's built a closet out of stacked moving boxes, what's wrong immediately becomes clear. Her piles of clothes are in disarray. Two pairs of pants are lying on the floor. Someone has rummaged through all her clothes.

Dora looks at the shifted piles in disbelief, as if, any moment now, she'll remember it was her. But it wasn't. She always folds her clothes neatly. Someone must have been in the house. When she came in from the yard, she didn't notice anything unusual. However, she went straight to the bathroom without looking into any of the other rooms. She has to make up for that now. She pulls underwear, jeans, and a striped T-shirt out of the mussed-up stacks and dresses in a hurry. Worst case scenario, there's someone else still in the house with her. But she figures there must be a harmless explanation. Franzi probably decided to play dress-up and just forgot to ask permission.

With hesitant steps, as if she doubted the floor could properly support her weight, Dora goes first to the kitchen, where she examines the sparse furnishings. Upon closer inspection, the changes are evident. Drawers have been pulled open and not closed. The coffee can is open, although Dora is always careful to close the lid so the aroma doesn't dissipate. A stack of magazines is lying at a different angle than before.

In the hallway, her jacket has fallen off the nail on the wall. In the bedroom, the mattresses are crooked, and a blanket hangs halfway off the bed. Since Dora owns so little, the whole thing looks like the cheapo version of a house search.

However, it doesn't exactly look like something

Franzi could pull off either. Whoever was looking for something here was systematic. They didn't try to cover their tracks, but they did make an effort to cause as little destruction as possible.

Dora saves her office for last. That's where everything of value is. She has no idea what she'll do if her laptop, tablet, and phone are gone. Those are her tools. She can't work without them, and she has to work. She doesn't even know if she has anything like homeowners insurance. Even if she does, who knows whether it would even cover a break-in of this sort.

The door is ajar, and Dora pushes it open with her foot. Her laptop is on the floor, right where she left it. Her momentary relief turns to horror when she sees what's changed instead. Now she almost wishes her laptop were missing. That would make this whole thing a normal, stupid burglary, including a police report, perplexity, and their pointless promise to get back to her as soon as their investigation yields results.

The large palm tree lies on its side, sprawled across the floorboards. Its outstretched arms reach halfway across the room. Power Flower, prostrate. Someone lifted the plant out of its planter and just threw it down. Someone with strong arms and an unbending will. Someone determined to find what they were looking for. Potting soil has fallen to the floor and been tracked across the room by the burglar's shoes. Dora doesn't need a forensic investigation to know whose shoes they were. She also knows what's missing now. Nevertheless, she goes to look. The wooden planter is empty. The keys to the pickup are gone.

48

Traffic Jam

He probably just wanted to go somewhere for a minute. He could have asked her, but he knew she'd have said no. Maybe he's doing so well, he's convinced he can drive safely again. Yesterday they went off into the forest together, Goth was behind the wheel, it was totally fine. Maybe he wanted to go visit his Nazi friends. Or to Schütte again, alone this time. Or he's planning a surprise for Franzi. Maybe the girl's birthday is coming up? Dora has no idea. In an hour and a half she'll ask Jojo if the strict ban on Goth taking the wheel can be relaxed a bit. Just so Goth doesn't have to break into her house every time he wants to go for a spin.

She takes a deep breath. Goes back into the bathroom. Combs her wet hair. Forgoes blow-drying it. To prove to herself how unworried she is, she cleans up the house first, which goes faster than expected. She even manages to set the heavy palm tree back on its feet.

Then she runs outside and over to the wall. She climbs onto the chair and peers over. The pickup truck isn't in the yard. Of course it isn't. Dora doesn't remember hearing the engine, but she's also been at the far back corners of her property for a long time, waging war on those tenacious nettles. Afterwards, she was in the shower and had water in her ears.

Franzi sits in the shade with a knife, whittling, Jay beside her, probably waiting for her next wooden bone.

"Where's your daddy?"

Both girl and dog raise their heads.

"Gone."

"Okay." Dora acts like this is perfectly normal, which is essentially true. No big deal. No problem at all. "When did he leave?"

Franzi thinks a moment, then shrugs. "Just now, I think."

That could mean anything, or nothing at all. Franzi is still in the blissful stage of childhood development where the notion of time is a foreign concept. For her, five minutes can last an hour and vice versa, depending on what she's doing at that exact moment. Humankind wasn't kicked out of Eden because it munched on an apple—it was kicked out when it invented the clock.

"Y'know where he was going?"

Franzi shakes her head. She doesn't think it's strange. Why should she? Her father drives off, leaves her alone, eventually comes back. The girl doesn't worry, and that's a good thing. Neither does Dora. Really. All that matters is that Goth be home when Jojo arrives, in case he wants to examine him again. Which he almost certainly will. If necessary, Jojo will have to wait. Jojo has no problem staying up late, until midnight and longer if necessary, especially if there's a good bottle of wine nearby. It's terrible timing, but not so bad in the grand scheme of things. Goth really could've asked her, she'd have found a solution. But that's Goth for you. He has his reasons, and does his own thing.

Anyone else, and she could just call on her cell phone. Or send a WhatsApp message, "Where the hell are you?" But Dora doesn't even know if Goth owns a cell phone. He's the only one she knows who isn't permanently fused to a communication device. Maybe that's the secret to his special presence. Still, Dora would give anything to be able to reach him right about now.

She goes back inside, sets the kitchen table for two, decants a bottle of red wine, just the way Jojo likes it, and then doesn't know what to do with herself. She keeps an ear out the entire time, in case she hears something outside. Not the elegant whirring of Jojo's Jaguar, but the sputtering of Goth's pickup truck. She paces the rooms, restless. Study, bedroom, hallway, kitchen, bathroom. They played tag along this route, Goth, Franzi, and her. It seems as if years have passed since then. Back then, the world was a different place. Dora was a city dweller in exile because of Covid, and Goth was the troublemaker behind the wall. Now she's a village-based solopreneur with an adopted daughter, and Goth is a friend with a tumor.

Friend. That's what she really thought just now. She walks faster. Study, bedroom, hallway, kitchen, bathroom. Was it Heidegger who said that, when facing the abyss, escaping back into everyday life wasn't a viable solution? Heidegger probably wasn't familiar with the *Error oxo*. The *Error oxo* is a handmade wooden bench right on the edge of Heidegger's abyss. The abyss is the knowledge that all Being is merely a transitory stage between not-yet-Being and no-longer-Being. The wooden bench is there so you can sit down next to each other and gaze into the abyss together. For the time being.

Shortly after six-thirty, the phone rings.

"I'm sorry, honey," Jojo says. "Looks like I'm going to be a little late. I'm stuck in traffic on the highway."

Tuesday night, Dora thinks. Commuter traffic, for sure.

"It's odd," Jojo says. "Nobody's commuting right now. Some people are working from home, others are vacationing on the Baltic." He snorts disdainfully. "There must've been an accident. I think they've closed the road."

Accidents happen on this highway all the time. That stretch of highway is a modern-day mass grave. Narrow lanes, no shoulder, lined with densely packed trees. Tractors, trucks, motorcycles, and oversized loads recklessly pass each other, even in the no-passing zone. There are several white crosses along the roadside, decorated with flowers or candles. Some days, Dora finds it interesting that people can be afraid of getting sick while driving 90 miles per hour down the highway with not a care in the world. Today, she doesn't.

"Would you mind if I eat some of this sushi?" asks Jojo. "I'm famished."

Another accident on this highway means absolutely nothing, Dora knows as much. Unfortunately, she doesn't believe what she knows.

"You have to go to the front," she says.

"What?"

"Get out of the car, go to the front, and see what happened."

"What kind of crazy idea is that?"

"I'm asking you to."

"Dora, I don't understand what this is all about. There's a fine for rubbernecking, and besides ..."

"You're a doctor, goddammit," Dora snaps. "You're allowed up front. Can't you just do what I ask?"

Jojo is silent for a moment.

"Okay," he says tersely, and hangs up. Dora resumes her pacing, but it's no longer enough for her. She runs into the yard, to the far corner, picks up the scythe and drops another thistle. That doesn't change anything either. Her thoughts can no longer be controlled. She pictures Jojo walking along the line of waiting cars. She pictures the faces of the drivers in the windshields who, despite their mounting impatience, don't dare to leave their vehicles. Some have the side window open and are vaping, creating clouds so massive it looks as if their vehicle were on fire. Breathing masks dangle from rearview mirrors. Jojo keeps walking. Up at the very front, ambulance, police, fire department. No helicopter. That could be a good sign or a bad sign. Just like the ambulance, which stays put, going nowhere. It's either very good or very bad. Men in uniforms are moving about on the roadway. They're getting ready to direct individual cars past the scene of the accident. Jojo has to hurry lest his Jaguar become an obstacle to the flow of traffic when things get moving again. Now he sees the towering rear of the crashed vehicle. It's a pickup truck. It looks huge in this strange stance, a bizarre sheet metal sculpture.

Dora tosses the scythe to the ground and runs through the yard, to the street, and over to Goth's place. Franzi and Jay are still sitting on the ground, barely looking up. Dora stays glued to the spot. She notices something she missed earlier when she peered over the wall. The she-wolf isn't where she was before. A carpet of scattered wood chips indicates where Goth diligently labored all night. But the she-wolf is crouching a few feet away, on the trailer steps, next to her companion. She's a bit smaller, slender and beautiful, with pointed ears and that amused expression on her face. Now Dora also realizes what the bump at the base was for. At the feet of the she-wolf crouches a wolf pup, chubby and cute, gazing up at its mother with adoring eyes. There they sit together, mother, father, child, and nothing is missing. Nothing will ever be missing for them.

At the very sight of the wolf family, Dora knows what has happened. But she needs certainty. She rushes over to the trailer, up the grate-metal steps, and leans on the door. It's unlocked. She steps inside. Her head and body feel numb. All the colors seem muted, sounds fall away. The trailer is tidy and cleaned, the bed carefully made. There's another wooden sculpture in the middle of the tiny dining table, presented like a gift. It's so small it fits on the palm of Dora's hand.

It's a mixed-breed dog, pug-like, with a curled tail. She's lying on her belly, lifting her panting face toward the viewer, and seems to be letting out a joyous laugh. Her hind legs are stretched out to either side, so that her squat body resembles the triangular shape of a ray.

Turning the figure over, she sees a carved mark on the underside. Two triangles, pointed like wolf ears.

Now it is completely clear what Goth, the idiot, has done. What he, in his boundless stupidity, thought was a good idea.

"You damn fool," Dora says loudly, but not loud enough to be heard outside.

She sinks into the chair and sits, frozen, pressing the little wooden Jay against her palm as if it were a living creature. Horror is a giant that likes to stare at its victims for a while before nabbing them.

When her phone dings, Dora's eyes burn so badly she can barely read the message. It's from Jojo.

"Proksch is dead."

49

Proksch is Dead

Two hours later, the plastic containers with Jojo's premium sushi stand on the kitchen table, untouched. Dora and Jojo haven't even managed to put the sushi in the fridge. Jay-the-Ray is the only one interested in it. She raises her head, again and again, sniffing in its direction. According to her notion of justice, at this hour, food that hasn't yet been consumed by humans clearly belongs to the dog.

Everything blurs around Dora, the contours of events as well as the contours of her house. Even Jojo blends seamlessly into the surroundings. He uses the bathroom without even asking, gets another beer without asking, because Bracken doesn't seem like the right place to drink wine, and has even filled up Jay's water bowl. He's clearly comfortable in Dora's new house, although she doesn't even know whether it's still her home. The last time he was here, he didn't see the interior. Now he's admiring the wide wooden floorboards, praising the sparse rooms, the minimalist furnishings, the building's good structure, and the fact that he's allowed to smoke in the kitchen. His unapologetic attitude is meant to stabilize the universe. It's the crisis-proof keep-calm mode of a seasoned doctor for whom conversations with bereaved families are commonplace. Jojo even manages to make jokes about Jay's sushi cravings.

Indeed, his demeanor does help Dora gain a bit of a grip. But that only leads to her falling all the deeper when the moment of truth hits. Every few minutes, the absurd idea that she'll never see Goth again settles over her like a black blanket. Goth has been "there" more than anyone else she's ever known. He can't just be gone. He can't. It's impossible.

Proksch is dead. A profoundly wrong sentence. Time and time again, she asks Jojo whether he could've been mistaken. And he patiently answers: "There's no doubt about it, honey. I recognized the vehicle and the man. Or what was left of them."

Dora still does her best to not believe him, but then her eyes fall on the little wooden dog lying on the kitchen table next to the sushi bowls. When she touches it and clasps it in her hands, she realizes all over again that it's true. Goth has left, never to return. Never again will they stand together by the wall and smoke. Never again will they go birdwatching or sit in the pickup truck together. Never again will she be able to see how happy Franzi is by his side. It's an outrage.

Dora tries out different sentences on herself: You didn't know him that well. Now Bracken no longer has a village Nazi. You couldn't have prevented it anyway.

Nothing works. When she touches the little wooden Jay-the-Ray, she plunges into the abyss.

When her mother's dead body was picked up, no one cried. They all sat silently in their rooms, each alone in their own space. A terrible silence descended over the house. It was as if her mother had taken everything with her: love, security, family. Nothing remained but rubble and night. Even the birds in the yard fell silent.

That's no good. You mustn't remember such things. The past, if nothing else, must remain in its oubliette, forgotten. With all her might, Dora pushes the hatch shut. She wipes her face with a paper napkin and smokes another of Jojo's unfiltered cigarettes, which are already giving her a sore throat.

About an hour ago, she brought a plate of sandwiches over to Franzi and invited the girl to spend the rest of the evening at her house. But Franzi wanted to continue carving. She didn't even ask when her dad would be back.

After that, Jojo forced Dora to get Nadine's number. She resisted. She said she wanted to tell Franzi herself. That she owed it to her. That she knew the girl better than anyone else by now. That they'd been living together like a family for the last few weeks. She'll take Franzi in. For the first night. After that, Franzi can spend the rest of her Covid vacation with her. And summer vacations. She can stay with her forever. She will go to school in Plausitz. Dora and Jay will accompany her to the bus stop in the morning, and if she ever misses the bus, Dora will take her to Plausitz in the pickup. She'll take the opportunity to go shopping. Then she'll enjoy a well-deserved coffee and work on one of her new projects, for small businesses in the region, for whom she's developing new business models.

"Franzi doesn't want to go back to Berlin!" shouted Dora. "She absolutely does not want to go back to Berlin."

Jojo looked at her like she'd lost her mind. He grabbed her by the shoulders and explained that she was not Franzi's mother. Loud and sharp: "You—are—not—her—mother! You have to call Nadine, right now!"

When Dora had no strength left to resist, she called Tom, who knew Sadie's number, who gave her the number of Mrs. Proksch.

Mrs. Proksch didn't speak Brandenburgish. None of the accent, none of the local lingo. She spoke with the slightly stilted care of a woman who trained hard to lose her dialect. She was happy to meet the new neighbor and to hear that Franzi was doing well. Dora didn't want to talk to her. Nadine Proksch is not Goth's wife, after all. Nadine Proksch is his ex, so she doesn't have the slightest idea what's going on. Dora is on the scene, Dora's the one taking care of everything, Dora's the one working away in the engine room to keep everything running smooth on the surface. This is her story, not Nadine Proksch's. If Jojo hadn't been there, she'd have hung up right away.

Goth had an accident.

How harmless it sounds. Downright dainty.

Nadine Proksch didn't say much. She just said that she was getting into the car right away. That she was already on her way to the door, cell phone in hand.

After a glance at the clock, Dora gets up. It can't be much longer now. Jojo follows her to the front of the house. Jay has to stay inside, it's better that way. They're standing on the steps when a red Honda Civic speeds down the main road from Plausitz, brakes hard at the edge of town, and comes to a stop in front of Heini's house. A blonde woman gets out and runs across the street. A very long, braided pig-tail taps her back as she runs. She doesn't say hello to Dora and Jojo. She didn't even see them. Dora considers going to the wall, but decides against it. It's unbearable enough as it is. She hears Franzi's surprised, happy voice, her happy Mama-Mama shouts, then a brief faltering, and then wild cries of protest.

"No!" Franzi screams. "I'm not going! I don't wanna!"

Dora and Jojo see Nadine Proksch drag her screaming daughter across the street and load her into the car with gentle firmness. Franzi doesn't know why, she can't possibly understand what's going on. All she knows is that she's suddenly being picked up. Taken back to the city. Away from here. She can't say goodbye to Dora or Jay. She can't say goodbye to her dad. She screams, and Nadine Proksch screams back. Finally the doors slam shut. The car starts.

Jojo's Proksch-is-dead message was bad. Finding the little dog figurine was awful. But this is the worst of the worst. After seeing that, Dora doesn't cry another tear. Crying would be totally inappropriate in the face of this catastrophe. Downright ridiculous.

Around ten, Jojo's stomach growls so loudly that it can be heard clear across the kitchen. He asks if it would be all right with Dora if he eats something. She sits down with him, opens the plastic boxes, unpacks the wooden chopsticks, mixes the wasabi paste and soy sauce, even though she knows she won't be able to get a single bite down. She has the impression she'll never be able to eat again. At the same time, she knows from experience that life has the stunningly peculiar property of simply moving on. The sun arcs across the sky, the rivers flow, and all living things eat and sleep, no matter what happened the day before. Jojo deftly grabs nigiri pieces and maki rolls with his chopsticks, tops them with ginger, dips them in soy, and shoves them into his mouth, whole. He chews for a long time before swallowing. Dora silently watches the spectacle. The fish used to be alive too. Jojo eats, unmoved, unemotional. His rationality, his ability to eat a huge portion of sushi in the face of disaster, acts like a sedative. Perhaps he does it all the time, even with the bereaved at the clinic. Maybe he eats right in front of them. Chewing, he embodies the great capacity of just moving on. Jojo has trained this ability like a muscle. All his gestures, even his way of consciously swallowing, convey the message that he has understood the secret of life, which isn't a secret at all: it's just life itself and its habit of continuing, going on until it doesn't, until it's over. Keeping going is the only meaningful response to how life always carries on. It's the only way anyone stands a chance of adapting to the sheer monstrousness of reality.

Dora wonders if Jojo is happy. She suspects that his trick is to not even pose the question. People who don't expect happiness aren't punished with unhappiness. No prickling bubbles rise up in someone like Jojo. Jojo drinks beer with his sushi and closes his eyes because it tastes so good. He's hungry, and that's all that matters right now. He proceeds to eat half of Dora's share, and gives Jay the rest. That makes two here who will attest to the fact that food is all that matters.

Jojo lights a cigarette and blows the smoke toward the ceiling. He obviously enjoys smoking indoors.

It's a form of time travel. You have to come to Bracken to do it. You're not allowed to in Münster or Berlin.

"Why do you think he did it?" asks Jojo.

Dora answers defiantly and promptly, "He didn't *do* anything. It was an accident."

"Honey. There were no skid marks."

"Maybe he passed out. Maybe that's why he didn't brake."

"No skid marks, no serpentine lines, no involved vehicles. Straight into a tree at 75 miles an hour."

Dora looks at the little wooden Jay. The figure is a parting gift. A request that she remember him. If your mutt digs up even one more potato, I'll kick his head in, Dora thinks. Besides, there's the wolf family. Goth worked all the way through last night because he was determined to get them done. Mother-father-child.

"He would've died soon anyway," Jojo says.

Dora almost laughs. This sentence is one of the most explosive mines in the entire Covid-debate minefield. Doctors, of all people, seem to have relatively few problems uttering this sentence. But the crux of the matter is that it doesn't apply to Goth.

"How do you know?"

"I guess I'm kind of an expert."

"He was getting better."

"That was because of the cortisone."

"Much better!"

"That kind of thing is temporary, I'm afraid."

"You didn't even know him!" Dora almost shouts. "You didn't know him at all!"

"I know from experience."

"Then why are you here?" Now she really is screaming. For a moment, reason loosens its grip. It's almost a relief. "You came to examine him again, didn't you?! Because you sensed the possibility he might recover! You didn't come to see me, just for fun, did you? I know you didn't!"

"Dora." Jojo looks downright startled. "It's all in your head."

"Why in my head, what about yours? What's in my head?"

The mass effect is all in your head. This neighbor is taking up too much mass in your head. You should demand a little more mass for your head. Power Flower, Dora thinks desperately, trying to replace one thought loop with another.

"I didn't come here for Proksch. I came for you." With both hands, Jojo reaches for hers. "I wanted to support you. You've done palliative work here. That's difficult, even for professionals."

"Palliative work!"

Dora spits the term out. Another one of those words. Yet again, all these words that poison life, and it's always Jojo who brings them. They spread like viruses. Maybe more people die from words than from Covid.

"I didn't do any work. I didn't do anything at all. We were just grilling. Bird watching."

Was that really just yesterday? The trip to Schütte? Obviously "yesterday" is no longer a temporal quantity, but the name of another dimension. Dora begins to cry again after all, this time softer and more regular, like a light rain steadily falling. Jojo strokes her hands.

"Maybe he did it to spare you the last few weeks.

To spare his little daughter, but maybe you, too. Not despite the fact that he was better, but *because* he was better. Because he could still do it now. No fading away, no disappearing while still alive, no agonizing last chapter in the hospital. Dying can be a damn ugly business."

Dora wants to yank her hands away from him, but doesn't have the strength. He isn't allowed to say these things, but says them anyway. She knows he's thinking about Dora's mother at that moment, and he mustn't, not like that.

"Now Franzi is a little girl who lost her father in a tragic automobile accident. From one moment to the next. Just a moment after they'd been playing together so happily."

"Carved wood together."

"Fine: carved wood together."

They're silent for a while as Dora just keeps crying.

"It's okay," Jojo finally says quietly. "He was just your neighbor."

"He was my ..." Dora's flare-up immediately collapses back in on itself. There's no term for what Goth was to her anyway. And no reason she needs to explain any of it to Jojo.

"You know what I was wondering earlier, back at the scene of the accident?"

Dora shakes her head.

"Whether your gym buddy would've gone and committed a mass shooting at a Berlin synagogue at some point."

Jojo deserved a good slap in the face for that statement, but then Dora can't help but smile through her tears.

"I've had that thought, too," she admits. Jojo squeezes her hands.

"He did it out of love," he says. "You can be sure of that."

Dora nods.

"You'll see, the pain will go away. Faster than you think. Today is the hardest. It gets better." He squeezes her hands one more time, this time with a finality that says, "We talked, we expressed our feelings, now we're getting back to work. Back to normal."

Dora thinks of a scene from a couple of years ago. Jojo and Axel were arguing about parenting methods, and Jojo, as usual, knew better than everybody else. All of a sudden, Dora felt the urge to ask him whether he had any children of his own. Just in time, she managed to hold her tongue.

Jojo stands up.

"I'll be off now. I have to be in the OR in a couple of hours."

Dora looks at her watch. It's just before midnight. She doesn't know if Jojo means the OR in Berlin or the one in Münster. She doesn't ask either. He'll make it, one way or another. She accompanies him to the front door, watches him walk through the front yard and open the gate. He turns around once more. Raises his hand in a wave. For the first time in her life, Dora feels like saying "Papa" instead of "Jojo." And she does.

"G'night, Papa! I mean, have a good trip."

He doesn't hear her. He's already in the car and honking the horn to say goodbye. Then the Jaguar carries him away, down the village street, toward the highway.

Dora wants to go to the wall. She wants to see if Franzi, the little night owl, is still in the yard. She wants Goth's head to appear over the wall once more. She wants to smoke one last cigarette with him. But there is nothing there anymore. Behind that wall lies only a silent emptiness.

What are you doing? Don't be an ass. This is exactly what you wanted. You wanted to get rid of everything. Family. Relationships. Responsibility. Closeness. All that annoying stuff. Berlin. Robert. The agency. Covid. Axel and all the anecdotes from the heroic life of a family man. Friends, acquaintances. The crowds, the chatter, the screens, the speed, the excitement. The mass media's alarmism. The arrogance of the big city. Parks with leash restrictions. Car sharing, bike sharing, and scooter sharing. Prickling bubbles and insomnia. All that shit. You also didn't want a Nazi on the other side of your property-line wall, nor did you want an annoying foster daughter. You wanted nothingness. And now you have it. Be happy.

She goes into the kitchen. Jay is curled up like a donut in her faux leopard-print doggy bed. Her body is slightly shivering. It can't be the temperature, because it's warm. Nor is it hunger, because she ate a ton of sushi. With every breath, she lets out a soft whimper. She misses Franzi. Already. Maybe Goth, too. So this is what remains. This is the result of the great liberation: a sad little dog.

50

Rain

It can't be true. But it is: Dora wakes up to the sound of thunder. She lies in bed and listens to a sound she hasn't heard even once since she has lived here. Pattering, roaring, the occasional sound of light knocking. Every now and then, a metallic clang. The bedroom looks different. Dull daylight colors the walls gray, her few furnishings cast no shadows. It smells different, too, damp and melancholy. Since Dora's move, the sun has shone day after day in Bracken, as if clouds, wind, and rain were a purely urban affair, or as if the village were covered by a large bell jar painted blue on the inside. And today, of all days, after months of dryness, even drought, it begins to rain. On the day of the funeral, of all things. No app had rain in the forecast. No feathery clouds rolled in, no southerly wind kicked up. The swallows weren't swooping, visibility was low. Sunset just the night before was spectacular, as usual. There must be some mistake.

Dora gets out of bed, steps up to the window, and sees it with her own eyes: it's raining. The raindrops fall from the sky in long, slightly slanting strings. Tree leaves tremble under its touch. The sandy earth is suddenly dark and heavy. The birds are silent. They must be all fluffed up, perched in their nests, their wings laid out, letting the drops roll off their rainproof plumage.

When the weather came up at the village block party, a woman said to Dora: "Bracken is like the desert. When it rains, nature explodes. Then everything looks totally different here. Just wait, you'll see."

Dora's not sure she wants to. She doesn't know what comes next. For the last few days, she couldn't think any farther ahead than this Sunday. As if the following Monday wouldn't even come. As if the story had to end on a rainy Sunday in June. She did not come to Bracken to meet Gottfried Proksch. But now she doesn't know if she can go on without him.

She walks to the front door and pushes Jay-the-Ray, who hates going outside when it's wet, outside with her foot. She breathes in and savors the smell of the damp lawn, which sends her back in time, to her childhood. The saying about her hometown back then was: "In Münster, it's either raining or the bells are ringing." She remembers what all those rainy days felt like: the steady rush, the muted light, the inertia that sets in immediately when life doesn't want anything special from you because of bad weather. You can just lounge around without wondering if there's anything more important to do. Rain puts the world on standby. Dora remembers hanging out next to Axel in the back seat of Mom's car, on her way to some afternoon piano or gymnastics lesson, hypnotized by the rhythmic squeaking of the windshield wipers, listless to the point of drowsiness. Behind the windows, the multicolored lights of the traffic lights radiated into stars. Dora traced the horizontal tracks of raindrops with her finger. The car smelled like a wet animal. She can still recall the radio babbling and her Mother's irritated remarks about other drivers' behavior. Boredom and bad moods can also be a piece of home.

She lets Jay slip back into the house and goes into the kitchen to make coffee. She feels like she's been shattered. In the last few days, she's nearly drowned in errands. Without Jojo's instructions, she would have been lost. He transmitted orders to her via WhatsApp, which she gratefully carried out.

The first thing he demanded was that, in spite of everything, Dora deliver her Power Flower presentation to Tom and Steffen. Somewhere outside her mind it registered that Tom was enthusiastic about her ideas and immediately assigned her to implement them. She would begin that, according to Jojo's timetable, after the funeral. The next thing to do was to call the Plausitz clinic and pretend to be Mrs. Proksch. No one asked any questions. Without further ado, she was told that Goth was still in the refrigerated room there, and they wanted him out as quickly as possible, since they were experiencing capacity issues. A postmortem hadn't been ordered, and the police had no doubts about their own findings. 79 miles per hour, tree trunk next to the highway, no others involved in the accident. Clear case. They had been waiting "all this time" for a mortician to "finally" get in touch.

Dora hung up, thinking that Goth's secret would indeed be kept without an autopsy, as he had probably wished. No one would know if, as Jojo claimed, "he would have died anyway."

Then she contacted the Last Journey Funeral Home. In accordance with Jojo's instructions, Dora bawled incessantly on the phone so they wouldn't ask her for proof of identity. When she could speak clearly again, she asked that all formalities be done over the phone or by email, because of Covid, to which Last Journey gladly agreed. She said she could pick out a casket on the internet, as well as floral arrangements, appropriate sayings, and the design of the funeral cards. Again and again she had to assure them that Goth, who since his death has been known only as "Mr. Proksch," really did not want a funeral, a speaker, or newspaper advertisements. With each rejection, Last Journey's morale sank. At the same time, Dora felt as if she were planning a wedding, even if, "in times like these," only on a small scale. She has never been anyone's wife, and certainly not a widow. Since Goth's death, it would seem the two of them officially belong together.

Last Journey cleared everything with Bracken Cemetery. They coordinated the date with Dora by phone and sent the contract documents by mail to Goth's address. They reminded her to send the copy of her photo ID, which she forgot yet again.

Tom and Steffen came by to tell her they would donate the wreaths.

"He was an absolute ass," Steffen said. "But he was one of us."

As for the sayings on the wreath ribbons, Tom wanted to write *One down*, and Dora wanted, *Here lies the village Nazi*. They laughed together, which did them a tremendous amount of good. Finally they decided on *Our friend and neighbor* and another, smaller bow, which would read *To my dear Dad, from Franzi*.

Last Journey's spirits finally plummeted when Dora called to cancel the flower arrangements. She chose the cheapest coffin made of pine. Goth would probably have preferred beech or oak, but as it was she didn't know where to get the money.

She brooded the longest over the invitation list she had to send to the funeral home. She had written down *Nadine and Franziska Proksch, Sadie, Tom and Steffen* as well as *Mr. Heinrich.* A text message from Nadine Proksch informed her that Goth's parents were dead and that he had been estranged from his brother for years. Dora's question about how Franzi was doing remained unanswered. On a walk through the village, she wrote down a few names and house numbers from mailboxes. After that, the list contained ten entries, which, thanks to Covid, seemed not sad, merely appropriate.

Jojo's next instruction was, *Clear everything out over there. Find documents!!!* with several exclamation points.

That's when the work really started. Dora spent two days at Goth's place. She cleaned up, disposed of food, thoroughly cleaned both the main house and trailer. She took the remaining keys, closed up the house, and shut down the water pump. She also found records: a manila folder full of documents that were amazingly tidy and well kept. Motor vehicle papers, land register deeds, divorce documents, old pension letters, an ID card, even a virgin passport, not a single stamp inside. She took it all to her place and spent an afternoon sorting through it. She called around and canceled contracts. Now Goth is officially signed out of the world of the living. Little Wooden Jay sat there, right next to Dora's laptop, as if she wanted to peek at the screen with her.

In between, Dora thought a lot. About love, for example. She had always believed that what movies and novels call "love" doesn't really exist. Or at least not in the form described. For her, at least, it didn't exist. She couldn't envision a scenario in which there were people who meet and immediately know they're meant for one another. Who stay together forever. Who make each other happy. Who feel excitement just looking at each other. Who argue and make up again. Who have great sex all the time. Who almost die of longing when they don't see each other for a while. Who sit next to each other on a park bench in their old age and hold hands. Dora doesn't even know if she really loved Robert. She doesn't know if any of the couples she knows really love each other. First and foremost, it always seems to be about who matches with who. Same background, same education, same good looks, similar preferences in sports, music, and politics. Like some rating system. Parameters, percentages. It provides easy content for conversations: He and she don't fit together at all. She was better suited to the other guy. Will he ever find another match?

Sometimes Dora thinks something broke inside her when her mother died. The ability to love another person from the heart, even though you know they're mortal. Sometimes she also thinks that the twenty-first century is to blame. Rating and ranking, match or no match, swipe left or swipe right. But mostly she thinks novels and movies simply lie.

She and Robert were a good match. They got along well and found a nice apartment together. Still, something was missing. They were all about functioning, but had a huge empty hole in the middle. And eventually they ceased functioning as a couple, too.

Then life prescribed her a neighbor. A Nazi behind

a wall. He was ugly and he stank. If he had been a product, he would have gotten only one star in the customer reviews on Amazon. He had terrible friends. He drank. He had a rap sheet: attempted manslaughter. Dora didn't like him. She was afraid of him. Saying they didn't match is an understatement. They would never have met on Tinder. The algorithm would have seen to that.

But Goth didn't just disappear, regardless of their 0% match stats. He stayed right where he was. At some point, Dora realized there was something to this being-there-and-staying-there thing. It can be shared. Goth's existence communicated itself to her. He shared it with her. In the end, they existed together. Connected by the wall that separated them.

Now he's gone. But he left something behind, a new little conviction in Dora's mind: if she could meet Goth, maybe she can meet someone else.

If, in truth, it's not about points, percentages, or stars after all, maybe there's someone out there for her. Someone who at this very moment is arguing with his kids as he tries to homeschool them in an apartment in Cologne. Or loading large crates into the cargo hold of an airplane at Leipzig Airport. Or washing out diving suits in the Maldives. Someone who doesn't yet know that, one day, they will meet.

She found out from Heini who drives the wheel loader in the village. It took only a short conversation, and on Friday evening the big machine roared up. Dora watched as the wolf family was lifted into the air on the huge shovel and driven down the road to the center of the village, where the cemetery is. Goth would have liked the idea, she's sure.

Yesterday, she tried to barbecue in his backyard. The fire wouldn't burn properly. She only drank half the beer, and fed the beef-neck steak to Jay. It just didn't taste good.

A couple of times she stood on the lawn chair against the wall and smoked before going to bed. On the other side, Goth, Franzi, and now even the wolves are missing. Dora thinks about quitting smoking. It's a pathetic prospect.

The rain is falling. It gets even heavier while Dora drinks her coffee. She stands by the window and notices how nice it is to just stare out into the rain with a cup in her hand and feel a little cold. It means she's alive. But she doesn't own an umbrella. No rain jacket either. No rubber boots, no cap, no rain hat. When it's time to leave, she puts on a thick sweatshirt and puts a bag from REWE on her head. The bag is made of paper. Before she even gets to the gate it becomes clear this isn't the way to go. The rain will soak through to her the skin in just a few minutes, and the temperature is fifty degrees at most. Jay refuses to put one foot in front of the other, and has to be dragged through the grass on a leash.

After briefly hesitating, Dora crosses the street and rings Heini's doorbell. He opens immediately, as if he'd been waiting for her. Behind him, a woman walks by down the hall, says a friendly hello, and disappears again. Dora is pretty sure she has never seen her before. Maybe she works odd shifts. Or maybe she's a secret lover. If Dora's eyes are to be trusted, she's a good head taller than Heini.

"Shit," he says. "What a bummer."

At first Dora thinks he means the weather, but then

she realizes he's talking about Goth. For a moment it looks like he's about to hug her, but then he remembers Covid. Or the fact that he's a man, and a Brandenburger to boot. Perplexed, he looks at her. When she asks for rain gear, the bustle returns. He scurries back into the house and takes a long time to come back. Dora listens to the drumming of the drops on the porch roof and occasionally glances at the clock.

"They can't start without us," Heini says when he reappears, and Dora wonders whether this is yet another joke.

Heini is now wearing yellow head to toe: oilskin jacket and trousers, plus rubber boots in the same color. He has pulled the hood over his head. Behind him, the tall woman appears in a dark green waxed-fabric coat and a wide-brimmed hat that makes her look like an English lord on a hunting trip. Heini extracts another pair of rubber boots in the same color and a rain jacket, which he passes on to Dora. She gets another yellow vest. When she finishes dressing, she picks Jay up off the ground and tucks her under the jacket. They walk off down the road together, even though, like most roads in Bracken, it has no sidewalk.

Because there are no ditches either, the roadway has turned into a river, with water flowing towards the center of the village. Next to Heini and his wife in their rain gear, Dora feels like a little girl on her way to vacation with her parents on the seal banks off the East Frisian islands.

At the cemetery, this fantasy ends with a thud. At the sight of the open grave, Dora is startled in a way that she hadn't thought possible after the way she had mourned over the past few days. That very morning, Jojo had texted her: *Those who accept death can live with it.* Dora felt like he was right, and figured she would definitely succeed.

But an open grave is a wide-open gullet and such sayings can't shut it up. It locks its jaws open and laughs at people. Dora presses Jay against her, as if the warm little body could protect her from the sneering pit.

The coffin she chose is on a wheeled cart, covered by a sea of flowers. Tom and Steffen have done a great job. The two wolves are already sitting at the head of the pit, like mourners who came a little too early.

Dora can't believe that Goth is really here. But then again, he also isn't here. In the deserted cemetery, the coffin looks like a prop. Maybe the pit is also part of the stage set. Her brain weaves the narrative: a small play was to be performed, but was postponed because of the rain. Dora wants to go home. Show canceled.

But then several figures detach themselves from the wall of the natural stone church where they had taken shelter. Some carry umbrellas, others have their hoods tied tightly around their heads. When Dora sees how many there are, a warm feeling flows through her. She didn't think it would mean anything to her. Tom and Steffen walk hand in hand, something Dora has never seen them do before. Sadie has brought two women who were also at the village block party. The firemen are there too. Two more figures approach under black umbrellas: the bearded man and jacket man. It's unclear how they learned of Goth's death, but around here the sandy soil has ears. They nod measuredly to the round and stand aside, as Covid guidelines dictate. Outlaws in adaptation mode. Krisse furtively wipes his eyes.

Motionless, the mourners surround the open grave. In the background, the wolves smile. The rain has subsided somewhat, has become finer, and now seems to come from all sides, like spray, rather than falling from above. The only thing missing is the priest. Dora shudders at the thought that she might have forgotten to book a priest. But then she remembers a message from Last Journey. Despite Mr. Proksch's lack of denomination, the Protestant congregation is prepared to organize the funeral; Pastor Heinrich will take care of it.

Dora looks around, glances at the clock, and sets Jay, who is fidgeting under her raincoat, on the ground. Next to her, she registers a movement and sees the tall woman take off her rain hat and pass it to Heini. Her hair is pinned into a tight bun, on which fine rain droplets immediately settle. She opens the waxed-fabric cloak, revealing a black gown with white Geneva bands. This transformation has something illogical about it. Pastor Heinrich and the Serial Griller. They probably wouldn't have met on Tinder. The algorithm would have seen to that.

"We are gathered here today," says Pastor Heinrich, and suddenly Dora senses a void next to her, powerful as a piece of dark matter. An absence contrary to the laws of nature, whose outlines correspond to those of a little girl. She wants to shout, "Stop, we can't start!" but at that very moment she hears a car approaching and abruptly hitting the breaks. A red Honda Civic stops in front of the cemetery's chain-link fence. As the passenger door opens, Jay begins tugging on the leash as if trying to slip out of her collar. Franzi runs through the gate, down the gravel path, and toward the mourners with giant strides. She wears a purple softshell jacket whose hood hides her long blonde hair, along with cut-off jeans and pink sneakers, which makes a nice contrast to Dora's and Heini's yellow oilskin garb. Reverend Heinrich smiles at the girl, Jay insists on greeting her with indignant jumps, and Dora looks for a way to hug her little friend without actually managing to.

When the situation calms down, Dora at least presses Jay's leash into her hand, which Franzi acknowledges with an absent-minded smile. The girl is as far away as the moon. All that's left is Franzi's body, which Berlin has briefly spat out in order to suck it back in as quickly as possible. Dora remembers the blonde braid as it flashed between the tree trunks in the forest. She can still picture patches of sunlight on the grass, and how Franzi and Jay would frolic across a meadow together. The smell of pine needles and mushrooms. The engine of the waiting Honda is running. It's the most hideous sound in the world.

"We are gathered here today to say goodbye."

No one cries. Everyone is silent, as if turned to stone. The wolves smile in the background: mother, father, child. During Reverend Heinrich's address, Dora wonders what species of birds can be found in Berlin, and in what quantities. There mustn't be too many, like with pigeons or sparrows, whose frequency renders them meaningless. But also not too few, as with wrens, who are so rare their existence is often forgotten. Blackbirds? In the process of extinction. Crows? Too noisy, too gloomy, too many. Magpies? Too aggressive. Swallows? Too high up. Kestrels? Too hard to spot.

When Dora notices a movement in one of the tall spruces standing between the graves, she knows the solution. She grabs Franzi by the arm.

"Look, there," she whispers.

Despite the bad weather, a red squirrel squats between the branches of the spruce, watching the action with black beady eyes.

"That's your daddy," Dora whispers. "He'll visit you as often as he can. And he'll always watch over you. He loves you so much."

Franzi looks blankly into the tree. She probably wasn't even listening. She doesn't look at Dora, and doesn't seem to notice the wolves either. She follows the priest's words with a blank look and even ignores Jay, who's licking at her knees.

When the ceremony is over, four men come to lower the coffin into the pit on long ropes. Everyone throws a bit of earth on top of it. Franzi even shovels in a few large chunks, which bang loudly on the lid of the wooden box. Dora leans down to the girl.

"You can always come here," she says, "To my place. To Jay's. During vacation, or whenever you want. We'd be happy to have you."

Franzi nods, and in that moment Dora knows she'll never see the girl again. The Honda honks its horn. Franzi presses the leash into her hand, tears away, and runs across the gravel path to the car. Dora turns away. She can't watch the girl get in.

She'd like to cover her ears so as not to hear the roar of the engine.

Everyone comes up to her, bows slightly instead of holding out their hands, and shares their condolences as if she were indeed the bereaved Mrs. Proksch.

"Thank you, Dora," Tom says, and she doesn't know what he means at first, but then somehow she does.

She walks home alone. Heini has followed his wife into the church, and the other mourners have dispersed. Jay walks ahead of her, looking forward to a dry spot. Today would be a good day to try out the wood stove. Goth would have helped her. He would have come over with a stack of logs and started a fire before she'd even have thought to ask him.

The rain continues to let up. It turns into a light mist, leaving a damp film on her face and hands. The stream of water on the road has dried up. The trees drip. The first birds resume their singing. Noisy storks can be heard somewhere nearby. In front of Tom and Steffen's house, two Portuguese guys are standing at the edge of a huge puddle, chatting, smoking, and waving to Dora as she passes by. Goth's house is silent.

In the future, someone has to look after things here. Tend to the right-hand neighbor. Peer through the windows every Friday. Maybe also air out, heat up, turn the water on and off, and take care of other practicalities you can read about on the internet. Dora has the keys. The orange tabby sitting on the wall turns and looks at her.

ALTA L. PRICE runs a publishing consultancy specialized in literature and nonfiction texts on art, architecture, design, and culture. A recipient of the Gutekunst Prize, she translates from Italian and German into English. Price's translation of Juli Zeh's novel *New Year*, also published by World Editions, was a finalist for the 2022 PEN America Translation Prize as well as the Helen & Kurt Wolff Prize.

Book Club Discussion Guides on our website.

World Editions promotes voices from around the globe by publishing books from many different countries and languages in English translation. Through our work, we aim to enhance dialogue between cultures, foster new connections, and open doors which may otherwise have remained closed.

Also available from World Editions:

Breakwater
Marijke Schermer
Translated by Liz Waters
"A poignant story of love, autonomy, and the devastating power of secrets." —IVO VAN HOVE

The Drinker of Horizons
Mia Couto
Translated by David Brookshaw
"A rich historical tale that recalls Márquez and Achebe."
—*Kirkus*

Fowl Eulogies
Lucie Rico
Translated by Daria Chernysheva
"Disturbing, compelling, and hearbreaking."
—CYNAN JONES, author of *The Dig*

My Mother Says
Stine Pilgaard
Translated by Hunter Simpson
"A hilarious queer break-up story."
—OLGA RAVN, author of *The Employees*

We Are Light
Gerda Blees
Translated by Michele Hutchison
"Beautiful, soulful, rich, and relevant."
—*Libris Literature Prize*

On the Design

As book design is an integral part of the reading experience, we would like to acknowledge the work of those who shaped the form in which the story is housed.

Tessa van der Waals (Netherlands) is responsible for the cover design, cover typography, and art direction of all World Editions books. She works in the internationally renowned tradition of Dutch Design. Her bright and powerful visual aesthetic maintains a harmony between image and typography, and captures the unique atmosphere of each book. She works closely with internationally celebrated photographers, artists, and letter designers. Her work has frequently been awarded prizes for Best Dutch Book Design.

The cover has been edited by lithographer Bert van der Horst of BFC Graphics (Netherlands).

Euan Monaghan (United Kingdom) is responsible for the typography and careful interior book design.

The text on the inside covers and the press quotes are set in Circular, designed by Laurenz Brunner (Switzerland) and published by Swiss type foundry Lineto.

All World Editions books are set in the typeface Dolly, specifically designed for book typography. Dolly creates a warm page image perfect for an enjoyable reading experience. This typeface is designed by Underware, a European collective formed by Bas Jacobs (Netherlands), Akiem Helmling (Germany), and Sami Kortemäki (Finland). Underware are also the creators of the World Editions logo, which meets the design requirement that "a strong shape can always be drawn with a toe in the sand."

Printed in the USA
CPSIA information can be obtained
at www.ICGtesting.com
JSHW081419220923
48999JS00002B/70

9 781642 861334